RS03

D0108599

SEP 4 26 2001

LONDON BRIDGES

London Bridges

Jane Stevenson

HOUGHTON MIFFLIN COMPANY

Boston • *New York*

2001

Copyright © 2000 by Jane Stevenson

First published in Great Britain
in 2000 by Jonathan Cape.

All rights reserved

For information about permission to reproduce
selections from this book, write to Permissions,
Houghton Mifflin Company, 215 Park Avenue South,
New York, New York 10003.

Visit our Web site: www.houghtonmifflinbooks.com.

Library of Congress Cataloging in Publication Data
Stevenson, Jane, date.
London bridges / Jane Stevenson.
p.   cm.
ISBN 0-618-04934-7
1. London (England—Fiction.) I. Title.
PR6069.T4535 L66 2001
823'.914—dc21   2001024993

Printed in the United States of America

QUM 10 9 8 7 6 5 4 3 2 1

M.S.

MARGERY ALLINGHAM

This novel could not have been written if I had not known Dominic Montserrat and Robin Smith: I am most grateful to them both. I would also like to thank Peter Blegvad, Peter Christopher, Andrew Durant, Arnold Hunt, Dan Franklin, Maureen Freely, Pat Kavanagh, Harjit Kaur Khaira, Carol Morley, David Morley, Alan Oxer, Tracey Potts, Jamie Reid Baxter, Alison Shell, Winifred Stevenson, Jane Treglown, Rory Young, and above all, Peter Davidson and Frank Thackray, for technical advice, essential facts, insights, support and encouragement. I would also like to thank Dr Laura Wright: if she ever happens to read this, she might like to know that her paper on 'Historical Linguistics and the River Thames' given at the University of Sheffield in 1995 was one of the more unlikely of the seeds from which this story grew. The quotation in Chapter XV is from Sean O'Brien's 'The Politics of', in his *Ghost Train*, published by Oxford University Press, p. 8.

The China Governess, which Margery Allingham published in 1963, includes the following page of text, in Chapter 10.

The child which, Campion saw, was tall and fair, suddenly turned its head and looked at him directly. His heart jolted and dismay crept over him. There it was, just as he had feared, the face again! Prunella Scroop-Dory herself, Luke's lost enchantress, had not had higher arches to her brows nor the promise of a rounder, more medieval forehead.

Mr Campion had not disliked Prunella for her own sake but for Luke's, and now he pulled himself together hastily and said all the right things with the best grace in the world.

'What is her name?'

Luke grinned. 'Hattie,' he said. 'Her Mum, God bless her, wanted her called Atalanta, which is sweet but silly in a daughter of mine. It was after a character who was always being chased. This is the best we can do.'

Old Mrs Luke beamed happily at the visitor.

'My daughter-in-law wasn't chased enough,' she remarked. 'A sweeter woman never drew breath but she didn't think enough of herself, being too well trained. That won't happen to you, Love, will it?'

The baby, appealed to, laughed revealingly as infants often do and the startled Campion found himself confronted by Prunella's aristocratic face with Luke's cockney intelligence blazing out of it like the sun in the morning. He went off feeling chastened and secretly apprehensive. It had occurred to him that in fourteen or fifteen years there might well be a personality of considerable striking force in Linden Lea. He put the thought from him; at the moment he had more immediate trouble to contend with.

I often wondered how she turned out, in the end.

I

London is a town for fog, mist swirling up from the river, the darkness between streetlights. But, although it is never summer in the London of the imagination, the streets are as answerable to sunlight and long evenings as those of any capital in Europe. There are hot, still, August nights in Mayfair, and on such a night, Jeanene Malone had just found out about the Greek optative.

On such nights, while visitors ebb and flow in vast human tides through London's centres of shopping, culture and entertainment, in Mayfair, though it lies between the sun-baked yet inviting grass of Hyde Park and the manifold entertainments of the West End, secret, flower-adorned mansions of stock-brick and stucco maintain a patrician silence; unguessed, unseen lives move in secret channels beneath the surface, and the streets are as deserted as the mountains of the moon.

As the Greek couple turned out of Park Lane and looked down the hot and dusty length of Mount Street, they saw nothing moving at all except a feral cat, white paws twinkling jauntily in the grey evening light as it slipped at its leisure from beneath a BMW to a new lookout-point behind the front wheel of a Jaguar. The woman's sharp heels set up flat, clacking echoes in the silent street. About halfway down, the Queen Anne Dutch frontages were briefly punctuated by a squashed-looking parade of shops built into the ground floor of nos. 40–48. The third shop remained lit, a little yellow beacon in the blue summer night.

'There it is,' murmured the woman. As they approached, they saw that the windows were bright with images of tanned and exquisite women, while the shopsign, running the length of the frontage, showed a mortar and pestle, and the words 'Mount Street Chemist's'. As they approached the shop, they found they were able to peer over the top of the window display into the lighted depths of the pharmacy. Within, a girl sat alone, resting her elbows on the counter, hands pushed into her dark, curly hair, studying an open book with great concentration. Her plain white blouse was obviously inexpensive, and she looked very young and small. The woman smiled to herself without humour. A student, she suspected, studying for exams. Ideal: with her mind full of her own problems, she would hardly notice that they had come in.

Taking a last look along the deserted street, the man stiffened, and touched his companion's hand warningly. A man had emerged from the side door of the Riyadh Gallery, and was rapidly approaching. The woman slipped her arm through the man's, and they turned away unhurriedly. Sebastian, as he came level with them, saw no more than a pair of elegant shadows, their faces obscure as they stepped away from the brightness of the lit window, and did not give them a second thought. He went up to the pharmacy door, and pressed the night bell.

Inside the pharmacy, Jeanene Malone heard the buzz, hastily shut her book and pressed a button under the counter to admit the late customer, who turned out to be an expansive and zestful individual, not unlike the late Oscar Wilde in appearance. He had longish dark hair, bright blue eyes, and an unEnglish ability to address a shop assistant as if she were a human being rather than a mechanical answering device, and she looked at him with interest. The man bought some Nurofen, and then suddenly decided to buy perfume as well, a transaction which took some time and involved frequent changes of mind. He thanked her courteously as he stuffed his purchases into various pockets, and was just about to leave when his glance swept across Jeanene's book. He flicked his heavy fringe out of his eyes with a practised toss of the head, put three fingers on it, and swivelled it on the counter till he could see the spine.

'I thought I recognised it. What on earth is an Aussie pharmacist doing with an ancient Greek Grammar?'

'I'm just about to start graduate work. At the Institute of Classical Studies.'

'Well, good for you. But that's ancient grammar, not just ancient Greek! Why Abbot and Mansfield? Everyone uses *Reading Greek* these days, surely?'

'Do you know the Institute people?' asked Jeanene, her heart lifting. 'I'm getting a bit of preliminary reading done for the Intensive Greek course. With Professor Beckinsale? It was what he asked us to get.'

Sebastian arched his eyebrows sardonically. 'Oh, *her*. In her dreams, dear. Actually, it's not even *Doctor* Beckinsale. Mister, and chippy about it. That explains it: our George is a bit of a museum piece in himself, as you'll find out in due course. The thing you've got to remember about old George is that he's rude to *everybody*, he doesn't mean it personally. Well, not usually. He can't stand me, of course, but I have to admit I wind up the poor old spook something shocking.'

'Do you teach at the Institute?' she said hopefully.

'I do a bit of Byzantine stuff for them. We'll probably bump into each other sometime – my name's Sebastian. 'Bye for now.'

The door whispered shut behind him, leaving her with the warm thought that she had just met someone she might meet again: after only four weeks in London, she knew practically nobody except her current employer, a fat and surly individual called Patel. She looked at her watch again: only thirteen minutes to lock-up. Was it really worth staying? Just as she was about to get up and go into the back for her bag, the doorbell rang once more. Two modish silhouettes, male and female, were dimly visible through the glass, and she buzzed them in.

'Good evening. How may I help you?' she said in her best professional manner. The man came forward, feeling in his breast pocket.

'Good evening. Can you fill this prescription, please?'

Jeanene took the piece of paper and studied it conscientiously, nibbling her thumbnail.

'I'll have to check on the computer,' she said apologetically. 'This is a high dosage, and I'm not sure we keep it in that strength.'

'It is very important,' said the woman, abruptly.

'Too right. If the patient's used to this amount, he's got to keep on with it.'

She considered the prescription more carefully. There was something else peculiar about it: the prescribing doctor's address was in Fife; and while Jeanene's education had not been big on British geography, Macbeth, she recalled, was the Thane of Fife. So, surely Fife was in Scotland? The man, watching her narrowly, saw her frown in puzzlement.

'We came down from Scotland on the night train,' he explained.

'Yes,' the woman cut in, 'and most unfortunately, we find our uncle has forgotten his pills.'

'So we rush out, and try to fill his new prescription this very night,' the man finished smoothly.

How did a pair of obvious foreigners end up with an uncle called Campbell? she wondered momentarily, and immediately answered herself: quite easily, no doubt, one of her own aunts had married a Hungarian, and she had relatives she couldn't even spell.

'I'll just go and see if we've got some – I'm just a temp here, so I don't know the stock that well.'

'Could you substitute another drug, if necessary?' asked the woman.

'Not without ringing up the doctor. I don't want to alarm you, but this stuff's a bit specific, and you can't monkey with it. If I get it wrong, you and the old gentleman could end up having a rough night.'

'Oh, it is too late to bother the doctor,' said the man hastily. 'If you haven't got the right stuff, just leave it.'

Jeanene excused herself and went through to the back of the shop. The couple puzzled her. '*Our* uncle?' They were both handsome, well-dressed and Mediterranean, but they did not look like siblings, and neither of them was wearing a wedding-ring. Well, none of her business. Probably some kind of weird extended family. She typed the prescription into Mr Patel's computer. It's not for mere pharmacists to criticise a medico, but she did wonder what this Scotch GP thought he was up to. The prescription before her was for a higher dosage than she felt comfortable with. It was within limits of the prescribable, but it occurred to her strongly that if the poor old bloke forgot and took two, chances were he'd not be troubling his kith and kin much longer. Perhaps she should check...? She reached for the phone, and rang the number given on the prescription. This, as she had fully expected at that hour of the night, gave her an answerphone with an emergency contact number. She scribbled it down, and rang it, but there was no reply. She put the phone down with a sigh, observing that the computer was flashing back at her victoriously: they had some in stock. She hesitated, in a quandary. But clearly, the stuff had been prescribed; and if the patient was used to it, he would be better with it than without it. All the same, she wished she had been able to check with the doctor. She went and took the bottle from its shelf, and returned to the front shop. The door which separated the pharmacy proper from the front of the shop was a heavy fire-door with a spring, which opened and closed slowly and silently, then clicked into place. Thus Jeanene, who was wearing light, rubber-soled sandals, was able to re-enter the shop without the couple realising that she had done so.

They were looking out down the road with their backs to her, and arguing under their breath in their own language, which (as she came gradually to realise) was Greek. She got an impression that the man was worried; certainly, the woman was insistent. Jeanene, apart from the ancient Greek she was laboriously acquiring, had a smidgen of modern Greek, initially acquired during a backpacking year after school, and kept in use during her undergraduate years because she lived in a cheap bit of Sydney. As she waited politely for a break in the stream of words, she found one or two making sense to her. θάνατος came up several times; δηλητήριο...poison, death. The whole thing was giving her the habdabs. They could be worrying about the prescription, but something about the way they were hissing at each other said not. Pull yourself together, girl, she said to herself. A sentence came over loud and clear: the woman's voice. What Jeanene understood her to say, unbelievably, was, 'Just shut up. Even if we killed him, it wouldn't matter. Who's ever going to know?' Then, as she stood doubting both the evidence of her senses, and her command of Greek, the door finally clunked shut. The couple whirled round, looking daggers. Jeanene opened her mouth, but nothing came out.

'I got your pills,' she squeaked, on the second try.

'Excellent,' said the man, too heartily. 'It is a very great relief to us.'

'You'll be really careful?' she asked, earnestly. 'Give him them one at a time, and make sure he takes them.'

'We will make very sure,' said the woman. She held out her hand for the little bottle. Jeanene handed it over, and she dropped it into a tiny Gucci handbag. The clasp snapped shut decisively, while the man got his wallet out again, and put a ten-pound note on the counter.

'Oh, and I want a tin of Andrews Liver Salts,' he said.

Wordlessly, she got one off the shelf, bagged it and put it on the counter, then rang it up and gave him his change.

'There you go,' she said, meaninglessly.

'Thank you very much. You have been most helpful. Come, Lamprini.'

They left; and as soon as they had gone, Jeanene locked the front door and pulled down the blinds. As she went mechanically through the motions of closing down, switching off and locking up, she thought furiously what to do next. Five to eleven; she'd shut a bit early. Well, whatever she was going to do in the wider sense, no way was she going back to her lonely little room to lie awake all night. What she needed was a drink, and human company.

Born and bred in the dry heart of Australia, Jeanene was sensitive to watering-holes, and had one staked out for emergencies. The big posh pub in Mount Street itself was closed for renovations, from which it would doubtless emerge posher and more expensive than ever. But, tucked unobtrusively into the tiny service streets and mews which fissure Mayfair's slabs of expensive architecture, there are one or two tiny, inconspicuous establishments. One such was the Horse and Groom in Balfour Mews, a distressing little saloon which had remained resolutely unmodified through so many changes in pub décor that fashion had practically caught up with it. Jeanene had been there only once, and had established two important facts. First, it was near enough that she could get to the bar before last orders. Second, the clientele consisted entirely of gay men. Still, she thought to herself, it had to be better than the echoing silences of a half-empty graduate women's hostel.

When she rounded the corner of the Mews, she saw light still spilling from the gilded, rococo window of the Horse and Groom, so she pushed open the door. The single bar was solid with male bodies, partially obscured by drifting veils of blue smoke. Heads lifted and swung suspiciously as she entered, like a herd of bullocks when a dog enters their field, and nobody moved.

Nonetheless, she began pushing her way through to the bar, past bodies which shifted only slowly and reluctantly out of her path. Elbowing her way between two beefy male backs, she was startled to see a girl's face through the crush: white, tense and big-eyed, framed by a mass of curly dark hair – it was, she suddenly realised, her own reflection in the mirror behind the bar. Moments later, she saw a far more welcome sight: her new friend Sebastian's elegant, grey-clad form, leaning on the bar in confidential conversation with a sulky-looking blond in a white T-shirt. He turned towards her, urbane recognition shading rapidly to concern.

'You look like death, dear. What's happened? Let me get you a drink. Gin?'

'Great,' said Jeanene gratefully.

'Larry, love. Double G and T, please, and two more Becks'. Stevie, this is one of our new students. She's working in the Mount Street pharmacy.' When the barman pushed the drinks across, Stevie curled his lip, muttered something inaudible, took his new bottle, and mooched off. Sebastian cast one wistful glance after his retreating back, and turned to Jeanene.

'Let's go and sit at that table in the corner, and you can tell me what happened. And your name, while you're about it.'

'This is incredibly kind of you,' said Jeanene, a little unsteadily. 'I'm Jeanene Malone.' Tears pricked her eyes, and the room dazzled around her as Sebastian piloted her through the crowd.

'Oh, rubbish. I'm just curious. Seriously though, you look as though you've had quite a shock. Was it someone on drugs?' Jeanene took a deep breath, and a reviving swallow of gin.

'No. That's always a worry, of course, when you're by yourself, but there's an alarm, and a video and stuff. This was something weird . . . Oh, I don't know if I can make it sound like anything at all.'

'Try me.'

'Well, there was this couple, you know? Greeks. They said

they were filling a prescription for their uncle, but the name was Campbell? Not impossible, but the whole thing didn't seem to add up. What's really given me the willies is, I overheard them talking Greek to each other when they didn't know I was there, and I got a serious impression that they're trying to poison someone.'

'How? I mean, what were they after?'

'Mellerox. It's an oral hypoglycaemic, for treating diabetes.'

'I thought diabetics got insulin injections?'

'That's right. Young diabetics get injections. But there's a kind of diabetes you get when you're old, and they treat that with stuff like Mellerox.'

'So, what's the problem? I mean, the stuff's not actually poisonous, is it? I thought the body made insulin naturally.'

'Well, yes. But if you get the dose wrong, then the patient can wind up in a diabetic coma. These are the highest potency pills on the market. Did I say the doctor's someone in Scotland?'

'No...' said Sebastian thoughtfully. 'It does sound as dodgy as fuck, doesn't it? I mean, if your punter starts frothing at the mouth or passes out, the doctor's going to have a job checking up on him.'

'Well, people do travel...' said Jeanene wretchedly, turning her glass round and round in her hands. It all sounded so trivial. Sebastian felt sorry for her, and decided she was due a little empowerment.

'Look, Jeanene. I've hardly known you five minutes, but you don't strike me as the sort to make a fuss about nothing. Where did you grow up?'

'Cootamundra. I did pharmacy at Sydney Uni, then I got a scholarship and went to Wollongong to do Euro Lit.'

'Well then. It sounds like you've pulled on your own bootstraps and got yourself out of the back end of nowhere. You've got two degrees already, and now you're starting postgraduate work at London. Right?' Jeanene nodded. 'So you're not exactly an airhead. And you're used to being alone, aren't you?'

'Yes.'

'Well, don't tell me you're seeing ghosts, dear. You can't possibly be that sort of girl. Unless it's that time of the month – it isn't, is it?' Jeanene shook her head, embarrassed, but beginning to feel much better.

'Well then,' said Sebastian, waving a hand magniloquently and knocking back the last of his lager, 'let's start by assuming you've got something to worry about.'

'Time, gentleman, *please!*' shouted Larry. Sebastian looked at his watch.

'I'm afraid I'd better go. I've got rather a lot on tomorrow. Where do you live?'

'I'm in Ellen Wilkinson House – you know, the women's hostel just off Bedford Square?'

'*Errgh*. You poor darling. I've got a flat in Stedham Chambers – opposite Pizza Express, just round the corner from the BM. It's incredibly convenient – I'm going to be devastated when they move the Library. Anyway, the point is, it's five minutes from Bedford Square. The Tube might be a bit nasty this late, so if you'd prefer to walk, I can go most of the way with you.'

'That's really sweet of you,' blundered Jeanene. 'Don't feel you have to. I mean,' she amended hastily, 'I'm used to going around by myself.'

'I know. But I don't suppose you usually attract villainous Greeks. Do you know what overseas graduate students are worth to a university these days? We have to protect our investment.'

She looked at him a little resentfully, disliking the feeling of being big-brothered, but there was nothing but goodwill and concern in his face. They drained their drinks, and prepared to leave. Sebastian blew the barman a kiss, and they stepped out into the hot, quiet night, heading towards the distant roar of Oxford Street.

'On they went through the shadows,' said Sebastian conversationally, after a while, 'beneath an obscured sun, through the empty halls of Dis and his phantom kingdom.'

Jeanene boggled for a moment, then suddenly realised that he was quoting the *Aeneid*. She shot him a cautious glance, not sure if he was just being pansy, or taking the piss: his expression, in the orange streetlight, was bland and innocent. 'I don't feel like a Sybil,' she retorted. 'Do you?'

'It's more the empty halls of Dis I was thinking about. London in August. Let's go up Great Marlborough Street, it's quieter. There's a bit of Oxford Street in our future, come what may, but we needn't rush it.' They ambled up Conduit Street in amicable silence, broken after a time by Sebastian.

'Actually, it must have been you who made me think of the Sybil. There you are, with a dark and formless prophecy of woe...'

'... I'm sorry...'

'Don't apologise, dear. It's the most exciting thing that's happened all week.'

'Okay, I'll skip the apology...but I hope he rings in the morning.'

'*Tant pis*. There's plenty more where he came from, surly little bugger.'

'It's sweet of you to be like that about it. But seriously, Sebastian, what do you think I should do?'

'Well, you could make a note of the data off the prescription, and I suppose make a memo of everything you can remember before you forget it again. Then I suppose if you're really feeling like Nancy Drew, you could ring the doctor's, and see what you can find out. That's about it, really.'

They went on in silence, but she was feeling better. The simple act of telling someone else had lifted the worst of the worry; she could already tell that by the morning, it would all feel like a lot of fuss about nothing. She had been so lonely, so isolated, that she just got herself into a state.

'Okay, Jeanene, I turn off here. You're all right the rest of the way, aren't you?'

'Sure.'

Sebastian fished in his wallet, and extracted a card. 'Here's my address and phone. If anything interesting happens, let me know. If not, I'll see you around the Institute one of these days.'

II

It is acknowledged by all right-thinking persons that an Old Etonian reduced to vulgarly scratching about for a living is a melancholy sight. One January day at the beginning of the same year, when Jeanene was still safe in Wollongong, dreaming of freedom, Mr Edward Lupset emerged from Holborn tube station in his customary state of rage, frustration and despair. As he strolled reluctantly towards the Inns of Court he found his gaze arrested, not for the first time, by Hackett's windows. The left-hand window was dominated by a coat: hard, brownish-green tweed, exquisitely cut, and for all its elegant lack of bulk, dense enough to stop the winds of Siberia. On the right, bright, soft cashmeres spilled in calculated disarray. And in both, his reflection returned to him by the dark background of the displays, was Edward, tall, slim, blond, and designed both by nature and nurture to wear such clothes. Fashion victims may be sad, sick people, but a frustrated dandy is a dangerous man. Looking with loathing at his reflection, he saw, perhaps, a sober-suited, dapper young man; not exactly shabby, no. But he was powerfully and resentfully aware that his was second-grade smartness. Trained as he was to pick up every nuance of distinction between the real and the false, the four-button cuffs, never undone, which must undo, the buttons which must be the right buttons, the cloth, the cut, the overwhelming mass of tiny details which distinguishes real tailoring from mere garments, he could have wept.

Climbing three flights of stairs and arriving (a little late) at Skinner, Catling and Barnacle, his place of detention, did little to cheer his mood. Betty, the senior secretary, an upright woman with her hair combed into a brittle grey shell who looked like a headmistress, was already shuffling papers. She gave him a curt greeting as he passed by. It was increasingly clear that Betty was underwhelmed by his talents: while Edward was not the sort of man who cared what secretaries thought of him, Betty had been with the firm for more than forty years, and her opinion counted for a great deal. The door crashed open again, and slammed shut, with a degree of racket which could only announce the arrival of the other assistant. A wintry smile flitted over Betty's austere features.

'Good morning, Mr Dhesi.'

'Morning, Betty, sorry I'm late. Hello, Ed.' Dil bounded in, briefcase under his arm, holding a minute paper cup of espresso from the Pret a Manger on the corner, and hurtled towards his own quarters. As usual, he gave the impression that the air had been left churning behind him like the slipstream of a powerboat. Edward looked after him with hatred. Dilip Dhesi dressed out of M&S, and didn't give a damn. His father and mother ran an Indian sweet business somewhere in Southall and had laughable curry-flavoured accents, yet he cheerfully admitted to them in public. Somehow, in other words, Dil appeared to be springing with effortless competence across the chasms which open in the way of an outsider who seeks to penetrate the Establishment, while Edward, insider born and bred, found himself increasingly left behind.

'At least he's not a fucking woman,' he thought to himself for the umpteenth time, and sat down wearily to examine the letter which Betty had left on his desk.

What he found himself faced with was a brief communication with a letterhead in Greek, addressed from a lawyer somewhere in Athens. Though it was written in excellent English, it appeared at first to make no sense at all. One Lamprini Polychronopolou (Jesus! what a name, thought Edward disdainfully) was apparently winding up an estate for a Greek client. So far, so good. It was the second paragraph which was, as they say, Greek to him.

The Mavrogordato family owned a certain amount of property in London, having had connections with England for many years. Most of this is easily accounted for, with one exception. My client's grandfather made over the rents of a row of properties on the South Bank for the maintenance of the fabric of St Michael Graecorum in that borough, while directing that any surplus was to go to the lavra of St Michael. However, we have some reason to believe that St Michael's was destroyed in the last war; and if this is the case, then the purpose of the trust is at an end. Capital (i.e. the houses themselves) and interest should therefore now revert to the Mavrogordato estate. Since your firm acted on our behalf in the initial transaction, we trust that you will be able to clear this matter up for us. If it is of any assistance, the principal trustees of St Michael Graecorum at that time were Eugenides & Co.

We look forward to hearing from you.

Edward read the letter three times, and then sat looking at it. Many things came his way that he did not understand, and it was his tendency, thus stymied, to float them past Dil as indirectly as possible, since the young Asian's comments generally indicated where the answer was to be found. But there was no way of bluffing an enquiry like this without admitting total ignorance. He got up, and roamed restlessly about the room, then drifted out into the main office, where Betty sat typing.

'Oh, Betty,' he began, with false casualness, 'ever heard of an outfit called Eugenides? Or the Mavrogordatos?'

Betty continued to type until she reached the end of her sentence, without acknowledging his presence; a subtle discourtesy, though the theoretical requirement that legal documents be letter-perfect meant that her typing rated higher in the scheme of things than in most offices. Only when she had come to the end, and marked her place carefully, did she turn and look at him over the top of her spectacles. After a lifetime with the firm, her omniscience was legendary; he had no doubt that she would know something. Her brows creased, disturbing the thick, old-fashioned layer of powder on her forehead.

'Eugenides? You'll have to let me think for a moment.' Edward did not reply, but leaned elegantly against the jamb of the door, and waited.

'The firm's done business with Eugenides & Company since the eighteenth century,' she said eventually. 'They're a tiny little merchant bank. We got involved with them originally because several important clients in our early days had Greek interests. I believe it was once quite a big concern, specialising in Greek business, of course. Now it's down to one old man, I think, but it must be a good ten years since we've had anything from them. There are a couple of boxes...' Her voice trailed off, and she took off her reading glasses to peer long-sightedly at the tin cases stacked on the high shelf above the picture-rail, labelled with the names of illustrious clients in white paint, whose purpose these days was essentially decorative. She pointed with a thick-knuckled but carefully manicured forefinger. 'There they are. Eugenides. In the corner by the fireplace. Any Mavrogordato records we have'll probably be in there as well. You'd better get the stepladder.'

'Where's that?'

She looked at him bleakly. 'In the basement. There's the key, on the hook near the door.'

Fifteen minutes later, Edward was in possession of two old tin boxes and a consuming sense of personal grievance. The boxes had lurked near the ceiling of the old room since the days when downtrodden clerks had stoked the grate with seacoal. They had been there through innumerable peasoupers, and had weathered the cigars of innumerable worried, or jubilant, clients. In other words, they were filthy with a very special adhesive, oily, urban filth, which had liberally transferred itself to Edward's hands, face, shirt and suit. The suit would have to go straight to the express cleaner's at vast expense the moment he had a chance to change; the shirt, he rather feared, might be a write-off. He scrubbed his hands on his handkerchief, which had gone in the course of the morning from a crisp poplin square to something more like an engineer's rag, and prised open the first of the boxes with his paper-knife, feeling very strongly that Mr Eugenides, and the lawyer Papadopoulos (or whatever it was) owed him plenty.

In the course of the morning, as Edward worked slowly through the archaic piles of documents, untying the faded pink string from one after another, he began to get slightly interested, despite himself. The firm of Eugenides, it appeared, was and had long been a small international banking house, dealing essentially with Greek mercantile clients. The house was already old when a representative had approached the first Mr Skinner in 1733. The Mr Eugenides of that time had been in occasional need of an English solicitor to deal with local business – which explained, at any rate, how the man Polychronopolou had come to ruin Edward's morning. But the church? Where did a church fit in with all this? As he read on, the story began to piece itself together. St Michael's itself was obviously older than the earliest of the documents before him, since a couple of transactions in the eighteenth century referred to gifts, in terms which seemed to imply that it was a going concern. No explanation, therefore, of where this all started. Edward shovelled the contents of box one back into it, and turned to box two: the Mavrogordato bequest, if indeed Skinner, Catling and Barnacle had any information about it at all, must be relatively recent.

He found it without too much difficulty: a confirmatory note, dated September 29, 1908, which he seized on with relief since it gave him the address of the property – St Michael's Road (unsurprisingly), Southwark. He began jotting down notes with a lightening heart. A quick visit to the Land Registry in the afternoon, and he would be able to confirm whether the property had been destroyed, and that would be the end of the matter. Oh, bugger. No it wouldn't. He extracted the original letter from beneath the piles of Eugenides bumf, and took another look at it. He still had to find out what had happened to the Mavrogordato bequest itself.

Seething, and emitting quite unconsciously a faint hiss like a pressure cooker coming to the boil, he turned back to the documents; and his interest quickened. The Mavrogordato bequest consisted of rents and ground-rents for a group of freehold properties in Lambeth. He fished his *A-Z* from the bottom drawer of the desk, and worked out where they must be: at this point, if they were still standing, their value must have rocketed. All good news for some greasy Greek plutocrat, no doubt.

Edward played with his pen, lost in fantasy. If a three-storey, flat-fronted eighteenth-century house came his way, now...he'd know exactly what to do with it. He could start living like a gentleman, not a fucking student. The man Polychronopolou seemed a bit uncertain that the property even existed... Reluctantly, he dismissed the fantasy. The deeds must be either in Athens or with Eugenides, either way, he stood no chance of putting himself in the way of them. A shadow fell across the desk, making him jump.

'Hi, Eddie. What's this, industrial archaeology?'

Edward forced a smile.

'Oh, hello, Dil.' His tone was repressive, but the young Indian paid no attention. He leaned forward, scrutinising the tin box with interest, flipping its contents over fastidiously with a slender forefinger.

'Fantastic. I don't think I've ever seen inside one of these before.'

'You can keep it,' snarled Edward. 'I'm going to be spending the next couple of days working out how to present a bunch of stinking-rich dagoes with a fat chunk of London real estate they lost track of before World War One.'

'How so?' asked Dil curiously.

'It's all endowment for some church the Krauts totalled with a well-aimed V2. There's been dosh piling up somewhere ever since.'

'Very nice. I say though, Ed. That's not going to be the only place dosh has been piling up.'

'What?'

'Well. I'm assuming your Greeks didn't hand over these rents totally out of the blue. And I don't think many Greeks are Anglicans, so I'm also assuming it's some sort of Greek church. When's it first mentioned?'

'Oh, ages back. It's before 1800, that's for sure.'

'Okay then. It's an old church, and rich Greeks thought it was important, and it was destroyed in the Forties. If the Church Commissioners haven't got their grabbers on it, then you could have a jolly good lot of endowments mounting up over that sort of time. There's absolutely nothing like obsolete charities for accumulating money. F'rinstance, if someone set aside money in thirteen-hundred for supporting six lepers in the diocese of Bermondsey, there isn't a use-by date built in. I had a case like that once. A charity for fishermen's widows somewhere on the East Coast, only the town fishing industry collapsed when the herring moved somewhere else, so there'd stopped being fishermen's widows. It goes on mounting up, see? You can't just use your common sense and distribute it to widows in general. There was shedloads of money in the fund by the time I got involved.'

'And it's all just got to sit there?' gasped Edward, shocked to the core.

'Oh, no. The trust-busting legislation in the Eighties did for the ancient charities. All kinds of pots of gold got hauled into the light of day and escheated to Ma Thatcher. The Treasury did jolly well out of my widows thing. If you do find there's a fund associated with this little lot, and you've run out of traceable owners, and it hasn't been nicked by the Church Commissioners, there'll be absolutely no difficulty sorting it out,' said Dil casually, glancing at his watch. 'Got to go, Ed. I'm in court this afternoon, and I need to grab a sandwich. Happy hunting.' Then he was off: the door slammed shut, as usual, and Edward distantly heard him galloping down the stairs.

He sat on for some time, sunk in thought, then returned to the first of the boxes. Dil's natter had sparked off some intensely interesting trains of thought, and he no longer grudged the Eugenides boxes his attention. Oblivious, as the clock crept from one towards two, he began reading carefully through all the documents in Box One which mentioned St Michael Graecorum. With the help of his *A-Z*, he located St Michael's Road; it was on the South Bank, no great distance from Southwark Bridge. There had also been a house for the rector, beside the church – had it gone in the Blitz, or was it still there? – and there was also a library, which appeared to be physically located in the rectory, since purchase of books for 'Sir Everard Digby's Library' was mentioned in more than one paper: the Greek titles meant nothing to him, but it gave him another name which might be useful.

'Betty,' he called peremptorily, emerging into the outer office, 'have we got a *DNB*?'

'Yes, Mr Lupset,' said Betty coldly, 'the compact edition.'

Edward opened his mouth to complain, thought better of it, and meekly lugged volume one back to his desk. Squinting at the miniaturised pages of the *Dictionary of National Biography* with the magnifying glass thoughtfully provided, he discovered that Sir

Everard Digby had been an antiquarian, adventurer and occasional pirate of the seventeenth century, whose adventures in the Middle East had included buying the future Lady Digby in a Circassian slave-market. After the Restoration, his main concern seemed to have been the forging of links between the Anglican and Greek Orthodox churches. Aha! 'He was instrumental in the setting up of an independent Greek Orthodox church in London, St Michael Graecorum, and endowed a splendid library of Greek texts for the furtherance of scholarly and theological debate between the two communities...' Edward began trying to assess the implications of this from a financial point of view. St Michael and its etceteras had been a rich man's pet project in the 1670s. He was vague about history, but he had a general sense that in the seventeenth century you could buy a horse for about threepence. If there was a money endowment for buying books and keeping the rector in retsina, if it had been at all well invested, three hundred years of compound interest would...Edward stopped to try and work out compound interest at two per cent on an initial £100 for three hundred years, and gave up, his mind reeling.

He had already overleaped the initial question of the Mavrogordatos' rents. Two much more interesting questions had presented themselves: who owned the church of St Michael and its rectory, and did they know? Somewhere, he could practically smell it, a large sum of money was sitting about unprotected, lost down the cracks of history, neglected and unclaimed. If no one knew they owned it, you could practically say it was unwanted. Now, these Athenian legal eagles were plainly on to the houses in Lambeth, but what about this Digby stuff? The notion of Dil's 'pots of gold' floated seductively.

As he continued to work through the heap of documents with these thoughts in mind, something caught his eye. A typed memorandum, on the firm's paper, dated September 30, 1940. Following the instruction of one Vassili Eugenides and other trustees of St Michael Graecorum, a number of items had been consigned to a safe-deposit box in the vaults of the City branch of the National Westminster bank. Item. Four pairs of silver candlesticks, weights ranging from six pounds or so down to two, with London marks, dating between 1662 and 1721. An altar-cross, weight fifteen pounds three and a quarter ounces, dated 1665. Edward's heart began to beat in slow, heavy thuds. This was treasure. His mother had, in happier days, collected silver; all gone now to fill the black hole of his parents' Lloyd's debts. He had a notion of what silver was worth; and seventeenth-century silver with weights measured in pounds not ounces, was worth a hell of lot. He read on. Chalices, cups, patens (what's a paten? he wondered, momentarily). A pirate's hoard of silver. And there was more. Five reliquaries, set with gold, enamel, and gems. An ivory statuette of St Michael, Constantinopolitan, height thirteen inches. And pictures – icons, rather. Names and technical descriptions meant nothing to him, but words such as 'fourteenth century' set off bells. Anything that old had to be valuable, surely? Really, really, valuable. Who knew about icons? How did you find out?

He went through the rest of the Eugenides material, twice, tremulous with excitement. The documents before him gave no indication that this hoard of stuff had ever been retrieved, though it was hard to imagine why not. It had been deposited by trustees; subsequent trustees could therefore presumably have claimed it at any time, and had probably done so. But for the time being, there, before his very eyes, was the treasure he had imagined. He looked round the office. Betty, back early from her lunch, was talking on the telephone with her back to him; no one else was in the room. He folded the thin, yellowish slip of wartime paper discreetly in half, and slipped it into his trouser pocket, against possible eventualities. As he was about to close up the box, it suddenly occurred to him that a paper outlining the constitution of the trust had passed under his eyes…perhaps it would be an idea to have that as well.

*

It was perfectly clear to Edward that the next item on his agenda must be to make contact with Mr Eugenides and see what he could find out. This proved easier said than done. He was not wholly surprised to find that the phone went unanswered, and decided to pay a personal call, which he thought it best to do on a Saturday. Edward always dressed with care, but on this occasion, the knotting of the tie, the shrugging into the jacket, the settling of the cuffs, were performed staring into the mirror, and resembled, in the deliberate formality of his movements, the donning of tilting armour. Visor down, plumes nodding, lance at rest, Edward was ready to do battle.

Mr Eugenides lived in Garlic Court, in the depths of the City. Among the mirrored monoliths of international finance, there are still a few enclaves of older buildings, and even a few little old houses not far removed in time from Sir Christopher Wren's great restoration. Garlic Court, reached down a narrow alley between Lombard Street and the Bank, proved to be such an enclave, a miniature square of half a dozen small townhouses looking into one another's windows round a tiny paved quadrangle. The houses had, perhaps, once accommodated rural landowners with business in the city. They had subsequently stagnated into Dickensian squalor, and still bore the scars, though post-war affluence had breathed new life into the old bricks, rosy beneath their layer of grime.

On a Saturday so early in the year, the City is deserted. The smell of money, humming on the wires, zipping through the air, is dissipated, and the pinstriped mobs who leap in and out of taxis talking urgently into their mobiles are presumably at home in Docklands or the Barbican, watching the rugby on TV, while the hordes of tourists who mill from St Paul's to the Monument during the summer months are, when the bitter winds of February whistle down the empty streets, still safe at home in Pasadena and Nagoya. As Edward strode briskly up Lombard Street looking for the entrance to Garlic Court, he was entirely alone.

He surveyed the court with interest. It bespoke a classic City mixture of grottiness and fabulous wealth. All but one of the six houses had clearly been taken over by brokers and money-men of some kind. Brass plates abounded, and one had been subject to a brutal, high-tech transformation which had replaced most of the ground-floor frontage with an enormous plate-glass window through which a modish jungle of tropical foliage was dimly visible. The last house also stood out from its fellows, but for the opposite reason: it seemed neither to have gone down in the world nor to have come up again in anything like the dramatic peripety experienced by its neighbours. It boasted its original wooden shutters, adorned with elderly dark-green paint, and firmly shut against the cold. The doorcase was crowned with an elegant fanlight. Edward stepped with some confidence up to the door, noted the words 'Eugenides & Co.' on a small, blackened brass plate beneath the bell-pull, and tugged the latter firmly. He heard a distant jangling from within, but nothing else happened at all. After a minute or two jiggling from foot to foot as the cold struck up through the thin soles of his shoes, his breath hanging frosty in the air, he rapped firmly on the lion-headed doorknocker. After his third assault on the lion, he exhaled in a great huff of frustration, and stepped back, hands on hips, to glare at the unrevealing façade. Just then, he heard a cough behind him, and spun round.

A little old man stood at the bottom of the steps. He was wearing a heavy dark coat, and a round fur hat with earflaps, which made him look like an eccentric small animal, a wombat perhaps. He was clutching a string bag which bulged with primitive necessities such as milk, bread and tinned sardines, and the expression in his soft black eyes was mildly enquiring, though he did not seem moved to speak. Edward, considerably irritated, drew himself up, gaining confidence from his commanding height.

'Mr Eugenides, I presume?' he asked, with a touch of sarcasm which he felt he was owed after the frustrations of the morning.

The old Greek considered this utterance for a minute, as if it were a proposition requiring examination from several sides.

'I am Eugenides,' he confirmed. Padding up the steps on silent feet, he handed Edward the string bag, in an oddly confiding gesture, stripped the heavy glove from his right hand, and fumbled for his key. As the door swung open, he gestured politely with his bare hand, motioning Edward ahead of him. 'My house is yours.'

Edward, still clutching the string bag, stepped forward gamely into the dark. Eugenides followed him in, and shut the door. His guest took an incautious step forward, and fell over a hall chair. Uttering an automatic 'po, po, po' of condolence at this mishap, the old man flitted easily past him, moving in the darkness with the confidence of a bat, and pressed a switch. The high-ceilinged hall was illumined, if that is the word, with an ancient electrolier thriftily fitted, in this late stage of the house's long history, with a single, dusty, forty-watt bulb. Before him, an elegantly curved marble staircase swooped up into total darkness. The hall itself was also floored in marble, as Edward's left knee bore painful witness, and was freezing cold. It contained four chairs as old as the house, a small Turkey carpet, and a number of tall, panelled doors.

Eugenides took the bag from him, opened the door to the right of the stairs, switched on the light, and revealed a parlour whose only concessions to the twentieth century were the electricity itself and the presence of smokeless boluses of anthracite rather than seacoal in the grate, where the fire was made up, but unlit.

'Please sit,' he said, motioning Edward to one of a pair of wing chairs set symmetrically on either side of the fire, and knelt before the hearth to bring the fire to life. Having achieved a curling wisp of smoke, he pattered off to deal, presumably, with his groceries in some unimaginable back quarters. Edward sat where he was bidden, a man in a dream, still huddled in his overcoat. The room had a dank smell of disuse, though the seat of the chair opposite was so moulded by the impress of Eugenides' slight body that it looked like a cocoon. The half-darkness of the room, the gradually penetrating warmth of the fire, and the stuffy dustiness of the atmosphere combined to produce an irresistible drowsiness.

Some minutes, or perhaps hours, later, Edward heard Mr Eugenides' slow tread in the hall. The old man shuffled in, wearing carpet slippers and a camel cardigan, carrying a small silver tray with a bottle of brown sherry, two minute and rococo gilt glasses, and a plate of obsolescent sponge biscuits. He put the whole thing down on an exquisite piecrust winetable, moved it bodily between them, and poured sherry with some ceremony. Having handed Edward a glass, and insisted that he take a soft, unpleasant biscuit, the Greek retreated to his own chair, and surveyed his guest with a bland, ambiguous countenance, much as a Byzantine city governor might have surveyed the white-skinned, ice-eyed lord of the barbarians encamped outside his walls.

'Well, young man, why have you come to see me?' he enquired, in a tone of scrupulous neutrality.

One of the most useful by-products of a public school education, especially to an acknowledged beauty and former toast of the Upper Sixth, is an expression of blue-eyed candid innocence which implies that its wielder is about to be snatched up to heaven by a choir of aggressively Aryan angels. It goes with an unspoken *sostenuto* of 'Yessir, please, sir,' and is the default position of the thus-privileged Englishman whenever he is in difficulties, or about to cause difficulties for others. Edward was wearing it.

'Well, Mr Eugenides. I've come to see what you can tell me about St Michael Graecorum. I've had some enquiries about a bequest in the Mavrogordato family. I do awfully need to sort it out. It's all landed on me, you see, and I'm afraid I don't have a clue about the background.' He stopped, dug out a small notebook and the silver propelling pencil which was one of his affectations, and looked hopeful, but with overtones of a puppy uncertain of its reception. The old man sighed, settled back into his chair, and held his glass up to the fire, playing with the light in its tawny depths.

'I think perhaps we begin about 1540.' The point of Edward's pencil snapped, but he recovered himself without comment. 'There was, as you know, a Greek community in Venice at that time. When the Venetians traded with London, Greeks also were involved in this trade. A branch of the Mavrogordato family established itself here in the mid-century and still flourishes, praise God. Our own house grew up at this time: we were involved in the fur trade between the merchants of Epiros and the market in this country, first as principals, and later as the agents of other traders. We have existed continuously as an Anglo-Greek banking house since that time, though with the troubles in Greece in this century, we came to close our offices in the Aegean. I am now all that is left. In 1667, however, we were privileged to assist Sir Everard Digby with his great enterprise. Our agents in the Levant helped him to gather his treasures, and we were involved from the beginning with the building of the church of St Michael. The Mavrogordato family have been most generous benefactors of the church over the centuries.'

'But the actual church was destroyed in World War Two?' Edward could not resist interrupting.

'That is correct. It was not, of course, the church of Sir Everard. That structure became unsound – the Greek mercantile communities who were its support became less important, you see, and it was sadly neglected – so it was rebuilt in 1868 to serve as an ordinary Anglican church, though it kept the name of St Michael Graecorum. From a legal point of view, however, the freehold and appurtenances were never transferred to the Church of England; the trustees, principally this house, considered that our responsibility was to preserve its independence in the interests of some possible Greek community of the future which it might serve. Apart from the superb icons which it still held, there was little in St Michael as I remember it which showed that it had once been a bridge between East and West.' The old voice, firm, beautifully produced, modulated in the gloom to a tone of elegiac regret.

'Then the Krauts blew it up?' said Edward inelegantly.

'It was destroyed by enemy action on December 14, 1940,' confirmed Eugenides. Edward's interest quickened. His memorandum was dated September of the same year: good timing on someone's part.

'It must've meant a hell of a lot of sorting out for you,' he observed, considering the old man thoughtfully. Seventy? Seventy-five? How old had he been in 1940?

'I was not personally involved at that time, of course,' explained Eugenides. 'It was the business of my absolved father. I was at school in the first years of the war, and from '43 I was on active service in Greece with the Signal Corps. My father unfortunately died in the Blitz some months after the destruction of the church, so the Dean of Southwark Cathedral acted in his stead until I was free to take over the reins.'

'What about the rector's house?' enquired Edward, changing tack.

'Now that, I am fairly sure, still stands, though it is untenanted. I have not crossed the river for a number of years, but it certainly survived the war. The last rector was killed attempting to rescue the icons from the flames, and the governing committee, headed by my absolved father, decided to present Sir Everard's priceless library to the British Museum, to ensure its safety.'

Edward looked at him, his mouth slowly drying. Eugenides clearly believed that everything in the church had been destroyed – and it was perfectly obvious how information could have gone astray. His mind raced, till it occurred to him suddenly that he was gaping like a codfish, and Eugenides was beginning to look at him with marked patience.

'Okay,' said Edward, pulling himself together. 'Let me get this straight. We've got a house, and a bombsite, and maybe some endowments, including this Mavrogordato money. Whose?'

'I beg your pardon?'

'I mean, who owned the reversion to this little lot?'

'Ah. You must forgive me. I do not often speak to young people, and contemporary modes of speech confuse me a little. The entire estate of St Michael Graecorum in London is a possession of the lavra of St Michael on Athos.'

'Come again? I mean, I'm sorry. Could you run that past me again, only slower?'

'Mount Athos,' repeated Mr Eugenides patiently. 'The Garden of the Mother of God. It has been the centre of the Greek Christian world since the tenth century. Sir Everard spent some years on the Holy Mountain during the English civil war, and was most impressed by the Athonites. He looked, therefore, to the lavra of St Michael – the monastery, you would say – for intellectual and spiritual support for his foundation. It was monks from St Michael who served as the church's first ministers.'

'So do they actually know that they've had a chunk of inner London real estate in their hands since 1941?' demanded Edward.

Mr Eugenides achieved a complex, Mediterranean shrug. 'Yes and no. Time matters little on the Mountain. The problem is really that although the monks are not lacking in worldly wisdom in the management of their immediate affairs, they know little of life beyond Athos, and less of life beyond Greece. England, if you will forgive me saying so, is a land of heretics and barbarians from their point of view. They would not seek to engage with such a problem. Do you know, another lavra of Athos has owned for some centuries a property on what is now Red Square in Moscow? I heard recently that following *glasnost*, it has been returned to them. The monks are very patient, and they wait to see the dispositions of God. Meanwhile, the firm of which I am the humble and now last representative, has always dealt with any practical problems which might emerge.'

'So, sir, can you confirm the details of the Mavrogordato bequest? The info I've got from Athens is that the purpose of the trust is now at an end, and the money ought to revert to the Mavrogordatos. Does that square with your records? Er...you are the principal trustee, aren't you?'

The old man sighed, and set down his glass.

'Principal, and indeed, only'. He shuffled over to the desk, and rolled back its top. 'After the church was destroyed, there was of course no rector, and the diocese of Southwark had no further interest in the matter. By agreement with successive abbots, I have therefore forwarded the rents of the Mavrogordato bequest to Mount Athos, but kept the other endowments in order to have a fund to pay rates and other charges as they occur,' he explained over his shoulder, 'The sums involved are not large, you understand. Let me see...the actual documents are kept elsewhere, but I should have a memorandum. Ah, here it is. You are quite correct. There is a certain ambiguity in the terms of the Trust. After the destruction of the church, my father interpreted the testator's intentions to define "surplus" as the entire revenue of the properties, and acted accordingly. I have followed him in this, but the situation certainly bears the interpretation your Greek colleague has put on it. As the trustee responsible, I would be happy to see this property revert to its original owner. I am an old man without an heir, and once I am gone, the abbot will be left without an agent, so the present situation will be difficult to maintain – if the Mavrogordato family wishes to continue to benefit the lavra, or the Church more generally, there are less cumbersome ways that they could do it.

'I will have to advise the abbot of the new state of affairs, of course, but I doubt if he will seek to contest, in the circumstances. In fact, I think I had better advise him in the strongest possible terms that he should make a final disposition of all remaining property which the lavra holds in London. Meanwhile, you may assure the Mavrogordatos' lawyers that I am holding the deeds of their properties, and that my accounts are available for inspection.' As he spoke, he was writing a brief note in Greek, on thick, yellowish paper. This he blotted, folded and sealed, then looked at Edward over the top of it.

'You are representing our friends Skinner and Catling?'

'Oh, yes of course,' said Edward, confused. 'My card...?' He struggled to his feet, and put the card on the desk. Eugenides did not trouble to glance at it.

'Please tell your Greek correspondents that their client's funds have in no way been misapplied. Assure them that I am the only steward, and that I have kept my trust.'

Eugenides turned, and handed the note to Edward, who stood towering over him. He began moving slowly towards the door, forcing his guest to fall in behind him. Mr Lupset, thus shown out into Garlic Court, heard the door close behind him with a soft, decisive click.

In the days that followed, Edward Lupset found his visit to Mr Eugenides recurring insistently to his mind. It had made it possible for him (with an air of conscious virtue) to send a fairly full reply to Polychronopolou, enclosing Eugenides' note, and answering, point for point, the questions raised. It was as a matter of mere professional self-protection that he suggested to the Greek that, given the age and eccentricity of Mr Eugenides, approaches to that worthy should go through himself.

In a wider sense though, the narrative of Mr Eugenides was one round which his mind repeatedly circled, in a mental action which reminded him of trying not to finger a pimple. He had consulted the Land Registry, and from the size and situation of the plot, the rector's house, even if it was a total wreck, was probably worth a small fortune, especially in combination with the still undeveloped bombsite of the erstwhile St Michael's. Business was booming all along the South Bank, and the value of land was rising by the week. Then, of course, there was the stuff on safe-deposit, forgotten by absolutely everybody, and worth – what?

And who owned it, pray? he thought to himself savagely,

whenever his thoughts came back to this point. A bunch of wild-eyed nutters with long woolly beards, who could never, quite plainly, be brought to any kind of sensible perspective on finance. Moreover, they neither knew nor cared. Edward, on the other hand, who knew everything and cared a very great deal, understandably felt that men attired in sackcloth and old sheepskins were but poorly fitted to become the inadvertent beneficiaries of an Englishman's generosity. Sir Everard, surely, with his priceless lace, his brocade coats and his clouded cane, must have known only too well how hard it is for an Englishman to dress. The whole thing offended Edward's sense of fitness.

Eugenides was the only trustee! – That was the real pebble in the shoe, for as he knew, and Eugenides patently did not, anyone who could demonstrate that he was the trustee of the estate of St Michael's could turn up at the National Westminster waving the memorandum which now sat in his wallet glowing, to his mind's eye, as if it were radioactive, and take a fortune in antique silver and icons away with him in a taxi. The bank, he knew, would not even want to see the box open: if anyone ever wanted to know what it had contained, he could say what he liked.

He had given the trust document he had extracted from the Eugenides box his careful consideration, and it was clear that Eugenides, as trustee, had the right to co-opt other trustees if he saw fit. The only problem was the Mavrogordatos, who, presumably because of their considerable benefactions, had at some point acquired a right of veto; a difficulty, but perhaps not insuperable. The frustrating vision of a forgotten fortune on the other side of a glass wall nagged at him, and soured his temper.

It was without pleasure that he found another letter from Athens on his desk a couple of weeks later. It turned out to contain a civil note from Lamprini Polychronopolou, saying that with his colleague Alexander Britzolakis, he would be arriving in London to sort out the final disposition of the Mavrogordato properties, and to put the houses on the market. Could they offer

Mr Lupset lunch?' Mr Lupset, after due consideration, decided that they could.

'Heard from your Greeks again?' said Dil cheerfully, seeing the letter in his hand.

'Yah. This chap Lamprini Polychronopolou wants to take me to lunch.'

'Chapess, surely? Lamprini's a woman's name, isn't it?' queried Dil.

Edward put his head in his hands. 'Oh, Christ. That just about puts the fucking lid on it.'

'Hey, don't worry, Edward. She might be really fit. Mediterranean girls go for blonds, you know.'

'Bugger off, Dil. Go and ruin someone else's day.'

III

In the opinion of Mr Edward Lupset, the holy mountain of Athos and its numerous inhabitants were infinitely remote from the concerns of civilised people. The only aspect of it which might have earned his grudging approval, had he known of it, was its complete exclusion of women. But as it happens, at the precise moment when the name of the mountain was first uttered in Edward's hearing, a person undeniably real even by Edward's standards, Dr Sebastian Raphael, was footslogging up to the lavra of St Michael swearing gently and monotonously under his breath. Athos was not Sebastian's kind of place. It is undeniably a long way from the nearest cappuccino, and while it is equally indisputable that some of the younger Fathers bring irresistibly to mind the sleek and perfumed Ganymedes of the court of Basil the Bulgar-Slayer, Sebastian personally found monks a turn-off. A spiteful, gusting rain was making inroads down the back of his neck, and where the land fell abruptly away on his right hand, he could see through the trees glimpses of a grey, oily, sullen sea. Somewhere on the other side of the straits, lost in the mist, was civilisation, and also a very dinky waiter back in Thessaloniki with whom he had reached an understanding.

Sebastian turned up his collar, wrenched his thoughts away

from the direction in which they were turning, and tried to get them in better order. Past experience suggested that infinite vistas of muddle and misunderstanding lay before him, and that the clearer his agenda was in his own mind, the greater the chances of getting away with at least part of what he was after. Or at least, of not rushing out of the lavra and throwing himself off the mountain, or throttling an archimandrite with his own beard.

Quite some time later, St Michael hove into view. He hammered on the gates, explained himself to the porter, and sent in his letter of introduction to the abbot. To his considerable relief, he was shown some minutes later into a square, high, roughly plastered room heated (up to a point) with a brazier, which at least took some of the rawness out of the air, and was provided after a further interval with a cup of treacly Greek coffee, and a plate of Turkish Delight and sticky little pastries. As he sat steaming by the brazier drinking his coffee, a number of monks appeared, impelled by curiosity, and to each in turn, Sebastian patiently explained his name, nationality, religion and purpose. They were perfectly friendly, but the gradually forming circle of owlishly staring black eyes over beards of every conceivable size, shape and texture began to make him feel as though he ought in some way to justify the attention he was receiving. As the atmosphere thickened with solemn monastic respiration, the urge to do something silly began rising in him like yeast.

Perhaps fortunately, the abbot chose to arrive just before Sebastian rose to his feet and treated the boys to his Wallis Simpson impersonation. A number of the younger and cuter monks promptly evaporated, leaving the abbot himself – a great hillock of a man, with a gorsebush beard and tiny, glittering obsidian eyes – accompanied by a phalanx of seniors. Sebastian began his introduction all over again, and then embarked on polite conversation, which pursued its circuitous path for some considerable time. He answered, as best he could, for the spiritual and physical welfare of the house of Windsor, and agreed with everything the abbot said, thus committing himself to a number of statements he privately considered true up to a point, if at all. Once the abbot had exhausted as many avenues of small talk as he saw fit, he condescended, eventually, to come to the point.

'Now, my son. What brings an English scholar among us ignorant monks?'

'The ancient reputation and glory of your house, kyrie Akakios,' answered Sebastian, deftly. The watching monks relaxed a little, and Sebastian began to hope that he was hitting the right note. 'You may remember,' he continued cautiously, or hoped he had: had he done the subjunctive right? Press on...'In the days of your most holy predecessor the absolved Abbot Athanasios, an Englishman, Sir Everard Digby, came to this lavra, and received baptism at the hands of the noble abbot. The English were at war with their king in those days, and Sir Everard spent some years here on the Holy Mountain. Once the king was restored, it was the wish of the kyrios Everard's heart to create harmony between the Church of the English and the True Church' (may I be forgiven, he added to himself parenthetically). 'Later in his life, he built a Greek church in London, for the use of Greek merchants as well as of converts like himself. It was men from this lavra who came to England to do this great work.'

Monks, whose attitude to time is essentially cyclical, often have little or no sense of history. Sebastian, watching the impassive countenance of Abbot Akakios and the solemnly nodding heads of his sidekicks, judged that they were probably all hearing this for the first time; that they were mildly interested; and that they were not in the least surprised. He was getting near his point now, and chose his words with care. 'The kyrios Everard was not concerned alone to bring true religion to our country. He wished also to bring back the true wisdom of the Greeks.' The social temperature began to drop. Brows beetled, moustaches quivered as the hidden lips beneath began to set in disapproval. What is *sophia* in the mouth of a pagan English kyrios but the Godless rubbish of the ancients? Sebastian hurried on before things got any worse. 'I mean of course,' he said firmly, 'the great works of the Fathers – John the Golden-Mouthed, Basil the Great, Gregory.' Good. The abbot even favoured him with a tiny nod; beetled brows returned to their former smoothness all round the room. 'The kyrios Everard bought many, many books of the wisdom of the most Christian Greeks, many here on this mountain, others from merchants and travellers.'

Abbot Akakios shifted impatiently, and steepled his thick, hairy fingers together, looking at Sebastian over the top of them.

'And what concern is this of yours, my son?'

Sebastian was momentarily afflicted by a wild desire to come clean, just to see what happened, but restrained himself.

'The library of the kyrios Everard went in the end to the British Museum, where I have seen his books. But in his letters, and above all, in his private enchiridion, his notebook, he speaks of Greek Christian books he read and studied, which are not now in the Digby collection. I have some hope that perhaps if I searched in your archives, I might find some clues, some memoranda, perhaps, to tell me where these other books might be...?' He trailed off, looking at the abbot with a wide-eyed stare which had melted hard hearts in its time. Because, he thought intensely, turning up the wattage of his hopeful gaze, dear old Diggers quotes some absolutely stunning lines from a totally unknown long poem by Nonnos of Panopolis, the best Greek poet for a thousand years either side, and I am going to find it, and make my fortune, whatever it takes, even if I have personally to seduce every abbot on Athos.

'You may look at our records,' decided Akakios.

'Thank you, my lord. I am very grateful.' Sebastian lowered his eyes demurely, and in his pocket, uncrossed the fingers of his left hand.

*

When Edward walked into the bar of the Connaught, he knew at once who his hosts were. Which was odd, since he had not had any picture in his mind at all, and the room hummed with business being done, one way or another. Ms Polychronopolou reclined at her ease, slim briefcase leaning up against her chair, her expensively shod feet crossed one over the other at the ankle, with the relaxed air of someone who is being paid a great deal of money just to sit there. Edward averted his eyes from her *soignée* but intimidating form, took one look at her companion, and immediately despised him. Everything the man wore, with the probable exception of the tie, was English. The blazer had come from Jermyn Street, not long since, as had the oxblood leather shoes; the grey flannels were elegant beyond cavil. Edward's nostrils flared with the absolute judgement of the dandy. The shoes were somehow fractionally too narrow; and the wrists appearing beneath the immaculate plain white cuff of the shirt were visibly hairy even from a considerable distance. Thus impeccably, soberly, and most expensively dressed, the fellow somehow made it absolutely clear that the essence of the appearance of an English gentleman is spiritual rather than material. Britzolakis was unmistakably a wog, though it was hard to say why.

A moment later, they had spotted him, though neither appeared to have been looking in his direction. Britzolakis rose easily to his feet, while Ms Polychronopolou remained seated, stretching out a slender hand adorned with an oversized, barbaric ring of pearls and citrine, and a pair of heavy gold bracelets. She smiled dazzlingly at him, displaying very white teeth, as he bent over her hand formally, and he was caught, with a shock, by eyes as amber as the necklace she wore.

Once all amenities had been observed and the trio was comfortably settled with their drinks, Ms Polychronopolou opened the batting, in excellent, slightly American-accented English, underscoring Edward's reluctant awareness that she was the one to watch.

'We are most grateful to you for making contact with Mr Eugenides,' she observed. 'You'll know, I am sure, how one small detail can hold up your business.'

'Glad to be of help,' said Edward blandly, swirling the ice in his glass and regretting, just a little, the fact that he was drinking Perrier water.

'From your letter, you found the old gentleman I think a little strange?'

'Well,' he said judiciously, 'a little eccentric, maybe. I rather formed the impression that he sort of hibernates. He's sharp enough once he gets going, but he probably lives in a dream most of the time. He's totally isolated, you know. He must be practically the only permanent resident in the whole of the City. The house is archaic too – all the shutters shut to keep out the cold and almost no lights. So there he is, you see, alone in the dark for week after week. God knows what he does with his time, but I'm not surprised he sort of coasts to a halt in the winter.'

'That is very interesting,' said Ms Polychronopolou. 'I didn't know he was so old.'

'Just out of curiosity,' said Edward, 'do you do much business with him? What kind of outfit is Eugenides & Co. anyway? When you got in touch with us, we hadn't heard from him for ten years or so.'

Ms Polychronopolou slanted her wolfish amber eyes at Britzolakis, who obediently replied.

'He is the end of a very, very old firm. The clients which they had, Levantine traders, fur merchants, they've gone either up or down. A few of the old Levant houses underlie the big shipping men of today; most of them have gone. Eugenides might have gone either way. Maybe round 1750, they had the clients, the know-how, to join the big league, but they settled for small. They got a lot involved with the Church, that goes right back.'

'And no one ever made money out of the Church, that's for sure,' commented Ms Polychronopolou, 'not without being a bishop.'

Britzolakis spread his square, hairy hands expressively. 'They've had this reputation, two-three generations now: honest, careful, they don't take risks. Like, you'd get them to sell your grandmama's pearls? But if you were doing deals, you'd maybe go somewhere else. Old Mr Eugenides, your guy's father, he wasn't cut out to be a banker. He wrote a lot of stuff nobody reads, and the word is, the son's just like him. How do you say in English, *anachronismos*?'

'Anachronism,' said Edward. Just then, a waiter arrived, and informed Ms Polychronopolou that her table was ready.

What followed was, from Edward's point of view, a sort of ordeal by dinner. He wished, if at all possible, to convey the impression that he was an *habitué*, but he was unable to work up a genuine indifference to exquisite food paid for by someone else. The Greeks' selections were from among the lightest and most austere items on the menu, and Edward, who lusted after tournedos Rossini, was constrained to follow suit by the fear that such an order would make him look like a greedy barbarian. The resentment thus engendered was deepened beyond measure when Ms Polychronopolou ordered a bottle of wine so expensive it gave him a faint sense of vertigo, and did not drink it. The wine stood in all three glasses, expertly poured by the *sommelier*, but the Greeks, after a token, indifferent sip or two, left it strictly alone. Edward was left in agony, trying not to look at his glass, knowing full well that if he sipped at it, he would empty it, and if he emptied it, he would empty the bottle; and that to do these things was somehow to lose game, set and match.

Ms Polychronopolou, meanwhile, nibbled indifferently at her julienned vegetables, and made conversation about skiing. It was only after coffee had been served and the waiter had gone away, that she permitted any business-related topics to be resumed.

'We will be interested to see the Mavrogordato houses,' she commented. 'It is clear from the original documents that the gift originally made was of substance, but how do I say it? Not great.'

'Modest?'

'Thank you. Modest is the word. Yet this area, once so modest, now commands great prices. Once the houses are sold, I expect to enrich the legatees for this not-so-great pious thought of the last century, by some millions in sterling.'

'Yah. It's amazing,' agreed Edward. 'Even a few years ago, you could get property well into the centre for next to nothing if you bought in the right areas. Now it's just impossible.'

'It's going to be a surprise for them,' she continued. 'This has just been going on from one generation to the next, you see? It was only that I noticed the trust could be wound up...' Her voice trailed off, and she moved a slender hand eloquently. Edward felt a momentary pang of sympathy: he knew only too well what it felt like to find a lot of money for somebody else.

'Pretty annoying for you,' he observed.

Her mouth twisted a little, and she looked at him consideringly. 'Edward...If I put the houses on the market, could I instruct you to act on my behalf?'

He looked up at her, then across to Britzolakis. Three sets of eyes, with the flat, hard brilliance of hunting carnivores, not one pair with anything to give away. The silence prolonged itself until Edward folded. He was pretty sure he understood her.

'I'm not sure I'm hearing what you're saying, Ms Polychrono-polou,' he fenced.

She shrugged. 'Call me Lamprini. I thought maybe we could do each other a little favour?'

'Put it this way, Lamprini. I'm happy to act for you, but on the level. There's no way you could get enough profit out of a deal like this to be worth the risk.'

'I was thinking, maybe twenty per cent...?'

'Still not worth it. An English solicitor's got to produce an audit certificate every year, you know. If you've done a bit of fiddling, it's a skeleton in the cupboard for the rest of your career. Can't be done.'

But, it occurred to him suddenly, the situation was one with definite possibilities. What she wanted was impossible, but there were much richer pickings to be had, and more safely. 'Mr Eugenides,' began Edward cautiously, 'was pretty clear that the guys on Mount Athos weren't taking any interest. They should've copped the lot in the nineteen-forties. I get the impression that he was saying they'd totally forgotten about their property.'

'Well, Edward, there could be reasons. The population of the Holy Mountain was at its lowest ever just after the war. St Michael's was maybe down to six old men, or something. It's not one of the big lavras. Just a little place. Anyway, London is a very long way from their daily concerns, is it not?'

'I don't know,' objected Edward. 'There's about tuppence-ha'penny in cash, apart from the stuff you're getting back, but if I owned a chunk of London real estate, I'd think it was pretty important. You can buy a lot of prayer-books with that sort of money.'

'But do you see,' chipped in Britzolakis, 'they do *not* know it? They know little of London, and what they know is very out of date. What their records will show, I think, is that they own a bomb-site which was once a church, in a poor part of the city, on the wrong bank of the river. How could they imagine such a property is of value? What they would care about, you know, is the icons that went with the church.'

Edward was in two minds: should he speak, or not? Abruptly, he decided to commit himself. It was all very well to know this stuff existed, but what it was worth, and how to dispose of it, was outside his area of expertise. It struck him suddenly and forcibly that Lamprini, who was acting for the Mavrogordatos, might have at least ostensible authority to approve the co-option of a trustee. And from the way Britzolakis spoke, Greek art evidently meant something to him. 'Mr Eugenides thinks the last rector was killed rushing into the church to try and rescue the treasures,' he said cautiously.

'Yes, and they will know that from the report of Eugenides. They maybe lost interest then.'

There was a thoughtful silence: Edward played with his cup, wondering whether to go on; Lamprini played with her bracelets, glancing at him covertly from under her long lashes, Britzolakis examined his immaculate fingernails. Lamprini spoke.

'Edward. "Mr Eugenides thinks." Are you telling us you know something he doesn't?'

'There's something else,' said Edward slowly. 'I found a note in one of the boxes in our office. The icons and silver stuff weren't destroyed. They were put in a safe-deposit a couple of months before the church went up.'

'Jesus Christ,' said Lamprini. 'Who knows about this?'

'Only me. I found the note, you see, trying to answer your question, and I hung on to it. D'you want to see it?'

'Very much.' Edward fished in his wallet, and brought out the memorandum. Lamprini examined it in silence, then passed it to Britzolakis, who raised his eyebrows, and said something under his breath. Lamprini was watching him narrowly.

'Do either of you know about icons?' asked Edward.

'Me,' said Britzolakis. 'I'm not a real expert, but I had to do some research for a job I was doing, you know? I was reading up this stuff, only last year. There's some good pieces here, that's for sure. But it's not the icons that matter. See where it says "ivory statuette"?'

'Yes?' said Edward and Lamprini in chorus, expectantly.

'You know how many in-the-round Byzantine ivories there are in the whole world? Two. One's in the Victoria and Albert, and this is the other. There's a photo of it in all the books. Everyone thinks it was destroyed.'

Edward's stomach flip-flopped, and he took a sip of his cold coffee. 'Serious money?' he enquired, a little hoarsely.

'You bet. Christ knows what it's worth. Millions. All the museums will want it. And the trustees could sell it, no problem. The provenance is perfect.'

'You're sure Eugenides is the only trustee?' asked Lamprini.

'Yes, positive.'

The three of them sat for a few moments, preoccupied with their own busy thoughts.

'Listen,' said Britzolakis slowly. 'If an English trustee, say, handed all this stuff to Greek agents acting on behalf of the owners, he'd be in the clear, right? I mean, he could swear he was acting in good faith they were the right people? In practice, you know, buyers aren't too fussy about the right to sell, as long as the object isn't actually on the Interpol list. J. Paul Getty, he's going to want this thing really bad, and monks don't read sale catalogues. They aren't ever going to find out.'

'Okay. That's all making a lot of sense. So, if I got everything out of the bank, how would you handle your end?'

'Well, there's nothing to say all this stuff isn't part of the Mavrogordato bequest,' observed Lamprini. 'If we sent you a letter claiming to recover this treasure on behalf of the Mavrogordatos, then if anyone ever asked questions, you could say you believed it. In Greece, of course, we don't tell this story; we're selling the things because St Michael is destroyed.'

Edward thought about this, and saw nothing wrong with it. 'Who knows about this at your end?' he demanded.

'We do,' said Lamprini, 'me and Alexander. You will understand, I think, that proving the Mavrogordato will involves many people? But one little tiny piece which is difficult, unthankable…?'

'A thankless task,' supplied Edward automatically.

'A thankless task. Yes! I get this thankless task, and my junior, who is Alexander. We look up books and records, we make a report. And our report, you understand, it deals only with the Mavrogordato interest. It says nothing of the Church of St Michael, or of English law on charitable trusts, or of Mount Athos. It only returns the houses and their rents to where they belong. How about you, Edward? You are also a junior, I think? You had in the same way a thankless task?'

The image of Dil came unbidden to Edward's mind; Dil flipping over the documents in the tin box with his forefinger. But Dil knew nothing; he had not been involved at any stage.

'I worked on it all on my own, Lamprini,' he said. 'No one in the office remembers anything about Eugenides except the secretary.'

'So,' said Lamprini deliberately, 'the knowledge of the great fortune represented by the estate of St Michael's sits with us three.'

'And with Mr Eugenides, of course,' pointed out Edward, looking her in the eye.

'And, of course, with Mr Eugenides,' she agreed. Lamprini pushed up her sleeve, exposing a wafer-thin, diamond-set wristwatch. 'Now, I think, we had better set out for Lambeth.'

'Send me a xerox of that thing,' said Britzolakis casually, as they stood up to leave. 'I'll do a little research on market rates.'

Think as he might — and Edward, who was circumspect by nature, thought long and hard — he could see nothing wrong with the conclusion they had tacitly reached. Eugenides and the modern world self-evidently had nothing to say to each other. The whole vast apparatus of late-twentieth-century knowledge-gathering had failed to gather up any of the facts now unexpectedly at his disposal. The Greeks — and it would be their necks on the block along with his, if they decided to do anything — were clear that no nasty surprises lurked at their end, and though he had disliked Lamprini on sight, she could plainly be trusted to do her homework where her interests were at stake. They were children of modernity, all three of them, lean, fit, young hunters. The idea that the past itself could hold concealed wolf-traps, snares and spring-guns, that the British Library, in holding the past, might also hold the future, was a notion wholly and absolutely alien to his theory of what constituted knowledge.

IV

What no reasonable person's assessment of Mr Eugenides and his position could have predicted on the basis of available information was that his long seclusion was about to be disturbed, as a direct consequence of a completely extraneous factor, apparently irrelevant to absolutely everything, but especially to the concerns of an ambitious young lawyer. Love was not something which Edward thought about much, but even if he had, the passion of one Nonnos of Panopolis, a distinguished poet of the sixth century AD, for a boy called Alexis who died too young, could hardly have struck him as relevant to his concerns.

However, the untimely death of the beautiful Alexis elicited from his grieving lover a long elegiac poem so uninhibited in the content and texture of its reminiscence that it would have been literally unprintable at any time before 1980. The fact that it was copied and preserved in itself seems almost miraculous – though the severe perfection of Nonnos's mastery of classical form may have been held in some quarters to offset the incendiary nature of his subject matter. Thus, some hapless monk, his blushes, perhaps, burning through his beard, was led to make a copy for posterity. As Sebastian, experienced in these matters, saw it, the existence of a medieval copy of the *Alexiad* was gratifying, but not astonishing.

What was not surprising in the least, on the other hand, was that seventeenth-century Athonites had found no use for the thing, and had offered it to Sir Everard. Equally, it was obvious that Sir Everard, a man steeped in Greek literature and a competent poet himself, would have pounced on it the moment he saw it.

Sebastian's scholarly interests lay largely in the Byzantine world. They had been led in that direction by an adolescent passion for the works of Constantine Cavafy, but as time went on, he found that Byzantium, that corrupt, fantastical, pragmatic civilisation, suited him very well. For one thing, unlike Classical Greece, a great deal of Byzantium still endures. And by a lucky chance, Sebastian, whose temperament was not academic in the ivory-tower sense of the word, was asked as a young postgraduate to date and authenticate some documents for an international auction house. Thus introduced to the murky and complicated world of dealers (not, in some ways, wholly unlike that of Byzantine politicians), he took to it with enthusiasm. Over the years, this interest metamorphosed into a second-string career of buying for dealers, and dealing on his own behalf in antique items such as textiles, intaglios and silver. Naturally, the time-consuming nature of this activity meant that he published less than, in an ideal world, he could have done. Sebastian's own view was that all this constituted a hobby; it took the place in his life of distractions such as football, parenthood, or building models of the Taj Mahal out of matchsticks. The fact that he made money out of it was, in his opinion, neither here nor there. He also pointed out, if the subject happened to come up, that even so, he managed to write more than a number of colleagues whose attention was theoretically undivided. No matter. The fact that he was known to make money over and above his salary as a result of piratical expeditions around the eastern Mediterranean meant that he was automatically dismissed as a dilettante by colleagues who spent their summers otherwise and on the whole, less entertainingly.

Sebastian's other problem besides simple envy and its complex ramifications, was that Classicists in general despise both Byzantium and Byzantinists. From a Classicist's point of view, the Greeks, having been offered Plato's *Republic* as the ultimate model for the ideal state, suffered a fit of collective lunacy and proceeded to reject it in favour of Christianity, emperors, eunuchs, and a degree of corruption and bureacracy which has become not merely a byword, but an adjective. The practical implications of this prejudice boiled down to the fact that if Sebastian were going to render his academic position impregnable, he needed to write an epoch-making book, for which he would need a very special subject, and the first sniff of anything suitable to cross his path was the *Alexiad*. With the current interest in the history of homosexuality, the amount he knew about Digby and Anglo-Greek relations in the seventeenth century, and the fashion for writing academic books which make visible the processes of discovery, he might be able to write a book which would at the same time establish his campus credibility and get reviewed in the Sundays. If, of course, he reflected bitterly, running over the facts in his mind for the umpteenth time, he could find the fucking poem.

His investigations on Athos had revealed some essential data. The manuscript had started there, bought fair and square from the lavra of St Demetrius, further up the mountain – Sebastian grinned to himself to observe that the *Alexiad* had been preserved in a volume of sixth-century religious poetry, sandwiched discreetly between the hymns of Paul the Silentiary and the holy kontakia of Romanos the Melodist. The copies of Digby's memoranda in St Michael's, kept just in case among the lavra's accounts, noted the purchase, what he had paid for it, and the date it left the mountain in a consignment of books bound for his new library in London, packed in straw and sealed in small barrels; all countersigned by the abbot of his day, Athanasios.

Sebastian had left the Holy Mountain well content. He knew where his story started. He did no business there: the monks, within their own specialist field, were extremely well-informed and far less unworldly than they looked. No one had got a bargain on Athos for forty years. When he permitted Abbot Akakios to sell him an early printed edition of the sermons of Gregory the Thaumaturge which might – just – have belonged to the kyrios Digby for twice what it was worth, this was more in the nature of a *quid pro quo*. He did considerably better, as he had expected, elsewhere in the Peloponnese.

But now, he sat at his desk in his elegant flat in Coptic Street, contemplating his notebooks. The *Alexiad* manuscript had left Athos in the spring of 1661. It reached London, that he was sure of, since it was mentioned in a private notebook of Sir Everard's begun in 1667, which he had used for jotting down odd reflections on his reading, and which had ended up presented to the British Library along with the other Digby manuscripts from St Michael Graecorum in 1940. It was this note, in fact, which was his only real clue that the poem had ever existed. He reread it, for the umpteenth time.

The Alexiad of Nonnus. Sweet and fantastical Numbers, much of luxury and looseness; ἡ παιδεραστία. Yet if this is of hell the devil hath music to move the mind to virtue – the eyes of ὁ καλός Alexis are lamps across a thous^d years – vide Plato Charmides et quoddam lasciviora apud Catullam. Are these not lines worthy even of Sappho?

– then Sir Everard quoted six lines, six lines which had affected Sebastian very much as if, idly turning over a stone during a walk, he had found it to contain a vein of gold. They represented, as far as anyone knew, all of the *Alexiad* which survived. Sebastian ran his hands distractedly through his sleek dark hair, clutching a handful of it at either temple as if this might help him think.

'*Concentrate*,' he admonished himself. 'Everything's got to be somewhere.' At the top of a page, he drew a small mountain ornamented with a cross, standing for Athos. He drew an arrow from it, pointing towards a square house with two windows and a door: the library. Across the line, he wrote 'Shipwreck. Pirates.' But it survived the perilous journey, that he knew. Then what? Great Fire of London? No: the notebook was begun in 1667, the fire was 1666. He drew another line, but this one had no confident arrow at the end, pointing to a known destination. He drew a rat, a big fat one with leering sharklike teeth. And a cloud, with rain pouring out of it. 'Damp,' he said to himself in despair. 'Insects. *Housekeepers.*' There is a special subsection of scholarly horror stories about cooks using old manuscripts to line baking-dishes... Okay, he told himself severely, scribbling over his drawing. Forget the rats. If it's gone it's gone. But what about if it survived? That's all you need to think about. What do people do with books?

The manuscript could have been in the church. Unlikely. St Michael's was essentially Anglican by the nineteen-forties; they'd not have been rocking round the clock with the holy kontakia of Romanos the Melodist. Another possibility: the rector might've kept it on his bedside table and got his rocks off thinking of the beautiful Alexis. But the poor old sod was burned to a crisp rushing into the flames to rescue his icons. So if he had had Nonnos tucked under his pillow, whoever picked over the wreckage would've sent it to the BL with the rest of the collection.

Whoever picked over the wreckage. Hang on to that thought. Who on earth was responsible for sorting it all out and making the bequest? Sebastian, stuffing the notebook in his pocket, dashed out of the flat and up the road to the Manuscripts Reading Room in the British Library. After a frenzied rummage through the index of personal names, looking for the right Everard Digby, he found something which might possibly be what he was looking for, posted his slip into the fetchers' room, and waited impatiently, drumming his fingers on the blue-leather-covered table, until he was prevented by a reproving glare from the austere West Indian lady who presided at the central desk.

Some time later, an overalled attendant brought him a box file containing the documents relating to the reception of the collection. The answer to his question stared up from the thin, yellowish wartime paper: Eugenides & Co., 3 Garlic Court, EC4. Sebastian carefully turned over the fragile sheets. Eugenides' letters spoke, between their formal lines, of deep affection; long-standing friendship between himself and the recently carbonised rector, but also, of passionate bibliophilia. One letter was particularly striking. 'In these desperate days,' Eugenides had written, 'I cannot consult with my principals on the Mountain. I must interpret my sacred trust on my own authority; and do so thus. These relics of the spiritual wisdom of my native land I now place with what is dearest and best in the great nation of my adoption, that they may share in the protection which the Library affords to the heart of all that is truly to be valued, as we stand once more, shoulder to shoulder, against the Barbarian.' The personality, the scale of priorities... 'He borrowed it,' breathed Sebastian, in the rustling, absorbed silence of the manuscript room. 'The old bastard borrowed it, and forgot to give it back.' He sorted the fragile papers back into order with automatic precision, and handed the box back to the superintendent with an absent-minded smile. Then he was off to the main reading-room to consult Pevsner and find out, as rapidly as possible, whether Garlic Court had survived the war.

Consequent to this series of discoveries, Dr Sebastian Raphael was to be found in EC4 at a suitable calling hour the following afternoon, beating a brisk tattoo on Mr Eugenides' lion-headed doorknocker. A minute or so later, the door opened, and Eugenides and Sebastian stood surveying one another with mutual curiosity. Sebastian produced his card with a flourish, and handed it to the old man accompanied by one of his most winning smiles. Eugenides considered the card at length, making small and inoffensive whiffling noises in his nose, then peered up at his tall guest.

'Why have you come to see me, Dr Raphael?'

'My dear Mr Eugenides,' said Sebastian, 'I have come to talk to you about Byzantine poetry.'

Eugenides considered this statement, took a step back, and motioned Sebastian into the hall. 'Perhaps you would care to come upstairs, to my private quarters?'

Sebastian padded up the marble stairs, carpeted with ancient drugget peeling away from long-unpolished brass stair-rods, full of curiosity. The house itself intrigued him considerably. When he emerged from the stairwell into a dusty but otherwise clean square upper hall, he felt he was ready for just about anything, but even so, Eugenides' drawing room came as a considerable shock. The big picture over the fireplace was a half-length portrait of Sir Everard Digby, all vulgar flash and polish; which looked as though it had been there since the day it left Lely's workshop. But as the eye travelled round the room, the Lely, despite its size and swagger, was completely set aside by a much smaller portrait hung between the two windows. A plainly dressed little girl, with the double eagle of Byzantium over her smooth, round head – my God! it must be Godscall Palaeologue, last known descendant of the Last Emperor – and the hand which recorded her was assuredly that of Mr Hogarth the face-painter. Sebastian, staring at the picture of the last heiress of the throne of Constantine, never noticed Mr Eugenides leaving the room. He came to himself only when the old man returned, bearing wine and biscuits. Having poured sherry and settled himself and Sebastian in a pair of Empire tub-chairs covered in worn-out yellow brocade, he peered quizzically from beneath thick and tangled brows, and enquired,

'Well, Dr Raphael, what do you wish to say about Byzantine poetry?'

His tone was mild, neutral, but Sebastian was not deceived. He leaned back in his chair (and leaned forward again hurriedly when an ominous creak was heard), sipped his sherry, and regarded Eugenides steadily.

'It's not a question of what I want to say, Mr Eugenides. It's what I want to ask.'

'My dear Doctor, how can a simple businessman expect to inform such as yourself?'

'Oh, Mr Eugenides. I'm quite sure you can.' Sebastian spoke with confidence. His host's private, ambiguous smile encouraged him, so did the room, replete with secrets, in which nothing appeared to have been changed in three hundred years, so did Sir Everard over the mantelpiece. The portrait would hardly be there if the relationship between Digby and the house of Eugenides was a casual one. He struck out boldly.

'Your firm dealt on behalf of Sir Everard Digby, didn't it?' The old man's heavy eyelids came down, signalling appreciation of this stroke of play.

'My ancestor, Mr Emmanuel Eugenides, was I think factor for Sir Everard,' he confirmed.

'And afterwards, after St Michael's was established, I think maybe you brokered the business between the church and the Athonites? You'd have had the contacts.'

'We did indeed,' agreed Mr Eugenides, smiling faintly. 'Our humble firm, I take it, has some place in historical record?'

Sebastian waggled a hand deprecatingly. 'I've been putting a few things together, Mr Eugenides. Sir Everard's notebooks, which are now in the British Library. What the *London Perambulator* has to say about St Michael's before the Germans got it. Your father's letters in the BL – I assume he was your father – some notes I found on Athos...'

The old Greek's shaggy eyebrows rose. 'You have been very thorough, Dr Raphael.'

'Lucky, Mr Eugenides. Lucky, and very interested. I was particularly struck by your father's letters. He was a remarkable personality, I could see that, and a great scholar. You can tell from the way he writes about books.'

'You are quite correct, Dr Raphael. He was indeed a remarkable man.'

Sebastian swigged the last of his sherry and leaned forward to put the glass on the winetable which stood between himself and his host. 'Very religious, very scholarly,' he continued. Eugenides pursed his lips, and nodded gravely. 'No one's going to make me believe that a man like that didn't have a library. Men like that *always* collect books unless they're moving once every six weeks, and it's absolutely clear to me that nobody's moved from this house since the Great Fire of London.'

'Dr Raphael, I appreciate your capacity for logical thought,' said Mr Eugenides. He got to his feet, taking his weight on his wristbones as old men do. 'Would you care to follow me through to the library?'

Sebastian, silent and triumphant, trailed after him across the hall to the other door, the back drawing room it must have been, and looked into the darkness. Eugenides crossed the room, moving confidently in the dark, and flung open the shutters. The room was lined from floor to ceiling with glass-fronted mahogany bookcases, and a fine library table stood in the centre. Sebastian had eyes for none of these things; he was transfixed by the dark, compelling gaze of a superb ikon of Christos *pantokrator* which hung over the empty fireplace, an image of such stupendous majesty and beauty that Sebastian, coming to himself, realised first that he had crossed himself, and second, that there was a tear rolling down his cheek.

'Sorry,' he said, mopping up and blowing his nose.

'Not at all,' replied Eugenides ambiguously. Sebastian turned on him.

'I'm beginning to get the impression, Mr Eugenides, that your ancestors were a lot more involved with Sir Everard and his activities than anybody really knows.'

'That is quite possible,' conceded Eugenides. 'But then, I do not know what everybody knows.' He crossed the room, opened a glass-fronted bookcase, touching the leather spines of the books thus protected with gentle, coaxing, fingers, and eased one out.

'That's an Estienne *Greek Anthology* I'm looking at, isn't it?' demanded Sebastian from the other side of the room.

'Yes, indeed. Printed by Stephanus – Estienne if you prefer – from the *Anthology* of the learned Maximus Planudes in 1566.'

Sebastian moved on to more delicate ground, feeling his way. 'I think I'm looking at one of the best private collections of early Greek printed books in the Western world,' he began cautiously. 'I didn't come here to find it, though. I'm here to back a hunch that printed books aren't the whole story. You've got some manuscripts, haven't you?'

'Oh, yes,' said Mr Eugenides. 'Would you like to sit down?'

Numbly, patiently, Sebastian sat at the table, while Mr Eugenides brought out his treasures. He admired, as it deserved, a very fine Greek bible of the twelfth century. A fifteenth-century copy of the *History* of John Zonaras; Chrysostom on the Statues. He praised lavishly, and asked technical questions only. Finally, the old Greek took pity on his good manners.

'I am forgetting myself, Dr Raphael. It is many years since I shared the pleasures of this library with anyone. It is poetry that is your interest, is it not?' Returning Chrysostom carefully to his shelf, he reached out a stubby, vellum-bound book. 'I have the *Alexiad* here. It is a very great treasure.'

Sebastian's heart lurched; he opened the book with a trembling hand, and bit his lip. It was the wrong *Alexiad*, the epic poem of that name by the princess Anna Comnena. It was, he had to admit, a very great treasure; dating perhaps to the fourteenth century, it had full-colour half-page illustrations in a splendidly antique style. Once he had dutifully looked through it – not without genuine interest – Mr Eugenides took it away and laid another anonymous, brown calf volume before him, with the Digby arms stamped firmly into its front cover in worn gold leaf.

Sebastian opened it, and knew instantly that he was sitting face to face with his heart's desire. The first texts in the book were hymns, the hymns of Paul the Silentiary. Flicking as rapidly as possible through Paul's work, he found, at last, the *Alexiad*. Looking on through, it was clear to see that the poem was huge, more than two thousand lines long; odd words and phrases, catching his eye, suggested that it was just as good as he thought it would be, and left him burning with impatience to read it properly. With immense self-control, he shut the book and looked up at Mr Eugenides, standing quietly by the bookcase.

'You have found what you were looking for,' stated the old man.

'I have indeed,' said Sebastian frankly, 'I was looking for Nonnos' *Alexiad*. If it survived anywhere, I knew it had to be here.'

'Ah, the *Alexiad*. It was a gift, you know, from Sir Everard to Emmanuel Eugenides; he thought it unsuitable for his library. I know it well.'

'You do, do you?' said Sebastian, looking at Eugenides appraisingly. The old Greek's sallow cheeks flushed a little, but he met Sebastian's gaze squarely.

'My dear young man,' he observed mildly, 'I was not always as old as you see me.'

Sebastian was covered in confusion. 'I'm sorry, Mr Eugenides. I'm being appallingly rude.'

His host lifted a heavy-veined hand in a gesture of deprecation. 'I have nothing to hide, Dr Raphael. After all these years, there is even a certain pleasure in frankness. I have lived a very sheltered life. I was a child of my times, and in my time, in London, there was no beautiful Alexis. You must understand, Dr Raphael, that I have the disease of Plato. The love of the Highest through what itself is high. I would not, if you understand me, settle for the shadow rather than the reflection of the Idea; and only the shadow was to be found in chance encounters with the bodies of sailors and workmen. I returned home to my father's library instead, and consoled myself, when consolation was needed, with the love of another for a boy who has long been dust.'

'I'm sorry...' said Sebastian, inadequately.

'My dear Dr Raphael, do not waste your sympathy on my frustrated youth. I did well enough, in my own fashion, which is not, I think, a fashion which a man of your generation would easily understand.'

'Mr Eugenides, I want to make it absolutely clear to you that I've been looking for this poem as a sort of quest. It's been important to me since I saw Digby's quotation, and I really think it's got to be published. You may not think publication very important, but I do. The poem's desperately vulnerable as a single copy. It's an absolutely brilliant piece of writing, quite as good as anything Classical, and it's about something important.'

'Perhaps its time has come,' observed Eugenides. 'I am an amateur of books and not a scholar; I could not have done such a thing in any case. But also, you will I think see when you have time to look at it properly, that if I had known how to approach a publisher, no one, I think, would have accepted it.'

'Would you let me copy it?' demanded Sebastian baldly.

'Dr Raphael, I will not stand in your way. I do not wish to let the book out of the house, but I am always here. If you came one afternoon a week – perhaps Wednesdays? – you would be welcome to sit in this room and copy the poem of the divine Nonnos.'

'Mr Eugenides, I couldn't be more grateful...' burbled Sebastian. Eugenides held out his hands; slowly, and with reluctance, Sebastian surrendered the book, and returned it to its owner.

'Dr Raphael, I do not want to hear of your gratitude. It is a very great pleasure.'

V

Mr Dilip Dhesi, when not occupied in being the bane of Edward Lupset's life, possessed a number of outside interests, one of which was the city of his birth. Dil's mum and dad lived out their lives in Southall, a small Indian town which has nothing in common with London except geography. While he loved and respected his parents, this struck him as, on the whole, a wasted opportunity, so when the mood took him, and his family had no particular demands to make on his time, he went and did something, or looked at something, almost always alone. Like another Kim, balanced midway between native and foreign, he went where he chose, and made many strange acquaintances.

One Saturday in March, he had spent an interesting morning in the Tate Gallery with the Turners when it occurred to him that he was hungry. But he had visited the café on a previous occasion, and had considered it so extortionate that he had vowed never to set foot in it again. However, Millbank (as the wily Tate well knows) is Café Desert. Dil disliked the feeling of being held to ransom, and had, moreover, recently committed himself to a mortgage which for the time being absorbed most of his salary, so he gave the matter a moment's serious thought. Millbank may be desert, but if you know your way around, most deserts have watering-holes… Moving with brisk purpose, Dil left the Tate, walked down to Lambeth Bridge and risked his life scuttling across the multi-lane junction of Lambeth Palace Road, then turned triumphantly into the small redundant church that is now the Tradescant Museum. This, as he well knew, gave you not only a look at a splendid collection of garden-related odds and sods, which were not without charm for him, but also a sort of cheery, W.I. café dispensing soup, rolls, home-made cake and sundry refreshments for sums which in the Tate, but five minutes away, would get you a cup of tea and a sneer. It was with a pleasant sense of having beaten the system, therefore, that he loaded his tray, flashed his seraphic smile at the nice lady in the pink pinny, and looked for somewhere to sit. In the gloom of the apse, dotted with incongruous Formica tables, he spotted a familiar blonde quiff rising above angular shoulders. Hattie, an occasional client who had gradually turned into a friend, was sitting hunched obliviously over a cup of coffee with an open notebook in front of her. At her feet, discreetly tucked under the table, lay her sandy-coloured lurcher. He walked down the church towards her.

'Hat,' he said, making her jump.

'Oh, Dil. Hi. I didn't hear you come up. How's tricks?' Hattie shuffled her papers together, and made room for him. He slid into the opposite chair, and they inspected one another with affection-ate interest. Hattie's long, lean figure was casually attired as usual, in a dark chenille jumper and leggings; severe, apart from the blonde hair, spiky with gel, and the big, sparkly earrings. She looked tired, but pleased to see him.

'You should get your earrings in Southall, Hat, love,' he remarked, gesturing towards her ears. 'Dowry gold; it never lets a girl down. My uncle knows this guy, I can get you top prices.'

'Nah. I'll stick with cheap'n' cheerful from Chapel Market. I'm always losing 'em; it'd just give me something else to worry about.'

'You look as if you're worrying about a bit much already, I

have to say. What're you doing, Hat? You need your Saturdays, you'll drive yourself crazy.'

Hattie shrugged and stretched, shoulderbones cracking as the long arms unfurled.

'Dil, you've no idea how frustrating it can be just trying to stop things getting any worse. I've got enough to do during the week with definite projects. What's got me out here is the other sort. Stuff that hasn't even got a file. Places that don't seem to belong to anyone. You'd be surprised how much no-man's-land there still is in the Smoke. And one day there's greenspace, the next there's a sodding great hole in the ground, and the day after, there's half an office block. There's an incredible amount of new building going on in London. I don't know where all the money's coming from. Anyway, I try and do a bit of walking around, checking up. The car won't do, you're past things too quickly. It's exercise, anyway, and Alice appreciates it.'

'You must know London like a taxi driver,' observed Dil.

'Just about. I'm not too brilliant on street-names, but I know where things are. Pubs, parks, statues, you name it.' Alice the lurcher stirred under the table, and he put a hand down absently: a narrow, coarsely whiskered snout was briefly laid in it.

'I'm surprised they let you bring her in here,' he commented.

'Oh, they're absolute loves. I asked, of course, and they said they'd stretch a point if she was good. I hate having to leave her at the door.'

'Why did you get a dog anyway? It's such a complication.'

Hattie shrugged, a little irritably. 'I didn't get her. She got me. She belonged to this *Big Issue* vendor in Islington I used to talk to. Lisa got a place somewhere, but they wouldn't take the dog. She was saying she wouldn't go unless she knew Alice was okay so I just thought why not, and said I'd take her.' Alice whined gently, hearing her name, and Hattie nudged her reassuringly with her foot. 'She's a bloody nuisance, but I've got quite fond of her.'

'Are you on your way to somewhere or are you on the way back?' asked Dil.

'On the way. I want a bit of a look round the South Bank. There's some bits and bobs I've got my eye on.'

'D'you fancy a bit of company?'

'Oh, sure, if you don't mind a long walk. Actually, come to think of it, I'd quite like you along. Anyway, 's all education, innit?'

Dil hastily finished his cake, and they got up. Hattie shrugged herself into the donkey-jacket which hung on the back of her chair, while Dil neatly stacked cutlery and crocks on his tray. They walked out together into the garden in the thin spring sunshine, the gravel crunching beneath Hattie's pink Docs and Dil's desert boots, and out to the Embankment. Together, they strolled up the river towards Southwark. Both of them were used to hiking about the city for hours on their own, so they walked for some time companionably, busy with their own thoughts. Beside them, the Thames was placid, grey, empty, spanned by bridge after bridge: Westminster, Hungerford, Waterloo, shadowed by the concrete Gulag of the National Theatre, Blackfriars. Crows bounced in the spring breezes amid the slicing, economical flight of the ever-present gulls, their calls echoing raucously over the water. As they went, the great panorama of Westminster and the City unscrolled on their left; too familiar to inspire comment, its theatricality a reminder of the long centuries in which the ceremonial side of London life was centred on, or viewed from, the river. But as they came out from under Blackfriars Bridge, Hattie caught Dil looking down at the blank, pearlescent water, and broke the long silence.

'It's one man who did that,' she observed.

'What?'

'He was called Malcolm MacLain, and he killed London River. He wasn't even thinking about it. MacLain invented a sort of steel box, eight foot by twenty. Shipping containers. They swept the world. You can fill 'em at source, Dil, and then they stay filled till they get to the buyer. That does in 25,000 dockers' jobs in London alone. All the people who packed stuff in ships, and the ones who got it all out again. Nothing's unpacked in transit. Another thing. No one needs warehouses any more, you can leave shipping containers out in the open. Of course, with containers, it's more efficient to use huge modern ships, and they can't make it up to the Pool. You can't put the clock back; but that kind of change means something. London was here because of the river for two thousand years, but now it's just here because it's here. That's why Dockland's full of yuppies, and the real docks are down at Tilbury which is practically in France. The Thames used to be a world, Dil. Now it's an under-used amenity.'

'Someone told me there's fish in the Thames again,' said Dil.

'Yeah. More fish, and a lot less people. I've nothing against salmon, Dil, but there's a lot of rivers with fish in around the place. This was something unique.'

'Hey, look. Talking of bringing things back. That must be the new Globe. What d'you think of bringing back a slice of Elizabethan London?'

Hattie stopped, and they looked together at the new theatre's high, plastered walls. She shrugged. 'Something and nothing. It's a tourist thing.' Her voice changed, suddenly vibrant with enthusiasm. 'Now, that's what I really like.' In the shadow of the recreated Globe there nestled a row of eighteenth-century cottages, and a prim, attractive house of about the same date, with a mansard roof and pineapples at the gable corners. There was a crest over the door, and a name, Cardinal's Wharf.

'Which Cardinal?'

'Oh, I dunno. Wolsey, most likely. The point is, it's not a museum of anything. It's not a London experience. It's just a house, and there's an old lady lives in it, experiencing London in her own way. You can't go in unless you know her or you're someone from the Gas Board. I'm not against tourism, but if we don't let places like Cardinal's Wharf just exist, we're going to end up like a pack of Red Indians on a reservation, playing at being ourselves. We're turning off in a minute. Look for Globe Walk.'

'Where is it we're actually going?' enquired Dil.

'Down a bit into Southwark. You'll like it. Come to think of it, it's providential you showed up, I wanted a word with you about it.' As she spoke, she was threading her way deftly and confidently through a maze of little streets. 'Here we are'. Dil looked about him. A world of soot-stained Victorian houses and Fifties flats. The nearest house was of substantial size, detached, but the windows were boarded up, the roofline was sagging like a hammock, and there seemed to be a small tree growing out of the chimney.

'It's a shame that place is being left to fall down,' observed Hattie. 'It'd make a good doctor's surgery, something like that. 'S next door we're interested in.'

Next door was a tall, larch-lap fence guarding what seemed to be a substantial gap in the surrounding brick environment. There was a blank door in it. Hattie put her hand through a hole left for the purpose, and flipped up a latch. They walked in together.

'Oh, wow,' breathed Dil, delighted.

It was a bombsite, of course. It must once have been a rusty nightmare of twisted metal and broken stock-bricks, a place for children to get tetanus and junkies to shoot up. Someone had got sick of the sight of it, and it had been transformed into a garden. Rubble had been hauled into piles to make rockeries, or flattened into paths. The earth thus bared was organised into brick-bordered beds studded with neat rows of vegetables, or raked and awaiting spring planting. Brambles were disciplined, and inter-planted with raspberries; daffodils winked and nodded from tin cans and everted tyres, answered by the pink of flowering currant.

'I thought you'd like it. You're a gardener yourself, aren't you? Some locals just took over,' explained Hattie. 'It's been going on for about twenty years. The coppers turned a blind eye, of course, since it was reducing problems for them, and no one's ever complained. What I really love about it is it's something a bunch of ordinary people just decided to do for themselves, to make their lives nicer. It wasn't laid on by the Council. There's some old people in the area who spend practically all their time here, specially when it gets warmer.'

'I think it's fabulous,' said Dil, sincerely. 'It's got no legal status, I suppose?'

Hattie shrugged. 'Doubt it. I've had a go at finding out for them, but I still don't know who owns the site, or why they haven't done anything with it. I reckon it's the same people as own the house next door, and my guess is that the original owners died in the Blitz. They can't've died intestate or the government would have copped the property, so maybe there's an heir nobody can find, or some kind of dispute.'

'I can try and find out about law and land-squatting for you,' offered Dil. 'All I know off the top of my head is, if anyone had moved into the house at the end of the war, tidied it up a bit, and started paying the rates, they'd have an excellent case in law if the original owners tried to evict them after all this time. But gardens don't come into the same category. Even if people have been using the space for twenty years, they don't actually live there, and it isn't anyone's livelihood, so squatter's rights don't apply. I've been into this recently for my dad and his mates. I was trying to work out whether allotment-holders built up any legal rights beyond the basic lease of the site to the Allotments Association, and I reckoned they didn't. This isn't even an allotment. If you were fighting this one, you might get a bit of help from "custom and practice", and I suppose the legislation on rights of way might get you somewhere. But this site is worth a heck of a lot of money, isn't it. Once someone realises they've got it, they'd be prepared to spend thousands on lawyers. It'd be worth it to them, you can see that. I'll do what I can, Hat, but the minute anyone wakes up and realises what they've got here, your gardeners are on borrowed time.'

Hattie wrinkled her long, aquiline nose. 'I didn't want you to say that.'

'Yeah, but you knew I was going to, didn't you? You don't come to lawyers for justice, Hattie. You come to them for law. Tell you what, though. You might just be able to put together a case that looked like long delays, and lots of money going to the lawyers. Look at it this way. Let's assume we've got a greedy punter. Everyone looks gift-horses in the mouth, it's only natural. He's got all this money suddenly he didn't know he had, and he can't realise it till the place is sold. He's going to want his dosh as quickly as possible, isn't he? So if you came along making a noise like a lot of timewasting and legal fees, you might just get an out-of-court settlement. Maybe enough to buy somewhere as a communal amenity, even if it wasn't as big. I think that's the best strategy: persuade the enemy it's better to spend 20k on you than 50k on lawyers.'

'I'm surprised at you, Dil,' said Hattie, mock seriously.

'Ah, but remember I'm not a fat cat yet, Hattie. When I'm a partner, I'll be singing a different tune.'

'Yeah, and you won't be talking to the likes of me.'

He picked up the playfulness of her tone at once, and responded in kind, grinning at her engagingly. ''Course not. You're just a troublemaker. One of Red Ken's little sleepers, isn't it?'

''Sright. Your dad'd be shocked you knew people like me.'

'I dunno. Mum'd be shocked anyway, cause she reckons you Western girls are only after one thing, but I'm not sure even Dad's going to be voting Conservative next time round.'

'Now *I'm* really shocked. Where are the Tories going to be if they can't rely on Asian small businessmen?'

Dil shrugged, pursing his lips. 'Dunno, don't care. They

should've looked after them when they'd got them, shouldn't they?'

Hattie looked at her watch. 'Oh, God. I hadn't realised it's got so late. Sorry to run away, Dil, but I'd better get myself back to Islington. I've got some dry-cleaning to pick up, and they're not open on Sundays.'

'You should live in Southall, love. There's seven days in the week there. See you around. I'll get in touch soon, when I've had a minute to think about your gardeners.'

'Bless. See you soon.' She touched his arm lightly, a casual gesture of farewell, and they parted.

VI

In the course of the following few weeks, Sebastian took his laptop to Garlic Court each Wednesday afternoon, plugged it into Eugenides' geriatric wiring, and transcribed the *Alexiad*. He arrived, on each of these occasions, with a small offering: the book he had bought on Mount Athos, a bottle of madeira, a bowl of spring flowers. Eugenides left him alone while he worked, but towards evening the old man would rap on the door, Sebastian would finish up, and for forty minutes or so, they would make conversation in the drawing room under Sir Everard's bold stare and the severe gaze of Godscall Palaeologue. He began gradually to become fond of the scholarly old recluse, to appreciate his gentle, archaic courtesy, and the almost Edwardian ceremony with which he deployed his fund of extraordinary knowledge.

Between Wednesdays, Sebastian did some preliminary work on the text, roughed out a synopsis; and after an exciting few days of faxes and transatlantic phone calls, got his *Alexiad* project accepted by Harvard University Press, a personal triumph which the old gentleman greeted with polite incomprehension. Sebastian, in consequence, found himself actually looking forward to the beginning of term. The idea of going back to work after a sabbatical is generally depressing, but on the other hand, a triumph's not a triumph until you've got someone to share it with – and Sebastian was further of the opinion that you really get the joy of it when you know full well that some of the people congratulating you are choking on their own bile. So, on the first Monday of term, he dressed with care. A bright blue shirt, and for once, a tie, his most irritating one, which was black and handpainted with Michaelangelo's David; a souvenir of a brief fling with a Californian. Jeans, loafers, a tobacco-brown cashmere cardigan, and one of his nicest intaglios, the one with Hermes, patron of tricksters. He admired himself in the bedroom mirror, pleased with the effect. On his way out, he paused, put down the briefcase and scurried back to the bathroom to spray himself lavishly with 'Jicky': true dandyism lies in attention to detail. Thus armed and fortified, he headed for the Strand.

After a tiresome couple of hours putting four months' worth of departmental memos unread into a recycling sack, deleting unwanted e-mails and generally tidying up, Sebastian decided he needed someone to talk to. He was just about to make a move in the direction of the coffee room, when the cheerful face of one of his best students appeared round the edge of the door.

'How's my favourite tutor? Ooo, *like* the tie. What've you been up to, Sebastian?'

'That's for me to know and you to find out, Ryan, love,' said Sebastian repressively. 'Have you been good?'

'Good-ish. Well, sometimes. It's nice to see you again.'

'You too. Actually, since I've got you here, you may as well tell me when you'd like your tutorial. I'm going to have to sort all that out today anyway.'

'Bless. What about Tuesdays? I'm signed up for "The Golden Age of Athens", and Mr Beckinsale's scheduled the class for nine o'clock in the morning! Honestly, Sebastian, I didn't know there *were* two nine o'clocks in the day. If I had something to look forward to after that...'

'I don't know why you're doing "Athens" anyway. I told you not to. Remember what happened last year,' grumbled Sebastian.

'Masochism, Sebastian. Pure masochism. Actually, Mr Beckinsale's so sweet when he gets cross, don't you think? Seriously, though. I thought it would help with sorting out all those political jokes in Aristophanes.'

'Hmmm...well, watch your step, there's a love. Let's say eleven o'clock on Tuesdays for your tute-group. Now piss off and do some work or something. I'm dying for a cup of coffee.' Ryan took the hint, and retreated. Sebastian looked after him with some misgiving, and left his office in search of gossip and sustenance.

He was delighted to find George Beckinsale himself in the staff common room at five minutes to eleven – that is, before his perfume had entirely worn off. George was a man with theories about many things, not excepting ancient Greek government, but among the most persistent, and fervently held, was that Sebastian would be none the worse for a good hanging. He was standing by the periodicals table with his back to the door, looking at the *TLS*, so he was unaware that anyone had come into the room. He recoiled skittishly as Sebastian came up behind him in a waft of Guerlain, as if he imagined you could catch queerness, like headlice, by contact.

'Hello, ducky,' said Sebastian cheerfully. 'Had a good Easter? How's the shop?' Beckinsale backed away, settling his tweed jacket nervously, shooting his cuffs.

'We have no significant problems with the students,' he admitted, with some reluctance. 'The second-year groups you're taking over from me have been told they're entitled to revision tutorials. They'll be expecting to start with Hesiod.' Thanks a million, sweetheart, it'd have been nice to get some advance warning, thought Sebastian to himself resentfully, though his expression remained childlike and bland. 'And what of your study leave, Dr Raphael?' He underlined the word 'study' with schoolmasterish sarcasm, looking pointedly at a postcard of St

Demetrius which Sebastian had sent the secretariat from Thessaloniki, and which had ended up pinned on the noticeboard. 'Profitable, I trust?' he expanded, his voice heavy with irony.

Sebastian fiddled with his ring, drawing attention to it, and wishing he'd worn two. 'Thanks so much for asking, George dear. I picked up a yummy little Hellenistic bronze in one of the hill-villages, just a day or two after I sent the card. And I got some very good jewellery – there's some excellent stuff around just now, and it's all kosher. It's gone to Phillips for their big sale in May, or I'd bring it in to show you. You really ought to have a ring, George. Or a tiepin, maybe, if you think rings are too sissy. I found a really beautiful chrysoprase Gorgon, she'd just suit you.'

Beckinsale flushed a dark, unbecoming brick-red during this speech, then exploded. 'I suppose it's too much to expect that you've justified the expense of the taxpayer's money in any way?' he enquired acidly.

Sebastian turned away.

'Oh,' he said airily, over his shoulder. 'I did a teeny bit of real work. I found a completely unknown, two-thousand-line poem by Nonnos of Panopolis.' He was moving towards the door as he spoke, and paused with his hand on the knob. 'I've got a book contract with Harvard University Press.' He opened the door, and slipped through it before George could open his mouth. His heart was singing as he waltzed down the corridor to pick up the gossip from the secretaries.

Down in the secretaries' room, Sebastian was greeted with cries of delight by Elaine, Moyra and Govinder. He was popular with them, since he was one of the few people in the department to treat them with any courtesy. He also enjoyed their company, so it was with a mixture of affection and calculation that he had taken care, when in Greece, to lay in some token items of silver filigree and amber jewellery, which he proceeded to distribute. Accepting in return a cup of coffee considerably nicer than the stuff which stewed in the common room, he hitched his backside on to the corner of Moyra's desk, and asked the room at large, 'What's going on then? I've just binned about five thousand memos without reading any of them. Ditto the e-mails. I appeal to you as my mates and partners in crime, was there anything in any of it I actually needed to know?'

'Very, very little,' said Govinder shyly. 'You know what it's like.'

"Course I do, dear. That's why I binned them.'

'Something you *should* know, Sebastian,' added Elaine, who was the senior secretary and knew everything, 'is that Mr Beckinsale has co-opted you on to a couple of committees. You're on the postgraduate review board now, replacing Andrew, who's gone on study leave, and you're with Katie and Clive on Academic Development.'

'And I wouldn't mind betting you never got a memo about either,' added Moyra dryly.

'Oh, I get you. One of George's little time bombs. I'm not told, so I don't go, then all of a sudden there's an outbreak of nasty little notes copied to Head of Department. Okay, love. Give me the dates, and I'll frustrate his knavish tricks for him.'

'Confound his politics, isn't it?' said Moyra.

'That too.'

Meanwhile, Elaine was leafing through the departmental diary, a heavy tome which functioned, for most day-to-day purposes, as the Tablets of the Law, jotting down dates on a memo pad. She ripped off the page, and handed it to Sebastian.

'Here you are.'

'Thanks, Elaine. Oh, *no*. I don't believe it. Look at this. He's scheduling meetings right into the vacations. How does he ever expect us to get anything done?'

'Academic Development has to meet after the Senate finance committee's published its estimates,' pointed out Govinder, who was tidy-minded, 'and I suppose he's thinking postgrads go on all year.'

'Okay, okay. You could still've got them into term. Nobody really minds meeting at six. And anyway, he's got totally the wrong idea about postgrads. I don't mind seeing the actual kids in the summer, but if we don't concentrate admin into terms no one's ever going to write a book again,' moaned Sebastian.

The corners of Moyra's mouth turned downwards in an ironic, Celtic smile. 'Ah, you're forgetting our Mr Beckinsale's a very busy man.'

Sebastian snorted. 'Oh, yes. Three ten-page articles in the last five years? I'm telling you, girls. Old Jim may have thought he'd fixed it delegating department business to our Georgie – I mean, I can see his point that we're at least getting some work out of the dreary old wanker, sorry, Govinder; but it's been absolutely disastrous. It's like putting a traffic warden in charge of London Transport Executive, he's thinking on totally the wrong scale.'

'Professor Savile did mention that he'd be giving the whole question of department administration further thought,' volunteered Elaine.

'Well tell Jimmy to hurry up thinking, then,' snapped Sebastian, 'before George drives us all barmy. Oh, well. I'd better go and sort out some seminar groups before the silly twit starts sending me more e-mails. Thanks for the coffee.'

Seconds later, he put his head round the door again. 'Oh, I forgot to tell you. I've got a book contract with Harvard. Something really exciting.'

'Sebastian, you dote! Congratulations. How long've you got?'

'Eighteen months. I should just about do it if you can help me keep Lovely Rita the Meter-Maid off my back. I'm not telling anyone what it's about, not even you. It's my special discovery. Ciao.'

VII

During the course of March and April, Mr Edward Lupset paid a couple of visits to Mr Eugenides. On both occasions, he was received in the old man's business room to the right of the stairs, and the rest of the house remained closed to him. He came, on these occasions, armed with sensible queries relating to the distant history of the Mavrogordato bequest, which Eugenides answered patiently, demonstrating a long memory and a clear, unencumbered intelligence. Edward, meanwhile, wrote down the answers absent-mindedly, preoccupied with the question of how on earth the old man could be induced to co-opt Edward as a second trustee when the trust itself was moribund, and indeed, its last significant reason for existing was in the process of being wound up. He was reluctantly forced to the conclusion that, since there was absolutely no reason for Eugenides to do so, the circumstances would somehow have to be altered. However, once one started thinking that way, there were definite plus points in the overall situation. Eugenides had no neighbours; while there was a certain amount of traffic during business hours in Garlic Court, there was no interaction between Eugenides and the offices that Edward could see. Casual questioning confirmed that the old Greek had no direct contact with anyone in the court, and more generally, there seemed to be nobody whatsoever who expected to see him in a particular place, or at any particular time. Following a suggestion from Lamprini, he contrived to ask whether Eugenides belonged to any church, and was relieved to discover that he did not. The impression that he himself was the only visitor to have crossed the threshold for years grew and strengthened.

As the old man shuffled out of the room on the second such visit, in search of the sherry he obviously considered an indispensable accompaniment to polite conversation, Edward watched him go with narrowed eyes. Eugenides was small, fragile in appearance; his hand, when shaken, was just bone covered in soft, papery skin, and his grip had no strength in it. He was completely vulnerable. It was easy to imagine him, for instance, falling down the stairs. A tragic accident. But what would happen if he did? Well, his affairs would be frozen, and Edward would have no *locus standi*. Any attempt to bring the St Michael's business under the control of Skinner, Catling and Barnacle would attract the attention of Betty, to say nothing of Mr Catling; it would be out of his own hands before you could say Mavrogordato. No, tragic accidents were not the way forward, even if anyone had the stomach for it. What was needed was a live Eugenides, but a less effective one. A Eugenides fielding demands he can't cope with, so he turns where? – to the obvious helping hand, a junior in the old and reputable firm of Skinner, Catling and Barnacle. Bob's your uncle. Thinking this over and over, he could see no flaw in it. Somehow, Eugenides' trusteeship had to become more than he could cope with alone; either because the work somehow became intractable, or because Eugenides himself became less able to do it.

When Lamprini paid a second visit to London, towards the end of April, he shared his impressions with her in the course of a walk in St James's Park. Wrapped in tawny fur, with high, glossy boots, she seemed to Edward to be taking an unnecessarily pessimistic attitude towards the mild mid-spring weather, but she insisted, nevertheless, that they should stay out of doors for the duration of their private colloquy.

'Business I can supply,' she declared. 'Alexander and me, we can invent some clients. Some kind of trouble, Anglo-Greek stuff, so you have a legitimate involvement. Don't worry. Details are for us.'

'Yes, but how can I get him to let me in with him?'

Lamprini shrugged, staring bleakly at a bed of early tulips. 'One thing I've thought of,' she said with uncharacteristic tentativeness. 'Old people, they fall over all the time, you know? The bones go thin. Brittle. So, if they have a little fall, they break a bone. And if you want someone confused proper, you send him to a hospital. My grandmama, she fell and broke her hip one day and they sent her to the hospital, and when she came back she was like half of herself.'

Edward was listening in horror. 'You mean you want me to break Mr Eugenides' leg?'

'I'm not talking about real violence, Edward. We're not monsters. I just think, if we could get him shaken up a little, into hospital for a while, maybe, then we can persuade him? What we got to be sure about, in this scenario, is you're there to pick him up. We don't want him to suffer, and anyway, you got to get him to hospital, so he don't just lie there and die, you know? Then you got the key, you see? And you say, you got nobody, Mr Eugenides, you need shoppings done, this and that. He'll want to get home, you bet, even if he can't look after himself. So you get to come in and out, like the son of the house. Alexander and me, we start sending the letters. We send you a letter too, at Skinner, Catling, you take it to Eugenides and say, oh Mr Eugenides, here's a big problem for me. He co-opts you as a second trustee, I send you a letter saying the Mavrogordatos don't dispute your right to act. Then you get over to the bank and we go into action, while Eugenides gets better and forgets all about it like it never happened.' Gazing past him towards the lake, she sounded earnest and reasonable, as if she was explaining the concept of multiplication to a kindergarten class. Edward stole a wary glance at her wind-pinkened cheeks and delicate, implacable nose, framed by the high fur collar.

'But you can't do things like that. It's so bloody risky!' he whined.

She turned to him, taking a step forward and looking up so that he realised, for the first time, that she was a full head shorter than he was.

'Have you got a better idea? Edward, I don't like this either. But the whole thing, it's like something sent from God, you know? I'm really, really stretched. I don't know what it's like in England, but for us, when you're still junior, the pay's pretty shit, and I haven't got a rich family. But if you don't look like you've already made it, the clients don't respect you, and the boss doesn't take you seriously. It's all about appearances. So I'm living in a dump, spending all my money on clothes, and my debts are getting out of control.'

'God, yes. It's just the same here,' agreed Edward fervently, looking at her, for the second time, with a modicum of sympathy. 'Well, that's the real world, isn't it?'

'When I saw this Mavrogordato thing, I just knew there was an answer for me somewhere. It's not as if we want to hurt the old gentleman, Edward. We just need him off balance for a while – I mean, you're *sure* you can't talk him into co-opting you, aren't you?'

'Positive. I mean, there isn't a shadow of a reason, is there?'

'Then don't you see? We've got to. It's just crazy. If we give old Mr Eugenides a little bit of a bad time and then get out of his life, we end up with a fortune. A real fortune, Edward. Like, millions. We could get ourselves out of this trap, and no one's ever going to find out how we did it. Trust me, Edward. I don't make mistakes. In my country, a woman in business can't afford to.'

*

It was the end of April. Sebastian had finished his transcription, and term was just about to close over his head. Weeks and weeks in which he would promise himself to call on Mr Eugenides, and be too busy to get around to it. Edward did not even know Sebastian existed, but if he had, he could have relaxed. Sebastian had seminars to prepare, at no notice whatever, on a variety of subjects hand-picked by George Beckinsale to make life difficult for him; he had chores which, similarly, were calculated to waste the maximum possible amount of time; he had students panicking about their finals and demanding tea, tissues, tact and time – and when not otherwise engaged, he had a difficult and complex poem in ancient Greek more than two thousand lines long to edit, translate and set before the world.

The random currents of human contact in the life of a great city bring people together for a time, then swirl them apart. Just as Sebastian was being borne away by the inescapable pressures of his own life, predators were gathering around his new friend, who for so many years had contrived to pass unregarded.

Edward, meanwhile, had taken to waking up in the middle of the night in panic. As he had long since realised, pushing Mr Eugenides down his own basement stairs would require nothing but a strong stomach, which he was not sure he possessed, but in any case, would avail them nothing. How one contrives a *slight* accident was a much more difficult question, to which he had no immediate answer. He had no access to the house unless he called; and when he did call, Eugenides kept him under his eye apart from the few minutes he took to toil down to the kitchen and back. The idea of trip-wires bristled with problems. How would you fix, let's say, an invisible bit of nylon fishing-line so that it would stay taut enough for Eugenides to fall over it, but be instantly removable, leaving no trace? In a minute, making no noise? He could, of course, make a trip across the front door, but then how on earth could he contrive to be the man on the spot? If he lurked round the corner in Walbrook Street, someone might spot him. It would be difficult to loiter – the idea of disguising himself as a street-person crossed his mind, only to be rejected. Street people avoid areas tenanted only by the massively rich, knowing full well that they are as mean as mouse-shit, and associate the term 'charity' only with corporate tax-avoidance. Wrapping oneself in a dirty sleeping-bag and sitting on a square of cardboard virtually guarantees invisibility in most areas of London; but he would collect curious glances in that particular setting. And besides, if Eugenides was left with any wits about him at all, which was the object of the exercise, he would at some point remember that the Edward who providentially just happened to be passing had also been most uncharacteristically dressed.

No. You want something natural, he decided. Banana skins kept nudging into his mind, but who's actually seen anyone slip on a banana skin? It was not till the following Friday that inspiration struck. He was in Bibendum in Lamb's Conduit Street, having an end-of-the-week drink with Julian, an ex-schoolfriend, now also a lawyer, who was his regular squash partner. Julian, who had a long evening's work ahead of him, had ordered a spritzer. When it arrived, Edward saw him looking around rather helplessly.

'Are you after more ice, Jools?'

Julian nodded. Edward, who was better placed by the bar, reached a long arm between the happy swillers, and pulled the icebucket within reach. The ice was the sort which is sold in off-licences, which is not in cubes, but in square tesserae. He watched idly as Julian grappled with the tongs, the slippery little squares eluding him triumphantly.

'Bugger the things,' he snarled, as three pieces, insecurely grappled together, exploded in different directions. Edward stared, transfixed. Julian caught him at it, and laughed to cover irritation. 'I give up. Cheers, Ned.'

'Cheers.' Edward took a long, luxurious swallow of his Scotch. Eureka.

About ten days later, he went to see Mr Eugenides again. As on all previous occasions, the old man went to fetch the ritual tray. This time, the moment he was safely across the hall, Edward was on his feet. In an insulated bag in his briefcase, there was a kilo of small, square pieces of ice, casually bought, a day or so before, along with a few bottles of claret and some lager. They had melted a bit in the course of the day, but that was to the good. He ripped it open with trembling fingers, and scattered the ice as evenly as possible just inside the door. Such light as there was, now it was spring, came from the window, and was cut off from that area by the door itself, which created a pool of dense shadow.

As Eugenides' slow steps returned across the hall, he scuttled back to his seat, and perched on the edge, too tense even to pretend to sit properly. He need not have worried. The old Greek came in with his eyes fixed, as usual, on the tray itself, concentrating on the perilous journey of his precious old glasses. One heavy foot came down squarely on a nodule of ice, which promptly skidded from beneath him.

'Ai!' The tray pinwheeled through the air; the bottle falling heavily to glug unregarded across the dusty floorboards, while the glasses arced and shattered against the door-jamb. Eugenides himself fell forward heavily, arms outstretched.

'My God!' cried Edward, on his feet in an instant, registering shock and concern. He could have spared himself the trouble. The old man lay crumpled on the floor in a pool of ice and sherry, breathing stertorously through his open mouth. He seemed to be unconscious. Edward paused briefly to scoop ice out of view and kick it along the walls on the dark side of the room – the sherry on the floor accounted quite naturally for the remaining moisture – and took the old man's wrist to check his pulse, which was threadlike, but reasonably steady. He drew the fragile limbs into something like the Ambulance Brigade's recovery position, checked (not without a squeamish shudder) to see if Eugenides had false teeth, which he did not, and ran out of the house, the model of a concerned and agitated young lawyer, to seek help at the nearest office.

The house next door was unresponsive to his knock, but the one with the plate-glass window, which turned out to be occupied by a firm called Pleroma, produced a couple of immaculate investment bankers, decently but humanly excited and not a little curious to see inside the mysterious house, together with an efficient secretary/receptionist who rang for an ambulance. Edward explained over and over again that Eugenides' foot had twisted under him as he negotiated the doorway. All three of them then proceeded to get dust and sherry on the knees of their expensive trousers, and Eugenides himself did not wake up to offer any contradiction.

When the ambulance arrived, Edward gave his card to the receptionist at Pleroma, and asked her to contact his office and explain that he would not be in for the rest of the day. Then he pocketed the door key, and departed with the ambulance in a blaze of glory and Good Samaritanism.

Once at Casualty, he did what he could to get Mr Eugenides checked in, and saw him covered with a blanket and wheeled off to X-ray by a strapping nurse. He signalled his intention of waiting around for news, retired to the waiting room, and fished out Haskins on the law of tort, which he had thoughtfully brought along with him. After twenty minutes or so, a thought crossed his mind. Casually, he fished in the bottom of the briefcase, and found the ice-bag. Wadding it into a little ball in his hand, he stood up, and deposited it in a hospital wastepaper basket. No one so much as raised their eyes from the contemplation of their private worries.

A good two hours later, he heard a cough. Raising his eyes, his gaze travelled up the lanky and slender form of a young black doctor, his pleasant face grey-toned and heavy-eyed with exhaustion.

'You're the chap who's with Mr Eugenides?' he enquired.

'That's right. He's okay, I hope?' Edward fished in his breast pocket, and offered his card as he spoke. The medic glanced at it briefly, and sat down beside him.

'You are a colleague?'

Edward became shyly voluble, meeting the dark, bloodshot eyes with a clear and candid stare. 'Yes, Dr...' he squinted at the man's lapel-badge '...Appiah. My firm has been involved with Eugenides' outfit for about two hundred and fifty years. As far as I know, we're the only people the present Mr Eugenides does business with. I've spent a lot of time with the old gentleman, and it's pretty clear he doesn't have any family or friends. Bit of a recluse, really. It's not exactly within usual terms of dealing, but since he hasn't got anyone else and he's an old client of ours, I feel he's sort of my responsibility,' he finished modestly.

Appiah massaged his own temples, shutting his eyes momentarily. 'It's most good of you to feel that way. Mr Eugenides is not in danger, you will be glad to hear, but the system has had a shock. He has broken his right wrist — I suppose he put out his hands to break his fall—'

'He was carrying a tray when he went over,' interrupted Edward helpfully.

'Ah. That explains a lot. Probably he could not see his feet, and tripped. Apart from the wrist, which is the only serious injury, he has sustained extensive bruising. The heart is strong, and for a man of seventy or more, as he seems to be, he's basically in good shape. He has, of course, also broken his glasses, which is disorienting for him. I take it he does speak English?'

'Of course,' said Edward, confused. 'He's lived here all his life, as far as I know.'

'Well, he's spoken nothing but Greek since he came round. We assume it's Greek, anyway. Something religious, I think; he's reciting, not complaining or making conversation.'

'Can't help you there. He doesn't go to church that I know of.'

The young doctor looked at him blankly, as if he had forgotten who he was, and scrubbed his long, pale-palmed hands over his face again.

'Sorry, Mr Lupset. It's the trouble with sitting down...Aphasia, or reversion to childhood languages, is a common response to trauma. Probably he's reverted to words familiar from very early in his life. It shouldn't last.'

Edward felt no impulse to pursue this, and changed the subject. 'Well, Dr Appiah. What can I do to help?'

'You've got access to the house, haven't you?'

'Yes. I locked up, and brought the key.'

'Oh, good. If you wouldn't mind taking a look around, see if you can find spare specs. The ones he's got aren't very strong, but blurred vision will contribute to his disorientation and impede recovery. Also, it makes it harder for us to see if there's any long-term damage. He's sedated now, but I hope we'll be able to get medical details from him tomorrow morning. He'd have to stay overnight in any case. Tomorrow, we'll see. If you're prepared to help out, then we might be able to get the old gentleman back home. Visiting hours are two till eight, by the way.'

'Tell him I'll be straight round after work,' promised Edward. 'He'll understand I can't just take the day off, and I've lost this afternoon already, you see.'

'Fine. I'll make sure he gets the message. Nice meeting you, Mr Lupset. We'll get your colleague back on his feet for you.'

Edward shook the proffered hand, and left the hospital. It was with a conscious effort of will that he left the premises looking subdued, brisk and thoughtful. Not prancing, punching the air, and yelling.

VIII

Meanwhile in Islington, Hattie Luke was getting ready to go to a party. She was not ordinarily a dressy woman, but she was perfectly well aware that her height, her narrow, sloping, medieval shoulders and long neck, her heavy-lidded eyes and quattrocento profile, could add up to something very like beauty if she put her mind to it – which ordinarily, she had neither time nor inclination to do. She was bothering now, because Anthony and Tim, the kindest of hosts, took such endless delight in the elegance of women that it was only polite to indulge them. Alice the lurcher watched tragically from her basket.

'There's no point looking at me like that, Al. You're not welcome. Not after what happened last time.' Alice's air of injured innocence intensified: could anyone believe, it seemed to say, that this neglected and suffering animal was capable of slipping into anyone's kitchen and eating an entire coffee-and-hazelnut gâteau and a side of smoked salmon in a minute and a half? Hattie could, and did, and paid her no heed.

Despite what she had said to Dil about the virtues of costume jewellery from the Chapel Market, Hattie did in fact own a pair of good earrings, one of the few relics of her mother's family which she possessed, and accordingly, cherished. They were beautiful, exquisitely matched drop pearls, which probably first glowed in the ears of some ancestral Scroop-Dory of the seventeenth century (when the family flat chest must have been a bit of a social disaster, Hattie mused, as she put them in, and double-checked the clasps). Otherwise, she was wearing a completely plain tunic dress in gunmetal-grey heavy satin which flattered her slender figure and brought out her pale, clear complexion, her grandmother's jade beads, and a pair of severe Ferrogamo pumps she had bought in a sale. Her hair was, for once, flattened into a sleek blonde cap, and no one could say she had not done her best with what nature had provided. There was a ring at the door: her taxi. She slipped a black leather jacket on over her finery, stuck her wallet in the pocket, and went out.

When she rang Anthony and Tim's doorbell in Highgate, Anthony came to the door, his lanky, towheaded figure elegant in a blue-and-white striped shirt, and kissed her formally on both cheeks.

'Hattie, darling. You look marvellous. Let me take your jacket. Come through to the drawing room, there's someone we'd like you to meet.'

Hattie followed him through, observing with mild amusement that it looked exactly as it had done for the last five years. The walls were still bare, age-discoloured, unpainted plaster, lavishly hung with engravings in heavy gold frames, the antique damask curtains, rotted in places by sunlight and sheer age, hung immobile in splendid swags of crimson streaked with faded pink, discreetly tacked into place, while the night was kept out by shutters. The effect, splendid in its way, had been created over a strenuous weekend in preparation for their housewarming party – and somehow, though resolutions had long been made that the curtains would be put up properly, and the appropriate treatment for the walls had been earnestly discussed on many a subsequent occasion, temporary grandeur had gradually solidified into the ordinary background of life.

Tim stood by the fireplace, short, dapper and bespectacled, in animated conversation with a tall, prematurely grey man and a small, stout, vivacious woman. The threesome fell politely silent as she approached, and Tim turned to greet her, stretching out a hand to draw her in.

'My dear Simon, let me introduce you to Hattie Luke. Hattie, this is Dr Simon Calverley, who is a colleague on the Survey, and Alicia Norton Calverley, who as I am sure you know, writes for the *Independent*.'

'Oh, yes,' smiled Hattie, advancing to shake hands, 'I knew I'd heard the name. Nice to meet you.' Ay-ay, she thought to herself, Tim's up to something. Which one of them's the reason they were asked – the journo, or the colleague?

'You're the Hattie Luke of the Bridge Trust, aren't you?' asked Alicia, who turned out to be American. 'I've never been sure what the Trust actually does...?' Her voice trailed off hopefully, and as Hattie considered her response, she heard a pop from behind her. She accepted an old cut-crystal flute-glass of sparkling wine from Anthony, who moved round the group, topping up the others' drinks, and took a sip while she marshalled her thoughts.

'We're a very old charity,' she began warily. 'Our funds originally derive from the chantry charities of the old London bridges, but in the last century or so, we've taken our position sort of metaphorically. We're set up essentially to facilitate things people want to do; ways and means, not beginnings or ends. When I first got involved, we were very much working with the Greater London Council, but fortunately as things turned out, we retained an independent standing. Basically, if anyone's trying to get a project off the ground, we offer support, paralegal, aesthetic, historic, we advise on planning applications, or how to put in a bid for Lottery funding. We publish, we broker information between groups. You might say my stock-in-trade's knowing things, making connections. I've always been nosy. It sounds like nothing, I know, but actually, our effect's out of all proportion to what we seem to be doing. We're for London, and our basic question is, is a new project going to make London life better or worse? If the answer's better, we're in there, stirring.' She sipped her drink. 'Why d'you want to know?'

This question, as she fully expected, went unanswered. Tim leaned forward and changed the subject, smoothly and adroitly, reinforcing her impression that he was up to something. In the course of the following ten minutes, while Anthony clattered about in the kitchen, she set herself to discover what she could about the other guests. She found out quite a lot more about the man Simon: he had known Anthony and Tim since Cambridge days, when he had been a junior fellow in architecture at their college. He had then become the London editor of *Arca*, before getting involved with the Survey of London. However, she found out nothing whatever about Alicia, who had the good journalist's combination of friendliness, charm and neutrality. While it was perfectly possible that Tim and Anthony had simply invited a group of people that they thought would get on, the fact that Tim's involvement with the Survey represented not only his source of employment but his other consuming passion besides Anthony, made this unlikely. The presence of an architectural old pal and a journalist, besides herself, was suspiciously suggestive of machinery in motion.

Anthony reappeared from the kitchen, smelling faintly of garlic, and holding out his empty glass for a refill.

'Are you expecting anyone else?' she asked him.

'Of course. I do like to get the numbers right, and we're still missing your complement. I hasten to add that we aren't matchmaking, nothing so vulgar, but he is someone we thought you'd enjoy meeting.'

'All the same,' added Tim, 'if he isn't here in the next two minutes, we'll start without him. I'm not having Anthony's dinner ruined.'

'Sebastian's always late. We should have remembered, and

asked him for seven for seven-thirty. You seldom think of these things at the time, and anyway, he probably wouldn't have believed us. Shall we go through?'

He led the way to the double doors which divided drawing room from dining room, and flung them open, politely motioning his guests to precede him. While they were arranging themselves, the doorbell rang. Anthony slipped off to answer it, and Hattie heard voluble explanations and apologies from the hall. Moments later, her host reappeared, cradling an enormous bunch of yellow lilies, and accompanied by a tall and substantial man in a loose, pale grey suit, with rather long dark hair flopping into his bright blue eyes.

'This is Sebastian Raphael,' announced Anthony. 'Excuse me a minute while I go and put these in water.' He left the room, and Sebastian surged forward to kiss his other host.

'Tim, darling, I am a *toad*. You must be so cross with me. Sheer inefficiency, as usual.' Tim performed introductions, and Hattie regarded the newcomer with interest. He was a bit outside the boys' usual range, she thought, and she wondered why he was there. Sebastian chattered continuously while Anthony dealt out plates of smoked duck breast, lentils and salad, creating a place for himself in the group by sheer force of personality. Tim led the conversation, according to established habit, since Anthony, as usual, was nervous and abstracted all through the first course, and remained visibly preoccupied until the main course (roast cod with grilled polenta and two sauces) was safely on everybody's plates. Once he was sure that there had been no disasters, he visibly relaxed, looking, at last, able to join in the conversation. Since it seemed as if Tim and Simon had more or less exhausted the subject of Quinlan Terry's architectural iniquities, Hattie turned to include him, with a sure-fire topic.

'Got any new gardens, Anthony?'

'Oh, yes indeed. I've come across something *quite* extraordinary. It's in front of a townhouse in Notting Hill, one of those rows of white stucco tombstones, you know. They've done it in a sort of white trash style. There's a sculpture in the front garden based on about one and a half motorbikes, with some lovely grasses and things. It's terribly well done, and such a witty comment on the urban scene, and the people actually want me to list it for once, but the neighbours are up in arms. They're afraid it'll bring down property values.'

'Isn't it usually the other way round? I mean, do you usually get resistance when you turn up and tell someone you're going to list their garden?' enquired Simon.

'Oh, yes, yes, yes. Almost invariably, when the garden predates the current owner. It reduces the resale value of the house, you see, because it acts as a restrictive covenant, and of course it makes them frightfully cross if the scheme's intrinsically expensive. Ghastly Gertie's one of the worst problems – I mean, it's all very pretty, and historically very important, but you need three fulltime gardeners and about an acre of glasshouses to keep each and every Jekyll border the way she meant it to be.'

'Don't you think it's all rather interfering?' asked Alicia.

Anthony's spectacles glittered with zeal, and he rose immediately to the defence. 'We entirely accept that the owners of irreplaceable old houses owe it to society to refrain from wrecking them. It's exactly the same principle. Old gardens are so fragile. Do you know, I came across the remains of an absolutely perfect Gardenesque plan laid out by Repton himself some time in the 1820s, on a site near Cambridge? It's survived by pure luck, and a series of old ladies with conservative tastes and not too much money. I shudder to think what could happen to it if the house was ever sold. You could restore the design to its original glory, serpentine beds and all, in about two years flat, because all the structure's still there. It's got a wonderful romantic walk, with mature yew-trees and cyclamen stools about a yard across. But a single oaf with a JCB and a half-digested book by Mrs Hobhouse could destroy it in a week.'

'Anthony dear, you're preaching,' Tim intervened gently. Hattie hastened to turn the conversation.

'I wish I could talk you into listing the garden in St Michael's Road. Remember, the bombsite garden and the ace gang of vigilante granddads?'

'Oh, Hattie. I wish I could. I do see that it's terribly important in human terms. But it's not *interesting*, you see. There's no idea behind it, and it isn't actually special in itself. I couldn't justify it.'

'What garden is this?' asked Simon. Hattie explained briefly; and the conversation drifted off on to gardening, and gardeners. It was not until sherry trifle had been succeeded by coffee and cantuccini that Tim broached the subject which had plainly been on his mind from the start. Conversation had drifted into a natural pause; and since it gradually became obvious to all of them that he was looking portentous, one after another, they found themselves looking at him, and waiting for him to speak. Sebastian fixed him with a knowing eye.

'All right, Tim, dear. Cough.'

'You've found something, haven't you?' asked Hattie. Alicia said nothing; but like the excellent journalist she was, missed nothing either. Her bright eyes tracked from face to face as Tim capitulated, and spread his hands wide.

'Actually, chaps. I think I've found something rather splendid,' he admitted.

'Something to do with the Survey?' asked Alicia.

'Absolutely.' Once launched, Tim's manner became easier, and he leaned forward confidentially. 'We're working on St Lawrence Jewry at the moment, and I was in an old cellar under a set of offices. No one had been down there for ages, and when we flashed a torch around, we found that part of the back cellarage was full of huge blocks of cut stone. I think people must have thought they were just part of the cellar itself. Anyway, to cut a very long story short, what we'd found was the remains of a fountain. We did a bit of digging around in the records, and it turned out that the thing had been commissioned by the Levant merchants to mark the coronation of Charles II. They'd meant to put it up in place of one of the usual conduit heads, and I expect it was meant to run with wine on the day. Only there was a typical London muddle about sites – the coronation must've been a bit of a scramble – I mean, half London must've still been asking themselves if they actually wanted a king anyway. One of the London livery companies – the Haberdashers, I think it was – said they'd earmarked the site for a triumphal arch or something, and the Levantines could just shove off. I don't suppose the thing cost that much in the first place, craftsmen came cheap in those days, so they let it go and put it into storage in case it ever came in handy. The Venice-Levantine trade wasn't very important by then, so they just had to swallow the disappointment.'

'That's awful,' said Alicia, listening in horror. 'All that work, and it never ever happened!'

'Clever old you though, Tim, for digging it all out,' said Simon. 'You've kept it very dark.'

Tim flushed, pink and pleased. 'It's taken me most of the last fortnight to work out what it was,' he confessed. 'I didn't want to say anything till I was pretty sure I knew what I'd got, but I found some correspondence about it in the Public Record Office, and it all came clear.'

'Well, Timmo,' said Sebastian, 'what have you collected us all up for? Time to come clean.'

'Advice, my dears. What on earth are we going to do with it? I thought of you, Sebastian, for two reasons. First of all, after that wonderful article of yours in *Past and Present*, I'm quite sure you know more about Anglo-Greek relations in the seventeenth century than anyone else in the country. I do rather hope to interest you in it. It's already clear that the carving is of high quality, and there are a great many mythological or symbolic people cavorting around in the architecture. When we get the thing properly assembled and dusted off, I would dearly like to pick your brains on the subject of who they all are, and above all, *why* they are who they are. What sort of message were the Greeks trying to send? You can see why I need you, but my more immediate concern is with the other side of your life. Let's say that someone approached you and asked you to sell it to Sotheby's for them. What sort of deal might you be talking about?'

'Well, I haven't seen it,' said Sebastian cautiously.

'Take my word for it, it's a splendid piece. Twelve feet high, six or seven feet wide, that rather touching coarse English baroque, but with great feeling and verve.'

'Okay. It's a beauty. Another question, I suppose, is who it belongs to. There's case-law about this, as I'm sure you know – things are usually the property by default of whoever owns the land. On the other hand, since the fountain's almost certainly been there since before whoever owns the site actually bought it, it might count as unadministered personal property and end up going to the government. I suppose it's also possible it's legally still the property of the Levant trading companies, though that's less likely. If it is, then I probably know the only man alive who'd be able to sort it out for you. Let's assume they go with the freehold, which is probably right. What are you trying to do?'

'Well, what I really want to work out, strictly off the record and without actually alerting any of the auction houses that it exists, is roughly what it's worth. I'm fairly sure we can get English Heritage to make an offer, and if it's pitched at a sensible level, there are political reasons why I think the owners might be prepared to do a deal rather than trying their luck on the open market.'

'Well, it's worth a lot of money. I'd have to see it to tell you how much. The trouble is, if it went to the salerooms, and it's really pretty, there's always the possibility that Donald Trump or someone would want it as a garden ornament, and then the price would go through the roof.'

'Let's assume you get it. What do you want to see done with it?' asked Alicia.

Almost in unison, Tim, Anthony, Simon and Hattie replied, '*Not* the V&A.'

'Absolutely not,' amplified Simon. 'They can't be trusted these days, now they've gone corporate. And they'd just stick it in that dreary courtyard of theirs and no one would get any good out of it.'

'*And* it costs five quid to get in,' said Hattie bitterly. 'I'm positive it's in breach of their charter.'

'If it did go to a museum,' said Tim, 'I'd much rather it went to the Museum of London.'

'That's not a bad notion. But what about that "if", Tim? What's really on your mind?'

Tim looked at his clasped hands, then up directly at Hattie.

'Could we get anyone to put it up?'

'What a wonderful idea,' she said immediately, then stopped to think. 'Where?'

'That's what I wanted to ask. There's no point trying to put it where it was originally meant to be, which is in Whitehall. I'm pretty sure it was supposed to be at King Street Gate, which was demolished in 1723, so it'd be somewhere underneath the Ministry of Ag. and Fish, I think. But you could put it up in some public space that needs a bit of magic.'

'Don't they all?'

After a minute's thought, everyone had an idea, and they argued happily till nearly midnight. Hattie, though cunningly plied with strong drink, refrained from committing the Bridge Trust to facilitating the erection of a pristine, seventeenth-century fountain. Alicia and Simon, similarly, kept their expressions of enthusiasm and interest just this side of definite promises of a feature. They were all too experienced to do otherwise. When the party finally broke up, Sebastian turned to Hattie.

'Would you like to share a taxi?'

'Love to.'

Sebastian rang for a cab, they kissed their hosts, found their coats, and started off home. Once ensconced in the throbbing sanctuary of the cab, Hattie heard Sebastian's voice out of the noisy darkness.

'What do you really think of this fountain project?'

She considered. 'I think it's just possible. Tim's committed enough and idealistic enough to bring it off, with a bit of help. You can see it'd break his heart if it was sold privately.'

'What about the Bridge Trust angle?'

'Well, it really will have to go to committee. But personally, I'd see it as something which makes life more interesting, so I think we'd be on its side. It sounds a good case for Millennium funding, and we've developed a lot of expertise in pitching cases. Also, I know an excellent young lawyer who'd be a good man to look at the legal side for him. If that ever becomes an issue, I'll put Tim onto him. There's another problem. Tim obviously wants it somewhere out in the open, where it was meant to be, and I agree with him, but there'll be a lot of pressure to put it somewhere under cover. He might have to settle for a site in an atrium somewhere, which'd be really boring. What do you think about it yourself?'

'Well, from the point of view of Anglo-Greek history, I think it's just fabulous. We've got so few physical traces of the Greek community in London before the nineteenth century. There was a Greek church in Soho which went a long time ago, and another one in Southwark which survived till World War Two, but neither of them was ever very fully described. Tim was being bloody coy about iconography, wasn't he? I've got to say I'm intrigued, and if I wasn't so busy I'd be saying I couldn't wait to get my hands on it. The way things are, though, even if it was served up on a silver platter with parsley on the side, it'd have to join the queue. If Tim's got a few months to spare, I think I could probably be quite a lot of help with the context – I can't do much if he insists on doing it this minute. By the way, you don't happen to know if the Survey pays consultancy fees?'

'I think they do, in theory, but you'll have to hint pretty hard. Tim'll try the old pals act on you if he thinks he's got the remotest chance of getting away with it.'

'Oh, don't I know it. It's not that I object to the brotherhood of queers as a principle, but when it comes to expecting a fortnight's work for nothing, I really do draw the line at being Rabbit's Friends and Relations.'

'Quite right too. It's always the problem with fanatics, however much you love them. They all expect you to make an exception for their own special cause. We get it all the time at the Trust.'

Sebastian peered out of the window. 'I'm not far from home now. It was very nice meeting you, Hattie. Can I ask for your number?' Solemnly, they exchanged addresses and phone numbers, scribbling on bits torn off the back of Sebastian's chequebook under the flickering orange glare of the streetlights.

IX

Edward let himself back into Mr Eugenides' house like a thief in the afternoon – which, in spite of what the Bible has to say on the subject, is the favoured time for modern villains, who have long since realised that this attracts less attention than creeping about in the dark with a bag marked 'Swag'. After some exploratory fumblings, he found the light switch, and looked around him with interest. The heavy smell of sherry hung sweetly in the air. One of the bankers had tidily set the bottle upright, and it stood incongruously by the jamb of the door. All the liquid had evaporated from the floor itself, leaving only a sticky dampness, already furring with dust. He opened other doors in the hall: one concealed stairs down to the kitchen, one opened into a dusty dining room.

He went on up the stairs. The atmosphere of the old house seemed to press against him, gently, ineffectually, in a dignified but helpless resistance to the invading barbarian, and he felt vaguely uncomfortable, a little nervous, as the old floorboards sighed and creaked beneath his feet. He opened the door across the upstairs landing curiously, his heart banging as it had not done those few hours before. The formal beauty of the drawing room was lost on him, but the probable value of the paintings it contained was not. He could not identify them, but they were obviously museum pieces. And nobody knows they're here, he gloated, running a lascivious eye over little Godscall Palaeologue, stern in her frame, who looked as if she was damning his impertinence. It struck him, looking around, that the only incongruous touch in a room otherwise completely self-consistent (however bizarre) was a bowl of pink hyacinths on the console table between the two windows under the little portrait, diffusing its ambiguous, artificial perfume. Edward dismissed it as an unanswerable problem: perhaps even the cobwebbed Eugenides was touched by some thought of spring. Giving the room one more comprehensive look round, he dismissed it. The obvious value of the paintings was offset by their almost certain unsaleability without a proper provenance. He tried the other door, and found the library. Its contents were literally and metaphorically Greek to him, and the only thing in the room which was recognisable was, fortunately, also what he was looking for. A pair of goldframed halfmoon glasses lay on a notebook on the table. Edward pocketed them, and went on up the second pair of stairs, wooden, and bare even of drugget, to have a proper look round.

There were three rooms on the second floor. The front bedroom was shuttered and completely dark, and the light did not work, but as seen from the landing, it appeared to contain a mighty carved bed, an equally capacious wardrobe, and a strong smell of disuse. The second door revealed a Spartan bathroom with a floor of bare boards, a tub standing on lion's paws, surmounted by a lethal-looking old geyser, and a few balding, elderly towels neatly folded on a rail. The third opened into what was clearly Eugenides' own bedroom. It contained an iron-framed single bedstead, a rickety rattan table with an alarm-clock, a clean handkerchief, a glass of water, and a small icon on it, a plain chest of drawers, an icon of the Virgin Mary, and a prie-dieu. Edward wandered around, filled chiefly with an amazed contempt for the idea of anyone living for so long in a house without exorcising the ghosts of his parents from the best bedroom.

One thing which he wanted to look into while he had the chance was Eugenides' personal habits, in case any aspect of them came in useful. A careful investigation of both bedroom and bathroom revealed that the old man took almost no drugs. There was a large bottle of aspirin in the bathroom cabinet, the faded label of which suggested that some considerable time previously, it had cost him four shillings and sixpence: in the twenty-five years or so since decimalisation, he had got through perhaps half of them. Eugenides' only Achilles' heel seemed to be Andrews Liver Salts: a large, new canister had a prominent place on the small table by the bathroom sink, beside his cut-throat razor and its strop, and substantial inroads had already been made in it. Thoughtfully, Edward filed this information mentally, wandered back down the stairs, and visited the basement to investigate the kitchen quarters.

The kitchen itself contained a well-scrubbed table, a gas cooker which looked as though it belonged in the Science Museum, an elderly boiler, and a number of cupboards. Meagre, dun-coloured garments hung overhead from a pulley. Opening the cupboards at random and poking about, Edward found that Eugenides' diet, as he had surmised, consisted largely of bread, sardines, corned beef, milk and tea. The cupboards contained a neat regiment of tins and little else: the whole room spoke of indifferent, monastic refuelling. To Edward, it all looked like wasted opportunity. He became almost angry with Eugenides – certainly contemptuous – for the extent to which he had failed to make himself adequately comfortable, despite an amount of space which Edward (who shared a flat in Belsize Park with a couple of similarly circumstanced young men, piglike in their personal habits) helplessly and rancidly envied. The kitchen, despite its scrupulous cleanliness, was evidently well used. A pair of slippers was tucked under the boiler, there was a wickerwork chair with a newspaper laid on the seat. It was relatively warm. Edward could imagine the old man sitting in the kitchen in his slippers, with three whole floors of empty space above his head, and decided he deserved no sympathy whatsoever. After a bit more desultory investigation, he located a brush and dustpan, and swept up the broken glass from the office floor. Once he had deposited it in the bin, he left the house.

Entering the ward the following evening clutching a token bunch of daffodils, he found Eugenides propped up in bed, very white and transparent, and pathetically fragile in appearance. His right arm, now in plaster, reposed limply on the counterpane. Edward regarded him without compassion, but arranged his features to represent decent sympathy. The old man was staring into space, lips moving just perceptibly, and when Edward laid the flowers across his knees, he jumped.

'How are you feeling, sir?' murmured Edward, pulling up a chair and sitting down. 'I've brought your other glasses. Hope you don't mind me poking about, the medics thought I should.' He fished in his pocket, and put them in Eugenides' left hand, which closed on them gratefully.

With his spectacles on, Eugenides began to look less other-worldly. 'They are my reading glasses,' he explained, 'but better than nothing. It was good of you to find them for me.'

'What happened, Mr Eugenides? One second you were coming in, the next second you were falling. I thought perhaps your foot twisted under you or something?'

Eugenides rubbed his forehead wearily with the heel of his good hand. 'I do not know, Mr Lupset. I have no memory of the accident. They tell me this is usual. A little seizure, perhaps, I am an old man. Tell me, were the wineglasses broken?'

'I'm afraid so.'

'A pity. They were very old, Venetian. It does not matter.'

Edward changed the subject, hugging himself internally in secret glee. 'Have they told you anything about how you are?'

'Yes. My wrist, as you see, is broken. I have bad bruising, especially on my right knee and hip, so I will walk with a stick for a little while.'

'Is it painful?' asked Edward, with childish, heartless curiosity.

The old man closed his eyes, and waved his good hand, dismissing the subject. 'There is nothing urgent about my case. The wrist will heal, and they will remove the plaster in due course. The bruises will go away. The hospital is more concerned with the *cause*, as indeed I am myself. I live alone, as you know. If I fall again, you understand, I am in danger. They have done many tests to see if I am becoming subject to blackouts. There are many diseases, they tell me, that can have this effect, but so far they have found none of them.'

Edward nodded soberly. 'I left a message for you, Mr Eugenides. If they're willing to let you go home, I'd be happy to keep an eye on you – do a little shopping, that sort of thing. I could do it on my way home.' Eugenides' black eyes regarded him steadily: his own gaze dropped, and he found himself blushing as he had not since he was a very little boy.

'That is most kind of you. They wish to keep me for another night. Some of their tests, you see, are very tiring, and all of them take a very long time. Tomorrow is Saturday, is it not? If you would have the great kindness to speak with the authorities, I think, with your help, I could go home tomorrow.'

Edward excused himself, and went in search of the ward sister, who turned out to be large, formidable and Asian. She confirmed Eugenides' impression that he was not, from the hospital's point of view, an object of great interest, and arranged that Edward should return to take him away immediately after lunch the following day. When he returned with these tidings, Eugenides was visibly relieved. 'It is all very modern here, very hygienic,' he said wistfully, 'but this is an awful place. Light which reveals nothing is a very terrible thing.' Edward took his leave. The whole thing, in his opinion, was going as well as could be expected.

X

Dil was sitting at his own kitchen table, carefully pricking out infant courgette plants into individual yoghurt pots, when the phone rang. It was Hattie.

'Look, Dil, I'd like a bit of a chat with you about something, outside of the firm's time, know what I mean? Is there any chance you aren't doing anything tonight? Or tomorrow, maybe?' Dil considered his grubby hands, cradling the phone between chin and shoulder, and thought for a moment.

'Tell you what, Hattie. Nip over, and I'll make you some lunch. I've just got a place of my own, you know. The paint's barely dry, and I still get a cheap thrill from asking people round.'

'Fabulous. I'd love to. I've got the address here...W5's Ealing, isn't it?'

'Yes. I'm just off the Broadway. About twelve?'

'Lovely.'

At half past twelve, therefore, Hattie parked her little red Renault outside the Polish church, let Alice out of the back, and stopped to look around consideringly. A nice area. Big, Victorian stucco villas with cast-iron balconies, mostly flats now, but mostly recently painted in shades of cream and off-white. Dil had done well for himself. She found the house, which was the sort that has stairs up to the front door over a half-basement, and rang the doorbell. Dil had the first floor, with the balcony. Looking through the glazed outer door, she could see the door to Dil's flat on the other side of the entrance hall. He had painted it bright, clear blue. Moments later, he charged through it, in jeans and an immaculate white sweatshirt, and let her in.

'Dil, it's absolutely lovely,' she said, looking around. Alice roamed about, claws clicking on the wooden floor, subjecting everything to a minute inspection. The floor was pale Ikea parquet, and the room, which was white-painted and very light, with double french windows on to the balcony, contained almost nothing but a boldly patterned black and white futon sofa and a television. Easily the most striking feature was the balcony, crowded from end to end with pots of all sizes, and seed trays. 'What've you got there?'

'Courgettes. Squash. Dwarf beans, they're to go up those cane wigwams. Runners; I thought I'd see if I could train them round the balcony itself. Tomatoes. That's about it.'

'My God, you're practically self-sufficient. Don't they pay you?'

Dil shrugged. 'It's just bloody-mindedness, Hat. Something to think about that isn't law. You see some guys getting very weird. Office, pub, telly, bed, week after week. Ten years of that, and they're brain-dead, and earning fifty grand. I'd rather grow vegetables than turn into one. If you've got something living to play with, you can maybe call your soul your own. I still help Dad with the allotment, of course – it's about the one thing we can all still do together without having a row. But it's important to have something here.'

'No flowers?'

'Not my scene. If you can't eat it, I can't be bothered growing it. Come through to the kitchen.'

Hattie followed Dil into his kitchen-dining room, which faced out over the neglected garden (an appurtenance, clearly, of the basement flat) and must have been made from the original morning-room. A miscellany of vegetables littered his worktop, together with a couple of beautiful and very expensive-looking knives. The kitchen was well though not lavishly equipped, and decorated only with a large and gaudy calendar representing the goddess Lakshmi. Dil saw her looking at it.

'Mum gave me that,' he explained. 'They get scads of things like that from their wholesalers. Would you like a glass of wine?'

'Please. Anything I can do to help?' He filled a glass and handed it to her, pouring himself some mineral water.

'Nah. I'm used to working by myself. Sit at the table, and talk to me.' He went back to chopping onions, the knife flashing through the crisp white flesh with mechanical accuracy. Alice wandered through.

'Basket,' commanded Hattie.

'Do you want me to find something for her?'

'No, it's okay. What that means is that she'll find somewhere out of the line of traffic, and lie down.' The dog investigated the kitchen, then tucked herself tidily under the table. 'I'm watching you,' warned Hattie. She turned to Dil. 'She's the most terrible thief,' she explained. 'She's just waiting for me to forget about her, then she'll pounce.' Alice rolled her eyes, looking misunderstood. The phone rang.

'Damn. Excuse me.' He reached past her to the wall-mounted phone.

'Dilip Dhesi. Oh, hello, Mum.' He rolled his eyes heavenwards, and made a complicated, apologetic gesture with his free hand. 'Making lunch…Yes, of course I washed the vegetables…No I didn't use soap, we're not in the tropics here, Mum. I'm…Oh, all right. Look, Mum, this isn't an ideal time. I've got someone over for lunch…No, just a friend…No, you don't know them…No, not someone from work…Female, as it happens… Look, Mum, she's actually sitting here, right? Could you just knock it off?…Sorry, sorry, sorry. Just calm down, there's a love. She's sort of a colleague…Anyway, she wouldn't have me if I asked…Listen, Mum. I've told you before. If I give you an English daughter-in-law, I'll send written notification in advance, okay?'

The phone quacked prolongedly. Hattie had given up any pretence of not listening. 'I'll try to get over tomorrow…Love you too, Mum. 'Bye for now.' He replaced the receiver. 'Families! Can I give you some more wine?'

'I know what it feels like,' said Hattie sympathetically, covering her glass with her hand. There was no possibility of pretending she had not heard him, so, having been forced into earwigging on his private life, she felt on the whole that he was owed something in return. 'I was brought up by my Gran, 'cause my Mum died of me. She must've been born about 1910, and she was a holy terror. Tiny little woman, but nobody ever got a thing past her. She'd been brought up in a different world, of course, it was hard for her to adjust. Dad was a copper, which didn't help. Between the pair of them, I didn't get my love-life off the ground till I went to university. They're both dead now. Mind you, it'd take a lot more than being dead to shut Gran up. I still hear her in my head.'

'Mum's dead suspicious of the flat,' explained Dil, turning the gas on under a blackened karhai, and dolloping in ghee. 'She just can't think why anyone would want to leave home unless they're doing something they don't want their parents to know about. But I've got four little brothers and sisters, and ever since the bhangra revolution no one's been able to hear themselves speak. I mean, I've got nothing against my people's culture, but if you're getting home at ten or eleven some nights and you're out again at half seven every morning, you need a bit of peace.'

'Oh, God, yes. I know exactly what it's like. Peace and quiet wasn't really a concept with Gran either. What let me get away was, when the last of my posh relatives died off, I inherited about twenty quid and a big house in Suffolk. It's in a really pretty village, and it's just off the A12, so there was no trouble shifting it.

Dad put his foot down. He said if I had a proper house, I'd always have something to fall back on. Then he asked round the copper-shops, and they reckoned that Islington was just about as good as you get for a girl on her own. Gran was left without a leg to stand on, so I bought the place in Bachelor's Row.'

Dil sighed, measuring out rice with casual expertise. 'I'd really like somewhere with a garden. But this'll do for now. The 207 goes past the top of the street, so Mum can hop on a bus and come over with fresh veg and mango pickle if she's getting worried. Spot-check for little mirrors and razorblades, steal my laundry, all that stuff mums do. But it's a bit too far for just dropping in, which suits me fine.' Dil's voice trailed off, as several different culinary operations came simultaneously to crisis point, and he turned his attention to his stove. A few minutes later, he came across to the table, and began arranging food.

'Pilau. That's just some raita. Brinjal bhaji, alloo sag. That's Mum's own lime pickle, it's really hot so be careful. Would you like some lassi, or water, or some more wine?'

'Dil, this is fabulous. It all looks beautiful. I'd like some water, please.'

Later, over milky, masala-spiced tea, Hattie told him about the Greek fountain. He was interested, up to a point.

'I'd really like to know why your pal thinks he ought to be able to just take the thing over,' he commented. 'Why shouldn't Hezza or Andrew Lloyd Webber or someone have it in his garden, anyway?'

'Don't you like the idea of public ownership?'

'I don't believe in it. If a thing doesn't belong to anyone, it just gets kicked about. There's no incentive to take care of it, is there? Like schoolbooks.'

'Dil, you're such a Tory sometimes.'

He shrugged. 'Pity I hate them so much, isn't it?'

'I just don't understand how you can vote Labour and think the way you do.'

'Simple. Rich guys, like I want to be when I grow up, can't really live well unless the poor have a social contract. What I reckon is, social justice and self-interest coincide, if you think about it. Rich guys've got two real choices. They can spend about a third of their income on tax and maybe still get to walk down the street on a spring day, or they can spend about the same on personal security and medical insurance and live in a ghetto. The second way, you don't even get to walk down the street without being mugged by some poor dude who wants to redistribute your wealth personally. See?'

'Dil, you sometimes sound absolutely Victorian.'

'Could be. The old Queen-Empress didn't half hang on back in the old country. Mum and Dad are proper little Victorians, into self-help and all that stuff. They're just getting round to noticing they've actually got less in common with yer modern Tory than they have with modern Labour, cause there's nothing conservative about Conservatives any more. Do you remember a sad, pathetic bastard at my office called Edward?'

'Seen him, I think. Cute, blond, sticking-out ears?'

'That's him. Now, Eddie's a modern Tory. As far as I can see, his dad made a fortune without getting his hands dirty. He had a bit to start with, got into some deals in the City, made money off moving money around, then punted the lot on Lloyd's and watched the dividends roll in. Ed went to a posh public school and got into Oxford on something dead easy, Land Economy, something like that, "for the contacts". What the rest of us'd call social life. He spent three years on champagne and boat-clubs with a bunch of other yahs, and I don't think he ever reckoned he'd have to work at anything. Then Daddy lost his dosh the way he'd made it, down the plug with Lloyd's. Sold the London house *and* the roses round the door in the jolly old Cotswolds, buggered off to the little place in France, and told Edward he'd have to look after himself. He got a crap law degree in some poly, 'cause he found out about then that you can't get into Harvard without good SATs. Daddy pulled strings and got him into Skinner, Catley, and he's been wandering round the office falling over his bottom lip ever since. That's where Tories have got to. Talk about featherbedding. They'll destroy a whole town and say it's just economics, but try introducing the middle classes to the idea you can lose as well as win! These people've got nothing in common with the likes of my dad, Hattie. They're just looters.'

'Lawyers' offices must be full of blokes like that,' commented Hattie. 'When I was a student, if you ever met someone really slimy, he turned out to be doing law. You went to Cambridge, didn't you? It must've been even worse there. How did you cope with them?'

Dil did not answer for a moment, and when he did begin to speak, it was with an uncharacteristic level of suppressed emotion. 'I bought it for a while, you know. It's hard not to, when you come from Southall. I was so impressed by the whole High Table bit, I actually believed they had the right to judge me as a person, just cause they wore the right sort of suits. But you've got to've got off your knees before you can really see what they're like. They're not all total berks, but I don't worry about them accepting me any more, 'cause I don't respect them, not personally. All I want from them is cash on the nail.'

Hattie listened to this outburst in silence. The rancorousness of his tone surprised her, and she wondered what lay behind it. Alice stirred against her leg, disturbed by the emotion in the air.

'And I hear you're not doing too badly,' she said lightly.

'Oh, I get by.' He was not looking at her, but past her: his face, with the light gone out of it, was dark, proud and secretive.

She smiled at him affectionately. 'I bet you do. Don't put yourself down, Dil, love. 'S a nice feeling, when you know you've won in spite of them, innit?'

He looked at her properly, and his expression lightened. 'You're right, Hattie. No point in going over old scores.'

XI

Edward awoke, late, slowly and reluctantly, that same Saturday. In the kitchen, one of his flatmates was frying bacon, and giggling with a Sloany girl who must have spent the night. Somewhere a radio was playing. Something had woken him: was it the shrill, neighing laugh of Alan's scrubber...? No, there was another element, a ringing bell...

'Edward! Edward!'

'Urrgh.'

'Ed, it's for you.' He got reluctantly out of bed, pulled on a pair of pyjama bottoms, and shambled into the living-room, which was littered with empty cans and full ashtrays. Chris, the third permanent resident, was standing by the phone looking stern: beyond him, the television was set to the latest stockmarket reports on Ceefax. He handed Edward the phone. 'I think it's your mother.'

'Oh, Christ...Hello?'

'Hello? Hello? Ned, is that you?'

'Hello, Mummy.' What could she possibly want? Since his parents had decamped permanently to the Dordogne, he saw, and heard, little of them. He could imagine her, sitting by the little marble table where they kept the phone, immaculately dressed, coiffed and made-up, one thin leg crossed over the other just so, her foot, in its elegant shoe, carefully pointed.

'Ned, have I got you up? What time is it over there?'

''Course not,' he lied automatically. 'It's about a quarter to eleven.'

'Ned, I want you to go to Scotland.'

'What! Mummy, I've got a bloody job, remember?'

His mother's voice acquired a dangerous edge. 'Don't take that tone with me, Ned. You know I simply won't have it. I'm not asking for gratitude, but after all we've spent on you, the least we can ask is that you put a hand out to help yourself once in a while. It's the height of the holiday season. Your father and I simply can't afford to come over, and anyway, it's about time you pulled your weight in this family.'

Edward scratched his balls through the thin cloth of his pyjamas, and boggled. 'Mummy, what the hell is all this about?'

'Your great-uncle James. As you very well know. Your godfather.' Light began to dawn.

'Uncle Jimmy?'

'Of course. I heard from someone who's seen him recently. He's failing badly. I don't know how much longer he'll be able to stay in that house.'

'But—! I can't just take off, Mummy!'

'Listen to me, Ned. I'm James' only niece. You're his only great-nephew. Blood's thicker than water. Someone's simply got to take charge up there before they end up getting the police in. You don't want him leaving the lot to a dog's home, or some sort of neighbour, do you?'

'No, but—'

'It's just as well it's me on the phone, Ned. Heaven help you if your father ever hears you whining like that. It's your own future that's at stake, you idiot boy. You must see that.'

What Edward was actually perceiving most clearly, at that particular moment, was a pressing, indeed, insistent, need to visit the lavatory. Alan and the girlfriend, refreshed by bacon, eggs and strong tea, lurched out of the kitchen, glueily embraced, and plainly heading back to bed. Edward cast an automatically appraising glance: she was insecurely wrapped in one of Alan's shirts, displaying meaty, horsewoman's legs. The thought of being trapped between those powerful thighs was actively repulsive to him, but he was offended by the blank indifference of her gaze as it flickered briefly over his naked torso.

'Ned, are you still there?'

'Yes, Mummy.'

The door to Alan's bedroom slammed shut.

The same evening, Edward betook himself to Euston, chanced his arm with his credit card, and got himself aboard the night sleeper, a routine which he recalled from the ritual family visits to Uncle Jimmy in his childhood. He felt deeply ill-used; but there seemed to be no alternative to the ruination of his weekend. The Eugenides business was stretching his credit with Betty to, if not beyond, its limit, and he simply had to hold any reservoir of sympathy which might remain for Eugenides-related business, something he could hardly explain to his mother. All the same, she had reluctantly conceded that his job might be at risk if he went to Scotland for a week, and energetic plea-bargaining had therefore reduced his immediate duty to this fiendishly expensive visit of inspection. The train moved off, and Edward almost immediately got up and struggled down the train to the bar, though not soon enough to be at the head of the queue. Surveying the train and its passengers with distaste as he went, he began strongly to feel that the whole thing would be more tolerable if he was slightly drunk, and decided firmly to lay in plenty of supplies. Safe in his seat once more, behind a small rampart of overpriced comestibles in nasty little brown-paper carriers, he began trying to do the *Telegraph* crossword, but abandoned it irritably as the train rattled and swayed, sending his pen skidding wildly across the paper.

Staring out of the window, trying to get his lager down before it foamed up and out of the can, he reflected that the romance of rail was well and truly dead. 'Here is the night-mail, crossing the border...' Pah. Night-mare, more like. Perhaps he should simply go to his berth and try to sleep.

'Tickets, please...all tickets, please.' The conductor was coming down the train, clipping tickets, smiling impersonally. 'Ticket, sir?' The man was standing over him, his eyes flickering disdainfully (or so Edward felt) over the mess of cans, crisp packets, sandwich cartons, and bits of newspaper on the table.

Edward handed up his ticket. 'When do we get into Edinburgh?' he asked.

'If we're on time, we should be in at approximately twenty past three.'

'*What?*'

'Not to worry, sir. The sleeping-car goes to a siding, and we don't take you into Waverley till eight.'

'That's simply ridiculous. I used to take this train about twenty years ago, and I don't remember doing anything like that.'

'Well, sir. Trains were a lot slower twenty years ago.'

'I don't know why I didn't just fly.'

'Can't help you there, sir. Here's your ticket.'

Edward subsided resentfully. He felt that he was not being treated with the respect that the amount he had spent should have entitled him to. Why didn't I fly? he asked himself rhetorically, and as soon as he did so, the answer was obvious: because he had simply, and without thought, duplicated the pattern set in his childhood, a realisation which did nothing to sweeten his temper.

The following morning, far too early, he hung irritably around Waverley, gnawing a limp, greasy, microwaved ham croissant and waiting for the grotty little electric train that would take him to Leuchars. What's wrong with these bloody people? he asked himself rhetorically. Having been dumped off the train, he had about forty minutes to wait before his connection came in, and even when it did, it would take him not to his destination, but to a dreary army base in the middle of nowhere. Why didn't the train go properly round Fife? It was typical of the general muddle and inefficiency of the whole place. The arrival of his train flashed up on the noticeboard and, grudgingly, he boarded it.

Fortunately, there was a taxi at Leuchars. It would cost him another twenty-five quid or so, but there was absolutely no alternative, so he felt, at least, glad that he had not had to wait for it. Sour-stomached and underslept, he watched Fife scrolling by, and firmly parried the driver's attempts at conversation. Familiar road, familiar bleak farmtouns, familiar cold grey sea. Memories welled up from his childhood, of appalling, cataclysmic boredom, kicking about on the beach mechanically chewing his way through hard little bars of McCowan's Highland Toffee and wondering if the day would ever end. In silence, they approached Crail, and in silence, drew up outside the tall house with its crowstep gables which he remembered all too well.

Once he had paid off the driver, and arranged for him to come back that evening to pick him up, he surveyed the frontage with misgiving. It was in no sense a pretty sight, and never had been. Scottish masons of the seventeenth century built to last, but even in their better moments, of which this was not one, they aimed not so much at elegance, as at harsh, penitential grandeur. No. 2 Cove Wynd bore not the slightest resemblance to a seaside villa as the term is understood in England. No painted stucco in fondant colours, no pretty, frivolous ironwork. The first adjective which came to mind was, rather, 'defensible'. But beyond an appreciable deepening of the erosion patterns in the big greyish sandstone blocks of which it was built, the basic appearance of the house had not changed at all. Its palpable air of being down on its luck was due principally to the fact that the exterior paintwork had not been renewed for many years, which meant that on the more salient surfaces, sand, salt and winter storms had not merely taken it back to the bare wood, but had begun to gnaw into the wood itself.

Dingy curtains hung limply half-open in the windows, and there was no sign of a light anywhere.

Edward trudged up the steps to the front door, wondering for the umpteenth time why old Scottish houses keep the front door on the first floor (floods?) and yanked cautiously on the tarnished brass bell-pull. Rather to his surprise, it failed to come loose in his hand. On his third attempt, he heard, to his relief, sounds of life from within. Someone was fumbling, slowly and ineptly, with the bolts. The door opened at last, and he and his uncle surveyed one another in mutual disbelief. Edward remembered a big, fleshy man, weather-beaten from long hours on the golfcourse, rather well turned out in a Pringle-ish sort of way. The man who now faced him was considerably smaller (because Edward himself was taller? Or had he actually shrunk?), unshaven, scrawny, and wearing a string vest, none too clean, a pair of pyjama bottoms, and a filthy striped towelling dressing-gown insecurely tied with a much-knotted piece of brown twine. His gnarled, heavily veined white feet were thrust into heelless old red leather slippers, and he smelt like a cross between a dog-fox and a four-ale bar.

'Piss off, laddie. I don't want any,' he snapped, and made to shut the door. The voice at least was familiar. Edward recovered sufficiently from his paralysis to insert his foot in the jamb, and the old man jerked the door open again, glaring at him.

'Uncle Jimmy! It's Neddie. Edward.'

'Never heard of him.'

'*Edward*. Your nephew. Great-nephew. I'm your godson, for fuck's sake.'

James Campbell wavered, confusion overlaying belligerence. Suddenly, he conceded the point, and opened the door properly. 'Oh, *that* Edward. Come away in.'

Edward followed him into the hall, and his uncle shut the door behind them. 'Come through to the kitchen,' he invited, with a flicker of his old manner. The hall was dark, dank, and cold, with a strange cheesy, yeasty reek, suggestive of some obsolete industrial process. Once the kitchen door was opened, the source of the smell became readily apparent. The kitchen was of old-fashioned design, with a long pine table and a deep stone sink, heated, if that is the word, by a one-bar electric fire. It was also in an indescribable state. For an indefinite length of time, the old man had evidently bought milk, made sandwiches, heated soup, and so forth, and forgotten about them. Milk-bottles perched here and there, their contents a spectrum of shades from yellow through various shades of green, and even brown. A bowl on the mantelpiece, above the old man's eye level, seemed to be on the point of spontaneously generating new life-forms. The cupboard to Edward's left seemed to be making a pretty special contribution to the atmosphere as a whole, so he opened it cautiously, observed a tin which had once contained corned beef and the remains of a chicken carcass, both of which were boiling with maggots, and hastily shut it again before he lost his breakfast.

'Who did you say you were again?' his uncle asked.

'Your nephew Edward,' replied Edward faintly. 'Your great-nephew, actually. You had a brother called Alexander, remember? He was killed in the war, but he had a daughter called Alison. She's your niece. My mother. She married Hugo Lupset. Okay?'

Uncle Jimmy sat down, with a certain dignity, at the kitchen table.

'I have to admit, dear boy, my memory is not what it was. Hang on, half a tick.' He rummaged in the pocket of his deplorable dressing-gown, and produced a small notebook and a biro. 'Run that past me again?' Edward repeated himself, grinding his teeth, watching his uncle write it all down in shaky capitals. 'Edward,' he said to himself, trying the name on for size, apparently. 'Edward.' The task completed to his satisfaction, he propped the notebook against a blue-and-white striped jug, where he could see it.

'Have some whisky, laddie. It's not every day I get a visitor.'

Edward looked at him warily, but he did not appear to be hinting at neglect.

'Love to,' he said, too heartily. 'I'll just wash a couple of glasses, shall I?' Without waiting for an answer, he seized a couple of marginally usable tumblers off the table, and went to the sink. There was no washing-up liquid, of course, but he found a cracked and fissured bar of kitchen soap, and made do with that, then watched with alarm as his uncle poured about half a pint of neat spirit into them both, and lifted his glass to him.

'Here's tae us, wha's like us?' he said, and swigged ritually. When Edward failed to respond, he completed the toast himself. 'Damn few, and they're a' deid.' He looked Edward in the eye. 'I can remember some things fine, eh, Sandy?'

'Edward.' Jimmy's face went momentarily blank, and he drank some more whisky to cover the awkward moment.

Edward took a sip of whisky, which he liked, but not at ten o'clock in the morning, and considered his uncle thoughtfully.

'How are you?' he enquired. 'You look as if you've lost a bit of weight. Do you see a doctor?'

'Doctors!' grumbled the old man. 'Every time I see the bloody doctor, he gives me more pills. Pills, pills, pills, it's all they ever think about.'

'What about a home help? It looks like you could do with a hand.'

'Home help?' The idea floated about in the old man's clouded memory, connected up with something, and promptly ignited. 'Don't talk to me about home helps. They tried that one on me, you know. Some sort of muscle-bound harpy in a nylon overall. She tried to give me a bath! Bloody cheek. Madam, I told her, I have reached years of discretion. If any female's going to give me a bath, she'd better be three Oriental popsies, not a fat Scottish peasant with flat feet and varicose veins. I may have got a bit forgetful, Sandy, but I'm not a bloody imbecile. That was the last I saw of the silly cow, and good riddance.'

'Er...but what about clearing up?'

'Yes, well, right enough. You can see for yourself I could do with someone, but you can't get servants in this blasted town for love or money. I thought there was supposed to be an unemployment problem. Not that I'd trust most of 'em as far as I could throw them, of course.'

'What about contract cleaners?'

'What?'

'You can hire a team of people to come in and spring-clean the place. Or get them to come once a month, or whenever.'

'Now that, young Sandy, is not a bad notion. It has got away from me a bit, I know. I put things down, that's the trouble, then I forget where I put them.' Edward regarded his great-uncle without affection. If only, he thought, old Eugenides was like this. Biddable, trusting, gaga. 'But can you trust these people?' persisted the old man, pursuing his own train of thought.

'Well, if they weren't honest, they'd bloody soon go out of business, wouldn't they? Honesty's their stock-in-trade.'

'I've got a lot of nice stuff here...Look, laddie, will you go round the house for me?'

'What d'you mean?'

'Make a what-d'you-call-it, a list thing. And, you know, if I've left a gold watch lying about, anything like that, you could bring it to me and I'll put it away.'

'You don't want a complete inventory, do you? I mean, you don't need me to list "six kitchen chairs, one table", that sort of thing?'

'No. Pictures, silver. The sort of stuff people steal.'

'Right. Fine.' Edward got up, reflecting that his mother would, in any case, be interested to know what the house contained. He had his Filofax with him, so he took out some note-pages, and pen in hand, licensed to pry, he began wandering round the cold and filthy house making notes.

The results were not too impressive. The furniture was nothing special, mostly bulky stuff from the Thirties, upholstered in horsehair, uncomfortable, and too big for modern interiors. There were quite a few pictures, all of which looked pretty crappy, and any amount of cut crystal and such things. Fortunately for Edward's sensibilities, actual squalor was pretty well confined to the kitchen and bathroom and the old man's bedroom: the rest of the house suffered mainly from dust and neglect. He wandered from room to room, notebook in hand, opening drawers, poking around. Uncle Jimmy trailed after him for a while, then lost interest, and went back to the relative warmth of the kitchen. He found all kinds of things tucked away: fossilised cigarettes, golf-balls, old spectacles, and gratifyingly, quite a lot of money, squirrelled away here and there a few tenners at a time in various table drawers and bureaux, some of which he discreetly pocketed. Above all, he found pills. Packets and packets of them; of various kinds, with date-stamps ranging from a fortnight previously to several years ago, mostly with a number of tablets missing from the foil blister-packs within. Edward took some sample boxes over to the window where the light was better, and squinted at them furtively. One lot were evidently heart pills, another lot seemed to be some kind of steroid. A third lot, called Mellerox, were apparently intended to treat diabetes. The leaflet included an awesome list of possible side-effects, warnings about mixing with alcohol or painkillers, and contra-indications. Even through the high-gloss finish of pharmaceutical company prose, it was very clear that the things were risky. There was a dire warning about overdosing, printed in bold, which ended with the following, arresting sentence: 'If you find that you become subject to episodes of memory loss or disorientation, please consult your doctor immediately'. Edward thought at once of Mr Eugenides: memory loss and disorientation in that quarter was a very attractive concept. He took out one of the blister-packs, and considered it thoughtfully. It contained gelatine capsules, with a plain white powder visible through the transparent coating, and the image which came immediately to Edward's mind was Eugenides' tin of liver salts. He had a shrewd suspicion that if he simply snipped open the capsules, and mixed the contents with Eugenides' burp-mixture, he would have a very useful aid to keeping the old Greek where he wanted him. It was worth a try – and presumably, if someone took the stuff for a while and then stopped, he'd just go back to normal? Edward made his mind up, and nipped back to the kitchen, where he found his uncle drinking whisky and reading a dog-eared paperback copy of *Casino Royale*.

'Uncle Jimmy.'

The old man looked up. Clearly, he could not remember who Edward was, but was disposed to accept him as a benign intruder. 'Mmm? One thing about being a bit absent-minded these days, I can never remember if I've read these before. This one's jolly good.'

'Uncle, have you any bin-bags, anything like that? I want to throw out some of the stuff I'm finding. Pills and things. You shouldn't keep old medicine lying around.'

'Help yourself,' said Jimmy absent-mindedly, his eyes still fixed on his James Bond. 'Stuff like that ought to be in the scullery,' he advised, waving a hand. Edward investigated, in the direction indicated, and found a roll of plastic bags. His uncle ignored him as he went out again, with a number of bags, and his briefcase. Efficiently, he evicted unopened letters, used hankies, coughdrops and the like from Jimmy's numerous caches and hidey-holes, but whenever he found Mellerox, he threw away the cardboard pack only, and dropped the foil blister-packs into his briefcase. A total of fourteen packs turned up, ranging from half-used to almost finished: still, he hoped, probably enough to have some kind of effect on a non-diabetic. Once he had made a clean sweep of the house (if the expression was appropriate, given the state of the place), he left his case discreetly in the hall, and returned to the kitchen, laden like Santa Claus.

'I've done a bit of a tidy-up,' he announced.

'Good lad.'

'Time's getting on, uncle. I've got to get back to London this evening, or I'd stay and help. Is it okay if I organise some cleaners for you?'

'Fine by me. It has got a bit much, I'll admit.'

'If you give me your notebook, I'll write it down, just in case.' Without waiting for an answer, he reached for the notebook, flipped the page over, and wrote the date at the top. Under it, in nice, clear capitals, he wrote: EDWARD LUPSET (MY NEPHEW) CAME TO SEE ME. WE AGREED I NEEDED SOME HELP WITH THE HOUSE. HE IS ARRANGING FOR SOME CONTRACT CLEANERS TO CALL. WHEN THEY COME, I WILL PAY THEM. He pushed the book back to his uncle. 'Will you sign it, please?' Uncle Jimmy read the message carefully.

'That seems to be right,' he confirmed, and signed the page.

'Have you got a chequebook?'

'Over there on the mantelpiece.'

Edward rose, and riffled through it. There were still some cheques. Good: that solved one problem. The senile old twit would at least be able to write the cleaners a cheque.

'It's nearly two. If I nip out now, I might still be able to get some lunch out of the Golf Hotel. See you in a bit.'

'My dear boy, I could open a tin. There's some quite nice oxtail soup somewhere about.'

'I wouldn't dream of troubling you,' said Edward, with weary sarcasm, and fled.

After a horrible but reasonably sanitary lunch and two pints of beer, he returned refreshed, to sweep most of the contents of the kitchen into yet more plastic bags, and carry them out to the yard. He contrived to be spotted, thus engaged, by one of the neighbours, introduced himself, and made it clear that the family was taking an interest.

Shortly after five, the taxi-man reappeared, so he said goodbye to his uncle, and left for London. Reclining smugly in the back seat of the taxi, he felt well pleased with himself. In the short term, though not insignificantly, given his cash-flow crisis, he had managed to reimburse himself for the cost of the fares, and quite a bit besides. Moreover, he had killed two birds with one stone: he now had a whole bucket of trouble for Mr Eugenides lurking in the bottom of his briefcase. His mother would, for once, be pleased with him, and so would Lamprini. He could be quite positive that great-uncle Jimmy, who he remembered as notably more unpleasant and difficult than he now was, had clearly been put into such a permanent position of giving the world the benefit of the doubt by the holes in his memory that he was unaware of the deficiencies of his kith and kin. Mummy would also be delighted to know that the silly old fart was extremely unlikely to take up revising his will – if the impulse struck him, he would hardly be able to remember what he'd gone to his lawyer for. More good news: the random cocktail of strong drugs and strong liquor which he consumed would probably see him off before anyone got around to trying to put him in a home.

XII

'If there's one bit of the year I hate and loathe,' said Sebastian to Elaine, 'it's this. Marking the scripts is bad enough, but I draw the line at bingo.' It was six o'clock in the evening, and they were in the Committee Room, sorting out an enormous pile of mark-sheets into sets, and putting one of each at each place. This was a 'secretarial' job: that is, perceived as demeaning, so it was assumed as a matter of course by George Beckinsale in his capacity of Exams Secretary and general departmental Milk Monitor, that 'the girls' would be only too pleased to spend their evening thus engaged. He therefore buggered off home to do whatever it is Georges do in the evening, without offering to help. Of course, it should not have been necessary to do it after hours at all: the whole job should have been over by five. Normally, in exam week, Govinder and Elaine spent the entire day on the eye-destroying task of entering first, second and third marks for each exam taken by each candidate on to the mark-sheets, leaving Moyra to field all other business as it came in. On this particular occasion, however, George mislaid all the Special Subject marks, and produced them only at quarter to four. Govinder and Moyra both had young children, and having made no special arrange-ments for their care, were forced, with many apologies, to leave at five. Sebastian, who had happened to put his head round the door just as the scale of the crisis made itself apparent, volunteered to help out. Elaine was duly grateful, but there was a glint in her eye which suggested that things would go very hard with Mr Beckinsale in future.

'Okay, that's Classics, Ancient History, Greek and Roman Studies, Classics with English. We must be winning.'

'There's the rest of the Duals still to go,' said Elaine grimly.

'What other Duals? Oh, God.' Sebastian took the sheaf of papers she held out to him, and looked at it unbelievingly. '*Classics and Ethnomusicology?*'

'Right. One student in the last four years. Here he is. You know, Sebastian, I must have been on the phone to SOAS about six times this week about that one student?'

'That's Duals for you. Hardly any students, and three times as much work,' commented Sebastian, dealing out copies of the marksheet. 'Oh, I know who it is. It must be that madman who was doing a dissertation about citharas. Tony Drakakis.'

'So much for anonymous marking.'

'Well, maybe everyone doesn't know. What next?'

'Classics with Anthropology, Classical Civilisation with Geography, Classics and Linguistics. Averaging two students each. Then we can go home.' They worked in silence for a while, shuffling efficiently round the table dealing out papers.

'Tell me this, Elaine,' said Sebastian after a while. 'Who got us into all these horrid little Dual degrees?'

'D'you want to guess?'

'Silly me. Gorgeous George, I presume. It's got the hallmarks, hasn't it? An incredible amount of trouble for all concerned, and not properly thought out. Anyway, that's him picked up after, for today anyway. C'mon, Elaine. Lock everything up, and then I can buy you a huge gin.'

The next day, the entire department assembled, contrary to its usual habit, at ten to nine, preparing themselves, in their various ways, for a long, hard day. At five to, Professor Savile turned up, beaming professionally and accompanied by the external examiners, and Elaine unlocked the committee room. The procedure they were following is basically a simple one, since with most students, a swift look at the marks is enough to decide which category they fit into: are their grades in the fifties, or the sixties? But there are always awkward cases – has student A achieved the top 2.ii or the bottom 2.i, has student B just scraped a First, has C failed? The arguments which result are extremely complex, especially when one decision has knock-on effects on others – if Mr Beckinsale, for instance, objects that the decision made on candidate 38 surely reopened the question of candidate 27, it can all take a very long time. Professor Savile had the University Statutes open in front of him, which he consulted in the spirit of someone approaching the Delphic Oracle whenever complete impasse was reached: unfortunately, like its predecessor, the utterances of the Statutes turned out to be susceptible to a variety of interpretations. But at last, some kind of decision had been reached with respect to each and every anonymous individual.

'Well, ladies and gentlemen,' Savile summed up briskly, 'we've got provisional marks. Now for the exciting bit. Elaine will de-anonymise the candidates, and then we will reconsider the difficult cases in the light of medical and other evidence.'

Elaine got out her secret list, and began reading out names and numbers with the detached clarity of the football results. 'One. Annabel Abbot, two-one. Two, Gavin Alexander, two-one. Three, Lucinda Bailey, two-two...' Furiously scribbling, everyone started writing in names, with occasional cries and whistles of disappointment or congratulation at unexpected results. Sebastian, like most of his colleagues, waited with interest for the names of those he had personally taught; moments of sadness, elation or *schadenfreude*, as a mature student didn't quite make it, a shy and silent victim of self-doubt got a First, or a chronically idle and arrogant boy got exactly what was coming to him. 'Twenty-three.

Ryan Mooney, two-one.' Oh, *no*, thought Sebastian, totally losing track of Fiona Morrison and Charles Morton as their names and achievements scrolled by. There was going to be a fight.

'Ryan Mooney,' announced Professor Savile, some time later. 'A bit of a problem. As I'm sure you will all have observed, Mr Mooney achieved a mark of eighty-five per cent for his dissertation. A good ten per cent above any other first-class mark given for any other paper this year, and there's no argument about him getting the Seatonian Prize. Two papers at 69, three others unequivocally first-class, one of them at 74. But unfortunately, Mr Mooney achieved a mere fifty-two per cent last year for "Greek City States". We have a convention, externals, that if performance in the final year is spectacularly better, some poorish results in the second year can be condoned. Unfortunately, he has also managed no more than fifty-eight for this year's paper on "The Golden Age of Athens" and the University Statutes suggest that if we are to award a first-class degree, only *one* mark can fall lower than 60 per cent. Over to you, ladies and gentlemen. I think we need to open this up.'

Sebastian shut his eyes. Ryan, he thought to himself with quiet vehemence, I could wring your fucking neck. How could you do this to me?

'I'd like to begin,' said George, 'by asking the externals what they made of the dissertation.'

'Well,' said Dr Seligman, the Greek external, flicking over his notes, 'it was an extraordinarily mature performance. Highly original, exceptionally well researched, very well written. I thought it was absolutely excellent.'

'What I'm asking, really,' persisted George, 'is whether the fact that the first internal marked it sky-high influenced the way you saw it. I mean, what's the difference, really, between seventy-five and eighty-five? How do you quantify it?'

'Well, that's rather difficult,' said Dr Seligman, nettled. 'All I can say is, I'd take the thing for *Classical Quarterly* tomorrow. I enjoyed the other First Class dissertations, but I wouldn't say that of them.'

'What I'm wondering is whether that's got to do with the subject. Frankly, the whole thing strikes me as the kind of fashionable filth that gets Classics a bad name. How on earth a respectable institution can go about *encouraging* students to work on homosexual pornography passes my comprehension.'

'George, dear,' said Sebastian, through his teeth, 'even you can't actually believe that Ancient Greeks spent all their time hopping in and out of cold baths while they waited for Miss Right. Ryan did a *superb* dissertation. It's balanced, scholarly and mature. He spent the entire summer researching it. What that means is that he went from museum to museum talking curators into letting him looking at thousands of pots in dusty basements. He was incredibly patient and thorough, and since he's included an excellent set of colour photographs, you can't even accuse him of making it up.'

'Gentlemen, gentlemen,' boomed Savile, genially. 'I think we're getting away from the point. Is there a general feeling round the table that the externals ought to reconsider the dissertation?'

Sebastian lost his temper. 'Chair, if the externals are going to start reconsidering Ryan's papers, I'd like them to look at "The Golden Age of Athens". George has raised the problem of the first marker giving a lead. I accept that. So it's quite worrying, don't you think, that the two papers this absolutely brilliant student has come down on were both taught and marked by George? Just to fill you in, externals, Ryan Mooney uses green ink and writes in a spiky italic you could recognise from the other side of the street. You might also like to know that he's not just out and proud, he's so camp he makes Julian Clary look like Will Carling.'

Beckinsale slammed his fist on the table, making everyone jump. 'I'm not bloody having it. You're accusing me of rank prejudice. I'll have you in court for it,' he roared.

'Sue and be damned,' Sebastian spat back. 'You've had it in for

Ryan since his first year. I *told* him he was an idiot to take your paper.'

'*Gentlemen*! Please. I suggest that neither Mr Beckinsale nor Dr Raphael give us the benefit of their opinions for the next fifteen minutes,' snapped Savile. 'Now, externals.'

'I would like to see "The Golden Age of Athens" paper,' said Dr Seligman, a little apologetically. 'I note that the second marker put it at 59/60. I am happy to admit that I did no more than sample the papers which did not appear to be problematic, and I am quite prepared to read it now.' Elaine got up, rummaged in the vast, tottering piles of paper which lurked on the table by the window, found the script in question, and gave it to Seligman. Then she escorted him out of the room to find somewhere quiet and private where he could give it his consideration. Sebastian crossed his fingers under the desk, and sent up a heartfelt prayer to St Joseph of Cupertino, patron saint of examinees.

'We'll come back to that one,' continued the Chair, efficiently. 'Now I think we'd better look at Karen Thompson, who was unlucky enough to break her right arm on the second day of Finals...' Sebastian stopped listening: one thing leads to another, and he was busy thinking about saints: quite a few obvious queers came to mind, but he was racking his brains for one who'd been out enough to take a kindly interest in little Ryan.

Twenty minutes later, Seligman reappeared, by which time Sebastian had silently committed Ryan's cause to St Anselm, St Hildegard of Bingen, and SS Sergius and Bacchus: St Sebastian, he felt, had had enough awkward jobs already.

'Well, what do you make of it?' enquired Savile.

'I do apologise for not spotting it the first time round, but there's more to this script than I had realised. The affectedness of the writing is misleading. There are actually some very perceptive points, particularly in the Pericles essay. I have to say, I'd be happy to put it at more like sixty-one or sixty-two. Say sixty-one.'

George flushed, a dangerous, unbecoming brick-red, always an indication that he was near the point of spontaneous explosion. Savile ignored him, but bent a warning look on Sebastian.

'It is the custom that an external's judgement overrides that of the internal markers, where this is appropriate. Is the Committee prepared to accept Dr Seligman's revised mark?' Murmurs of assent round the table.

George stood up abruptly, blind with rage. 'No it bloody isn't. A pack of buggers sticking together like glue, and you accuse *me* of prejudice!' he shouted, and slammed out of the room. In the ensuing silence, his chair fell over, and was quietly righted by a harmless archaeologist.

'My God,' commented Sebastian much later to his friend Katie Flaxman, when it was all over, and they were standing around drinking gin before the examiners' dinner, 'I was really beginning to wonder whether old George would actually accuse me of screwing the silly little twit.'

'Oh, Ryan's not a bad lad, really.'

'Of course not. I'm quite fond of him, some of the time, anyway. It's just that you'd think he'd *invented* it, the way he goes on. And it's a bit ripe for Georgie to jump to conclusions just because I'm a known bender.'

'Specially since about ninety-nine per cent of the trouble we have that way is with blokes like George falling for sweet little girlies.'

'Come to think of it, George isn't here, is he?'

'No. He must be sulking in his tent. Just as well, really.' Katie paused, and took a swallow of her gin. 'Sebastian, has it ever struck you that George is really quite mad?'

'Katie, darling, I've assumed he was as mad as a fucking fox from day one.'

'No you haven't. What you're saying is you took one look, and decided he was disobliging and eccentric.'

'I see what you're getting at,' said Sebastian thoughtfully. Clive, who with Sebastian and Katie, formed the Academic

Development Committee, and who had been with the department for nearly thirty years, drifted over to join them.

'What are you talking about?' he asked.

'Whether George is actually mad as opposed to barmy. What d'you think, Clive? You've known him a long time.'

'What a question. Actually, I sometimes think that quite a few middle-aged people are no longer quite sane, at least on certain subjects. It's the sort of thought that forces itself on the reflecting mind during long committee meetings. George is a classic example. Of course, he's a very disappointed man.'

'Why?' asked Katie curiously. 'He can't possibly have hoped to get further up the ladder than he did. He must *know* his work's crap, surely?'

'Ah,' replied Clive, 'that begs the question of what his work actually is.'

'You're hinting he's a spook,' said Sebastian immediately. 'I bet you're right. But if he's a spook, he's a pretty spectacularly useless one.'

'Well, I rather think that's what I'm trying to say. You have to remember how paranoid the establishment was about the new universities in the Sixties and early Seventies. I suppose you were both still in rompers, but I can assure you, there was a tremendous concern that they'd turn into hotbeds of Marxism. Paris in '68 had a lot of very important people extremely worried. It wouldn't be at all surprising to find that there were suitable types salted in here and there to keep an eye on things.'

'That would make sense. George really ought to have been a schoolmaster. I suppose someone pulled strings.'

'But think of it from George's point of view. I'm sure he was bursting with patriotism and good intentions. Can you imagine spending your working life guarding a gate which no one ever, in all that time, tries to open?'

'What a horrible idea. No wonder he's sour.'

'Sebastian, it's hard not to tease George. He's such a soft target, and he's so often a pain in the neck. But I sometimes wonder if it's quite fair.'

'Clive, dear, sometimes I worry about you. A quarter of a century of tantrums and cock-ups, and you're still prepared to be charitable. If you don't watch your step, you might find yourself snatched up to heaven by a choir of angels.'

'Oh, look,' said Katie, 'They've started going through.'

'Good-oh. All right, Clive. I'll try to be good. Let's talk about something else now.'

The following morning, Sebastian was blamelessly dealing with his laundry and nursing his hangover when the phone rang.

'Bugger,' he said, reaching for it. 'Sebastian Raphael.'

'Sebastian? Oh, good. I tried last night, several times, but I couldn't get through. Tim Claydon-Jones here.'

'Tim. Nice to hear from you. What do you want?'

This was too bald a riposte for Tim's refined sensibilities: for the next ten minutes, therefore, he punished Sebastian for his coarseness with polite small-talk and beating about the bush, which Sebastian endured with reasonable patience, holding the phone against his ear with his shoulder, and sorting his socks into pairs the while. Eventually, Tim condescended to come to the point.

'Sebastian, do you remember me telling you about finding a Baroque fountain under an office-block in St Lawrence Jewry?'

'Of course. What's happened to it?'

'Well, we're not absolutely out of the woods, but it looks as though the owners are going to let us have it, which is terribly good news. I wanted to talk to you, because I suddenly had the most wonderful idea, and I thought you might be able to help me.'

'Okay,' said Sebastian cautiously, reaching for a bottle of San Pellegrino which stood beside his bed, and opening it one-handedly.

'I remember you mentioning at dinner that you knew someone who knew all about the Levant trading companies and what happened to them? You wouldn't have an idea who knows about the old Greek church in London?'

'I certainly would. It's the same chap, actually. His name's Constantine Eugenides, and he is an absolutely charming old hermit living in a sort of time-capsule in the middle of the City. His firm's been looking after St Michael's since the days of Sir Everard. What d'you want to know?'

'Oh, Sebastian. That's absolutely marvellous. So he'd know who owns the site, and that sort of thing?'

'I'm absolutely sure he would.'

'The idea just came to me in a flash. As I'm sure you know, St Michael's Graecorum was destroyed in the War, but the site's never been developed. It's just a blank on the area plan. And it's in a rather dreary bit of London, without a lot of amenities once you're off the river-front. I suddenly thought, it would make the most wonderful millennium project if the site was landscaped into a permanent memorial of Anglo-Greek contact and co-operation, with the fountain as the centrepiece. I'm sure Hattie Luke would help with drawing up the proposal, and we might even be able to get some money out of the Onassis Foundation or someone like that. But obviously, I can't make any moves at all until I have an idea of who owns the site, and whether they're happy to have it used in this way. Could you possibly get in contact with your Greek friend, and try and find out for me?'

'Actually, I think I can answer that one myself. It almost certainly reverted to the lavra of St Michael on Mount Athos. I was reading my old chum's father's letters in the British Library, and it's pretty clear from what he says that it's the Athonites he's acting for. He couldn't contact them, of course, in the middle of the Blitz, but he mentions them, and seems to be implying that he's acting on their behalf.'

'Oh, Lord. Who on earth do you know who knows anything about Mount Athos?'

'Me,' said Sebastian smugly, beginning to enjoy himself. 'I was chatting up the boys in St Michael's in February. The one you need to know's the abbot, kyrios Akakios. He's a good enough sort of chap as long as you keep him where you can see him. I think he quite likes me, actually. I'm respectful about St John Climacus, and I never ever mention Classical Athens.'

'Oh, Sebastian, you are a wonder. You couldn't bear to write a lovely letter in Greek for me, could you?'

'I could, but not this minute. I'm off to Berlin tomorrow for the big conference on Byzantine art at the Kunsthistoriches Museum, and staying on there to do some research till the end of the month. I'm still not properly sorted out after the end of term. We did only finish yesterday, Tim, and everything just piles up during the exams. It's a nightmare getting turned round so quickly, but I need to teach this berk in my department not to organise meetings outside term. I'll get in touch with Eugenides after I get back, just to make sure, then I'll write you a lovely letter to the Abbot, full of curly bits – "very reverend and learned", "ardent advocate with God", all that sort of stuff. They don't half go on, you know.'

'Couldn't you do it while you were there?' It crossed Sebastian's mind, not for the first time, that if Tim had ever grasped the meaning of the word 'negotiate', he might have got a lot further in life. He decided not to give way, it only encouraged him.

'Hang on a minute, Tim. You're miles further forward than you were five minutes ago. You're ninety-nine per cent sure who owns the site, and you've got direct-line access to the lucky boy in question. Don't be greedy. I'm going to be *working* in Germany, remember? If I'm going to make maximum use of my time, I can't spend the best part of a day doing something I could just as easily do in London.'

'I'm so sorry.' Tim's tone was offended rather than penitent: it was perfectly obvious that he could see no reason why Sebastian should not just drop everything in order to oblige him.

'Listen. I do sympathise. I know what it's like when you're

really on the track of something. I *will* write your letter, cross my heart and hope to die. Only not now. It's going to take ages. And after all, the fountain's waited three hundred years already, and he Athonites haven't done anything since World War Two. If it has to wait another three weeks, it's not going to make any difference. I'll be in touch after I get back.'

'Thank you so much,' said Tim, with a faintly sarcastic inflection, and rang off. Sebastian looked at the phone, shrugged, and went back to sorting out his laundry.

XIII

'...and the temperature in London today is 20 degrees Celsius, warm and fine. On behalf of the Queensland and Northern Territory Airway System, let me wish you a very pleasant stay in London. Hope we'll be seeing you again...'

Jeanene Malone, tired, stiff and jaded, tuned out of the captain's farewell speech, and scrabbled under the seat in front for her shoes. She felt vaguely that she ought to have some sense of excitement, but after more than twenty-four hours in an economy-class seat, there wasn't the energy to spare. If there was one thing she felt more than anything else, it was nauseated: part of that was the insult to her internal clocks, while part was a cloudy, unfocused apprehension that, somehow, the whole thing would turn out to be a gigantic mistake.

In a daze of unreality, she managed to retrieve her luggage and get herself through Passports and Immigration, who seemed to be under the impression that claiming to be a graduate student was some kind of cunning ruse aimed at battening off the British state. When at long last they were through with her, she changed some dollars, and followed the signs to the Tube. In the confusing, echoing underground space of the station, she leaned her rucksack against the wall and peered dubiously at the map. The British

Museum was her reference point, but there wasn't a Bloomsbury Station. Looking around for help, she spotted a couple of uniformed women, air-hostesses going off duty, most probably, and appealed to them.

"Scuse me. D'you know how to get to the British Museum?'

'Cor, you're starting the way you mean to go on, aren't you? Tottenham Court Road's the nearest.'

'Go to Russell Square,' advised the other kindly, 'then you won't have to change. It's not much further.'

Thanking them, she turned back to the map again, and checked it out. It seemed right enough.

Once she was safely ensconced on the train, surrounded by weary fellow-travellers and their mountains of baggage, she was free to contemplate the other passengers; on the whole more interesting than the tracts of scrubby bush and undistinguished suburban row housing that flashed by outside the windows. Obviously, the passengers picked up at the airport were mostly foreigners like herself, but what intrigued her, as the train meandered through West London, the Heathrow contingent gradually struggled off with their luggage, and miscellaneous other travellers got on, was the extreme variousness of the other people in the carriage. Londoners, she could see, came in almost every conceivable variety of physical and ethnic type. It was disconcerting – in a vague, childish way, she had somehow expected the English to look English – but she found it comforting. Surely, amongst all that diversity, a small Australian student could pass unnoticed?

Jeanene fished in her pocket for the university's letter, and read it for the umpteenth time.

We are pleased to be able to offer you accommodation for your first year in Ellen Wilkinson House. Ellen Wilkinson is a University of London hostel, established in 1947 specifically for the reception of female postgraduate students from the Commonwealth, advantageously situated near the British Library (see enclosed map). A copy of the rules for residents is also enclosed: please note that they are designed to enforce mutual courtesy and respect for the cultural traditions of others. Please confirm your estimated time of arrival with the warden. If this is within reasonable hours – i.e. between 9 AM and 11 PM – please go directly to the ground floor flat to pick up your key. If you expect to arrive in London at unsocial hours, please let the university know at once so a suitable arrangement can be made.

Not exactly warm and welcoming, but clear. It at least meant that somewhere in this gigantic city full of strangers, there was a lockable door, with behind it, a bed designated for her use. She would be a lot happier once the key to that door was in her pocket.

By the time she had negotiated the lift in the Russell Square tube with her heavy rucksack, suitcase and briefcase, discovering in the process with a sort of retrospective panic just how far underground she had been, she was ready to cry with tiredness and stress. Emerging on to the busy crossroads of Southampton Row and High Holborn, she looked at the scurrying cars, the tall, dirty slabs of red-brick building marching away in all directions as far as the eye could see, the complete absence of any landmarks, and panicked all over again. A friendly newspaper-vendor told her how to hail a cab, which turned out to be the same as at home, and more importantly, how to identify one available for hire. After only a few minutes' anxious hovering, she found rather to her surprise that it worked. Once tucked into the taxi with her luggage, she peered out of the window curiously at the unfamiliar streets which were to be her new neighbourhood, and a few minutes later, she was deposited at the door of Ellen Wilkinson House, a plain slab of yellowish stock-brick with old-fashioned metal windows, just off Bedford Square.

According to her watch, which she had set to London time on

the plane, it was apparently half past three – she had, herself, no sense of what time it was, or might be. Since she had told the warden that she expected to be in between two and five, if all went well, she felt duly pleased with herself. There were two buttons by the door: she rang the one labelled 'Warden's Flat'. Moments later, she heard heels clicking across the floor, the door opened, and she found herself confronting a tall, slender, dark-skinned woman, with an immense coil of glossy black hair, brilliant, birdlike dark eyes and a severe, high-arched nose. She was wearing a cream-coloured cotton blouse and a dark blue batik skirt, so immaculately starched and ironed that she made Jeanene feel that she ought to start off by apologising for being grubby, sweaty, and probably smelly.

'Hi,' she began nervously. 'The name's Jeanene Malone. You're expecting me?'

The other woman bowed her head, a formal gesture of welcome from some unidentifiable culture.

'I am Miss Jayastardena, your warden. Please come in, and I will show you your room.'

Jeanene lumped her baggage into the hall, while Miss Jayastardena darted into her own quarters, and emerged with a pair of keys on a ring.

'Follow me, please. Your room is on the first floor.' Jeanene trailed after her, as she moved briskly down the hall and up the stairs. The hall was dingy, and in serious need of a lick of paint, but clean. When she emerged on to the first-floor landing, she found Miss Jayastardena patiently holding open a door. It was, as she expected, a totally anonymous little room with cream-coloured paint, pockmarked with drawing-pin holes, containing a bed, a desk, a sink, and a clothes-cupboard. It was all right.

'Let me show you the kitchen and the bathroom.' Together, they inspected these amenities, spartan, but acceptable. A smell of exotic spices hung around the kitchen, perceptible even beneath the basic odour of bleach.

'If you would like to knock on my door,' offered Miss Jayastardena, 'I would be happy to give you a cup of tea. But you will perhaps want to unpack?'

'Thanks a million, but all I want right now is to have a bath and pull myself together. Then I think I'll probably go to sleep,' said Jeanene, realising uncomfortably that she sounded ungracious.

'That is very understandable. I will leave you to rest. I hope you feel better in the morning.' Miss Jayastardena gave another of her formal little bows, and vanished.

Jeanene sat down on the too-soft, springy bed, and kicked her shoes off. She was home. Everything else would have to wait. Getting up again, she pottered about for a bit, putting things in drawers. She was feeling slightly faint and sick, but too wound up to try and sleep, so she poured herself a glass of water, which tasted flat and unpleasant. Too much chlorine, but it was probably wholesome. She remembered suddenly that she had a bottle of duty-free Scotch. A good slug of that, and at least she might get some rest...

By the end of a week, she was feeling a lot better. She'd got over the worst of the jet-lag, found out where to buy things, and started proceedings to get herself registered as a qualified pharmacist, the essential preliminary to having enough to live on. Ellen Wilkinson House began to make more sense. She was the only native English speaker who was resident. Over the years, as the Commonwealth disintegrated, it had evidently adapted its admissions policy, and now accommodated women whose only common ground was that they were single, and came from a long way away. Miss Jayastardena, who was Sri Lankan, was the most capable of making conversation in English, but that severe lady was frankly uninterested in anything but systems analysis, and clearly considered the study of ancient literatures completely pointless. The two other rooms on her landing were occupied by a pair of Indonesian computer scientists, almost extinguished by wimple-like headscarves, who seldom uttered a word in public, though occasional outbreaks of tinkling oriental laughter from behind closed doors suggested that they had formed a defensive alliance against the iniquities of London. As neighbours, they were completely inoffensive, and unspeakably boring. The friendliest member of the household was the Estonian agronomist from upstairs, who liked to stop and chat when they met, but she had an accent so impenetrable that Jeanene had yet to understand a word she said. The remaining rooms were empty, though they would presumably be filled before the beginning of term.

It was clean, it was quiet. God, was it quiet. Bashfulness, language difficulties and courtesy combined to prevent anything else. If Jeanene surprised the Indonesians cooking curry in the kitchen, they smiled and apologised breathily, and made no attempt to draw her in. The Estonian woman, whose name seemed to be Jadwiga, was sometimes to be heard droning interminable Slavic songs in her bath, but immediately stopped if she heard anyone else moving about. It struck her that given recent history, it was perfectly possible that in ten years time, she might open a paper and find that one of her housemates had suddenly become the President of somewhere, but in the meantime, considered domestically, they were as dull as a month of Sundays.

Jeanene spent a number of unsatisfactory evenings exploring various facets of the Australian network in London, but found the experience depressing, on the whole. She felt increasingly strongly that she had not gone halfway round the world in order to spend her whole time talking to Australians about Australia. Furthermore, the Oz homes-from-home that she investigated were too noisy, too boozy, and too expensive. But, having given up on the Backpacker and the Redback, she found herself spending long, lonely days and evenings: she signed up at the local library and got herself a British Library card, she explored London, she met no one. When a part-time evening job came up in a Mayfair pharmacy, her interview with Mr Patel, its fat, rude, and indifferent manager, felt like the nearest thing to human contact she had had since she left home.

The Monday after his return from Scotland, Edward went to Garlic Court after work. He rang the bell, opened the door with his key, and stepped into the hall, calling, 'It's only me.' A faint voice answered him from above, and he went up, to find Eugenides in his study. His arm was still in a sling, and he had lost weight, but it was clear that, now he was back in his own environment, he was rapidly returning to normal.

'I've come to see if you need anything, Mr Eugenides. I brought a pint of milk, just in case.'

'That is very kind, and most thoughtful. I have some tinned milk in the cupboard still, but I am very glad to have fresh. If you could bring me two loaves, I would be most grateful. And perhaps half a dozen eggs and a little bacon? Tomorrow would do perfectly well, if it is more convenient.'

'That's okay. I may as well nip out now.'

'I hope very much that I will not have to trespass on your kindness much longer, Mr Lupset. It still takes me some time to get down the stairs in the morning, but if I move with care, it is very much easier than it was. The arm, also, is not so painful. I hope that I will soon be able to manage a shopping-bag as well as a stick, and then I will be able to fend for myself.'

'Great. I mean, I don't mind doing it, but I'm glad you're feeling better.' Edward spoke as heartily as he could, but realised with discomfort that the old man was looking at him assessingly, his dark eyes unreadable. 'That's cool. Er. Mr Eugenides, before I go out again, do you mind if I use your loo?'

'Of course not. You know where to find it, I think?'

'Top floor right?' Edward got up, glad of the diversion, and went upstairs. In the bathroom, as he had hoped, he found Eugenides' tin of Liver Salts. No wonder the old bastard takes the stuff, he reflected, he hasn't eaten any fresh food since he came out of hospital. Flipping the lid off with a ten-pence piece, he set it down, and fished in his pocket for a little black plastic Kodak canister, opened it, and compared the white powder it contained with the stuff in Eugenides' tin. They looked much the same. The previous night, he had spent a careful half-hour locked in his bedroom, opening capsules with a razor blade and decanting the contents. He had even gone so far as to taste a minute grain of the stuff: it was faintly bitter, but probably unnoticeable beneath the strong, alkaline flavour of the salts themselves. Crossing his fingers for luck, he tipped the stuff in. There was a spoon lying beside the tin, so he stirred it through as best he could, and pocketed the now-empty canister. He was a little concerned about dosage, but since he knew neither how poisonous the stuff was, nor how much of the salts Eugenides got through in a day, all he could do was hope for the best. There was nothing in his mind but a faint, scientific curiosity. He flushed the lavatory, washed his hands noisily, and went downstairs again.

'I'll just nip out to the shops now,' he said, putting his head round the study door. Coming further into the room, he picked up his briefcase, looking down on Eugenides as he sat at the table reading something in Greek. 'I'll put the stuff on the kitchen table, okay? And the milk in the fridge. Then I won't need to bother you again.' He stood there, swinging the case, shifting his weight from foot to foot, tall, young, impatient.

'Thank you very much. Then I will bid you goodnight.'

As Edward clattered down the stairs, Eugenides laid down his spectacles, and listened. The heavy, careless feet receded down to the hall. He heard the latchet of the kitchen door, then a minute or so later, the slam of the door to the street. He was profoundly uneasy. The boy had no education and no real manners: enough upbringing, presumably, to account for his taking on the chore of looking after an old man – a job which Eugenides was determined to relieve him of at the earliest opportunity. But something was not right. Was it simply the extraordinary manners of the times, hiding clumsy goodwill beneath a façade of brashness? Such a boy could not, could never be, a friend, but why, when circumstances had thrown them together, did he feel that somehow, there was no connection at all? When he looked into Edward's eyes, it was as if no one was there; but was he imagining it?

Eugenides sat brooding, praying a little as his habit was, but alert to the sound of the key in the door. The fact of his temporary helplessness, the possibility that the fall represented the beginning of the end of his autonomy, weighed on him with paralysing effect. Only after Edward had returned, visited the kitchen, and left again, did he move. Painfully, he got up from his chair, and, leaning on a stick, shuffled clumsily across the room to the mantelpiece, where he retrieved Sebastian's card from a majolica bowl, and then toiled across the landing to the drawing room, where he carefully lowered himself on to the sofa which stood beside the telephone table. He dialled the number, which rang twice, then clicked into connection.

'Hello. May I speak to Dr Raphael?' He was bewildered to realise a voice was speaking alongside his own, and fell silent in confusion:

'...Raphael. If you'd like to leave a message, please do so after the beep.' The phone clicked and muttered, then buzzed penetratingly.

Eugenides collected his wits, and said, 'I would be most grateful if Dr Raphael could call me.' Only when he had put the receiver down did it occur to him that he had not given his name.

When Sebastian did not reply, Eugenides concluded that he had not realised who the message was from. Pride, the feeling that he had given way to a moment of weakness, prevented him from trying the number again – the fact that his voice and diction were immediately recognisable had not of course occurred to him. And Sebastian would certainly have answered, if he had not been in Germany, dividing his time on the whole pleasantly between working in the Kunsthistorisches Museum, auditing conference papers, shopping in KDW, gossiping with international art historians, and scouring Berlin for a decent restaurant.

As the days went by, Eugenides became more and more afraid. Sometimes, when he arose in the morning, the stairs down to the first floor held for him the menace of the Cresta Run. A sort of black dizziness seemed to hover about him, and sometimes overcame him entirely. He found he was reaching for things, and grasping the air beside them. It was harder and harder to remember what he had done, and what he had merely intended to do. Even his writing began to get away from him. He had a beautiful script, neat, precise, regular; a source of pride. Sometimes – not always – when he looked at what he had written, the letters looped and staggered drunkenly across the page. Edward Lupset continued to visit every few days, and Eugenides struggled with all his might to conceal the mysterious deterioration which was coming over him. He dreaded above all being returned to the hospital, and was very much afraid that this blank-eyed boy, in his simplicity and good intentions, would simply ring up some doctor and dump him back in the hygienic hell where he had endured two days of torment. He was not aware that, with increasing frequency, he addressed Edward in Greek, or that his attempts to cover lapses of memory or concentration were as obvious as those of a drunk. Lost in the solipsism of mortal terror, he did not even perceive Edward's expression as he looked at him.

When Sebastian got back, having stayed on in Germany for a few extra days to finish a piece of research, he found Eugenides' message, with many others, on his answerphone. It surprised him considerably, but he interpreted it accurately, as a cry for help, and felt an immediate twinge of compunction that, what with term, exams, Germany and the general horrors of life, he had not seen the old man for three months or more. He had a great deal to do, but was sufficiently concerned to abandon his pile of unanswered and mostly out-of-date correspondence, and go straight round to Garlic Court, pausing only to buy a bunch of carnations from the flower-seller by the Tube.

It was getting on for four when he rang Eugenides' bell. Nothing happened. After waiting a couple of minutes, he tried again, wondering if he might have gone out. He was beginning to think he might go and find a cup of coffee and then try again, when he heard a faint shuffling noise from within. This was followed by a sort of scrabbling and clanking, as if Eugenides were trying to put the chain on, or perhaps take it off. Eventually, the door opened, and Sebastian's stomach lurched in disbelief as he looked down at the shaky, unshaven wreck of his old friend, bowed over a stick, with his right hand and wrist bandaged and held protectively against his chest.

'Mr Eugenides? My God, what's happened to you?'

Eugenides peered up at him confusedly, his tufted white brows knitting with the effort of memory.

'Sebastian.' He gulped and, shockingly, burst into tears.

'Oh, Jesus,' said Sebastian under his breath, tossing his ridiculous bunch of flowers on to the nearest of the hall chairs, and catching the old man in his arms. He felt peculiar and insubstantial, like a bundle of sharp little bones wrapped in musty cloth. While Eugenides snuffled wetly down his shirt, Sebastian fumbled for a hanky, which was rapidly becoming Priority One. 'Come on, Mr Eugenides. Blow. Let's get you sat down, and you can tell me about it.'

'Upstairs,' whispered Eugenides.

'Fine. Lean on me. I'll take your stick.' He kicked the door shut, tucked the stick under his left armpit, and put his other arm round Eugenides, and thus clumsily embraced, they shuffled across the hall and tackled the stairs. He found he was having to take most of Eugenides' weight, such as it was.

'I am ashamed,' said Eugenides wretchedly, as they paused on the landing for him to catch his breath.

'Oh, rubbish,' said Sebastian, nudging him into motion again.

By slow degrees, he managed to get him into his chair in the drawing room. Eugenides leaned back with his eyes shut, breathing hard, the wrinkled skin beneath his eyes still moist. He looked wretchedly ill. Sebastian got one of the hard chairs which flanked the portrait of Godscall Palaeologue, and sat down beside him, taking his good hand. Eugenides' grip was tentative at first, then strengthened as if Sebastian were literally a lifeline.

'Can I get you anything?'

'No, nothing,' said Eugenides, in Greek. He seemed to be unaware that he had switched languages.

'What's happened to you?'

'I cannot remember. I fell, I think. Yes, I fell.'

'And hurt your arm?' Sebastian prompted.

'Yes.'

Sebastian looked at him, baffled. That accounted for the stick, anyway.

'Look, I'm sorry to pry, but do you know why you fell?'

The dark eyes flew open, and stared at him, wide with panic.

'I cannot remember. I cannot remember things, Sebastian. God have mercy on me. "Εἰς τὸ σῶσαί με Κύριον, Ὁ θεός, εἰς τὴν βοήθειάν μου πρόσχες"...'

'Oh, God. I'm so sorry, Mr Eugenides.' Brain tumour? he wondered. Alzheimer's? Does it come on so fast? *Something* must be causing this. 'Look, have you got a doctor? Would you like me to find someone?'

'I have seen a doctor,' snapped Eugenides, with a sudden access of vitality. 'They did many tests, and they have found nothing wrong.'

'But that's crazy. I mean, something *is* wrong.'

'It is the will of God,' said Eugenides flatly. Sebastian looked at him thoughtfully. Well, that had put some lead back in his pencil. Quite clearly, nothing short of a team of men in white coats was going to get the old darling out of the house while he was still conscious. The threat of medical intervention had him positively galvanised into life.

'Don't worry. I won't try and interfere. Have you got anyone to look after you?'

'I have a young colleague, who has been very kind. He looks in on me twice a week. And I am getting stronger. Perhaps this confusion will go from me when I am well again.' Like hell, thought Sebastian, but forbore from comment.

'Excellent. Actually, there's something I wanted to ask you, if you're feeling up to it. It's something legal. Don't worry if you're too tired.'

'My dear Sebastian,' said Eugenides, with something like a return to his old manner, 'you cannot imagine what a pleasure it is to think about something other than this poor failing body. Please ask what you like.'

'It's about St Michael Graecorum. I don't know if that rings a bell...?'

'Oh, yes. Curiously, it came up quite recently. What about it?'

'Who has the reversion?'

'The lavra of St Michael, on Mount Athos.'

'That's exactly what I'd guessed. Thank you ever so much. There's something I need to write to the Abbot about. I've met him, you know. Would you like me to ask him to pray for you?'

'Please do. I became estranged from the Church as a young man, because of my nature, but as I have become old, it has become very clear to me that I never left it in spirit. I have been corresponding with the Abbot on business matters for a number of years. He may remember me.'

Sebastian glanced at his watch. 'Mr Eugenides, I'm afraid I'm going to have to go in a minute. I'm just back from Germany, and you know how it is when you've been away. There's a million and one little jobs. But I'm going to be in London for at least the next two months. Do just ring up if you want anything, and I promise I'll come. Is there anything you need, while I'm here?'

'Thank you. Could I ask you to buy me some Liver Salts? Since I am taking no exercise at the moment, I fear they have become a necessity. The key is on the mantelpiece, if you would not mind letting yourself in and out.'

XIV

It was a Saturday, and it was half past eight in the morning, so in Hattie's view the phone should not have been ringing, but it was. Resentfully, she put down her toast, and went to answer it.

'Hi,' she said, without enthusiasm.

'Oh, hello. Hattie?'

'Yes?'

'Hattie, it's Tim. Are you busy?'

'Tim, it's Saturday. I've got to get to Sainsbury's, and I've got to do my ironing. And if I don't walk Alice, she'll fall over and die.'

'Oh, good.'

'Tim,' said Hattie warningly, 'I don't think you're hearing what I'm saying.'

'Oh, Hattie, darling. Don't be cross. *I've got the fountain.* We've just got it out of the City, and it's in store in Willesden. I couldn't possibly persuade you to come and see it? I'd love to know what you think of it. You can bring Alice, and I'll take you to lunch.'

'But ...' Hattie considered this proposition, and abruptly changed her mind. It was certainly intriguing. 'Okay,' she decided, 'I'll come. But there's got to be a proper dog-walk in the deal somewhere, or my weekend collapses. Tell me how to get there by Tube. If you're taking your car, there's no point me taking mine.'

'Of course. We can nip down to Richmond afterwards. We'll have a nice lunch, and then Alice can have a run in Richmond Park. Go to North Acton or Willesden Junction, and find Victoria Road. You want the Victoria Road Industrial Estate, unit five. Can you be there by half-past eleven?'

'No problem. See you there.' Hattie turned to glare at Alice, who was lying in her basket with an air of conscious virtue, and observed, without surprise, that the toast had mysteriously evaporated from her plate.

'All right, mutt. You win this time.'

Alice raised her eyebrows. Who, me? she seemed to say.

By half past eleven, Hattie had done the worst of her ironing, got herself to Willesden, and was walking up Victoria Road, with Alice pattering happily at her heels. The area was classic West London wasteland: shabby factories, viaducts, urban clearways, and patches of run-down housing – the kind of thing, on the whole, that she spent her life trying to prevent. There seemed to be absolutely nobody around, but the industrial estate was, unusually, adequately signposted, so she kept on up the weedy asphalt private road until she spotted Tim's Citroën parked outside an anonymous, hangarlike building.

'Tim!' The door opened, and Tim emerged.

'Hello, Hattie. Come in. I've put the lights on.' She walked in, looking around curiously. The building was subdivided into aisles, with numbered sections marked out in paint on the floor, lit by flickering neon bars mounted on the roofbeams. Some sections were piled high with dusty packing-cases, others were empty, or held a variety of mysterious items: a piano, a collection of brass beds, a flock of wardrobes. Planks of wood. It all had a dusty, neglected look.

'What is this place?'

'General storage. You can hire so much floorspace, short or

long term. Quite a few antique dealers use it, for example – people who handle big items of furniture. There's a security man for the estate, and you've got to go to him to get the alarm switched off and the door open, so it's fairly secure, but you can still get at stuff quickly when you want it. It's not like Pickford's, where it all goes into containers, and you can't get an individual bit out if you need it suddenly.'

'Useful.' They walked together up the left-hand aisle, their footsteps echoing flatly on the concrete.

'Here we are.' Hattie came to a halt, and surveyed a heap of pale grey, cut stone blocks, tied round with sacking and bubble-wrap, with numbers painted on them in white gouache. The sharp, earthy smell of limestone came to her through the general ambience of dust and chemicals. Tim, watching her face, said, 'It doesn't look like much, does it?' She bit her lip, and shook her head. Tim produced a Maglite from his Barbour pocket, and flicked it on. 'Look'. The powerful white beam spotlighted a sexily rounded little goddess holding a cornucopia. She was solid, blocky, none too elegant, but the roughly-sketched stone face was smiling joyously, and the vitality of the figure made up for any lack of grace.

'Tim! She's *lovely*.'

'She's on the left side. I'm not sure yet if the scheme's classical and she's meant to be Hebe, or if the whole thing's emblematic and she's something out of Alciati or Ripa. She's a good sample. Most of the sculptured sides of the things are still wrapped up, but when we were moving the bits in here, I put a couple of pieces face out where I'd be able to show them to people.'

'All right. I'm nearly sold. It's all like that, is it?'

'Yes.'

'And you've got all of it, cross your heart and hope to die?'

'Yes.'

'Have you got a sketch?'

'Of course.' Tim pulled a notebook from his pocket, and rested it on one of the blocks, shining his torch on the page. 'Here.' Hattie looked with interest at his drawing, which had the precision of his architect's training, and was executed in fine pen. 'I'm sure this is right. The blocks have actually got numbers carved on them, on the undersides. Once we'd sorted out we were meant to read from left to right, it wasn't hard to sort out the bits. Look. You've got a Byzantine eagle sort of presiding at the top. The basin is shell-shaped, supported by dolphins, and then there's the lion of St Mark at the front here, for Venice. And up the sides, you've got all these symbolic bods. It seems to be quite eclectic, but I'm hoping that Sebastian will take one look at it and tell me it all refers to current politics or something. I'm positive it all means something.'

'I think it's wonderful. How tall is it?'

'Oh, eleven or twelve feet?'

'Fab. Big enough to notice, but not absolutely enormous. Even with plumbing it in to run water, it wouldn't cost a fortune to get it up.'

''Scuse me,' said a voice from behind them. Hattie turned, and saw a burly man in a fleece jacket. He was wearing crêpe-soled shoes, which had allowed him to join them unheard. 'Are you going to be much longer?'

'Hello, Craig,' said Tim, hastily. 'Sorry to have kept you. I think we're about ready to go. Have you seen all you want to, Hattie?'

'Oh, yes.' She smiled at the security man. 'Sorry to bugger up your Saturday.' He was profoundly underwhelmed.

'That dog didn't ought to be in here,' he grumbled. 'What if it cocks its leg on something?'

'She's a bitch. They don't do that. Heel, Alice.'

'Hattie, I really think we should be going,' said Tim warningly. They walked out together, with Alice slinking behind them, conscious of Craig watching them out of the building.

'Keen, isn't he?' she said sarcastically, once they were safely out of earshot.

'Well, you've got to be grateful for it, really. Some of them don't give a toss. I'm sorry he was rude about your dog.'

'Oh, don't worry about it,' said Hattie wearily. 'They tell me with kids it's even worse.' Tim opened the car, and let Alice into the back.

'Let's go to Richmond. Is the Three Pigeons okay?'

'Lovely.'

'Do you mind if I talk rubbish till we get there? I'm not absolutely sure of the way, and I need to concentrate on driving.'

Half an hour later, they were safely drinking beer and looking at the Thames when Tim dropped his bombshell.

'I'm so glad you saw the point of the fountain. I've had this absolutely marvellous idea about where to put it. I see it as having two functions. One's just being a great big beautiful thing cheering up a dull bit of London. The other's acting as a sort of memorial. It's the only sizeable material object to survive from the premodern Greek population, so it might help to stop people going on as if immigration started in 1950. What I thought was that it ought to go on the site of the old church of the Greeks, which was destroyed in the war. I've had a look at the area plan, and it's still wasteland.'

'Where is it?'

'Southwark.'

'Good idea. The area's on the up, and you're getting more tourists through. Mostly on Bankside of course, but I can see "exciting, historic Southwark" getting people interested. You might get Greek money in, too.'

'I'd thought of that,' said Tim, with a trace of smugness.

'Where is it exactly, then? I thought I knew Southwark pretty well, and I've never heard of a Greek church.'

'St Michael's Road.'

'*What?* Oh, Tim. This is ridiculous. It must be my bombsite garden I was trying to talk Anthony into listing. I should've thought – St Michael's Road, and no church to go with it. Not even a Marks and Sparks. What a fabulous idea – it's the handle I need to get it turned into a permanent amenity. Who owns it, then? I've wanted to know for ages.'

'It belongs to one of the monasteries on Mount Athos.'

'Got you. What an amazing thing, though. I suppose you're trying to get in touch with the owners?'

'Sebastian's writing a letter. In his own sweet time, of course, and if he gets round to it. He says he knows the abbot.' Tim's tone was resentful, and Hattie divined that it represented a battle lost.

'That's a piece of luck for you, all the same,' she pointed out.

'Oh, all right. I shouldn't get cross with Sebastian, really. It's just that he's so *casual.*'

'Does he think they'll play?'

'They might. He thinks they've barely registered they own it. But if it's put the right way, and we get the link to the old Greek community across to them, they might just let us have it. They're monks, after all.'

'Oh come on, Anglican. You don't really think monks are unworldly, do you? If they're anything like Catholic monks, they'll be a pretty organised bunch. Strikes me you'd better do some praying. I'll put a couple up myself, and light a candle. I'd really, really, like this to happen.'

'Oh, absolutely. Nothing's settled yet at all. But Hattie, it would be so lovely…'

The same morning, Edward was sitting on a bench in Green Park, unhappily contemplating the prospect of an imminent Lamprini. A shadow fell across him, making him jump.

'Lamprini! Great. You look fabulous,' he said, standing up.

'Hi, Edward. I've got half an hour. Then I'm somewhere else.' She was dressed in white linen, a long coat over a short shift-dress, with a white hat and strappy little shoes, but the result was anything but sweet and demure. There was a suggestion rather of nurses' uniform, and at that, the kind of nurse that applies discipline for a big fat fee. Furtively contemplating her, Edward decided that this impression was generated not by the clothes, which were very good, but somehow by Lamprini herself. 'How's it going?' she asked casually, as they strolled off together.

'Pretty well. After the accident, you know, he let me keep the key. I drop in twice a week. And I had a brainwave. I got some stuff from my great-uncle's house. Before you ask, the old bastard's absolutely senile, he doesn't know it's gone. It's for diabetes – the leaflet says it had side-effects, confusion, disorientation, etcetera, so I thought it might be worth a try. I put it in Mr E.'s liver salts, so he's dosing himself with this muck every day, without me lifting a finger. It's working like a charm. He's got pretty confused, and I think he's seeing about two of me.'

'But he's basically okay?'

'Yah. I don't see why it should do him much harm. I mean, it's a prescription drug. He's just got a bit too much insulin knocking about in his system.'

'That's great. You've done very well. Okay. We'll start sending a lot of letters from Greece. One to you too. What we planned. Just keep up the pressure. Once he's given you signing rights . . .'

'Yah, yah, of course. As soon as we've got his signature, we can just stop giving him the stuff, and he'll never know anything happened.' Though he believed what he was saying, it struck him forcibly, as he spoke, that with respect to this operation, even though he did not allow himself to think of it as anything which might constitute dirtying one's hands, if one did think of it in that way, the dirty hands belonged exclusively to him: whatever else happened, he must be sure to get her actively implicated. And that sod Britzolakis, too.

'Fine. You got any problems?'

'Well, one. He's ripped through those bloody salts a lot faster than I thought he would. When I was last there, I saw he'd nearly finished the tin. I'll need to get hold of some more stuff, and it's obviously prescription only, so I'll have to nip up to Scotland.'

'Scotland?'

'Where my Uncle James lives. They're his pills. I nicked all the packets he'd left around the house half-finished, but I put all I'd got in Eugenides' burp mixture. If I lift what he's got in the house now, he'll just think he's lost 'em somewhere. He usually forgets to take them, you know. I don't think it'll make a ha'porth of difference to him.'

'Okay, I see. Can you do that?'

'It's the weekend. I should be able to get a flight to Edinburgh tomorrow, drop in on him, turn round, come back. He won't remember I've even been, and if any of the neighbours see me, they'll just think I'm doing the concerned relative bit. My parents live abroad, you know. There's only me to keep an eye on him.'

'Sounds good. And there's no problem with leaving our guy to himself for a few days?'

'I don't think so. I read the leaflet, and they were talking about "long term" effects. I'm sure he'll actually start getting better, but it'll be a while before he actually notices.'

Lamprini looked at her watch. 'Fine. Look, Edward. I'm going to be in London with Dmitri for a couple more days. Till Tuesday or Wednesday, maybe.' She took a card from her white bag, and scribbled a number on the back. 'You can contact me here. I'd better go now.' For the benefit, presumably, of hypothetical observers, she took Edward by the shoulders and air-kissed left and right, before turning on her heel and leaving him in a waft of designer perfume.

There was no difficulty about getting a standby to Edinburgh; in fact, it was so easy Edward was left wondering why anyone ever bothered with the train. Since he was fairly certain that, given the old man's habits, he would leave Fife slightly richer than he had arrived, he decided to take a taxi all the way from the airport, and reclined luxuriously in the back, enjoying the contrast with his previous journey north.

Cove Wynd looked no better than when he had last seen it. He rang the bell. To his considerable astonishment, it was answered almost immediately. To his even greater astonishment and disquiet, the door was opened by a policeman.

'Er…'

'And who might you be, sir?'

'Edward. Edward Lupset.'

'Sergeant Mackintyre. We've been trying to contact you, sir. We found your name in a wee book he had.'

'What? Look, what's going on?'

'I'm sorry to tell you, sir, your uncle (great-uncle is it?) was found dead this morning.'

'My God. I must have been at the airport. I thought I'd come and see how he was doing.'

'Very proper, sir. A shame you didn't see the last of him. Come away in.'

'Er. He's not still here, is he?'

'Och, no. He's down at the…I mean, we've taken him away. Ye ken, when a body dies unsupervised, as you might say, we've got to get an autopsy.' This fact had not come Edward's way before: it struck him now, with a nasty chill, that it was something to bear in mind. 'Not that we're worried,' continued Mackintyre chattily, 'I wouldn't like you to go thinking that. It's been clear enough from the neighbours your uncle was failing for a good wee while now.'

'It's all a bit sudden,' said Edward, who had had time to collect his thoughts, walking into the house after the policeman. 'Obviously, I was worried about him. But I didn't think he was that bad.' He looked around him: the level of squalor was definitely reduced from his previous visit. 'I organised some cleaners to come and sort him out,' he added, anxious to establish his righteousness.

'Aye, you did. We knew about it from his notebook, of course, and we heard about it from the neighbours. They were glad to know the family was taking an interest. It was a neighbour that found him. Mr Stewart, you'll maybe want to go and have a word. He hadn't seen Mr Campbell for a wee while, two or three days maybe, and when he couldn't get an answer, he broke the kitchen window, and got into the house that way.'

'It's not easy,' said Edward defensively. 'We're all a long way away. I'm working in London. Mummy and Daddy are in France.'

'That'd be right. I'm sure you did your best,' said the policeman neutrally, but it was clear that the Lupsets had been weighed in the balance and found wanting.

Together, they walked down the hall, and into the kitchen. This was, compared to its unspeakable state the last time Edward had seen it, clean; with merely a surface encrustation of milk-bottles and mugs of no more than a few weeks' growth. He was angry and alarmed. His great-uncle's squalid and unregarded death did not touch him, since he had felt nothing for the old man when he was alive: the question which filled his mind was how on earth could he do what he'd come to do, under the eyes of this well-intentioned bluebottle. It was answered almost immediately.

'I'll be away back to the station,' said Mackintyre. 'I'm glad I caught you. It's a sight easier for us if we can raise a member of the family to take charge.'

'Oh, God! But I don't know anything about Uncle James's business!' wailed Edward.

'Take a wee look around,' advised Mackintyre, with an air of fatherly tolerance. 'Start with the desk. If you notify his lawyers and the bank, they'll tell you what to do. Good luck, son.' He stuck his hand out; Edward felt constrained to shake it. Some moments later, he was left in the empty house.

In a sense, he realised unhappily, he had got exactly what he wanted. Freedom to rummage unopposed; positively encouraged to do so by a passing guardian of law and order. Yet it was horribly apparent the whole thing was about to let him in for a great deal of trouble. He went up to Jimmy's bedroom and stood in the doorway, contemplating with a sort of superstitious, nauseated distaste the bed in which the old man had presumably died. The room held a sour fug of unwashed old man, with overtones of something even nastier. Mac-thing, he recalled, had said the old man was *found* that morning...For Edward, the vengefulness of the dead was easier to believe in than the rights of the living. He had been reluctant to enter the house; he found it impossible to consider entering the death-room, especially now he was alone. Irritating though the chatty copper had been, he was at least human.

What on earth should he do? Retreating from the bedroom, which he did not want to enter except as a last resort, and closing the door, he decided to follow Mackintyre's advice, and look for the desk. This, as he recalled, was in the relatively neutral territory of the front room. He ran downstairs, and went to look. The desk produced an address book of sorts – which, he realised, would make the next bit a lot easier – and a couple of lawyers' letters, which gave him a contact name for winding up the old bastard's affairs. But nothing helpful. Just chores. The kitchen, he thought. He lived in the kitchen. If there are spare pills, that's where they'll be.

He was right, in a way. There was one loose packet of Mellerox, half-finished, lurking in a chipped cut-glass biscuit-barrel on the mantelpiece. But behind the said biscuit-barrel, there was something much more to the point; a repeat prescription. Three months' supply. He pocketed it. Fine. He was not displeased. It gave him, most conveniently, a cast-iron reason for persuading Lamprini to do some of her own dirty work.

Edward returned to the front room, and dug Lamprini's card out of his wallet. 'Ms Polychronopolou, please,' he said to the answering voice. 'This is Edward Lupset.'

'Please hold.' A minute or so later, during which Edward was favoured with a random excerpt from *Swan Lake*, Lamprini came to the phone.

'Hello?'

'Lamprini. Thank God I've got you. I'm in Scotland. My great-uncle's just died. I'm afraid I'm stuck here for a while.' (It occurred to him suddenly, to his immense irritation, that this might be true; and what would Betty say?) 'I'm next of kin. I don't know when I'll be able to get back to London.' He could hear, or sense, her drawing breath to object. 'But I think I've got an answer,' he continued triumphantly. 'I've got a repeat prescription for the stuff. I'll send it down registered post, and you can get it filled. I'll send it off first thing tomorrow, and you should get it first thing on Tuesday.'

'Look…'

'Don't worry. It's dead easy. You don't have to sign anything. You just take the prescription to a chemist, say it's for someone who can't get there on his own, and they give it to you. It's a diabetic drug, for Christ's sake. It's not like Methadone or something. They won't be worried you're trying to resell it, so they won't think twice.'

'Edward, can't you…'

'No.' He had the whip hand for once, and he was enjoying it. 'Just think a minute, Lamprini. This is the one place on God's earth that people know the man it's for is dead! I *can't* fill it. And I can't get out of here in the foreseeable future. My mother's flying in from France.' (Or she will be, when I get around to ringing her …he thought, parenthetically). 'I'll have to go and meet her, so what the hell am I supposed to do? I don't think there's another chemist nearer than St Andrews, and I haven't got a car.'

Lamprini conceded defeat. 'Okay. Send the thing down now. I'll deal with it.'

'First thing tomorrow. There's no post on Sunday.'

'But you will have to give it to him. Only you can get into the house.'

'*Okay*. But we don't want any more delay than we can help, do we? Look. You get the stuff. Empty the capsules, and mix the powder through a can of Andrews Liver Salts. Parcel it up in something, and leave it at my flat – I gave you the address. Then the minute I get back, I can get it to him.' Lamprini put the phone down without a farewell; an indication, Edward was rather inclined to think, of how pissed off she was. Which, in turn, confirmed him in his initial feeling that he had been wise to draw her in. Buoyed up by the cheerfulness of this thought, he felt he could almost face ringing his parents, at least if he had a drink in his hand. Whatever other amenities his uncle's house might lack, there was no shortage of whisky.

XV

A few days after her adventure with the mysterious Greeks, Jeanene was sitting peacefully in the British Library when, on filling in a request slip for a book, she suddenly realised that it was the fifteenth of August – which, as all good Catholic girls know, is the feast of the Assumption of the Virgin, and a holiday of obligation. She considered her options. If she was going to get off her bum and go, and she felt on the whole that she should, the neatest of the possibilities available was to go to Evening Mass with the Jesuits at Farm Street, just round the corner from the pharmacy, even though she'd then have half an hour or so to kill before starting her shift in Mount Street. But it was a still, hot day, and she could always take a book and read in the garden. That decided, she returned with a clear conscience to Murray's *Greek Religion*. It was a good day, it occurred to her, to be reading about mysterious and terrible goddesses.

As she emerged from Bond Street tube station, heading for Jesuit HQ, Jeanene mused that nothing, not even Christmas, underlined so completely the essentially European mindset of Christianity as the shape of the Virgin's year. This was an idea which had first struck her in the after-school year she spent backpacking round Europe, and today seemed to confirm it.

Mary's Day feels like the hottest day of the year even if it isn't. It is breathless, the turn of the summer. The day when the green of the trees and the grass begins to lose its freshness and starts looking dusty, the start of the slow slide towards autumn. May is Mary's month the world over, but it is in Europe that it is a month of optimism and unfolding, when the late tulips meet the early roses, while by mid-August, when the Goddess's reign is over and she ascends to heaven, the forces of entropy gnaw and nibble at all that has been achieved. Okay, boys, you can hear her saying, as she gathers her sky-blue robes around her and thankfully departs, you try running this lot, and see what kind of a bollocks you make of it.

With which thought, Jeanene reached the chapel, pushed open the door, dipped her fingers in the holy water stoup, and tried to turn her mind into more reverent channels. The dim, religious light of Farm Street closed round her, its subdued, glittering opulence presided over by a small army of life-size polychrome marble statues. She chose herself a seat near the back, where she stood some chance of not being suffocated by incense, near St Margaret of Scotland. Farm Street is probably the smartest Catholic church in London. As six-thirty approached, the Feast of the Assumption flushed an extraordinary number of elegant ladies from Mayfair and the embassy quarter. They flowed in, heels clicking, diamonds flashing, adjusting tiny cobwebs of priceless lace on immaculate coiffures. As the church got fuller and fuller, and warmer and warmer, an expanding cloud of expensive perfumes filled the air, suppressing the church's basic odour of incense and furniture polish.

About five minutes after Mass had actually begun, Jeanene became aware from the corner of her eye of a late arrival, and obligingly budged up to give her a seat. In the ensuing minutes, she became dimly aware of a cockatoo-like shock of blonde hair, a long, patrician nose, a smell of honest sweat, and a strong singing voice – this last was extremely obvious, since most of the congregation, Jeanene included, were unfamiliar with British hymn-tunes, and remained completely silent. Her neighbour's pleasant soprano added an unexpected descant to the otherwise unsupported tenors of the Jesuit fathers. At the Pax, she had a chance to turn and look at the woman properly, while they shook hands and murmured 'Peace be with you'. She was tall and thin, dressed in running shorts, Nikes, and a T-shirt which said, 'If I were you, I'd be afraid of me'. The face was a long, pale oval, with grey eyes hooded beneath heavy lids and high, arched brows; in repose, concentrated on the business of the Mass, you would say it was a medieval face. But the grey eyes had a diabolical sparkle which led her to doubt that their owner's expression was always so demure. As the stranger's long, strong, fingers wrapped themselves confidently round Jeanene's small, hot paw, she felt a cool shock of interest and attraction. Tearing herself away, she shook at random a number of immaculately manicured hands presented languidly for her attention, but her heart was not in it.

At the end of Mass, as the congregation broke up into small, chattering groups, Jeanene decided she had nothing to lose by being un-British, and said hello.

'Hi,' responded the other woman, with a friendly smile, her eyes flicking up and down Jeanene's figure, taking in her plain blouse and cotton skirt.

'Do you live round here?' asked Jeanene.

'No. Not my kind of place, even if I had the dosh. I had some business over this way, and I thought I'd just fit in a run in the Park. Timed it a bit wrong though, I'm not up to speed these days. That's the worst of good intentions. How about you? You don't look like an embassy type, not even the Aussies, though I know they aren't big on formality.'

'I'm filling in at the Mount Street pharmacy. My name's Jeanene.'

'I'm Hattie.' They strolled out together into the dusty Mayfair sunshine. A sandy lurcher, which had been lying flattened in a patch of shade, got to its feet without undue haste, and fell into step behind them. 'And this is Alice.' Jeanene was mildly surprised: lurchers, in her experience, were working dogs, and she did not expect to be introduced to one. Come to that, she didn't expect to see one.

'Hi, dog,' she said, a little at a loss. The creature ignored her.

'Do you fancy a drink?' Hattie offered politely. 'I'm parched.'

'That'd be great. I'm on duty at half seven. If we went to a pub, maybe I could pick up a sandwich?'

'Tell you what. Let's go down to the Marble Arch Pret, they won't mind the way I'm dressed. Pubs tend to be a bit smart round here, cause of trying to keep the barristers apart from the workmen. Someone's always doing up a house, so the place is crawling with plumbers and plasterers, but the posh boys don't like to find them at the bar. Too much like admitting they're people. Or do you really need a drink? The Farm Street Js can take a girl that way.'

'No, Pret'd suit me. Coffee and a sarnie's all I want.' They ambled companionably eastwards towards the park, Hattie considerately shortening her stride so that Jeanene could keep up with her.

'Hattie,' began Jeanene cautiously.

'Mmmm?'

'I know you Brits think questions are rude, but can I ask you something?'

'Ask away,' said Hattie, amused.

'Are you a cockney? I mean, is the way you talk what they call a cockney accent? People sometimes say Australian's like cockney, but you don't sound like us at all.'

'Cor, stroike a loight, miss, I dunno. It is, I suppose. Not that I was brung up within sound of Bow Bells. My gran and my dad were proper cockneys, but by the time I came along, he'd parked her in Linden Lea. One of those little postwar developments out west where nothing ever happens till someone runs amok out of sheer boredom. They were both real characters, and I suppose I just copied them. Anyway, by the time I was growing up, middle-class kids were all desperate for common accents so they'd sound like Mick Jagger. I went to North London Collegiate on a scholarship, but my mates thought I sounded great. Instead of learning how to talk proper, I had 'em all saying "fink" and "froo" like the revenge of Liza Doolittle.'

'Do English people still care about how you speak?'

'Sort of. Like I was saying, for some people it's kind of gone into reverse. Dad always said you could talk how you liked as long as you were making sense, but if I'd come home saying "Yah, thanks aw'fly," he'd've put me across his knee. And I don't suppose my mates' parents liked it much.'

'I really don't understand about class,' confessed Jeanene. Hattie's aristocratic eyebrows rose like croquet hoops.

'It's not complicated. My dad always said there was nothing wrong with toffs. My mum was a toff, and he had some nobby friends. He reckoned it was the ones in the middle who caused the trouble. The ones who always wanted to be something they weren't. That's what I remember from school. I'd take girls home for tea sometimes, and there they'd be, parked on the sofa, drinking it all in – Gran didn't have a set of flying plaster ducks on the wall, but she might've had. They thought it was really authentic, going home by bus and everything. They'd drink Gran's 'orrible tea, and sit there waiting for her to say something working class. Then their dads'd turn up in the Rover to collect them.' They turned into Pret a Manger.

'If you grab a couple of stools,' said Jeanene, 'I'll get. What'd you like?'

'Can I have two bottles of water? I haven't half worked up a sweat.'

''Course.' Jeanene went round the cabinets, collecting up Hattie's water, a chicken sandwich, a chocolate brownie, and a cappuccino, and brought them back to the counter where Hattie sat waiting. She drank the first of the bottles in three long swallows, then started on the other. Halfway through it, Jeanene caught her eyeing the brownie hungrily, and pushed it over.

'Thanks. I shouldn't, but what the hell.'

When Jeanene said goodbye, shortly afterwards – praying that she could make it to Mount Street inside four minutes – she had Hattie's phone number tucked into her back pocket, and an invitation to a party. Pounding up Oxford Street, dodging the tourists, she began to feel London was a friendlier place.

Hattie's party, which she had been planning when she bumped into Jeanene, was scheduled for the following Saturday. No cook, she preferred to work off her hospitality debts by taking people to lunch in pubs and restaurants, and having a twice-yearly bash. She had reached the last stage of her preparations, disposing strategic bowls of dips, tortilla chips and crudités throughout her sitting room. It was a good house for parties: a miniature townhouse with two rooms on each floor, and the kitchen in a semi-basement. Though the original rooms had been small, the original first floor drawing and dining rooms had long since been knocked into one, so there was plenty of space for people to mill around. Interior design, like dressing up, interested Hattie only up to a point: she had, she knew, insufficient flair and taste to impress genuine aesthetes, so she had settled for pleasing herself. She had kept a few nice pieces of furniture from her mother's family house (all a bit big for the rooms they now occupied), but items which were glorious without being practical, such as fragile but lovely antique chairs, had gone their way to the saleroom. In their place were neutrally contemporary pieces from Habitat and Ikea; the walls were painted off-white, and the furnishing fabrics were all simple and neutrally coloured, set off with a few bright cushions. Not a smart room, but even Anthony and Tim could hardly deny that it was comfortable.

The windows stood open, admitting the hot summer air, Ella

Fitzgerald was singing Cole Porter on the CD player, and there were flowers everywhere. She was wearing a new, short red dress, Alice was shut in the spare bedroom upstairs (much to her disgust), and it all looked very nice. The doorbell rang, startling her, and she looked at her watch: a bit early for guests; so who was it?

'Hi, Hattie.' Dilip Dhesi stood there grinning, loaded with mysterious Tupperware containers.

'Hi, Dil. What's – oh, you haven't. Oh, you sweetheart. What've you brought? Come down to the kitchen.'

'There's about a kilo of Dad's best barfi,' said Dil cheerfully, following her in, 'and I made some samosas and onion bhajis. They never go to waste, do they?'

'Oh, Dil. It's really, really, nice of you.' She excavated some big plates from the back of the cupboard, and together, they unpacked and arranged Dil's offerings. 'I ought to marry you, really. You're a fabulous cook.' She unwrapped the barfi, which turned out to be vibrantly striped in red, yellow and green and decorated with silver foil. 'Cor, those're a bit special, aren't they? Look, I've got this George V jubilee plate of Gran's. I'll pile 'em up on it, and they'll look a treat.'

'How are things?' asked Dil.

'Pretty good. Hey, something I meant to tell you. You remember that garden in Southwark? It turns out it belongs to some Greek monks on Mount Athos. My mate Tim's got this fabulous scam worked out. He's trying to talk them round to letting us turn it into a memorial to the Greek community in England. That way, we could make it something permanent.' She picked up the biggest two plates, and carried them up to the sitting room.

'It's a nice idea,' said Dil, following behind her with the rest of the food.

'But you've got your doubts. I can hear you not saying something again, Dil, love.'

Dil put a plate of onion bhajis down on Hattie's nice mahogany sideboard, and centred it carefully. 'I don't know anything about Greek monks, Hattie, but I suppose they've got some human nature like everyone else. They may've ignored this property for fifty years, but if you start writing letters, they're going to start thinking about it, aren't they? And as soon as they leave off praying and start thinking, they'll realise it's an asset, and they won't want to part with it. That's what people are like.'

Hattie nodded. 'I'd thought of that. Tim had this mad notion that just because they were monks, they wouldn't mind giving it away. I've talked him out of that. We're organising a bid to try and raise the cash to buy the site. That's a bit different. We'll be going to them and saying, dear Father Whatsit, why not take this big wad of drachmas instead of a property you can't do anything with.'

'That's a bit better. But I told you before, Hat. Everyone looks a gift horse in the mouth. Bet you a quid that they look at your offer and say, Hey, someone wants this site. Someone else might want it lots more. How are you going to pitch your offer? I doubt if you could raise anything like what it's worth as building land.'

'No. You're right. We'd be offering for waste ground, which is what it is.'

'Well, there aren't any restrictive covenants on it, are there? And I can't see a lot of problem with planning permission, in that area. You'll just have to hope they don't put two and two together,' commented Dil. The doorbell rang again.

An hour later, the party was in full swing, and it was no longer possible to see across the room. Hattie drifted from group to group, with a bottle of wine in one hand and a bottle of water in the other, making sure that everything was all right, and periodically answering the door. Snatches of conversation drifted past her.

'...When you've got total faith in your shoes, it gives you this divine *confidence*...'

'...the trouble with all this stuff you hear about free radicals is they sound as though you ought to be *for* them, know what I mean?'

'...Well, we're all little windsocks fluttering in the gale of the *Zeitgeist*, aren't we? Look at Thai cuisine. One minute no one's heard of it, and two minutes later, Findus are doing Thai-style crispy pancakes and pot-noodles...'

Hattie passed on, and saw her friend Daniel, talking to her other friend Valerie, and a woman she didn't know. '...So I said, why don't you stop fantasising and give it a try?' he was saying, dismally. Something in his tone suggested an often-told tale. She stopped to listen.

'Did she?' asked Valerie.

'Yes.'

'More wine, anyone?' said Hattie, dispensing Chardonnay into out-thrust glasses. 'What are you talking about?'

'Daniel's ex,' said the woman she didn't know, smugly.

'Karen? The one who works for the Midland?'

'Now she's Karen the professional belly-dancer,' said Daniel, gloomily. 'I think she calls herself Zuleika.'

'Wh—' The doorbell sounded again, and Hattie tore herself away. It turned out to be Anthony and Tim.

'Hi. I'm so glad you could make it.' She drew them into the room, and took the bottle which Anthony gave her. 'There's someone I'd really like you to meet.' Once she had got them settled by the window with a glass apiece, she went in search of Dil. She found him at the other side of the room, talking to the cheese-buyer for Selfridges and the manager of the Pont Street Gallery. When an opportunity offered, she cut in, and carried him off to talk to Tim. It rapidly became clear that this had not been a good idea. Tim clearly found Dil abrasive; Dil just as obviously thought Tim negligible. When she heard a strange voice, it came as a welcome relief.

'Anyone want one of these?' Jeanene was standing there, with a plate of Dil's samosas, heaven-sent. Anthony accepted one.

'Mmm,' he said, surprised, after the first bite.

'Dil made them,' said Hattie. 'Dil, I know two really fabulous cooks. Anthony's the other one. And he's interested in gardens too.' Deftly, she moved a little to one side, forcing them to adjust their positions, and grouping Dil, Jeanene and Anthony as a threesome. 'This is Jeanene. She's just arrived from Australia.'

'What do you do?' asked Anthony courteously. Good, she thought, as Jeanene opened her mouth to answer. They'd look after themselves. She turned to Tim, who was visibly sulking. 'Tim, I wanted to ask you something,' she said, racking her brains for what she was going to say next. 'If you can't get the monks to co-operate, have you thought about alternative sites?'

'I do hope it won't come to that,' he said crossly. 'Did you ask Sebastian, by the way? I'd rather hoped to see him here.'

'Yeah, I thought of that,' casually drifting a step or two away from the others, and forcing him to follow her. 'I did ask him, but he said he'd got to be away this weekend.' Much though she loved a bit of good gossip, she refrained from further details in the interests of peace. ('Hattie. I'd love to. But I met this wonderful man at a symposium on plaster conservation. An old-fashioned English rose in corduroys and a tattersall shirt – he's carrying me off for a dirty weekend in Gloucestershire...') 'He's very busy', she finished, diplomatically.

'I'm terribly fed up with Sebastian,' Tim complained. 'I don't think he's even written my letter yet.'

'Well, he might've,' said Hattie soothingly. 'I don't suppose the monks are brilliant correspondents.'

'At least he's confirmed that it's the monks we're dealing with, or I think he has. I got a postcard about three weeks ago, and all it says is "Bingo. We were right." I just wish he'd be more serious.'

'Well, if he was any swishier, you could hang curtains off him, but he's really quite serious in his own way,' protested Hattie. 'I mean, when I talked to him, he'd just been at this all-day conference on restoring frescoes and stuff. It's not the kind of thing you do if you aren't pretty dedicated.' She was, she knew, wasting her breath. Tim continued to pout. About to open her mouth again, she stiffened. Somewhere on the other side of the room, she caught a glimpse of a slim, sandy form slipping deftly through the forest of legs. 'Oh, shit. Some cretin's let Alice loose. I wonder what she's eaten? Tim, help me catch her.'

They ran her to ground finally in the upstairs bathroom. She was standing beside the bath, paws apart and head down, looking at her loving mistress sullenly.

'What a theatrical-looking animal she is,' commented Tim, once he had caught his breath. 'It's those black rims to her eyes, against the pale fur; they make her look like Sarah Bernhardt.'

'That's why she's called Alice,' said Hattie. 'Lisa, the girl I got her from, named her after Alice Cooper. Remember? The one with all the mascara, back in the Seventies.' Alice shuddered, and answered Hattie's most immediate question by suddenly heaving, and sicking up a multicoloured mess of semi-digested Indian sweets.

'Well, at least you've done it on the vinyl,' said Hattie resignedly. 'Alice, if you've broken that plate, I'm going to be really cross.'

'I'll go and find out, shall I?' said Tim, beating a hasty retreat. Hattie unreeled many yards of lavatory paper, scooped up the mess, and flushed it down the loo, then gave Alice some water, which she lapped eagerly.

'It's fine,' reported Tim, returning. 'It was under the sideboard.'

'I'd better shut her in the bedroom again. Come on, hellhound.' Having stashed Alice out of harm's way, she followed Tim back downstairs, and gave some thought to cheering him up. Fortunately, scanning the nearest faces, she spotted a restoring architect and his mouselike wife: they would definitely get on. She introduced him; they did. Anthony, Dilip, and Jeanene were still an animated threesome at the other side of the room, no problems there.

By midnight, things were beginning to wind down. Hattie, not wanting to break things up, but equally, quite keen to reduce the chaos, discreetly collected up empty bowls and plates that had once held dips, chips, and so forth, and carried them down to the kitchen.

It's a funny thing about parties, she reflected, as she came through the door. However organised you are, someone always ends up in the kitchen. Jeanene was perched on the sink-unit, a full glass neglected beside her, while Dil stood over her. Both of them were holding mugs. It struck her suddenly how attractive Jeanene was. She was very simply dressed in a pair of chinos and a white sleeveless blouse, but her slender figure was graceful, and the girlish prettiness of her face, animated by conversation, with flushed cheeks and sparkling grey eyes, was altogether more striking than she had observed on their earlier encounter. Dil, lounging elegantly, propped against the wall by one long, outthrust arm, was evidently exerting himself to charm, and to some effect.

Jeanene saw her come in and smiled: unembarrassed, Hattie (who found herself suffering a tiny, unacknowledgeable pang of envy) was pleased to note. Dil, also, was in no way disconcerted.

'I made us some tea, Hat. Hope you don't mind.'

''Course not. Actually, I could murder a cup of tea. Is there anything left in the pot?' Dil bestirred himself, and went to look.

'You're in luck,' he reported.

'Don't let me interrupt,' said Hattie, accepting the mug which he filled for her. 'What were you talking about?'

'I was just asking Jeanene why she works as a pharmacist. It's such an Asian thing to do.'

'Why do you, Jeanene?' asked Hattie, interested.

'Well, the same reasons Asians do it, I reckon,' said Jeanene. 'It's pretty boring, but the great thing about it is, it's the fastest professional qualification you can get. So I did that first off, then I was able to put myself through an arts degree, and got hooked by Classics. But with pharmacy under my belt, I could get the hell out, y'see, and always be able to support myself. It pays much better than shit jobs, and once you're on the local list, it's easy to pick up part-time or locum work, so you can keep your head above water without committing too much time.'

'Cool. Where are you working?' asked Dil.

'Mayfair. The Mount Street pharmacy?'

'I don't believe it. The manager's a man called Patel, isn't he? A big fat guy, with a birthmark on his face?'

'That's right.'

'His wife's one of my mum's best friends. They must've known each other for thirty years. I think they came from the same village or something.'

'I've never seen her. I didn't know he even had a wife.'

'Well, you wouldn't. They're very traditional. I hope he's not too shitty to you.'

'Oh, well. You know how it is. He's okay really. It's nice to think of him having a home life – basically, I just get to see him as this drongo who shouts at me when I screw up, you know?'

'Doesn't sound too good,' commented Hattie.

'No worries. It's better than the other sort, who try and get you to go out with them,' said Jeanene practically. 'Look, do you want a hand with the clearing up?' At that moment, heavy feet were heard on the stairs, and someone put his head round the door.

'We're saying goodbye, Hattie, love. And we're giving Susan and Val a lift to Paddington.'

''Scuse me,' said Hattie, and hurried out. This, it turned out, was the start of a general exodus. When she returned, after having said all the goodbyes, she found things very well under control. Dil was squatting by the dishwasher, loading it up efficiently, while Jeanene binned leftovers and handed him glasses.

'This is great,' said Hattie, 'thank you ever so much.'

'First in, last out, that's the rule for you lefties, isn't it?' said Dil amiably.

'That's right. I'd better join the production line while I've still got the chance.' She picked up a tray, and went back up to the sitting room to collect more glasses.

'This is about it,' she said, returning. 'Once I've got the place aired, I'll be practically straight.'

'I've ordered us a taxi,' said Dil. 'Jeanene's a long way from home.' And probably can't afford one on her own, Hattie reflected. Dil was not one of the city's champion taxi-takers. It was nice of him to have thought of it.

'It's been great,' said Jeanene.

'Well, nice you could come. Sorry we haven't had a chance to talk, that's the trouble with parties. We must sort out another time.' She meant it. She was interested in people who seemed to be inventing themselves as they went along, and Jeanene intrigued her. There was a ring at the door. 'That'll be your cab.'

When they had all gone, she released Alice from the spare bedroom. Her house had a pocket-handkerchief back garden, which contained practically nothing except a magnolia tree which long predated her tenure, a bit of patio paving on which she could in theory put a barbecue, and some dank grass. Dil would doubtless have made himself self-sufficient out of it, and Anthony would have turned it into a work of art, but as far as Hattie was concerned, it functioned mainly as Alice's latrine. The dog trotted down as soon as she opened the back door, and Hattie sat on the top step in the velvety midnight air to watch her pale shadow as she pottered fastidiously about before choosing a spot. Having relieved herself, she climbed back up to Hattie, and sat down beside her, leaning against her, with her head on Hattie's shoulder. Hattie rubbed her cheek against Alice's soft ear, and hugged her. They sat together for a long while.

XVI

A few days later, Jeanene received a letter from Mr George Beckinsale, inviting her to come and introduce herself. When she knocked on Beckinsale's door, she was greeted by a red-faced, dark-haired man in a shabby tweed jacket, regarding her fixedly from the safety of the far side of a desk. He looked more English than anyone Jeanene had yet seen, so English that she immediately suspected him of being some kind of colonial. Nervously, she introduced herself and begun to describe her project.

'I got this idea about looking at the Athenian *gynaeceum*. What women's quarters were actually like, using archaeology? Then bringing in literary evidence for how people lived in them, legal evidence, stuff about what women were supposed to do with their days...'

Beckinsale steepled his fingers, and frowned at her headmaster-ishly.

'What *for*, Miss Malone?'

'Well, I think women's lives are important. And, you know, people talk about women's lives in Classical Athens, the way they were really repressed?'

'Do they?' enquired her supervisor, coldly; she looked at him in bewilderment. 'Miss Malone,' he went on sternly, 'I am happy to say that I don't read the kind of thing you are no doubt referring to. I can help you on the archaeological side and probably suggest some things you might read. But I can only help you if you are prepared to be guided by the evidence.' She opened her mouth to defend herself, but he overrode her. 'There is a great deal of so-called theory about, Miss Malone. Perhaps, coming from a rather far-flung part of the world, you have been spared that sort of thing' – oh, sure, thought Jeanene sardonically to herself – 'but I have to warn you, it is endemic here. And I have no time for it, Miss Malone. Sound, fact-based scholarship. That is the *only* way into the past.'

He was glaring at her as if he hoped to convert her to a new religion, or sell her an insurance policy she didn't want. As she looked back at him, his expression softened into misty avuncularity, and she realised with horror that her face had let her down: she must be looking sweet and appealing again. He's completely loony, she thought. Still, I've got so much to learn, I'm sure he can teach me something. And there's a way you can change supervisors, I'm pretty certain.

'I'm sure we'll get on very well, Miss Malone.' Like hell, she thought, standing up and offering him her hand, which was briefly engulfed in a surprisingly damp and nervous grasp.

Jeanene wandered dispiritedly down the corridor, looking at obsolete posters. The place was strangely quiet. Term would start soon, and doubtless the corridors would fill up with chattering, surging hordes clutching files and notebooks, but for the time being, it was almost untenanted and looked like the vasty halls of death. Just when she was beginning to think she might burst into tears, she saw a name on a door which she recognised, and before she could think twice, knocked.

'I'm not here. Oh, all right. Who is it? Come in.' No single reply suggested itself, so Jeanene turned the handle, and went in. Sebastian Raphael was sitting in front of his desk, which unlike Mr Beckinsale's was pushed back against the window wall, wearing a pale linen suit with a yellow waistcoat, and spreading cream cheese on a bagel with what looked ominously like the wrong end of a nail-file. He caught her looking at it, and hid it hastily in the bagel-bag.

'Hi. You know, bagels are ninety-nine per cent fat free?' he offered. 'When I found that out, it absolutely made my week.'

'Well, sure, but if you spread 'em with cream cheese, you might as well be eating chocolate eclairs,' Jeanene pointed out.

'I suppose so. Oh, to hell with it, anyway. I can still get into this suit, so I don't know why I'm bothering. I may not look like every boy's dream, but I'd rather have my last relationship with a Mars Bar than a mirror, wouldn't you? What can I do for you?'

'I just came to say hi. I'm Jeanene. Jeanene Malone?'

Sebastian's eyes narrowed. 'Oh, yes, I remember. The pharmacist, right? Met any dodgy Greeks lately?'

'No, thank God. But I've just met one bloody weird Englishman. Sebastian, I don't know if it's rude or against the rules or something, but where is Mr Beckinsale coming from? How do you change supervisors?'

'So soon? You must have two supervisors, surely? George not having a PhD himself, they can't have left him alone with you. It's against the rules.'

'The other's Dr Katherine Flaxman, but I got a letter from her, and she said just to see Mr Beckinsale for now.'

'Katie? But she's a darling, and terribly clever. I can't think — shit. She's on study leave, isn't she? I'd forgotten.'

'That's right. She told me she's going to be in Princeton for six months.'

'Oh, dear. Have a bagel.'

Jeanene took one, judging that he would not eat unless she did so, and worried it into very small pieces while Sebastian got on with his lunch, staring absently over her shoulder and apparently thinking hard.

Suddenly, he said 'Jeanene, dear. Tell me a bit about your project while I get this lot down. I can't think when I'm hungry.'

Feeling rather foolish, Jeanene outlined her ideas about woman's space for the second time that morning.

'Mmm,' said Sebastian thoughtfully, 'what started you off on this track?'

'Well, we've got lots of communities in Australia which keep women pretty much under control. Muslims, mostly. But if you talk to the women, it's clear they've got some compensations. Okay, some of them want Western-type freedom, but some of them're happy the way they are. That surprised me, and it got me thinking. I want to look at how ancient Greek women made their lives viable, even if they look incredibly frustrating and depressing to the likes of us. I don't think you can just say that they were oppressed, and quote female infanticide records, and sort of leave it all there.'

'Well, the good news is you'll really get on with Katie when she gets back, that's the way she thinks too. I'm sure she's not angling to stay in the States, by the way. She's got a very nice partner here, with a good job in London, and they won't be wanting to move. Look, try not to worry. George will get your Greek grammar straight. He'll help you sort out the physical evidence. He's not totally useless, you know, even if he is a bit bonkers. If it's a matter of dull facts about Athenian life, he's got 'em under control. And in your first year, you basically need to learn a lot of ancient Greek and do some reading.'

'But I've got to write something, haven't I?' wailed Jeanene. 'A sample chapter?'

Sebastian waved half a bagel dismissively. 'Look, dear. Just write up a sort of school project on the physical evidence. In sixty-five per cent of known cases, the women's quarters were upstairs, in fifty-two per cent of known cases, the entrance was at the back, blah, blah, blah. All that stuff. George'll pass it with flying colours, then when Katie gets back, you can take the research and use it for something.'

'Is that okay, really? I mean, it doesn't have to be a chapter?'

'Oh, no. It's just got to look like one. Just put up with it, Jeanene, and try not to let him know what you're thinking. He's got a nasty, vindictive streak sometimes when he's crossed, but he's not hard to get past. If you can bring yourself to keep your mouth shut and just sit there looking like Little Miss Muffet the way you do, it'll never occur to him that anything's going on behind those big grey eyes.'

Sebastian got to his feet, and made an ineffectual attempt to clean his nail-file with a bit torn off the paper bag. Abandoning the problem, he swept the remains of lunch into the wastebin, and said, 'Come on. I'll introduce you to the secretaries, and they'll give us a cup of coffee.'

Ten minutes later, as they sat in the secretaries' room chatting, the door opened and admitted George. Jeanene said hello, but he ignored her, stalked across the room to collect some papers from his pigeonhole, and left as abruptly as he had arrived. Sebastian raised his eyebrows as the door banged shut.

'Well, *she*'s not been reading Miss Manners this week,' he observed.

'I must throw you out, actually, Sebastian,' said Elaine. 'We've got a lot to get through this afternoon. Mr Beckinsale may have thought that was a gentle hint.'

'I must go,' said Jeanene hastily, 'I've got stuff on reserve in the library.'

They went their separate ways, but a minute or so later, Sebastian was still thinking vaguely about Jeanene when he bumped into George in the corridor.

'I saw you,' hissed George, falling into step beside him. He was red-faced, shaking, and apparently beside himself with rage. Sebastian looked at him in amazement.

'George,' he said wearily, 'you can't possibly think I'm after her virtue. As you very well know, I'm a notorious woofter. Try to be consistent, dear.'

'I'm not having it. Miss Malone is a decent, well-brought-up, pure-minded little Colonial. The poor child's hardly been in the place five minutes before I catch you trying to fill her up with your filthy ideas.'

'Oh, for goodness' sake. Ever heard of being civil? She's new. She needs to meet people. I'm not corrupting the youth of Athens, for crying out loud. So you can keep your hemlock cocktail, sweetheart. I don't want it.'

'I'm warning you, Raphael. Keep away from her.'

'*Quelle mélodrame. Goodbye*, George, missing you already,' said Sebastian, nipping deftly into his office, and slamming the door behind him.

'What was all that about?' he asked the plaster bust of Antinous on the mantelpiece. But as usual, Antinous (glancing sulky and heavy-lidded from under a wreath of plastic grapes and vineleaves which had been made for him by Mr Ryan Mooney as a farewell gift) had nothing to contribute. Sebastian selected a postcard from the heap in the top left-hand drawer of his desk, addressed it to Princeton, and scribbled on it: 'Katie – remember what you said at the examiners' dins? You were right. Barkity bark bark, woof woof woof. At this rate he'll be bowling down the corridor like a hoop foaming at the mouth by the time you get back – something to look forward to, no? Love & kisses, S.' He nibbled thoughtfully at his left thumbnail, looked at it critically, then remembered his nail-file was *hors de combat*. It was no good: he would have to do some work. Sighing, he turned on the computer, activated the Greek alphabet facility, and began trying to remember how you chat up an archimandrite.

Sebastian's letter, though possibly not the most punctual piece of correspondence in the history of the world, was something of a masterpiece. It was a far more difficult brief than Tim imagined, since the monks, as Sebastian very well knew, cared about only four things: God, the Virgin Mary, the internal politics of the Holy Mountain, and money. Their interest in art was nil, their interest in history was nil, and their interest in the world beyond Athos, except insofar as Greek politics affected them or their way of life, was minimal. Ideas such as heritage, antiquarianism or improving the quality of life in London, meant absolutely nothing to them; and the notion of an appeal to Greek patriotism, which had seemed so obvious to Tim, was as Sebastian well knew, likely to cut as much ice as a chocolate hacksaw.

His approach was therefore Machiavellian, and stressed the following considerations. The total absence of effort involved for anyone in the lavra. Getting something for nothing – which is to say, transforming a piece of wasteland, neglected for fifty years, into hard cash. Current South Bank property prices were not a subject on which he chose to enter. And – this he considered his masterstroke – by careful choice of words, and selective omission, he conveyed the impression that the God-loving Greek merchants of the seventeenth century had created a work of religious art, and that the garden which was planned was essentially intended as a shrine, the fact that he had not actually seen the sculpture aided him in this Jesuitry. All this was wrapped up in the Byzantine *politesse* still current in Greek Orthodox circles.

For all its deep cunning, this letter would probably have gone as unanswered as any of Mr Eugenides' correspondence over the previous fifty years if it were not for the fact that it was the second letter out of England the abbot Akakios received in the same week. Pursing his lips, he got the first one out of his desk drawer, read it again, and then compared it with Sebastian's. It was a formal missive, on thick laid paper, and came from the secretary of the Friends of Mount Athos. It recalled the old connection between England and the lavra of St Michael and extended an invitation to join a delegation of distinguished Athonite bishops for a visit to the Prince of Wales at Highgrove. He considered it thoughtfully.

The abbot's knowledge of the outer world was highly selective, but by no means nonexistent. A rumour of the Prince of Wales' interest in Greek Orthodoxy had reached the mountain some time before, and had caused no great surprise, since His Royal Highness is, after all, of Orthodox extraction on his father's side. At that time, Akakios had taken no great interest in this fragment of gossip. Now, it gave him seriously to think. St Michael's was a relatively small and unimportant community in terms of the life of the mountain. To be included in a diplomatic mission headed by some of the most distinguished figures on Athos . . . It might well, he considered, be worth the appalling inconvenience of having to go to England. He spared a moment's benign thought for Sebastian, who had so clearly come to him as a messenger from God.

Stroking his beard, he thought about the proposition which Sebastian's letter had offered, and realised, again, that it was providential. If he accepted the invitation, then he would also be able to go to Southwark, and see the situation for himself, at someone else's expense, which was very satisfactory. He had always been reluctant to make an irrevocable decision about an item of monastery property whose value he could not gauge; but it was high time that something was done. In the New Year, he had received a long letter from Constantine Eugenides, explaining in careful detail why his regular remittance of money from the Mavrogordato bequest was about to cease, and asking for instructions. This letter he had ignored, since he did not at the time see his way clear. But the loss of this regular item of income represented an effective breaking of the monastery's tie with England, so he had had it in mind for some time to do something about the problem, and had awaited guidance on the matter. When taken together, the two new letters made the will of God very clear, he decided. He would go to England.

Reaching for two pieces of paper and a fountain pen, he began to draw his *chrismon*, a dense and complex arrangement of calligraphic arabesques which ran across the top of the paper, and contained within it his name and title. This took him some time, and gave him thinking space. Contemplating it thoughtfully, he rolled it into his elderly typewriter, and began the first of two letters.

To the honourable committee of the Friends of Mount Athos, grace and peace from God the Father and our Lord Jesus Christ.

Our Humility, responding most gladly to a devoutly expressed request, addresses commendation and blessings to Your Honours from the Garden of the Mother of God. By this our letter, we express our personal gratitude for your invitation, and that of our Holy Patron, the Archangel most pleasing to God...

A week later, the letter which he subsequently wrote to Sebastian reached Coptic Street. Sorting through the morning's post, Sebastian recognised it for what it was at sight, and, since he knew it represented a fair commitment of time, put it on one side. By about eleven o'clock, he was ready to deal with it, so he took it over to his desk, found his modern Greek dictionary, and slit it open. The *chrismon*, despite its intrinsic impenetrability, gave him no trouble because he recognised it; but he knew he would have to keep his wits about him working through the rest of the document. The trouble, as he well knew, with Athonite phraseology was that it was extremely easy to miss the actual content, if any, so he opened a notebook and began to jot down a rough translation as he worked through it. To the honourable and most learned Sebastian, pleasing to God...commendation and blessings...'Well fuck me sideways!' he said aloud. He reached for the dictionary to double-check, but his eyes were not deceiving him. Abbot Akakios was undoubtedly saying that he intended to visit Britain, and hoped (i.e., assumed) that Sebastian would make himself available for an indefinite length of time as interpreter, and doubtless, as general dogsbody. The thought was horrific. But what on earth did the old sod think he was doing? Sebastian ploughed on through the letter, wondering if he had taken leave of his senses....The most Christian and magnanimous Prince...He couldn't mean—...to Iggróvi. Highgrove? Oh, shit. He *did* mean.

'Well, thanks a million, your Walesness,' muttered Sebastian resentfully. 'That's all I bloody need.' He translated his way through to the end of the letter, just in case, but there was nothing else in it of any substance. Flipping through his phone book, he rang Tim at the Survey of London.

'Tim? I've heard from Abbot Akakios.'

'Oh, that's marvellous. What does he say?'

'You're not going to like this,' warned Sebastian. 'He's coming over to take a look for himself. That bloody idiot the Prince of Wales has had one of his "anything but the C of E" funny turns, and he's invited half of Mount Athos to Highgrove. Akakios is coming along, and he's using it as a chance to look into the Southwark business.'

'But that's good news, surely? I always feel you've got a better chance of persuading people if you can show them what you're doing. We should have some lovely plans ready by then.'

'For one thing, it's going to hold you up indefinitely. You can't really go looking for sponsors till the owner's expressed a willingness to sell, and this way, old Akakios is certainly not going to decide anything till he's been, and the whole thing could take months. Or fizzle out, if Prince Charles goes off the idea. And I have to say, he's not going to like what you're planning.'

'Why not?' Tim sounded offended.

'It's not holy. Look, Tim. What you're setting up is a totally secular monument. As far as Akakios is concerned, we're dealing with what's basically still consecrated ground. I didn't exactly tell porkies, but I did sort of give him the impression that we were talking about a sort of shrine or sanctuary. You simply can't expect him to be interested in anything else. This fountain doesn't by some wild chance have religious imagery on it, does it?'

'No,' said Tim curtly.

'Shit. It sounds like we might have to make two sets of plans. If we don't bootleg God in somewhere, he just won't see the point. I'll design a lovely *temenos* for you, and as long as he doesn't actually want to see the fountain itself, we might just get away with it. At least the old bastard doesn't speak a word of English.'

'Really, Sebastian. I sometimes think you're totally unscrupulous.'

'Well, you want this to happen, don't you? I'll send you my translation of the abbot's letter, so you can see it for yourself. But if you want to get anywhere with him, you'd better do it my way. The trouble with you is, you think monks ought to be interested in old stuff because they're anachronisms – you don't understand the way he's thinking at all.'

'But monks are concerned with tradition, surely?' said Tim stuffily.

'Not the way you think they are. They don't really think their lives are traditional. I mean, they're not very conscious of history. Monasticism's a reflection of eternity within time, therefore things are either in the here and now, or they don't matter. It's only because you're an Anglican you get religion mixed up with heritage.'

'Oh, thank you,' said Tim sarcastically.

'Ciao, dear. See you soon.'

XVII

Edward, having returned from Scotland, went to call on Mr Eugenides. He was extremely cheerful. First of all, his mother, after a great deal of whingeing and squealing, had reluctantly recognised that sorting out the late James Campbell's affairs was a job which must fall primarily to her, since she was not otherwise employed, and not a great deal of his time had, in the event, been wasted. He would have to go back for the funeral, though: a prospect which was considerably mitigated by the fact that Uncle Jimmy had, in fact, not attempted to reassign his property to a cat's home before death overtook him, and in consequence, he and his mother would soon be richer by a large, if scruffy, house in a seaside village popular with retirees, and a variety of incompetently managed investments. He had in his briefcase a tin of Mellerox-laced liver salts, handed over to him by Lamprini. All in all, things were looking pretty hummy.

He let himself into Garlic Court, and called up the stairs. To his mild surprise, Eugenides answered from his business room to the right of the hall. Edward opened the door and went in, untroubled by memory. Eugenides was sitting at his desk, which was silted up with bits of paper. Edward looked at this with approval: Lamprini, presumably, had begun her campaign. Mr Eugenides covered the page in front of him with a bit of clean notepaper, and turned slightly in his chair. He was thin, and looking very unwell, but his hand and arm were clearly functional again.

'Mr Lupset, would you be kind enough to witness my signature?'

'No problem.' Edward put his briefcase down on a chair, extracted his fountain pen, and walked across to the desk. He signed his name, 'Edward Lupset' in an unformed, schoolboyish, hand, and watched while Eugenides wrote his own name in his elegant script. Edward frowned a little. The old bastard had clearly bounced back faster than they might have wished: he was looking well in control. Never mind. The answer was sitting in his briefcase, biding its time.

He made conversation for a time, took Eugenides' meagre shopping list, and went out again, somewhat surprised, and perturbed, to find that it did not include a new tin of liver salts. When he returned, he made an excuse to go upstairs. To his relief, there was a fresh tin in the bathroom: an indication, presumably, that the old Greek was feeling sufficiently better to manage a little of his own shopping, and also of the depth of his addiction to the filthy stuff. It's an ill wind that blows nobody good, reflected Edward. He had been wondering how he would get past the fact that the tin he had brought with him was obviously tampered with, and had been reduced to the hope that Eugenides would simply fall on it and rip the paper aside without observing that it was, in fact, slit carefully halfway round the rim. He compared the two, picking Eugenides' original tin up in his hanky, and ladled surplus salts out of the other can into the bog (where they fizzed cheerfully), until the two tins matched precisely. Then he pulled the paper away from inside his own tin, wiped it carefully, and put it where the other had been. The first tin he intended to keep in reserve: once the vital transaction had taken place, he could swop it back, and Eugenides would be none the wiser.

The following day, to his infinite alarm, Mr Eugenides found himself subject to a return of the nightmare symptoms which had haunted his summer. In the haze of confusion which threatened to overwhelm him, he struggled downstairs to answer a repeated knocking on the door, and found himself facing a special messenger with a registered letter. He scrawled an unrecognisable travesty of his signature on the form which was held out for him, took the letter into the house, and opened it. It was in Greek, he could see, though the letters starred and dazzled before his eyes. He was feeling extremely ill, but the word 'urgent' caught his attention. He tried to concentrate, but the sense kept skittering away from him. He put it down, as a problem he was simply unable to deal with, and toiled upstairs to his study. Some time later – he was losing track of time – the phone began to ring in the drawing room. It was a phone of considerable age, made of bakelite, and did not so much ring as rattle. He did not always hear it, especially if he was on another floor of the house, and in general, made no particular effort to answer its summons, but on this occasion, he guessed that it must be ringing in connection with the morning's letter. Helplessly, he tried not to hear it: if he could not even read the letter, how could he answer? It rang for a long time, then stopped, but for the rest of the day, he was half-convinced that it was still ringing.

In the course of the days which followed, he came to the conclusion that he was probably dying. The dizzy spells continued, there were black-outs, when he found himself in a room with no idea of how he had got there, or what had happened in the last few hours. Eugenides did not greatly fear death, but he feared dependence; and above all, he feared dishonour. He received several more communications from Greece, and made some effort to understand them; but the story, as far as he grasped it, was an appalling tangle of international property law which he was unable to reduce to sense. Something would have to be done; but before he tried to tackle this new problem, it seemed to him that he must put his failing mental and physical energies into dealing honourably with the things which were specifically his concern. He had not been brought up to tackle the problem which shouted loudest, but to deal with things in due order. He had already written to his solicitor, whom he had not contacted for twenty-five years, and brought his will up to date, because he was greatly concerned that his two icons should go to Athos, where they belonged, and that his library should end up in a place of safety. His private business having thus been taken care of, in the precious hours in which the darkness receded from his mind, he grimly, meticulously, sorted and filed all the business which remained in his hands, determined above all that no one who had trusted the house of Eugenides should ever have cause to regret it.

By far the largest problem remaining in his hands was the estate of St Michael Graecorum. It was clear to him that the monastery must be persuaded to reclaim its property, as indeed he had already advised it to do, while he was still capable of dealing with it. And, he realised, by the great kindness of God, he knew someone who could help, so accordingly, he laboured up the stairs to the drawing room, and rang Sebastian.

'Mr Eugenides? How nice to hear from you. How are you?' said Sebastian, holding the phone against his ear with his shoulder, and continuing to read through the half-finished article on his computer screen, adding commas here and there.

'In poor case, I fear, in general terms. But the condition is one which comes and goes, and at the moment I am well enough. My dear Sebastian, I think I need your help.'

'That's fine, Mr Eugenides. Any time.' Damnation, thought Sebastian, who had two overdue reviews and the article to finish by the end of the week. 'What can I do for you?'

'Are you in contact with the abbot of St Michael?'

'Ye-e-e-s,' said Sebastian, cautiously. 'Did you know he's coming to London?'

'God be praised. And you will see him, I hope?'

'Actually, I think I'm going to be seeing as much of him as I can stand. He wants to rope me in as his interpreter.'

'Sebastian, my health is failing me, as I think you have realised. When His Holiness comes to England, can you speak to him on my behalf, and ask him to authorise me to sell the remaining property of St Michael and take the proceeds into his own hands? It would be a great relief to my mind to know that I was no longer responsible for this property, which is now worth a very great deal of money.'

Oh, *hell*, thought Sebastian. Tim wants me to talk the old bugger into giving it away, and Eugenides wants me to talk him into selling up...He wished very heartily that he had had the sense to keep his mouth shut in front of Tim; the whole thing looked like a great steaming heap of unnecessary trouble. Glumly, he closed down the computer, and gave the old man his full attention.

'Sebastian?'

'Yes, I'm still here. Just having a think. The abbot's turning up in about six weeks' time. There's a whole delegation of Athonites coming over, but Abbot Akakios is planning to split off and get his business sorted out at some point. I'm not sure about the timing. The big thing is that the Prince of Wales has asked them all to Highgrove, so once that date's fixed, we can sort out everything else round it.'

'I see. I had begun to wonder what would bring them so far from the mountain. Sebastian, you would be doing me the greatest kindness if you would take charge of a set of memoranda, and give them to the abbot.'

Sebastian sighed inaudibly. 'What sort of memoranda?'

'A summary of the monastery's property in England, and notes of where it is deposited. I have this material in good order. If you could possibly come here and let me explain it to you, then you could explain it to His Holiness. I would feel very much happier if this information was held by someone other than myself.' It was bloody inconvenient, but beneath the steady tones of Eugenides' thin, courtly voice, there was a note of genuine appeal.

'Of course I'll come. Don't worry. Look, will Friday be OK? I've got this blasted article to finish, and I've run right up to the final submission date as usual.'

'I am very sorry to be troubling you. Friday will do very well.'

'Do you want to fix a time? – Let's say half past twelve. If I haven't got the thing finished by then, I'll have missed the deadline, so either way, I might as well come.'

Some time after noon on Friday, therefore, Sebastian, who had faxed off his article at the eleventh hour, and was feeling pretty pleased with himself in consequence, took himself off to Garlic Court, and rapped hard on the lion-headed knocker. There was no answer. After fifteen minutes of continuous effort, there was still no answer, and Sebastian started to get a funny feeling in the hairs on the back of his neck. He stepped back, and surveyed the other houses in the court. Most of them were blank and uncommunica-tive, but there was one, mysteriously called Pleroma, which had replaced the original sashes with a picture window, through which he could see a forest of lush tropical leaves, and ensconced dimly beyond it, some kind of secretary/receptionist. He strode across, and rang the bell. When he was buzzed in, he asked the woman, whose name according to the plaque on her desk was Yvonne Kolinsky, and who looked basically kindly under her high-gloss finish, whether she had seen Eugenides go out.

'No, sir. He hasn't been out that I know of for weeks. I've hardly seen him since the accident.'

Sebastian gnawed his lip. 'I made an appointment with him for half-twelve, and it's getting on for one, Ms Kolinsky. He's not given the key to anyone here, has he?'

'No, 'fraid not. He's not really in touch with anyone else in the Court, that I know of.'

'I think I'd better ring the police,' decided Sebastian. She did not volunteer the use of the phone, which indeed began to ring almost immediately, so he mimed a farewell while she picked it up, and trotted hastily off to look for a functioning payphone. When he explained the situation, the police were sympathetic and helpful, and agreed to meet him at the house, advising him to ring a locksmith immediately to repair the damage they would necessarily do.

Once back at Garlic Court, Sebastian tried the knocker again, with little hope of a reply. When none came, he sat down on the step in the sun to wait. At twenty past one, he heard a car stopping in the street, and a young, shirt-sleeved policeman came into the court, carrying a toolbag.

'Dr Raphael?'

'That's right. Thanks for coming.'

The young man surveyed the door with a professional eye. 'Good, solid stuff this. What we like to see, generally, though for a job like this it's a bloody nuisance. Do you know what the owner's got on the other side? Bolts top and bottom, or just the locks?'

'Just the locks, I think. He's about five foot five and pretty fragile. I think the bending and stretching's probably beyond him.'

'Fingers crossed, then,' said the policeman cheerfully, getting out a dangerous-looking chisel and a hammer, 'we'll try the locks.'

The door was of Baltic pine, hardened by the centuries to something more like the toughness of oak, but the constable, whose name, Sebastian discovered, was Nugent, worked away at it manfully. Sebastian saw the receptionist watching them through her window and waved: she promptly retreated. The wood splintered, and a final blow of the hammer sent the door shuddering open.

'Timber!' said Nugent cheerfully.

'Mr Eugenides!' called Sebastian, pushing past him, and shouting up the stairs.

'Start at the bottom,' advised the constable. Together, they searched the basement premises and the ground floor, then went upstairs.

Eugenides was in his study, sprawled on the carpet. By mere accident, he had fallen loosely curled on his side. His glasses lay bent out of shape beneath his cheek. Sebastian hurried to kneel beside him, and put a hand in front of the old man's mouth and nose. A faint breath, like a kitten's, still stirred.

'He's still alive,' he reported breathlessly. Nugent knelt on the other side, and gently pulled back an eyelid, revealing only a sightless white.

'He's in a coma. I'll ring for an ambulance,' he said practically, scrambling to his feet. Sebastian pulled the glasses gently from beneath the old man's head, and put them in his pocket.

'Mr Eugenides!' he called, as urgently as he could. There was a sort of flicker of response: it was hard to identify what, if anything had moved, but from some infinite distance, the spirit of Constantine Eugenides had registered his presence, he was sure of that. Casting the Girl Guide Handbook to the wind, he scooped the old man into his arms as if he had been a baby, and held him tight, rocking unconsciously to and fro.

'Mr Eugenides!'

'You won't do much good like that,' said Nugent, with a hint of sympathy. 'He's better laid flat.'

'Bugger that,' snarled Sebastian. 'He needs to know someone's here.'

'Well, ten to one you won't do much harm either,' said the young policeman pacifically. Sebastian, past caring, barely heard him.

'Mr Eugenides!' The mouth twitched; the slight body in Sebastian's arms tensed perceptibly. 'I think he's coming round.' The lips moved again, as if to form a word; Sebastian, straining, thought he heard 'Ssss...' as soft as a whispering mouse. Then the old man began to breathe hard, and the mouth fell open slackly. The stertorous breathing suddenly stopped, while the body in his arms seemed suddenly to double in weight. 'Oh, my God.'

Nugent squatted down beside them, and took the limp wrist, feeling professionally for a pulse. 'He's gone,' he confirmed. 'Poor old bastard.' Slowly, Sebastian laid Eugenides down. The eyes showed a flicker of white between the lids, where the old man had struggled to open them; he shut them. Crossing himself, he said the prayer for the dead, while Nugent, embarrassed, scrambled to his feet, and stood awkwardly by.

'We'll be needing the ambulance anyway,' he volunteered. 'Best if a doctor looks at him.'

'Stay there,' said Sebastian curtly. Later, he knew, he would weep, and probably get extremely drunk, but for the time being, he was full of nervous energy. He ran upstairs, three at a time, and looked in the top-floor rooms. It was not hard to identify Eugenides' bedroom. He took the icon off the old man's night table, and looked around for a clean sheet. The linen press, as he could see from the door, was in the front room: so he went in and blundered across to the window, where he opened what turned out to be a wartime blackout, still in use. In the bottom of the press, he found some real linen sheets, thick, smooth, weighing a ton. With a sheet over his arm, he went from room to room, shutting blinds and curtains, before going back downstairs.

He entered the study, where Nugent stood guard, looking with vague incomprehension at the leather backs of Eugenides' books, and put the icon carefully on Eugenides' chest, folding the small, arthritic fingers round it. Then he covered the body carefully with the sheet. There seemed to be miles of it, unfolding as stiffly as cardboard. It had been in its folds so long, it lay on the floor like a huge, discarded map, the lines of the old man's corpse almost invisible beneath it. Sebastian took a deep breath.

'Look, Constable. I don't know Mr Eugenides all that well, but I don't think there's anyone but me to look after things. I know he's been worried about his health. In fact, I think he's been afraid of something like this. The reason I'm here is that he asked me to take a memorandum about some property he's been administering to the chap who owns it. If you wouldn't mind coming with me to see I'm on the level, do you think I could have a look around, and try and find out who I ought to be telling? And maybe find the stuff he wanted me to have?'

'It'll be somewhere in here, I expect,' said Nugent, 'to judge by all these books.'

'Actually, I don't think so. He was a scrupulous old dear, and I don't think he'd mix business and pleasure.'

'This is pleasure? Jesus.'

Sebastian walked over to the worktable, and looked over the papers that littered it. 'There's nothing about business here,' he reported. 'It's technical stuff; notes and scholia on Greek literature.'

'Some people!' said the constable, shaking his head. After a little further investigation, they found the downstairs business-room, and its desk.

'Oh, excellent,' said Sebastian. The top of the desk was rolled back, and lying in the centre was a bulky envelope addressed to Dr Sebastian Raphael. 'Do you mind if I take this? I'll sign for it, if you like. Here's some identification.'

'Don't worry.'

'I'd better go into the desk a bit,' said Sebastian, pocketing his envelope. 'It all looks pretty organized. He said he'd been sorting stuff out, poor old coot. Ha! Bless him.' Questing through the neatly docketed packets, he had found one clearly labelled, 'In the Event of my Death'. 'I'd better open it.' It turned out to contain the name and address of Eugenides' bank, his solicitor, who was also named as his executor, and a list (short) of everyone with whom he had any sort of active professional involvement, headed by a firm in Athens, and Skinner, Catling in Holborn, which rang a faint bell. Oh, yes. Hattie had mentioned a friend who worked there. All most respectable. He turned to Nugent. 'I'll contact these people, shall I?'

'It's good of you, sir.'

'Well, to be honest, I've got a terrible conscience about all this. I was rather fond of the old darling, and he did me the most terrific favour once. I've kept meaning to come and see him, and I knew he wasn't well.' Sebastian felt the truth of what he was saying rising over him like a thundercloud; tears, he knew, were on their way, almost unstoppable. Say something platitudinous quick, for the love of God, he prayed, as his eyes began to prick hotly, and his nose bunged itself up.

'I'm sure you did your best, sir. We're all busy these days.'

Bless you, thought Sebastian, blowing his nose ferociously. All that could wait. Fortunately, at that point a knock at the door announced the emergency locksmith, and a few minutes later, the ambulance arrived.

'I'll stay here,' Sebastian said to the policeman. 'When the lockman's finished, I'll send the keys off to the solicitor, and he can take it from there.'

'Thank you, sir.' There was a soft bumping, as the two ambulance men manoeuvred the stretcher and its burden awkwardly round the bend of the marble stairs.

'Be careful,' called Sebastian. 'The stairs are slippery.' He watched, biting the inside of his lip to distract himself, as they carried Eugenides out of his house, the locksmith standing politely aside. He followed the little cortège out on to the step, and became conscious of movement, out of the corner of his eye. It was Yvonne Kolinsky from Pleroma, hurrying across the square on her high, thin heels.

'He's dead, isn't he?' she asked, breathlessly. Sebastian nodded. 'I had an awful feeling. Look...' wordlessly, she held out three strelitzia, hard, modish flowers, like art-deco peacocks' heads. She must have cut them off one of the plants in the office, Sebastian realised suddenly. One of those silly, decent impulses people have.

'That's sweet of you, dear,' he said gently. 'He'd appreciate it.' He swung himself up into the back of the ambulance, and laid the flowers on top of the still figure. When he jumped out again, an attendant pulled the doors to. The ambulance pulled smoothly out of the square, and moved off without haste.

'I'll follow it in the squad-car,' said Nugent. 'Here's the station number, if you want to contact us about anything. We'll keep an eye on the place.'

'Here's my card.' They shook hands, and Nugent left in pursuit of the ambulance.

'It's nice to feel you've done something,' observed Ms Kolinsky.

'I just wish I'd done a bit more,' said Sebastian.

'Don't worry yourself,' she said, with intent to comfort. 'He had a friend who came in sometimes. A lawyer. He was visiting Mr Eugenides on business when he had that stroke or whatever it was, and he came rushing round to us, the way you did, to use the phone. I saw him a few times after that, I think he was doing the old man's shopping. It was sweet of him to get involved – I'd been thinking I might have to do something, you see, so I kept an eye out, but when I could see he was being looked after, I didn't worry. It's dreadful to think of him lying there all alone. Do you think he suffered much?'

'No,' said Sebastian. 'He just went into a coma. He died in my arms.'

'You poor thing.' Her easy-come, easy-go sympathy was beginning to annoy him. He's dead, he wanted to say. The point is, he's dead, and he was lovely. He was sweet and patient and kind, and now he's just a heap of meat. But it was hardly fair, when at least she'd come out and made a gesture. He looked at his watch, to give himself something else to think about, and she caught the movement. 'Oh, I'd better get back to work,' she said at once. 'They'll be going mad. Goodbye.' She scuttled across the square, and popped back into her office.

'I'm just about finished here, sir,' said the locksmith from behind him.

'Good-oh. If you give me an invoice, I'll write you a cheque, and send the bill on to his solicitor with the keys.'

This transaction duly completed, Sebastian put the keys in his pocket with the stuff for Akakios, and plodded away in a state of black depression and self-loathing. When it came to the crunch, it struck him forcibly, he was right down there with Yvonne Kolinsky. He was halfway home before it occurred to him, just to add the final touch to his mood, that by the time he was going to need to check the proofs of his book, the *Alexiad* manuscript would probably have disappeared.

The next day, Edward called on Eugenides, bringing with him the prearranged letter from Lamprini to himself. A man little inclined to look carefully at the familiar, he was all the way up the steps, with the key out of his pocket, before he noticed the mess that had been made of the door. He tried his key, without optimism. It didn't work. A dreadful qualm came over him. The outline of the situation was clear: someone had broken in. But was Eugenides now in hospital, or was he dead? What was going on? How could he find out? Since it was Saturday, the offices were all shut, and Yvonne Kolinsky was not available to enlighten him.

The full horror of the situation began slowly to dawn on him. If Eugenides was dead, the whole thing was up the spout; an abject failure. What was worse, they had killed him, and evidence of the scam was in the house, locked away from him – the doctored liver salts, but also the letters. Please God, let him not be dead, he prayed, panic-stricken. What could he do? Frantically, he tried to think. Get a grip on yourself, Neddie, he admonished himself. Start the motor. Eugenides must have been well enough to dial 999 or shout out of the window or something. Then he'd collapsed, and someone had bashed the door in and found him. So he'd have been found a few minutes after he made contact with the outer world. It wasn't likely he was dead. He'd be in a hospital somewhere, surrounded by machinery. He was tough...he'd just better not be dead, that's all.

Folding his arms, he thought furiously. There wasn't much he could do over the weekend. On Monday he would have to be in Scotland for his great-uncle's funeral, organised by his mother with typical lack of consideration. He would just have to hope that in the next few days, the old Greek would return home, where he could be dealt with.

XVIII

On the same Friday, Dil finished the letter he was writing, printed it out, signed it with a flourish, then collected up the morning's correspondence and took it to Betty.

'Betty, can you get this lot off for the eleven-thirty collection?' he asked, dropping the letters in her in-tray. 'I've got the McGill job done and dusted.'

'Thank you, Mr Dhesi. There's something else come in I'd like you to have a look at. Here's the letter. I'm sorry to have to ask you to do it, when you're so busy, but it needs to be sorted out quickly, and Mr Lupset's not going to be here on Monday.'

Dil took it from her, and glanced at the clock above the door automatically. 'Where's he going to be?'

Betty sniffed, conveying scepticism. 'He's going to his great-uncle's funeral, or so he says.'

'He had a couple of days off a little while ago for family business, didn't he?'

'Yes. That's right. He rung in saying his great-uncle had died, and he was stuck in Scotland. It's not like our Mr Lupset to get caught that way.'

Dil shrugged. 'Well, people do die. And the family's got to do

something. Even Edward's little lot. I suppose he got his mum and
dad over from France?'

'I'll tell you one thing, Mr Dhesi,' said Betty darkly, 'He's up to
something. I wouldn't expect Mr Lupset to lift a finger unless he
saw some profit in it, and he's been running around all summer as
if he was working for a Boy Scout badge. It's not just his uncle,
there was all the hoo-ha with that Greek as well.'

'What Greek?'

'Oh, yes. You were in Birmingham that week. Mr Lupset was
sorting a bit of business out with Eugenides. They're a little firm
in the City we've been dealing with since goodness knows when.
He rang in to say that Mr Eugenides was taken poorly, and he was
taking him to the hospital. I believe he's been round once or twice
since.' Her tone suggested her firm belief that no altruism could
conceivably be involved.

'But if someone collapses in front of you, you've got to do
something, haven't you?' protested Dil.

'Well, you would, Mr Dhesi, and I suppose I would. But I'm
not sure our Mr Lupset would, unless he saw something in it for
himself.'

During the course of the day, Dil found himself thinking about
Edward from time to time. Like Betty, he found, once Edward's
activities had actually been shoved under his nose, that the official
version sounded barely credible. The notion that upper-class
Englishmen get decency walloped into them along with cricket
and grammar, gleaned from the somewhat old-fashioned childhood reading his parents had hoped would be good for him, was
one he had long since dismissed as myth. In his experience, a
goodly proportion of posh boys would do absolutely anything if
they believed they could get away with it, and Edward was
undoubtedly thick enough and opportunistic enough to think he
could get away with murder. On the other hand, his cautious
streak would probably do him instead of a conscience as long as
nothing actually walked in front of him wearing a sign saying

'steal me'. Dilip remembered the name of Eugenides because of the box, since it was the only time he'd ever actually seen one open, and vaguely recalled having a conversation about obsolete charities which, in retrospect, maybe hadn't been too clever – thinking it over, he hoped he hadn't given Edward any bright ideas. But, as he gave the matter a little further consideration, fishing in the depths of his memory, he recalled there'd been someone else involved, a Greek woman, much to old Ed's disgust, with an idiotic name like Lampshade. He was scared of women, so he could hardly have got into much trouble with some Greek bint's beady eye on him, surely? Perhaps they were all maligning him. Dil was possessed of an orderly and logical mind; illuminated by two minutes' real thinking, his suspicions melted like September frost. The trouble, he reflected as he dismissed the subject, with going around suspecting pathetic gits like Edward of serious mischief was if you started down that road, you'd end up suspecting practically everyone.

The other person whom he found coming into his mind from time to time was Jeanene. Unlike Edward who was, he considered, pretty transparent, she mystified him. In some ways, she seemed exactly the kind of thing he knew most about; an ambitious outsider, making it under her own steam. In other ways, she baffled him completely. Powering herself to London from the Outback was a phenomenon he recognised, since it was the same basic story as that of his parents and their friends, but doing it in order to study ancient Greek (a subject he associated exclusively with privileged pointlessness) was completely opaque to him. Yet it wasn't a snob thing, he was sure of that. She made him curious.

One of Dil's axioms was that if you become aware that you've been thinking about someone more than three times, you ought to do something about it. He need do nothing in order to see Edward, who would be in to work by midweek, no doubt, but he'd have to do something about Jeanene. He considered possibilities. On Saturday, he had promised to put in an afternoon's work with his dad on the family allotment, and he didn't want to ask her out in the evening, because it looked too much like a date, which he couldn't really afford at that stage of the month, and wasn't sure he wanted anyway. Sunday, on the other hand, was free. Accordingly, when he got home, he rang Ellen Wilkinson House, and waited patiently while someone went to find her.

'Hello?' said her soft, husky voice, suspiciously.

'Jeanene? It's me. Dilip Dhesi. We met at Hat's party.'

'Oh, Dilip! Hi. Sorry I sounded so snotty. Practically no one rings Ellen Wilko except the police and the Home Office, so when we hear the phone, we all run around like a bunch of chooks. How're you doing?'

'Oh, fine. I was wondering...Look, if you aren't doing anything on Sunday, would you like to meet up? We could go for a walk. I could show you a bit of London.'

'I'd really love to. I've been exploring a bit on my own, of course, but it'd be great to see things with a real Londoner.'

'Excellent. If you don't mind an early start, I was thinking I might take you to the flower market in Columbia Road. It's quite a sight, and it's a slice of real London. Then maybe we could get ourselves down to Chapel Market in Islington? There's plenty of time, 'cause the flower market happens so early, and I know a nice place there – everyone calls it Indian Veg. It's not glamorous, I mean, don't dress up or anything, but the food's good. Wear comfy shoes, it'll mean a quite a bit of walking.'

'Sounds great.'

'Okay. I'll meet you just outside Liverpool Street tube. Shoreditch and Old Street are nearer, but you'd have to change several times from where you're starting, and it's not worth it. Could you manage half past eight?'

'Sure.' Jeanene put the phone down, her spirits lifting. The message 'I'm not really asking you out' came over loud and clear, but all the same, it sounded like fun. And she wasn't exactly in the market for a boyfriend; there weren't enough hours in the day as things were.

Meanwhile, on the Saturday of that week, Hattie rang Sebastian. Tim had told her about the threatened abbot; and she wanted to know if there was any further news from that quarter. Clearly, nothing could go forward with Plan A until the abbot's agreement had been secured; and from her point of view, it would help to have some idea of the timescale they were looking at. The phone rang for a long time, so long, she began to wonder if he was away for the weekend, and had forgotten to put the answerphone on. She was about to give up when he picked up the receiver.

'Sebastian? It's Hattie.'

'Oh, God.' The voice was thick and muzzy with something more than sleep.

'Sebastian? Are you all right?'

'Hang on a minute. Let me go and have a pee. Oh, my *head*.' Hattie put down the phone, went and got the *Guardian*, and sat flicking through the magazine until a tinny voice from the receiver warned her to pick it up again.

'Sorry, Sebastian. I've obviously picked a bad time. I hope the night before was worth it.'

'It was fucking terrible. I had an old man die in my arms.'

'Jesus, how awful,' she said, automatically crossing herself with her free hand. 'Was it someone you knew? Or a road accident?'

'Someone I knew. A sweet old Greek,' said Sebastian, miserably. 'That was in the afternoon. I suppose I coped. I mean, I did all sorts of good citizen stuff, and saw him off to the morgue. Then I came home, and got absolutely pissed out of my brain. I can't even remember most of the evening, and now I feel like the living dead.'

'Oh, Sebastian, I'm really sorry. Get as much water down you as you can, and go back to sleep. I'd like to talk to you – if I ring this evening, perhaps we could sort something out?'

'Fine,' said Sebastian wearily. 'Oh, Christ.'

'What is it?' said Hattie, alarmed.

'There's a half-empty bottle of ouzo on the desk. I must've drunk it. My God, no wonder I'm feeling like this. Some nit brought me it about three years ago. I'd forgotten I had it.'

'Water. Sleep. I'll talk to you later.' Hattie replaced the receiver gently, and thought for a minute. It would be only decent to take him out: he obviously needed cheering up. Sunday lunch, maybe, nothing too smart.

On Sunday, Dilip emerged from the exit from Liverpool Street underground at twenty past eight on a crisp, blue, autumn morning, and leaned against a wall to wait. Jeanene did not keep him waiting long: they'd both tried to make it a bit early, he noted approvingly. She looked a bit different; though he couldn't at first put his finger on why: she was simply dressed as usual, in jeans and a thick blue sweater. He suddenly realised that she had put her hair up. Without that mass of dark curls round her face, she looked less girlish; and the knot of hair at the back of her head accentuated the slenderness of her neck, flexing gracefully as she looked round for him. With a sudden little shock, it occurred to him that he might actually fancy her, a thought he had been trying to avoid putting into words. He dismissed it from his mind, and walked forward, smiling.

'Oh, hi. I didn't see you there. Which way do we go?'

'Up towards Shoreditch,' said Dil, gesturing. 'Then we turn right towards Hackney.' They set off, keeping pace easily.

'You were born in London, weren't you?' Jeanene ventured. Dil nodded. 'I don't know if you can understand what I heard when you said that. I did the Shakespeare paper at the Uni, and Shoreditch means Shakespeare to me. You know, the Globe started here? Then they took it down and carted it over the river. It's hard to think of it as an actual street – you sort of expect to see Richard Burbage coming round the corner.'

'He'd get a bit of a shock if he did,' commented Dil. 'Shoreditch is Shoe City now. There's nothing but wholesale shoe and leather merchants for about a mile. Anyway, he'd get himself run over first thing, wouldn't he?'

'But all that's still here, underneath. It's not just me being romantic.' She stopped and gestured at the pub they were passing, very ordinary-looking, apart from its bright blue paintwork, with a flat, tiled frontage. 'Look at this notice beside the door. It says it's been here since 1462. Shakespeare probably drank here. See what I mean? Even the bars turn out to be historic.'

'I never noticed that. But why shouldn't it still be here?' objected Dil. 'Getting thirsty's one of those things that just goes on happening. 'S not really worth noticing. If we come back at opening-time, we won't find a bunch of Elizabethan actors quaffing sack, it'd be the guys from the wholesalers tipping down lager.'

'I know that really. But literature's realler than life for a lot of us resident aliens. It's only talking to someone like you I can really get myself focused in the here-and-now. I've met a few Aussies since I got here, and I can see that some of 'em just don't believe in the place. They get through the week thinking about their work, whatever it is, then they spend the weekend getting rat-arsed in the Redback. It's as if they think real life's what happens at home. I don't want to be like that. I'll probably go back to Australia – unless I get a career-type job here, the Home Office'll throw me out as soon as I've got the degree. But while I'm here, I want to try and live here properly.'

Dil looked at her curiously, and did not immediately respond. 'I suppose my story's sort of the opposite,' he said after a while. 'Mum and Dad live in Southall. I don't suppose you've heard of it, but it's London's Little India. They're like your Oz friends, I suppose – home's India to them. They talk about it all the time, so I grew up knowing "home" was somewhere I'd never been. Mum and Dad wanted me to get ahead, and I did exactly what they wanted. I worked hard, stayed out of trouble, went to Cambridge, got assimilated, learned how to pass. Now they're tying themselves in knots because I'm not Indian enough. But I can't please them, you know? I decided the same as you, in the end. To be at home in London, I mean. Talking of which, we turn right here.'

Together, they walked up the Hackney Road. Someone was walking towards them, carrying a six-foot stand of bamboo in a pot, which nodded regally with every step. Looking ahead, other people were to be seen, almost invisible behind armfuls of greenery.

'Here we go,' said Dil cheerfully. 'It's a proper slice of Shakespeare, isn't it? Burnham Beeches come to Dunsinane, or something. Didn't you just know the English are crazy?'

Jeanene began to laugh, as they approached the market. 'I've never seen anything like it. People don't garden like this where I come from. There isn't the water.'

The narrow street opened up in front of them, lined on both sides with stalls set with towering greenhouse staging, packed with plants. People tacked erratically from stall to stall, laden with carrier-bags and pots. It was incredibly noisy, and very crowded.

'Lilies! Pahnd a bulb, top quality lilies...' 'Chrysanths! Best spray chrysanths. Just look at the buds on 'em...' 'Spring bulbs! Daffs two pahnd a pahnd, 'elp yerselves. Get 'em in now, summing to look forward to...' The voices came from all sides, as the stallholders outbawled each other, and gardeners leaned eagerly forward to bargain with them. Buffeted by oblivious punters, dazzled with colour, Jeanene began to enjoy herself. She touched Dil's arm, which tensed involuntarily, and he cocked an ear towards her.

'Are you tempted?' she asked. He shook his head.

'I'm a veg man,' he shouted back, 'I don't do flowers. I just thought you'd like it.'

'Too right. I think it's great. Ellen Wilko's like the bloody tomb. I haven't heard anyone shouting since I left home.'

Dil beamed at her, delighted at her pleasure, a sparkling, white-toothed grin which lit up his dark face, and she looked away, suddenly shy.

'Hey, Dil.' The speaker was a thin-faced man, his face burnished dark by the sun and ground-in dirt, with his hair in a mass of tiny plaits. Despite the early-morning autumnal chill, he was wearing nothing but ancient army-surplus fatigues and a grubby Oyster Band T-shirt. Celtic spirals were tattooed on his cheeks, and round both upper arms. Jeanene surveyed him with interest. 'How's tricks? Your dad doing OK?'

'Hi, Digger. We're all fine. Dad's got brinjals growing like weeds this year. Thanks for the tip about plastic bottles. You should come and have a look sometime.' Digger waved a farewell, and they strolled on.

'Who was that?' asked Jeanene curiously.

'He's an eco-vigilante, a total mad bastard. We're sort of mates. We met when Railtrack was trying to sell off the allotments where my dad's got his patch. That was the weirdest thing. Tories, crusties, my dad and his friends, Rastas, Digger's lot, all on the same side, and talking to each other for once. I wrote the letters, Digger organised the demo, and we saw 'em off between us.'

'Allotments are kind of hired gardens, aren't they?' asked Jeanene.

'That's right. And the trouble is, most of them date to before the war. They were set up on what was wasteland at the time, but a lot of it looks like prime development sites now. The land belongs to all sorts of people, local councils, the Church Commissioners, railway companies. Most of them've got an incentive to realise assets these days. Digger's so far round the bend he's practically coming back, but he's right about needing to defend what we've got. An allotment's a community, not just a place.' He lapsed into silence, perhaps afraid that he was sounding sententious, and they ambled along together for a couple of minutes without further conversation.

Looking around her, a stall caught her eye. 'Hey, look at those!'

'Sweet, aren't they?' The stall was piled high with tiny orange trees, about two feet high, covered in miniature oranges. Kumquats, they must be. They shone brightly against the dark leaves, on the sturdy little trees. Jeanene, who had never in her life owned so much as a spider-plant, found herself hesitating. There was something immensely appealing about them.

'Fifteen quid,' shouted the stallholder, immediately observing her interest, 'best price in London.'

Jeanene turned to Dil, appealingly. 'Are they easy to look after?'

He laughed. 'Fallen, have you? If you've got a table where it'll get some light, it should be okay. He's right about the price, it's a real bargain. They're forty or fifty quid, most places.'

She hesitated, and was lost. 'Do you take cheques?'

'Well, that's you going native with a vengeance,' remarked Dil, picking up the chosen tree which, Jeanene suddenly realised, they would have to carry about with them for the rest of the day.

'I'll take it,' she insisted anxiously. 'I don't want you to carry it for me.'

'No sweat,' said Dil amiably, tucking the pot against his lean hip, and strolling on, with a nod to the stallholder. Jeanene, half-pleased, half-mortified, hurried to catch him up.

'Sure you don't want one of those?' he said teasingly, gesturing towards a group of twelve-foot trees with their rootballs wrapped in grubby sacking, leaning together like brooms.

'Right. I could plant it in the bloody washbasin. And…oh, a couple of those nice big bush things, over there. And some dirty great heavy pots. There's some dinkum ones a couple of stalls back.' Dil looked at her sharply, and grinned. 'On the other hand, I might just settle for the orange tree, y'know?'

'Look,' said Dil, pointing with his free hand. 'Proof it's really Disneyland-on-Thames. Mary Poppins'll be round the corner any minute.'

'*Jellied eels?* They're taking the piss. It's got to be a front for something.'

'No, it's straight up,' insisted Dil. 'I've even seen people eating 'em. This is proper East London.'

Jeanene shook her head. 'Orange trees, and jellied eels. The unreality quotient's off the top of the scale.'

'That's just hunger talking. Let's turn back, we're nearly at the end anyway. It's a bit of a hike to Islington.'

'Righto.' They turned, and began threading their way through the crowd.

'I'll say one thing for you,' commented Dil, as they were walking up the City Road some time later, 'at least you fell for something practical.'

'*Practical?*'

'You can make jam with these. Don't let 'em go to waste.'

'I just wanted to look at them,' she protested. 'They make me think of Andrew Marvell. "Like golden lamps in a green night".'

'Well, look at them for a bit. Then eat them, before they go off.' Jeanene was on the verge of pointing out that her biggest pan held all of two pints, but decided against. He was, after all, the one carrying the tree. 'We'll go down here,' he said, gesturing towards the vast curl of white plastic which sheltered the entrance to Old Street station. 'The only tube station that looks like a bit off Sydney Opera House. Specially to make you feel at home. One stop to the Angel, then we're nearly there.'

When they got out at Islington, Dil led them across the road, right, then left again down Chapel Market. 'Look,' he said, a few minutes later, 'There's Indian Veg.'

'And there's Alice,' said Jeanene suddenly, seeing the pale, sphinx-like shape of Hattie's lurcher waiting patiently outside the restaurant.

'So it is. 'Course, this is Hattie's home turf. I'm not surprised she eats here, it's one of the best places in this bit of London.' Dil patted Alice on the head as she lay by the door, her dark-rimmed eyes tragic, pushed it open, and went in.

'We're looking for a friend,' explained Dil to the waiter who came forward to seat them. Peering round the room, he spotted Hattie sitting near the back of the restaurant, with a tall, dark man, unknown to him. For a moment, he wondered if they might be interrupting something, but looking again, he thought it on the whole unlikely. Jeanene, meanwhile, recognised Sebastian, look-ing rather haggard and puffy round the eyes, as if he'd had a heavy weekend. They were talking quietly and earnestly, completely absorbed by their conversation.

'Hello, Hattie,' Dil said cheerfully as they came up, 'mind if we join you?'

'Hi, Sebastian,' said Jeanene, while Hattie said simultaneously, 'My God, Dil, what're you doing with that bush?'

Jeanene slid in beside Sebastian, and Dil, having parked the orange-tree beside her, sat down beside Hattie. Hattie introduced Dil and Sebastian, and turned to Jeanene. 'I didn't know you knew Sebastian.'

'We know each other from the Uni,' explained Jeanene.

'Oh, of course. I'd forgotten you were doing Classics.'

'Actually, we met at a pharmacy, didn't we?' said Sebastian. 'I'd been in the Riyadh looking at some textiles for them, and when I popped in for some headache pills, there was Jeanene, getting stuck into a Greek grammar. It was such a surprise, we got talking.'

'How do you two know each other?' Jeanene asked Hattie. 'Sorry if that's rude? I mean, I spent my first weeks in London wondering how you ever get to know anyone at all, and now I find there's some sort of connection between two people I met in totally different places.'

'Oh, we met at a dinner party. There's a lot of special interest

groups connected with London and the built environment, and
with a job like mine, I meet quite a few of them. If you get onto
the circuit somewhere, you meet other people who're interested
too.'

'And where do you fit in, Dilip?' Sebastian asked Dil
courteously.

'Oh, I met Hattie years ago, when she was working for the
GLC. She came to us for legal advice about something, I handled
the case, we got on.' He turned to Jeanene. 'It's self-service here.
We'd better get ourselves some food.'

'I'll come round with you,' said Sebastian immediately. 'I had
such a hangover yesterday, I couldn't face anything, so I reckon
I'm owed a second helping. Dilip, maybe you can tell me what I'm
eating? It's all fabulous, but I'd quite like to know.'

'Sure.'

Once they were sat down again with high-piled plates, and
even Hattie had been tempted to a couple more pakoras, she
turned to Dil and Jeanene.

'We're having a think about strategy,' she explained. 'I don't
know if you've heard about this, Jeanene, but we're involved with
trying to create a new public amenity in Southwark, on some
ground which belongs to a bunch of Greek Orthodox monks. I'm
involved because the people who're trying to get it off the ground
want me to help them to draw up a proposal. Sebastian's our link
with Mount Athos, and he's just telling me what the abbot's likely
to make of all this. Dil knows a bit about it too; I've bitten his ear
for legal advice once or twice.'

'It sounds great,' said Jeanene. 'I mean, if you think there's
anything I can do, count me in.'

'I don't know that there's anything at the moment. Unless you
can prescribe something for this abbot which'd get him strolling
around London saying "yes" to everything…but I suppose
there's nothing legal which'd help. Anyway, I'm glad you don't
mind us boring on.'

Dil, meanwhile, took advantage of the general conversation to watch Jeanene. He was profoundly conscious of her. Her eyes disturbed him – clear grey, dark-rimmed, with long, dark lashes, striking against her pale, Celtic skin – and he was charmed by her independence. Since his Cambridge days, a number of girlfriends had passed through his life, mostly white, and all briefly. While he rejected his parents' comprehensive dismissal of these, to them, shadowy figures as 'dirty women', there was still a deep-seated fastidiousness in him which was repelled by their lack of dignity, their vulgar zest for experience as an end in itself. How did Jeanene fit in to what he knew about the opposite sex? She was probably not inexperienced, but certainly not a dirty woman… Musing thus, he let his eyes linger a little too long, and feeling his gaze on her, she looked straight back at him. He dropped his eyes at once, but the moment of contact remained with him like a physical shock. Jeanene, her colour a little heightened, turned to talk to Hattie, but as she opened her mouth, she was forestalled by Sebastian.

XIX

Edward, meanwhile, had entered a state of abject, bowel-liquidising terror which he remembered only too well from his schooldays; the terror that stalks by day whose name is Nemesis. A cloud of memory engulfed him: incidents both wincingly present in his mind, and obliquely filtered out of full recall by protective amnesia. The exam revision put off, the rabbits left unfed, the cricket-club tea-money borrowed; and all the dreadful, endless times when the exam had to be sat, the dead rabbits, or the empty cashbox, explained...each such moment so painful, so lost in red, burning shame that it was almost instantly forgotten, along with his tearful promises never to do it again.

The weekend passed in a blur of alcohol and indecision. On Sunday, he flew to Scotland and met up with his parents, never a pleasant experience in itself, but the usual litany of complaint and fault-finding washed over him virtually unheard. He was thinking, urgently, endlessly, about Eugenides. The scenario which had first occurred to him still commended itself – perhaps he was worrying about nothing – but it was hard to make himself believe it, not when the other possibilities were so dire. The thing which he kept coming back to in his mind was the Mellerox. The doctored tin was still sitting in Eugenides' bathroom; if the worst had happened, would anyone think to test it, and if so, what for? Surely no one *would* think of it – and if they did, he had a vague idea that insulin wasn't detectable as a poison, an Agatha Christie sort of fact, and therefore quite possibly untrue.

If he was dead…Painfully, Edward began to try and think it through. Though the idea of the old man's death was agonisingly and continuously present in his own mind, looked at rationally, if he was dead, was there any reason for anyone to think twice about it? An old geezer, living alone, has a fall, gets a bit shaky and confused, dies. Who's going to be worrying? Let's say someone gets suspicious. There's no sign of violence. No one in the house. And if someone gets really, really suspicious and does blood-tests, what are they going to find? Probably zero – insulin's a natural substance, isn't it? What copper's going to think of chasing up a pile of correspondence from a big Athens law-firm to find out it's a heap of bollocks? a) it's all in Greek, b) why should they? The address was all right, who'd want to go into it? And anyway, there wasn't a single thing to connect him personally with Eugenides. The chaps in Pleroma had seen him, of course, because of the 'accident', but no one in the City actually knew who he was. He was almost certainly in the clear.

The principal aspect of the Mellerox question which haunted him was dosage. That had been a serious problem with the scam from the start; the absence of any way of finding out how much of the stuff would keep the old Greek off balance without doing much harm. Even if they'd known, there was no way of controlling how much burp-mixture Eugenides got through in a day. His own efforts had successfully left the old man not knowing if it was Tuesday or breakfast-time – but how much of the stuff had he actually given him? Frantically, in the privacy of his uncomfortable hotel bed on the Sunday night, he reckoned up. He'd had about fourteen packs. Two getting on for half-full, several with only one or two capsules in. Sweating, he switched on the bedside light, and scribbled sums on the back of his chequebook. The best guess he could make was that he had doctored the first of the tins with the contents of about forty or fifty capsules, apparently, by sheer luck, about the right dose for their purposes. A scarifying thought struck him. Lamprini had cashed in a prescription for three months' supply. That was... God. Ninety-odd capsules. Had she put the lot in? More than double? And if so, what had happened? Even the extraordinary combination of muddle and wishful thinking which constituted Edward's attempt to grapple with his problem was not proof against the laserlike directness of this reflection, and cold sweat trickled down his spine. Sickly, it began to occur to him that between them, they might have killed the old man by mistake. Had he (he thought, racking his brains) said anything about dosage? – No, he realised, he hadn't. As he remembered the conversation, he had been focused almost entirely on the fact that he had at last managed to shift some demonstrable criminality on to her, and so had she: she'd been so pissed off she'd banged down the phone. His squirrelling thoughts came to rest gratefully on one essential point: it was therefore her fault. If the old bastard was dead, it was she who'd killed him, though the thought of explaining this to her made him quail. The whole thing had got them precisely nowhere; the best they could hope for was that no one would ever find out about it. Assuming Eugenides was dead ...Edward, in despair, realising that his thoughts had gone right round to where they'd started, got up, liberated two miniatures of whisky from the hotel fridge, and poured them both into his toothglass. Somehow, he must get some sleep.

The one thought which crystallised with absolute clarity during the course of the hellish night was that he would have to ring Lamprini. First, though, he must get himself back to Eugenides' house, and find out, if possible, what had actually happened. Having thus contrived to insert a procrastinatory stage between the present moment and a deeply unpleasant moment to come, he found himself able to give at least a moment's thought to the business in hand, which was bad enough to be going on with.

He got through the whole funeral, the grim business of carrying the coffin to its place of sordid interment, the ghastly reception at the Golf Hotel, the platitudes, and the complaints of his parents, on automatic pilot, so preoccupied with his own thoughts that the whole experience barely registered. With each rotation of the tortuous wheel of his thoughts, he gradually talked himself into a more optimistic stance towards the whole mess. If Eugenides was dead, the whole thing could be written off. A bad moment. A mistake. At least he had uncle Jimmy's dosh; things weren't as bad as they had been. Almost, he had resigned himself to letting go of Eugenides' fairy gold. It was a learning experience; chalk it up. And what he had learned from it was, never, whatever the provocation, to get involved in this sort of thing with a woman. But perhaps Eugenides wasn't dead after all...His train of thought set off again, round, and round, and round.

'One really sad thing about all this,' said Sebastian to Hattie and Dil, swallowing the last mouthful of his fourth pakora, 'is that the person who really knew the whole story's just died.'

'Who was that?' asked Jeanene.

'Oh, an absolutely sweet old thing called Eugenides. I got in touch with him about a manuscript – I thought he might know about it, and he did. He lived all alone, in the most fabulous old house in the middle of the City, like a sort of urban hermit, but when you got to know him, he was incredibly kind in a faded, courtly sort of way. He was the last survivor of a sort of Anglo-Greek merchant bank which went right back to the Restoration.'

'What happened to him?'

'I don't know. I didn't see him for a few months, and then when I saw him again, he was terribly shaky. I wondered if he'd had a little stroke or something. He certainly knew something was wrong – he'd asked me to do something for him, and when I went round to see him, he died in my arms.'

Sebastian's voice thickened and wavered out of control, and he burst into tears. Jeanene put her arm round him as he sat shuddering and sobbing into his paper napkin, unaware of covertly curious stares from other diners and the consternation of the waiters. Hattie fished out a packet of tissues, and handed them over silently once the flood showed signs of abating.

'Thanks, Hattie,' said Sebastian, sniffing richly and mopping up. 'Sorry, chaps,' he said apologetically, turning to Dil and Jeanene. 'It was only on Friday, you see, and it was a hell of a shock.'

'I'll bet,' said Jeanene sympathetically. 'It'd be a real bummer even if it was a total stranger, never mind someone you liked.'

'I'll just nip off to the boys' room and wash my face,' said Sebastian. 'Would someone be an absolute darling and order me another beer?'

When he returned, he was visibly calmer. 'It's not just that I'll miss the old darling,' he explained, taking a reviving swig of his lager. 'I spent quite a long time chatting to him last Easter vac., and it was clear from what he said that he had archives of letters and things going right back to the beginnings of the firm. I thought at the time it was an absolute pot of gold for a real historian, which I'm not, really – I mean, I do a bit of history, but I'm really a literature person, so we mostly talked about poetry. The fountain project didn't get off the ground till May-June, and of course, I'd got no idea that there was any urgency about getting stuff out of old Eugenides. Actually, I thought he'd live to a hundred.'

'Eugenides?' said Dil, thoughtfully.

'Yes. Is the name ringing a bell?'

'I think so. Hang on. There's a strange little Greek outfit in London we've got some sort of relationship with. Pretty dormant, but I've seen the old tin box open. I'm sure the name was Eugenides.'

'Well, there can hardly be two, can there?' observed Hattie practically.

'I've not been involved personally,' Dil explained further. 'One of my colleagues was going through the Eugenides box for something back in the New Year. I remember, because it's the only time I've seen one of the boxes down off the shelf. Come to think of it, Betty mentioned that Ed had been seeing Eugenides. The Greek guy had a fall or something, and he got sucked into doing his shopping.'

'Mmm,' said Sebastian thoughtfully. 'There's a receptionist in one of the offices in the square where Eugenides lived who told me someone had been going in. It must've been this colleague of yours. Look, Dilip, you couldn't let me have his name and phone number, by any chance? I know it's absolutely useless now the poor old thing's dead, and probably a bit irrational, but I'd really like to talk to someone who'd been seeing him over the summer. It was such a transformation, you see.'

'Well,' said Dil cautiously, 'Ed's not the world's sharpest observer, but he might give you some idea of what happened. If you let me have your number, I'll give you a bell this evening.'

'Fabulous. I've got a note of Eugenides' solicitor's name – he'd had the sense to leave an "in the event of my death", bless him. I'll be ringing him to find out if Eugenides left any directions for his funeral, you see, and if there's a proper church do somewhere, I'll pass the message on to your colleague in case he wants to turn up. I don't think the old boy had any friends. In fact, I got a distinct impression that your chap's the only personal contact he's had for quite a while.'

Dil said nothing, but his expressive mouth twisted a little.

'What's wrong with the bloke?' asked Jeanene.

Dil shrugged and laughed, slightly embarrassed. 'Nothing, really. He's not my type. I suppose what went through my mind when you said that was, poor old sod if Ed's all you had to depend on. I don't mean there's necessarily anything wrong with him, but he's the sort of guy you want to keep where you can see him.'

'Aren't we all?' said Sebastian sadly. 'I mean, I really liked old Eugenides. He was sweet to me, and we got on terribly well. Then term started and I was very busy, and I just didn't make time to go and see the old love, which I perfectly well could've. As far as I can make out, your colleague didn't owe him a thing, but he rolled up his sleeves and got involved all the same. I owed him a hell of a lot, and I did sod-all when he needed someone. The real reason I want to get in touch with Edward is so I can say thank you. If old Eugenides had ended up lying at the bottom of his own stairs starving to death, I'd be feeling ten times worse than I am now.'

'You couldn't know, Sebastian,' protested Hattie warmly. Sebastian shrugged.

'That's no excuse,' he replied, and drained the last of his lager. Hattie looked round, and flagged a waiter to bring them their bills.

When Edward got into the office on Tuesday, the backlog of work from Monday's absence kept him there till half-past eight in the evening, by which time there was clearly no point in getting himself over to Garlic Court. On Wednesday, however, he broke for freedom at half past four, and was in the City shortly before five. Eugenides' house remained, as he had last seen it, shuttered and secret; he looked up at it, wondering what to do next. Turning away disconsolately, he noticed out of the corner of his eye that the receptionist in Pleroma, phone clamped to one ear, was waving at him frantically through her plate-glass window. He crossed the little court, and, after she had buzzed him in, stood waiting impatiently for her to get off the line. When she put the phone down, they opened their mouths to speak simultaneously. He overrode her.

'I—' she began.

'What's happened to Mr Eugenides?' he asked.

'That's what I'm trying to tell you,' she said, her tone sharpened by irritation. 'I'm afraid he's passed on.'

He had been half-expecting it, of course; but he still felt a jolt of the heart at hearing it confirmed, and bit his lip.

'When?' he demanded curtly.

'On Friday—' She might have said more, but the phone began to ring again. ''Scuse me,' she said, picking it up. 'Pleroma. How may I help you…?' Rather than wait, Edward nodded to her abruptly, and walked out of the office. He desperately needed to think.

He took the Tube back to Holborn, brooding. Unappealing though the prospect was, he was definitely going to have to phone Lamprini and tell her that the whole deal was cancelled. The habits of a lifetime screamed at him to put this off, since the news could get no worse, but his better self dictated otherwise. The only mitigation, not an inconsiderable one, was that once the phone call was made, he would never have to see, hear from, or think of her again.

Accordingly, he bought a couple of bottles of wine on the way home, and braced himself. The situation back at the flat was on the whole propitious. When he looked into the kitchen, it was clear that Alan had been in and gone out again, on the evidence of the ravaged foil containers containing remains of egg fried rice, something sticky in black bean sauce and chewed spare ribs which shared the central table with mysterious bits of his beloved motorbike, marinating in a pool of engine oil. Chris was standing at the stove frying sausages, generally an indication that he intended to spend the evening at the pub, and the air was thick with spicy, greasy, smoke.

Edward refrained from sarcastic comment, closed the door, and went to his room to change out of his work clothes. Once he was comfortable, he pottered in his bedroom, sorting out laundry, until he heard the door slam, indicating that he was at last alone in the flat. He opened his address book and a bottle of wine, poured himself a big drink, and took a deep breath. His hand was actually descending towards the phone when it rang, startling him considerably.

'Edward Lupset.'

'Oh, hello. You don't know me, I'm afraid. My name's Sebastian Raphael. I'm sorry to be disturbing you at home like this, but I was a friend of old Mr Eugenides...'

Edward's knees gave way under him, and he dropped heavily into a chair, gaping at the phone in helpless dismay.

'What?' he croaked, his mouth suddenly dry.

'Oh, I'm sorry. How clumsy of me. You did know he was dead?'

'Er. Yes.'

'I was terribly fond of the old dear,' the voice rushed on. 'I gather you were a colleague? – Look, I was just ringing up, basically, to say how glad I am there was someone to look after him. I didn't know how ill he was, you see.'

'But who are you?' demanded Edward, caught agonisingly between panic and total bewilderment, but regaining some control over his voice. 'I didn't think he knew *anybody*.'

'Oh, God. You make me feel such a toad. Time just flies past during term. I used to see him quite regularly, to talk about Greek poetry. If you knew him professionally, then I suppose it'd never've come up, but the place was an absolute treasure-house. We talked for ages, sometimes, and I was constantly surprised by the things he said. He was a lovely, lovely man, and an absolutely natural scholar. He told me the most extraordinary things about the Greeks in London. All kinds of stuff I don't think anybody else knew about at all.'

Edward was not listening. The idea of Eugenides as a person had no meaning for him, indeed, it was a thought he was anxious to avoid. In any case, his mind was completely occupied with digesting the wholly unacceptable fact that this man knew exactly who he was, and how to contact him. *How?* He could hardly ask, but he desperately wanted to know.

'Why have you rung me?' he demanded baldly, aware only once the words were out of his mouth how lame and peculiar the question sounded. The madman on the other end of the line fortunately misinterpreted him.

'Oh, I'm sorry, Edward. I should've asked if you were busy. Have I caught you at a bad time?'

'No,' said Edward reluctantly. Much though he wanted to put the phone down, and pretend that none of this was happening, it was obviously essential to find out as much as possible. Moreover, out of the welter of words, one caught unpleasantly at his memory; the word 'treasure'. 'It's okay. I'm a bit tired though,' he managed, covering for himself as best he could. 'I'm just back from Scotland.'

'Oh, I do understand. I'll try and keep it short. I was really ringing up to ask if you knew what had happened to the poor old dear.' Edward seriously wondered for a moment if he was going to be sick: he could feel cold sweat forming on his brow and back.

'Happened?'

'I gather he fell, or something? The thing is, Edward, when I was spending a lot of time with him back in the spring, he was as bright as a button. Then I didn't see him again till late summer, and he was totally transformed. I wondered if he'd had a mini-stroke, or something like that. I've been thinking about it a lot. I suppose there'll have to be an inquest? You don't happen to know when it is?'

'I don't know. I'm not a medic. The people at the hospital never got to the bottom of it,' said Edward desperately. 'I mean, he did have a fall. I happened to be there on business, and since he seemed to be totally on his own, I sort of looked in from time to time. Er – there weren't lots of friends, were there?'

'Oh, no. He wasn't leading you up the garden path. I think I was probably the only person he'd seen for quite a while. He'd pretty well retreated into the past, though he couldn't have been nicer when I actually went looking for him. And I'm afraid I didn't exactly tell people how to beat a path to his door. It's awful, really, but he was a tremendous find, academically speaking, and I didn't feel like sharing him around. And I thought he'd go on forever, you see.'

Edward made an indeterminate noise, unable to formulate any sort of reply to this.

'Edward, you must be knackered. I'll get off the phone and leave you in peace. The only other thing I wanted to say is that I'm going to be finding out about Eugenides' funeral from his solicitor. Would you like me to let you know?'

Edward recovered his wits: this was an opening. 'Yes. But I'd like the name and phone number – and I'd like to know where to contact you, if you don't mind.'

'Oh, of course. Have you got a pen?'

Numbly, Edward sat and stared at the letters as they formed under his hand, as if he had never seen writing before. His tormentor continued to make small-talk for a few minutes, then brought himself to ring off. He sat on, in a state of physical and intellectual paralysis. What on earth was he going to do about this? Who, in any case, was Sebastian – despite the amount the man had had to say for himself, he had not been exactly clear about his profession or way of life. All that was clear was that he knew far too much.

And now he would have to phone Lamprini and tell her the good news. Oh, God. He dialled her number. The phone rang for some time, while his heart banged against his ribs: an odd, purring tone: was it actually an engaged signal? He was just about to ring off when it was picked up, and he heard her voice saying something in Greek. She sounded extremely pissed off. When it stopped, on a peremptory upward inflection, he said 'Hello'. There was a pause, while she collected her thoughts and switched languages.

'Edward?'

'Lamprini, have you got anybody there?'

'Of course not. It's late. I was just going to bed.'

'Oh, sorry,' said Edward perfunctorily, 'I forgot you're in a different time zone. Listen, Lamprini. There isn't a good way to say any of this. The deal's off, and we've got a huge problem.'

'Shit, Edward, how've you screwed up? What's happened?'

Edward lost his temper. 'Listen to me, little miss I-Don't-Make-Mistakes. It's not me that screwed up. You've murdered the poor old bastard. What d'you expect me to do about it?'

'Jesus God.' Lamprini was silent for an appreciable space of time. 'Okay, Edward,' she said evenly, 'leave this shit about who's to blame. Just tell me what happened.'

'When you doctored the liver salts, did you use all the pills you'd got?'

'Doctored? Oh, yes, I see. Yes, of course we did, Edward. You didn't say to do anything different.'

'That's because you put the phone down on me,' riposted Edward smartly, and took a healthy swig from his glass. He could hear her seething quietly, far away in Athens. 'The essential fact is, Lamprini, the dose I gave him left him pretty confused and pretty well where we wanted him. You must've just about doubled it. I don't know how much of the stuff it takes to poison someone, but that's what you did.'

'You're sure he's dead?'

'Absolutely certain.'

'Okay, Edward. Let's just say that none of it ever happened, eh? I'll talk to Alex. It's been nice knowing you.'

'Hang on a minute! Lamprini, I haven't got to the bad bit. There's someone who knows about it.'

'*What?* Oh Jesus, Ed, what have you done?'

'I don't know! This chap rang me up, absolutely out of the blue. He's known Eugenides for ages, and he knows I've been visiting, God knows how. I haven't thought of a way of asking him where he got my name from, maybe Eugenides told him.'

'What sort of a guy?'

'Some kind of academic, I think. He was banging on about Greek poetry. So I suppose he's pretty bright, and not very clued up.'

'Why was he talking to you?' asked Lamprini, with a dangerous edge on her voice. 'Use your brain, Edward.'

Edward felt his stomach knotting up with tension. 'He wanted to know about the old bastard's illness,' he admitted sullenly.

'What did you tell him!'

'A lot of bullshit. Look, Lamprini, it was fucking difficult, you know!'

Lamprini, wincing, took the receiver away from her ear, noting the hysterical crack in his voice: if this mystery man hadn't been suspicious at the outset, she had an ominous feeling that if Edward had reacted as he was doing now, he would have become so. A larger and larger proportion of alarm began to be superadded to the chagrin and anger which threatened to suffocate her.

'Tell me more. What did he say about the relationship?'

'Oh God. He said they used to talk. He said Eugenides knew all kinds of stuff no one else knew about—' A ghastly thought suddenly struck him. 'Christ, Lamprini, d'you think the old bastard was stringing us along? He said something about treasure – mean, I know the pictures are pretty good, but that's bloody strong. He was hinting he knew all sorts of things. And he was worried about the change in him. He was asking about the inquest.'

'Edward. We're going to have to do something about him.'

'Oh, Jesus,' he wailed, slumping despairingly in his armchair. The really terrible thing was, he knew she was right. The whole mess was only bearable if nobody knew about it. He did not formulate in any way what the 'something' might be; for the moment, all he allowed himself to realise was that they needed to eliminate him as a risk.

'He's clever, he's worrying about Eugenides, and we don't know anything about him,' she insisted, pressing home her point. 'For Christ's sake, Edward. We don't know what he knows. He's a researcher. Maybe he found another copy of the memo. Think of that. You'd better talk to him soon, and find out all you can.'

XX

Jeanene, meanwhile, had troubles of her own, the most significant of which was her supervisor. At the outset, she had been most unclear how much she was supposed to see of him, but she expected on the whole that she would see him only once or twice a term. In practice, she saw him at least twice a week for Advanced Intensive Greek, once for his undergraduate Special Subject on the Greek city, which he had suggested she sit in on, and often at evening lectures, or in the pub after such events. If she had either liked or trusted him, this would doubtless have been joy and jam: as things were, she found it increasingly difficult and embarrassing.

Learning ancient Greek is hard work at the best of times, but George made matters worse by outbreaks of petulance and heavy, schoolmasterish sarcasm, as if he thought that ritual humiliation would somehow make the aorist subjunctive of λύω easier to remember. Jeanene coped with all this better than most, because she felt sorry for him, but it was not enjoyable.

After one of these ghastly sessions, in which a bleeding chunk of Thucydides' *History of the Peloponnesian War* had been mangled out of all recognition by a class of otherwise intelligent people hounded into temporary stupidity, Jeanene was shovelling books and notepads into her backpack when she realised that George had approached and was standing in front of her. He seemed to have something on his mind.

'Jeanene. I wondered if you'd care to come for a coffee?'

No, she thought, I really don't want to. But he's my supervisor …'Thanks. Could it be a quickie? I've got a lot lined up for today.'

'As you should, as you should,' said George, with uneasy heartiness. 'I've noticed, of course, that you're always properly prepared, unlike these little animals. They get worse every year. No discipline. Slackers and whingers. Have you noticed that the Yanks are the worst?' Fortunately, he did not seem to want an answer. 'Let's go.'

Once they were duly wedged on either side of an ugly formica table in the building's little café, with the coffee she did not want in front of her. George resumed his one-sided conversation.

'I'm very pleased with you, Jeanene. You're making excellent progress.'

'I think my Greek's really coming on,' volunteered Jeanene shyly. 'I mean, I've got to the point where I can sometimes look at a passage and just know what it says? It's a great feeling.'

'Excellent. All down to hard work. If the others had a tenth of your application, my job would be a damned sight easier, I can tell you. What I wanted to ask you, though, is about your real work. Any progress on your first chapter? Early days yet, I know, but I'm keen to see a draft of something. I want to be sure you've started off on the right foot.'

Oh, God. Just what she'd been hoping to avoid. She felt herself beginning to flush, a wave of hot pinkness travelling across her forehead and down her neck; she stared at her cooling coffee, holding the mug in both hands. Unexpectedly, George reached out, and touched her arm. 'Don't be frightened, Jeanene.' His voice and the damp hand on her wrist both trembled; she dared not look at him.

'Um. I'm doing a lot of reading, and putting together a bibliography…' Her voice trailed off. She had thought of giving him the bibliography, but it was full of stuff which would drive him bananas. And if she faked up a biblio with Julia Kristeva and Amy Richlin and so on pruned out of it, she'd just look as if she hadn't been doing anything much. George, fortunately, misunderstood her hesitation.

'My dear. It's very proper to feel a little nervous at this stage. But it's your supervisor's business to guide you through. And frankly, I want to see you well under way before Dr Flaxman returns from her little jaunt in the USA. I'm not asking for anything much. A few thousand words, either a sketch of a chapter, or a section of material. But I'm determined to get you working on your own before you're contaminated.'

'Contaminated?' she echoed, stupidly.

'Dr Flaxman, as you will discover in due course, if she ever sees fit to return, is a purveyor of fashionable feminist filth. I want to see your work set on a good, sound basis before she gets back and tries to fill you up with nonsense. By the same token, you would be well advised to steer clear of Dr Raphael.'

'He's been very kind,' said Jeanene defensively.

'You are very young, Jeanene, and very innocent. I could tell you a thing or two about that sort of kindness. Take it from me, Jeanene. He's not a fit person for you to associate with.'

'Do you mean because he's a poofter?' demanded Jeanene.

George recoiled from this bluntness, his face darkening. 'Because he's degenerate, young lady. His private life is none of my business, or yours either. The point is, that sort of thing's a symptom of moral and intellectual rot. I'm sure it all looks very nice and harmless to a young girl like yourself. That's why I'm taking the trouble to tell you there's a lot you'd be better off not knowing. You're a churchgoer, aren't you?'

'Yes?' said Jeanene cautiously.

'Then you should know better than to go anywhere near him.'

George glanced at his watch, and rose. 'I have to go. I'll be expecting to see something from you by the end of the month.'

Damn, damn, damn, thought Jeanene furiously. She'd have to drop everything she was trying to do, and write a lot of bullshit about archaeology.

'Hello, Jeanene. What's wrong?'

'Oh, hi, Sebastian,' she said, in some confusion, as he slid into the seat recently vacated by George.

'I saw you through the glass door, looking like thunder,' he offered.

'George has gone bush. He just warned me not to talk to you,' she blurted.

Sebastian raised his eyebrows. 'Sweet of him. Why?'

Jeanene told him the whole story, while Sebastian leaned his chin on his hand, and listened carefully. When she had finished, he sighed.

'I'm beginning to wonder if George is cracking up,' he commented. 'He's never liked me, but I think this is getting out of hand. Oh, well. Try not to provoke him. If you can just manage to save up the row till Katie gets back, you'll have someone on your side. I can't get involved since I'm part of the problem, so it really wouldn't be a good idea to try and unpick all this before Christmas. It'd have to go to the professor, and he wouldn't necessarily be sympathetic. It all looks like trouble for the department, you see.'

Jeanene sighed. 'O-kay. I'll cope. Forget it for now. Tell me some good news, if there is any. I could do with some.'

Sebastian grinned broadly, and unexpectedly burst into song. 'I'm in love with a wonderful guy!' he carolled, *sotto voce*, though even so, people at adjoining tables turned round surreptitiously to stare.

'That's great! Tell me about him?'

'Oh, I'll introduce you some time. He's called Giles Penne-thorne, and he's so lovely he'll make you cry. You must meet him, actually. You'd find him very educational – he's like Old England on its hind legs.'

'What does he do?'

'Oh, wonderful things. Specialist plasterwork, restoring old buildings, making models. He knows all about limewash and stuff. He wears corduroys and old jumpers, and he's terribly sweet and earnest. I don't know what he sees in me.'

Jeanene laughed, looking a bit more like herself, and pushed away her cold coffee.

'I'd better get going. I suppose I shouldn't be seen with you.'

'Bye, then.'

Sebastian let her go, then went out of the café in his turn, waving at a number of students, the odd colleague, and the woman behind the counter. He had plenty to think about. Dismissing George and his questionable sanity for the time being, he gave his mind to the subject of Abbot Akakios, due to arrive in England in three weeks' time. Once he was back in his office, he sighed, and rang the secretary of the Friends of Mount Athos to see if anything had been finalised, so that he could reschedule classes if necessary. The secretary, fortunately, sounded cautiously optimistic.

'I think we're pretty definite now, Dr Raphael. We've got three days in London set up for them. They're meeting His Eminence Archbishop Gregorios, and His All-Holiness Kallistos Ware, attending a number of services, and visiting a monastery. His Holiness Ephraim Lash has been tremendously helpful at this end. We've set aside the Friday for general sightseeing, which probably means resting, since most of the abbots are rather elderly – we thought they'd probably be glad if the programme wasn't absolutely crammed. If Father Akakios has personal business in London, that'd be the ideal day. We're going to Highgrove on Saturday afternoon. We'll have lunch in Tetbury, at the Talbot Hotel, and His Royal Highness will be expecting us at about three. I thought you'd probably like to come along, so I've already given your name to the equerry, and I'm sure you'll be hearing from them in due course.'

'Okay,' said Sebastian, relieved. 'That sounds pretty stream-lined. I'll join the welcome committee at Heathrow on Monday morning, and get a few words with Akakios when I can. Then I'll roll up to the hotel and collect him on Friday morning. As for Saturday, perhaps I could hitch a ride with you' – the thought of sitting among a busload of abbots for a couple of hours presented itself in its full horror, and he abruptly revised what he was saying – 'or on second thoughts, perhaps I could arrange to meet you at the Talbot?' Gloucestershire topography was not his strong point, but it occurred to him suddenly that Giles's cottage was somewhere in the area and probably not far from the Walesery, and that Giles ran a car.

'Well, if you prefer. There will certainly be spare seats on the minibus if you change your mind.'

Having got the secretary off the line, after due exchanges of civilities, Sebastian rang Tim Claydon-Jones.

'Tim? I've got the abbot set up. He's got a free day in London on October the thirtieth – we'd better plan our campaign.'

'It's not a lot of notice,' complained Tim.

'It never is when you're dealing with the Holy Mountain, they're as solipsistic as bloody gyroscopes. Think yourself lucky you've got most of a month. The dates aren't negotiable. He's tied up with millions of bloody-minded English archimandrites from Monday to Thursday, and we're all seeing the Prince of Wales on Saturday.'

'I'll have to think about it,' Tim said.

Sebastian sighed. It was all very well Tim insisting on being the one to set the agenda, but what did he expect anyone to do about it?

'We'll all have to think about it,' he said, more sharply than was his wont. 'But if we can get the old bugger to a decision, it'll all be worth it. I think we might just pull it off, because his agent in

London's just died. He's got every incentive to get out while he can. Our line's got to be that if he's got an offer, he just ought to close with it, on the bird-in-the-hand principle. Talking of which, have you actually got a deal to give him? And an independent valuation of the site? He's not a fool, you know. He'll want to see that in writing.'

'Yes, I have. Hattie's been extremely helpful. She's mad to save the garden, of course' – his dismissive tone spoke of another battle fought and lost, and Sebastian grinned to himself – 'so what we've worked out between us is a set of costings based on levelling the vicarage site, and using that for the fountain and memorial garden, while the existing garden stays as it is. The house is a write-off, you know. The main roof-beam's obviously gone, and the dry rot going up's just about met the wet rot coming down. It'll have to come down whatever happens, and we've pulled strings with the planning officer about change of use. Hattie's trying to talk the Bridge Trust into agreeing to underwrite an offer on the valuation, while we try to raise money from various sources. The Onassis Foundation have been very sympathetic, and we've got some private backers as well, who don't want to be named at this stage. As far as the other lot's concerned, the St Michael's Garden Committee and the Southwark Residents Association are doing all they can, but you can't expect them to raise that sort of money themselves. The borough council's said they would be prepared to match an offer of funding to save the garden, if we get external input. Hattie's lobbying like mad, and co-ordinating both campaigns.'

'What a pity Eugenides is dead,' commented Sebastian. 'I mean, it helps in a way, since we can use it to force the abbot's hand, but I'm sure he had plenty of money tucked away. Since Eugenides & Co. were connected with the church from the beginning, I'm sure he'd have wanted to contribute. Actually, Tim, I've just had a brainwave. I've got to ring his solicitor anyway, to find out about the funeral, and I could ask what the terms of his will are. It's just possible he's said something unspecific about charitable uses, you see, and we might be able to talk ourselves into a share of it. He hadn't a soul to leave things to, that I know of.'

'That's a wonderful idea,' said Tim, audibly brightening.

'Don't get carried away,' warned Sebastian, who could hear that Tim's perception of his words was ineluctably moving in his own mind from possibility to certainty. 'I'd better ring the lawyer now, just in case, but for Pete's sake don't go counting chickens till I talk to you again.'

'Of course not. Talk to you later.' Sebastian rang off, and cracked his knuckles.

'One more tiny phone call,' he said to the bust of Antinous, glowering reproachfully from the mantelpiece, 'then I really will get down to some work. Cross my heart.'

He fished out his diary, in which he had scribbled the address on Eugenides' last letter, and rang Directory Enquiries.

'A business number, please...'

In due course, he was put through to Eugenides' solicitor.

'Hello,' he began, 'Mr Cowan? My name is Sebastian Raphael.'

'Ah, Dr Raphael. Glad to hear from you. We were wondering how to get in touch. Were you aware that you were Mr Constantine Eugenides' only personal legatee?'

'*What?*'

'Mr Eugenides has left you a book. He describes it quite carefully, but to be honest, we could do with some expert help in identifying it. No one in the office reads Greek, I'm afraid. I presume it is something familiar in some way? A volume of Greek verse in manuscript?'

Sebastian's heart expanded within him. 'Oh, God,' he whispered, mostly to himself. 'He's left me the Digby manuscript. Oh, the darling.' He sniffed, and blew his nose.

'I gather it means a lot to you? A lot more than it does to us, I'm afraid. That's excellent.'

Sebastian shook himself from his daze, pinched the bridge of his nose hard, and tried to answer coherently.

'Yes. It's something he let me use. I couldn't be more pleased.'

'You'll have to wait till after probate before you get it, of course. But if we could perhaps ask you to come and identify it for us informally, we could put it on one side, and make sure it's kept for you.'

'Fantastic. That's absolutely no problem. I know exactly where it is, actually – it's in the glassfronted bookcase to the left of the fireplace, fifth shelf up, about fourth in from the right. But just give me a time, and I'll come and confirm it. Actually, though, I wasn't expecting this: I was ringing up to enquire about the terms of the will in general.'

'It's a very simple document. Two ikons are to go to the lavra of St Michael on Mount Athos. Apart from the book which is going to you, all other manuscript and printed books are to go to the British Library.'

'Gosh, they'll be pleased. It's a fabulous collection. The manuscripts must be worth literally millions.'

'You relieve me considerably! It can be very embarrassing for the executors if a testator makes a bequest of this kind, and the library refuses to accept it. There's another similar bequest, if I could just run it past you – a Lely of Sir Everard Digby, and a Hogarth of Godscall Palaeologue, for the National Portrait Gallery?'

'They're kosher. I've seen them.'

'Excellent. Thank you so much. The residue is simply left to the Greek Orthodox Cathedral in London, which is also where he's directed his funeral should take place.'

'I think I can help with a lot of this,' offered Sebastian. 'I'll be seeing the abbot of St Michael towards the end of the month, and I'll almost certainly be meeting the Dean of the Cathedral; do you want me to tell them? The abbot doesn't speak English, though I'm sure the Dean does.'

'That would be most kind. We haven't really any relevant expertise, I'm afraid.'

Sebastian, meanwhile, had thought of something else, and also that, having done the man a huge favour, it was a good moment to mention it. 'What about the firm's archive? Papers? Has he said anything?'

'Um, no. It's a bit of a grey area, isn't it? I suppose we ought to hang on to recent stuff, in case of enquiries.'

'No! I mean, that's not the point. Eugenides & Co. have got records going back continuously to the English Civil War. They're *priceless*.'

'Oh, I see,' said Mr Cowan politely, in a tone which suggested that on the whole, he didn't.

'I suppose he didn't think about it. He wasn't a historian, and he won't have realised the value of this stuff. Look, it's not your kind of thing either. Let me ring up the Public Record Office. Gervase Hood's the chap who'll know what to do. If he doesn't want them for the PRO itself, he'll certainly be able to tell me where they ought to go. Can you think of any objection in principle to putting all but the most recent papers on deposit in a public archive? We're not talking monetary value here. I don't see why it should influence probate one way or another.'

'Let me think about it,' said Cowan. 'I have a feeling we might be able to offset it against his tax liability. I'll get some advice.'

Sebastian said his goodbyes, and rang off, well satisfied. Apart from the fact that Eugenides had left him the Nonnos manuscript, the enormity of which was yet to hit him, thanks to his intervention, it was fairly certain that anything of the slightest use was going to end up in a public collection, where he, since he was currently the only person to know of its value, would be at the head of the queue. It crossed his mind briefly that it was bad luck for old Tim's charity scam, which he had practically forgotten about in the course of the phone-call's excitements, but he could always try his luck with His Holiness in Moscow Road.

XXI

Lamprini put the phone down carefully. She was feeling rather sick; partly from fear, and partly from fury. Edward had got rawly under her skin by quoting her back at herself. Moreover, the realisation that she had indeed done something stupid in not checking with Edward about dosage upset her quite disproportionately, since her pride of self was based on faultless competence in all professional matters. It was this pride, rather than simple pragmatism, which left her instantly determined, the moment Edward first uttered the fatal news of a potential witness, that he should cease to exist, as he should never have existed in the first place. This was not a decision based on the calculus of rational self-protection, but a much deeper, essentially irrational instinct for the defence of her identity in her own eyes. It was midnight in Athens, and she would have to be up before seven, but sleep was obviously out of the question. She wrapped a robe around herself for comfort, poured herself a little brandy to settle her stomach, and sat down on her sofa to try and collect her frantic thoughts.

The Eugenides project had seemed, as they entered into it, one of potentially very high gains for a very low risk. They'd known all along that it might not work, in the sense that the pressure they were able to apply was indirect, and the old man's responses, both physical and psychological, necessarily unpredictable. But across the whole spectrum of possible outcomes which they had thought about, while success could only result from some configurations, no risk appeared to attach to any. It had never seriously crossed her mind that they would kill Eugenides: the thought of herself as a murderess was so bizarre, so inexplicable, that she simply rejected it. The important thing was that they had lost the game; and, at least, it should have been possible to draw a line under the whole incident, learn some lessons, and forget about it.

However, this friend of Eugenides was a wild card, and spelt disaster. It was absolutely imperative that no one should ever know how fatally she had compromised herself, and this man Raphael was in a position where he might do so. Lamprini, as she reviewed the situation, did not trouble herself with the questions Edward was asking: who he was, or why he had suddenly appeared. He existed, she would move forward from that. As she thought, the gut conviction she had started with was augmented by a number of bleakly rational considerations. It seemed probable, from Edward's hysterical account, he suspected nothing at the moment, though he quite evidently knew a great deal. Equally clearly, Edward's reaction to him was one of such guilty panic that suspicion might eventually lodge in his mind. The situation was unacceptable; it left her personally at risk. She was under no illusions about Edward himself. If he was confronted in any way, he would go to pieces, and would certainly seek to throw the blame on her as far as possible. In the whole of her orderly and rational life, she had never been in such a mess.

'Shit!' said Lamprini to herself, in frustration and rage. The sheer unfairness of the situation left her on the verge of tears. She got up, and went to get her work diary. Standing by the window, unconscious of the glittering lights of Athens against the velvet night and the ever-present noise of the traffic coming up from the streets far below, she gazed bleakly at pages covered with meetings and appointments. Something would have to be done about Sebastian Raphael, and Edward could not be trusted. Somehow, she would have to find time to go to England and assess the situation. She was unwilling to involve Alexander, for a number of reasons. His sudden attack of compunction over the actual buying of the Mellerox left her feeling that she would not be wise to trust him any further: she certainly didn't want him to have anything more on her. Better if he knew nothing about it.

Sebastian arrived at Haghia Sophia, five minutes late. Wise in the ways of the Orthodox, he was sure nothing would have started on time, as indeed, it had not. He kissed the icons which stood near the door, giving them an automatic dealer's once-over as he did so, and lit a couple of candles. The church opened out before him, an inexplicable splendour of Victorian green and gold after the dreary streets of Notting Hill – dim, richly ornamented, and glittering with gold-ground mosaics. A single figure was sitting in the front row of chairs, with his hands clasped together, apparently lost in thought, facing the iconostasis and the pathetic coffin which stood in the centre, in front of the Royal Doors. No one else was visible at all, except an overalled caretaker tinkering with one of the silver hanging lamps and two old ladies talking to each other in a back pew. It was immediately obvious who this man must be, but in some ways, Sebastian thought, as he walked noiselessly up the central aisle looking curiously at him, he was a bit of a surprise. The generally Sloany air was much what he had been expecting in a young lawyer, so was the severe elegance of his dark suit. He was prettier than the standard model, girlishly fair, with short, well-cut blond hair and a sulky, vulnerable pink mouth, tougher and fitter, also, than the general run of his kind. But as Sebastian came closer, significant cracks appeared in the façade. The cheeks were not smooth, but marred by minor nicks, rashes, and outbreaks, like a teenager's, and scurf marred the collar of the suit. Sebastian wondered momentarily if he were on drugs, though this seemed fundamentally implausible.

Sebastian walked past him, and went up to the open coffin. Eugenides' face was barely recognisable now the lids were sealed fast over the expressive, sloe-black eyes. The nose stood away from the face like a knifeblade, and the cheekbones strained the pale, yellowish skin. He knelt to kiss the cold, waxy forehead, then turned to slip into the chair beside Edward, who was gazing at him with petrified revulsion.

'Sorry,' whispered Sebastian. 'You're supposed to kiss the corpse, I'm afraid. But you're allowed to kiss the little icon tucked in with him if you really don't want to. I'm Sebastian Raphael.'

'Hi. Edward Lupset,' said Edward faintly, shaking the proffered hand. Sebastian manfully resisted the temptation to wipe the clammy sweat off on to his trousers, smiled encouragingly, sat down, and tried to cheer him up a bit before one or other of them burst into tears.

'We've probably got a minute or two to chat. You'll know something's going to start happening when the priests come through at the side there. The Royal Doors stay shut for funerals – the altar's behind them. Have you ever been here before?' Edward shook his head. 'Wonderful, isn't it? It was basically built for the community which grew up here after the War of Independence, and they put a lot of money into it. The congregation's probably mostly Cypriots these days, I think.'

'I don't know anything about Greek stuff,' said Edward defensively.

'Oh, sorry. I thought you might, since you were doing business with Eugenides?'

'We weren't really connected. Well, there was a connection, but it was basically in the eighteenth century. He got in touch with us about something this year, but before that, we hadn't heard from him since the Seventies.'

'Oh, I see. And you were just the proverbial concerned citizen who happened to be passing?'

'That's right.'

'A bit rough on you. It must've been quite a strain. Oh, look. Someone's come through. I think something's happening at last.' He stood up, and Edward followed suit.

In ones and twos, a group of cantors drifted into the church in the casual way that an orchestra enters the pit, and assembled to the right of the ikonostasis. One after another, a number of priests, black beards dramatic over white robes, entered from the left, padding up and down the church with an absolute lack of urgency. It all struck Sebastian as unnaturally quiet. The vociferous crowd of mourners who ought to have been there were an insistent absence, but even given that Eugenides had no known family, in some indefinable way Anglican restraint seemed to have seeped in from the very stones of Notting Hill Gate.

As the reader began to sing Psalm 91 and the slow, interminable ritual of a Greek Orthodox funeral got gradually under way, Edward and Sebastian settled down to endure it, according to their respective lights. Sebastian prayed intermittently, thought about Eugenides, listened to some of the hymns he particularly liked, and admired the mosaics. Edward, who could not understand a word of what was going on, simply suffered, shifting his weight restlessly from foot to foot, wondering if he was allowed to sit down, boredom warring with tension till he began to feel he might faint or suffocate. The Dean of the cathedral, magnificent in white, gold-embroidered robes, chanted psalm after psalm monotonously in a resonant baritone, which bounced metallically off the curve of the dome, filling the church from all sides, while a small group of cantors answered him reedily from the right-hand side, crossing themselves repeatedly with sweeping, whole-arm gestures in perfect unison. The dim light and green marble of the church gradually gave Edward an oppressive sense of being under water.

Considerably more than an hour later, he was roused from sullen preoccupation with his aching feet and sore back when, as the Dean advanced to the head of the coffin to say yet another prayer, Sebastian nudged him discreetly. 'We go up for the last kiss in a minute,' he hissed. 'Just follow me.' Edward stumbled nightmarishly forward when Sebastian began to move. He knelt clumsily in front of the coffin, and kissed the icon, as Sebastian had advised. The idea of touching the body was unendurable to him, though he was squeamishly relieved to see how like a thing, and unlike a person, the little husk in the coffin now looked. People, mostly old and mostly women, who had gradually swelled the congregation in the course of the service, filed up behind them to do the last honours to a stranger. As Edward scrambled, swaying, to his feet, Sebastian discreetly took his elbow, and piloted him back to the chairs. 'Where are now his kinsfolk and his friends?' sang the choir. Where indeed, reflected Sebastian sadly.

That, mercifully, represented the beginning of the end; from that point on, the service drew almost swiftly to a close. Once the last prayer was said, they followed the coffin out of the church, and as the hearse moved slowly away, Sebastian blew his nose, and, reaching gratefully for his fags, turned to Edward. 'Come on. You must need a drink. I must have a huge gin, or I'll *die*. There's a dreadful place called the Leinster just on the corner of Pembridge Square.' Edward did not even bother to reply, but merely fell into step; and they walked down Moscow Road together. Sebastian, forced to keep his mouth shut for the best part of two hours, was bursting with chatter, which was just as well, since Edward, though his mind was racing, was completely at a loss to think how to extract the information he needed.

As promised, the moment the Victorian redbrick of Moscow Road gave way to the stucco of Pembridge Square, the Leinster appeared on the corner, rendered almost invisible by dripping mounds of petunias which cascaded from every possible point of support. Sebastian surveyed it dubiously.

'Do you mind sitting outside? If there's big screen sports on offer in the bar, I don't suppose we'd be able to hear ourselves speak.'

'Fine by me,' said Edward.

'Super. You grab that bench, I'll get them in. What do you want?' he called back, already halfway to the door.

'I kept thinking,' he remarked once he had returned with their drinks, 'what a shame it was there was just the two of us.'

'Well, he didn't know anyone else, did he?' offered Edward dully.

'Not here in London, as far as I know, but he did have associates on Mount Athos. I don't know how much you know about the old dear, but the firm had a long-standing connection with the monastery of St Michael there. Eugenides was still looking after some property in London for them. The abbot's coming over at the end of the month, and I've got roped in as interpreter – hey, Edward. Are you feeling all right? Try putting your head between your knees.' He broke off, in justifiable concern, for Edward had gone ashen, and swayed in his seat.

'I'm all right,' he croaked, attempting a smile.

'Let me get you some more whisky.' Sebastian bustled off, and while he was at the bar, Edward drained the remainder of his glass at a gulp, his mind wincing away from the pit which had opened up before him. Thank God things had gone no further, was his first thought, his second, that he was finally and absolutely convinced Lamprini was right. Though the thought made him quail, they would have to get rid of him. He tried to pull himself together. It was imperative that he discover Sebastian's points of vulnerability; and he considered him covertly as he returned with the glasses. A little taller than his own six foot nothing, quite a bit heavier. While he was obviously no athlete, he was still formidable, and Edward simply could not think what to do about him. Not even an Oxford education had taught him about the practicalities of assassination; and unlike the wispy, otherworldly Eugenides, Sebastian was inescapably practical-looking, near his own age, and with all his wits about him.

'Thanks,' he managed, as Sebastian put another double Scotch down in front of him. 'It's been a long morning, and I must've gone a bit woozy with all that standing around. You were saying something about an abbot?'

Sebastian was happy to talk. 'I got to know the chap over some research I was doing on Athos,' he explained. 'The stuff which led me to Eugenides. Then when he decided to come over and look into this property, he just assumed I'd help him out. I might've told him to bugger off, only some friends of mine are keen to buy the land the monastery owns here, and turn it into a public amenity.' Edward, listening to this, began to wonder if he had taken leave of his senses. Did the whole of fucking London know about this property? *How?* 'So,' continued Sebastian obliviously, 'I ended up as muggins in the middle. I'm taking the old coot round Southwark on Friday week, to try and talk him into a deal. It's incredibly inconvenient. You've just had a taste of the Orthodox grasp of timekeeping, and the Riyadh needs me at about five to look at some Byzantine silver for them before the weekend. I'm somehow going to have to get a wrap on the deal by four-thirty at the latest.'

'Couldn't you do it on Saturday?' suggested Edward, feeling for information.

'Would that I could, Edward, but he's over with half the bigwigs from the Mountain. We're just doing a bit of private business on their one day off, then we're all supposed to be in Gloucestershire on Saturday, meeting the Prince of Wales.'

'So you're all driving up to Highgrove on Saturday?' guessed Edward.

'In theory. Actually, flesh and blood revolts at the thought of spending the morning on the M4 with a load of archimandrites, so I'm going to go and spend the night with my friend in Rodmarton, just up the road. I'll have to get poor old Giles to drive me to Tetbury in my best suit and catch them at the Talbot. We're not meeting His Walesness till three-thirty, thank God.'

'Where in Rodmarton?' asked Edward, with a pretence of

vagueness, committing the name to memory. 'My parents used to have friends there.'

'He's got the old grooms' lodgings on Manor Farm,' replied Sebastian guilelessly. 'Do you know the place I mean? Down by the school.'

'No. I think Mummy's friends were up by the church somewhere,' said Edward, improvising wildly. 'I was quite young the last time we went. I can't really remember.'

'I don't suppose it's changed much,' observed Sebastian. 'It's a classic so-called unspoiled Cotswold village, and they're desperately trying to keep the clock set at "warm beer and cycling to Evensong". Anyway. That's enough of my affairs. The point I was working round to, really, was that it's a pity Akakios wasn't here. I'm sure the old dear would've liked to be prayed down by a proper abbot, and not just the likes of us.'

A few days later, Jeanene, with butterflies in her tummy, was walking misgivingly towards George's office. He had had a preliminary draft of her first chapter for a week, and this was the unavoidable meeting to discuss it. She reached his door, and hesitated. Get it over with. She knocked, and went in.

George was sitting behind his desk, looking betrayed. She could see her typescript, lying flat in front of him in its folder.

'I have read your work, Jeanene,' he began abruptly. 'I have to say, I am very disappointed. Very disappointed indeed.'

'I—'

'I think you will have to admit that I have done my utmost to guide you,' he went on, ignoring her attempt to speak. His voice rose, and little bubbles of spittle gathered at the corners of his mouth. He swallowed hard. 'This essay is proof positive that you haven't listened to a blind word I've said since your arrival.'

'Look, Dr Beckinsale. I think you're being totally unfair—'

'Unfair! I'm trying to educate you, you mindless little bitch!'

Jeanene had had enough. She stalked over to the desk, and

stared down at him, arms folded. She was quaking internally, but determined to have it out with him before things got any worse.

'Look here, Dr Beckinsale. You say I haven't listened to you, but you haven't even let me open my mouth. You've been acting like you could do a Pygmalion on me just because I'm Australian! They did *teach* us at Wollongong. I'm not straight off the backblocks.'

George's mouth opened and shut; it looked for a moment as if he was meditating some kind of appeal, and she braced herself to deal with it. Then his face hardened, and set into the mulish, contemptuous expression she knew only too well, though it had never before been directed at her. 'I decline to supervise you,' he snapped.

'Good,' she fired back. She turned to leave, then hesitated at the door. 'Look. I do realise you meant it for the best. Thanks for your time.' Then she was gone.

The door closed gently. George dropped his head in his hands, and stayed in that position for a long time. He was near to tears. She had seemed to him so entirely the promise of something different, unlike the dismal procession of louts, pansies and trollops he normally dealt with. Since the moment he had first seen her, an unaffectedly lovely girl who was also serious-minded and hard-working, he had thought of her, or at least told himself that he thought of her, as the dream pupil, biddable, diligent, yet intelligent. But in his dreams and fantasies, the moments when his conscious control of his mind slackened, his feelings for her had gradually developed an emotional and sexual charge which he was not prepared to acknowledge even to himself.

In his pain and anger, he was unable to believe that a young and attractive girl could possess such a thing as a mind of her own. Therefore, as he saw it, if he had failed to shape her in the way she should go, she was necessarily the creation of someone else. It was thus in a spirit of pure vindictiveness (though he did not recognise it as such) that, having dismissed her from his mind and turned to his administrative duties, he went to find Elaine and the department diary, and fixed a graduate studies committee meeting for five o'clock on Friday week, in the unacknowledged hope of ruining Sebastian's weekend.

It gradually became clear to Edward, brooding intensively on Sebastian, his obvious intelligence, his energy, his esoteric knowledge, his contacts, and above all, his loquaciousness, that there was only one realistic solution to the problem he represented. At no point could he be said to have consciously made a decision; the process more closely resembled the imperceptible seepage of water which suddenly results in an overflow. But once he had reached that point, he had a clear idea of what to do about it. As he knew from conversations with other lawyers discussing their more adventurous clients, there were pubs in parts of London such as Brixton and Newham where a sizeable bundle of fivers could be exchanged for a gun and some ammo with no questions asked. His squash-partner Julian, who special-ised in criminal law, had a story…what was it? The punchline was something about 'West End murders at East End prices', but it included some fairly specific details, so he could probably get the information he needed in the course of a game and a couple of beers just by getting Jools to tell it again. He could shoot, fortunately: he had been a fair marksman in his teens, courtesy of his school's OTC, and while he disliked the thought of owning anything as incriminating as an unlicensed gun, the thing could be dumped in the Thames after only a week or two in his possession.

He had rung Lamprini, and passed on Sebastian's agenda to her: she had agreed to come over for a long weekend. One thing in their favour, as she pointed out at once, was Sebastian's obvious homosexuality. The police might well take the attitude that a wealthy and flamboyant queer found dead in a public place had in some way brought this fate upon himself, or was, at least, randomly rather than specifically victimised. Another plus-point which she also dwelt on was Edward's youthful complexion and delicate features. Since he was also tall and slim, if he dressed down appropriately, he could pass for a lot younger than he was. Edward saw the force of this: clothes, and their transformative power, were something he believed in absolutely. He already owned a pair of jeans, so he went to The Cut, and bought a pair of lurid trainers, a rip-off Arsenal shirt emblazoned with the name 'WRIGHT', a baseball cap mysteriously inscribed 'Falanx Lacadaimonicus,' and a green and purple fleece jacket with good deep pockets. Dressing up in the privacy of his bedroom and admiring the effect in his full-length mirror, even he was surprised by the extent of the transformation. If the feds were ever actually looking, they'd be going after a lad in his early twenties, not a thirty-something posh boy. Well pleased, he piled the disgusting stuff back into its carrier bags, and hid it in the bottom of his wardrobe.

It was also a very different Sebastian from the usual model who was to be sighted in Southwark on a dull and overcast Friday at the end of October. He had, not without a pang, had a haircut; and he was wearing his best formal suit, charcoal with an almost invisible chalkstripe, a good, plain white shirt, and no jewellery. His manner, as he followed Akakios out of the taxi, was murmuring and deferential, in the best traditions of the Byzantine Civil Service and Harrods Food Hall. Akakios, stately as a galleon, was responding well to treatment. After several days of being a minor player, he was evidently enjoying being the centre of attention.

A welcome committee of Tim and Hattie was waiting for them on the pavement. Briefed by Sebastian, Tim was soberly suited, while Hattie was wearing a severe grey-and-white woollen dress which came up to her collarbones and well below her knees, and had combed her yellow hair unassertively flat, back from her high, medieval forehead. She looked older than usual, and more formidable, Sebastian was pleased to note: it was unlikely that Akakios would listen to a word she said in any case, but she'd certainly improved her chances.

Akakios beamed graciously, and Sebastian performed introductions. Hattie, to his delight, did not offer her hand, but sketched a little convent-school curtsey, her eyes demurely downcast. Doubtless Tim would get the bill for this unnatural conduct in due course, he reflected momentarily, then concentrated on the business in hand. Opening his briefcase, he gave Akakios Eugenides' memorandum of the property held and administered by him. While the welcome committee shivered on the pavement, trying bravely to maintain expressions of respectful interest, he took the abbot patiently through the document until he was absolutely clear about the way what he saw corresponded to the paper description. Tim and Hattie watched him carefully through this lengthy process, but the fraction of his countenance not obscured by hair was unrevealing.

Eventually, the abbot signalled his desire to go through into the garden. Tim opened the latch, and held the door for him. Though the day was dreary, it was looking very nice. Leeks and Brussels sprouts stood in rows; late roses, flourishing in a variety of unorthodox containers, still made a brave show. A couple of old men were working on a bed of winter cabbage in a corner. Akakios walked round without comment, acknowledging their greeting with a dignified bow. Hattie several times opened her mouth to speak, but subsided in response to Sebastian's urgent signals behind the abbot's broad back.

'I would like to inspect the house of the rector,' he announced in Greek, once he had toured the garden and they were back on the pavement.

'I'm afraid that is not possible, Your Holiness,' explained Sebastian. 'You can see for yourself that the main beam of the roof has rotted – look at the way it sags. In this damp climate, houses cannot be left empty for so long. It is not safe to enter, and the surveyor employed by Dr Claydon-Jones' committee has told us it is dangerous and beyond repair. The grounds are head-high with briars and brambles, and absolutely impenetrable, so we can't even walk round the outside. It'll all have to be pulled down.'

Akakios absorbed this information impassively, but it was evident that, used as he was to buildings made to last a thousand years or so which could be deserted for indefinite periods of time, the state of it had come as an unwelcome surprise. 'Why is the site of the Church not also wasteland?' he asked.

'Hattie, explain about the garden. Now's your chance,' hissed Sebastian. She smiled charmingly at the abbot, and began to talk: with Sebastian interpreting sentence by sentence, she told him about the reclamation project.

'But they have no right in the English law to use my land?' asked the abbot, searching for clarification.

'No, Your Holiness. Just custom.' Sebastian glanced at his watch. 'If Your Holiness permits, we have booked lunch at a suitable restaurant. If you have seen all you want, perhaps we could go, and resume after lunch in Miss Luke's office?' He was privately worried about time, and determined to keep things moving along. Things were going quite well, but he wanted to leave plenty of time for negotiations in the afternoon, and he'd have to be out of the place by four-thirty for George's farcical meeting, about which he was as sore as a boil. He was in no doubt, having spoken to Jeanene, what lay behind it, and perhaps imprudently, he had complained to Professor Savile, who had elected to treat it as an issue of discipline in the ranks, and insisted he go. His friend at the Riyadh had not been pleased.

Tim conducted Akakios and Sebastian to his car. Behind the abbot's back, Sebastian gave Hattie a thumbs-up sign to indicate that things were going as well as could be expected, and was rewarded by seeing her medieval countenance illuminated by a cheeky cockney grin.

Once Akakios had been fed — a lengthy process — he finally

condescended to talk business. Hattie got them all round a table in the Bridge Trust's conference room, and brought in a couple of experts: Michael Portman, the surveyor who worked for the Trust, and Dilip Dhesi. Once they were all settled, Akakios turned to Tim, and said, 'Tell me about your plan.' Sebastian cued Tim, who rose, and spread out a series of architectural drawings for Akakios's inspection. Since he had reluctantly followed Sebastian's advice, his drawings indicated the size and position of the fountain, but did not describe it in detail. Sebastian took over.

'As you can see for yourself, Your Holiness, the plan is for a monument to the happy relation of two nations: a fountain made for the most Christian Greek merchants of three hundred years ago, in honour of the joyful restoration of King Charles II to the throne of his father, and of the Mother of God. There are funds available for erecting it as a monument on some suitable site, due to the generosity of a number of Greek merchants of our own day, and of the English Millennium Fund. As Dr Claydon-Jones has suggested in this document, if the fountain is erected on this site, it will have a double association with the Greeks of London, to the honour of God and His Mother, and also of the lavra of St Michael.'

Akakios stroked his beard, and considered.

'Your Holiness, there are four choices before you. You can defer any decision, but following the death of the absolved Eugenides, you have no agent in London. Mr Dhesi could advise you, or we could try to find you a Greek-speaking lawyer, but you will need to commit time, and, I fear, money. You can put the two sites on the open market. Perhaps that will be the most profitable, but you will need to employ an agent, and again, it will commit an indefinite amount of time and money. Or you can consider the offers before you. Dr Claydon-Jones is empowered to offer you the price of the Rectory site; and Miss Luke advises me that the Southwark Residents Association, together with their Borough Council, are able to make a bid to buy their garden.

They are not wealthy people, and the bid is a little below the independent market valuation. You can, of course, accept one offer, but not the other; they are independent, but if you do, you are left, again, with the problem of disposing of the unwanted property. If you accept both these offers, then you will be able to conclude this business and go away knowing that affairs in England need never trouble you again. You will also have the satisfaction of knowing that a site long under the protection of St Michael is permanently consecrated to holy uses, and will carry the name of your lavra for ever. May I leave you to think, Your Holiness, while I explain to the others what I have just told you?' Akakios nodded, and Sebastian swiftly translated. When he fell silent, the abbot raised his head.

'Did you not say that you had got an independent assessment of the value of the land?' he asked.

'Yes. Mr Portman is a surveyor, whose credentials I can explain to you. The funding bid for Dr Claydon-Jones' project is based on meeting this valuation, and as you will see, the funds raised for the garden are within ten per cent of the valuation of that site.' Sebastian brought more papers out: Portman's valuation, the memoranda of funding pledges, and his own translations into Greek. Akakios put the papers side by side, running a thick, hirsute finger down the figures, his lips moving soundlessly in their thick nest of wiry hair. Hattie and Tim sat on tenterhooks, not daring to move, staring at his face.

'Dr Claydon-Jones, Miss Luke. I will accept the offers,' he said, finally.

'That means yes,' said Sebastian.

'Oh, that's super. Sebastian, tell him it's marvellous.'

'Dr Claydon-Jones and Miss Luke are very pleased.' Sebastian indicated Dil, who had been sitting patiently waiting for something to happen, drawing little pictures on the notepad in front of him. 'Mr Dhesi here is a solicitor. He has drawn up draft deeds of sale, with a notarised translation – we realised that your time in England is extremely short. If you want to act immediately, both Dr Claydon-Jones and Miss Luke are empowered to act on behalf of their committees, or alternatively, we can recommend a solicitor for you, and you can exchange contracts later. Dilip, love, can I have the contracts?' he added, switching into English. Dil produced his paperwork, sober-faced, and pushed it across the table. Sebastian glanced at the clock, which told him it was ten to four, and fretted internally.

'I will act now,' the abbot decided, after a pause for thought. Everyone round the table relaxed, except Sebastian, who had been rather hoping Akakios would choose to defer, thus bringing the meeting to an end. Oh, get a move on, he adjured silently, while the abbot applied himself to the documents, asking an occasional question, which Sebastian patiently referred to Hattie, Tim or Dil as appropriate. While Akakios read slowly through the contracts, he gradually achieved first a state of resignation to the inevitable, then a realisation that despite the inconvenience to himself, they had achieved something to be pretty pleased about. He scribbled a note on a piece of notepaper, and discreetly sent it round the table. When it reached Hattie, she found that it said, 'Darlings. PARTY. We must celebrate. At mine, eightish. I have to run after I've got old bloody off – ciao, xxx'.

Finally, Akakios nodded. Tim rose, and shook his hand, and so did Hattie. In turn, they clustered round, signing the deeds where Dil told them to, with Sebastian and Michael Portman as witnesses.

'Hattie,' hissed Sebastian, as soon as she had finished, 'can you call me a taxi? I've got to be out of here in less than five minutes.' She nodded, and slipped out to the phone.

XXII

Sebastian, having dropped Akakios off at his hotel, took the taxi on to the Institute of Classical Studies, where he hoped to make George's idiotic meeting with about a second to spare, if he had any luck at all with the traffic. Since the day was overcast, most of the vehicles on the road already had their lights on, making it look even later than it was, and he gave himself up to bad temper. An absolutely ridiculous hour to be going in; and made no better by the row he'd had with Professor Savile, who to his immense irritation, had quoted back at him an acidulous memo of his own (a response to some earlier outrage, now forgotten) about the advisability of getting admin into term rather than letting it dribble on into the vacations, even if it meant meeting in the evenings. He sighed gustily, and conscientiously began to rack his brains for constructive thoughts about graduate student recruitment, item one on the agenda.

He would doubtless have felt quite different about the meeting, and about George, had he been in a position to know what was going on in Mayfair. Edward, who was of course quite unaware of this development, was loitering in Mount Street. He wondered whether he dare go into the Mount Street Tavern for a drink, till it occurred to him that the place had got so smart since its refurbishment that dressed as he was, they would probably throw him out, and that even if they did not, he would be very conspicuous.

His office clothes and briefcase were in a locker in the Tottenham Court YMCA, where he often played squash. On this occasion, he had simply changed into shorts, walked out one door and in the other, and changed again into his yob gear. Since both yuppies and yobs abounded at the Y, no one had looked at him twice in either guise. A gun lay heavy in his right-hand jacket pocket. It was the hour of the dog and the wolf, when it is hard to tell friend from foe, and the first nip of autumn frost hung in the air, which was to the good. It meant that there were few people on the street, and those that there were, were absorbed with their own affairs, but it also made for a desperately uncomfortable wait. He had had trouble getting away from the office, and reached Mount Street later than he would have liked, so he had not seen Sebastian going in to the Riyadh Gallery. He shifted from foot to foot, trying to ignore the tension in his bladder and bowels. Just cold and stress, he told himself. Certainly, there was nothing to be done about it without taking his eyes off the Riyadh, which he was not prepared to consider. Shit, he really wanted to go... Desperately, he tried to think of something else. The two or three times he'd gone shooting with his father in happier days came back to him. The experiences were similar: aching boredom, sudden, swift movement...But as time went by, and the streetlights came on properly, he became increasingly uneasy. How long could looking at a few bits of silver possibly take? He'd've had to've been in there before five, or Edward would have seen him...He couldn't have got in much earlier, not with a day pissing about in Southwark, but he had certainly not come out. Visibility was not wonderful, but Sebastian's jaunty, loping walk would surely have been instantly recognisable?

It was only when the last light went out in the gallery, and a single man, manifestly not Sebastian, came out, got into a

Mercedes, and drove away, that Edward, angry and baffled, was forced to admit defeat. Walking down towards Oxford Street, where he thought he would be less conspicuous, he wondered what to do next. He would have to go back to the Y and pick up his clothes, and then go and consult with Lamprini, waiting for him in her hotel room. As he jogged along, gradually getting some circulation back into his half-frozen limbs, a second plan began to evolve. It depended on whether Sebastian lived alone, and was therefore risky, since he didn't know if he did or not. But if he did, then a very good scenario presented itself. A gay man, found in his flat... The police would almost certainly assume a pick-up who'd turned nasty, especially if he used something lying around rather than the gun, a long, heavy candlestick or something. Potentially, it was even an improvement on the Mount Street hit. If Sebastian turned out to have someone there, well, he'd just have to say that he'd dropped in on his way somewhere. It was risky, but not ridiculous.

Sebastian, blissfully unconscious of all this, rang home as soon as his meeting was over, and, as he had hoped, the phone was answered by Giles. He warned him of the imminent arrival of a band of thirsty and triumphant English aesthetes. Giles was unperturbed, and promised to tidy up.

'Don't go buying stuff, sweetheart,' warned Sebastian, 'I'll collect supplies on the way home.'

'Righto,' said Giles equably, and rang off. Sebastian then rang Jeanene, and asked her along to cheer her up: though it was obvious to everyone, including her, that she was better off with no supervisor at all than with George, she was understandably miserable, and anxious about her work. Sebastian, cursing himself for taking anything more on, had therefore offered to keep an informal eye on her progress till Katie got back. He felt sorry for her: she was a likeable little soul, and coming all the way from Oz only to be confronted with the likes of Mad George struck him as a somewhat undue dose of bad luck. He also had another reason for inviting her. It was obvious to any disinterested and reasonably observant bystander (though he was not sure it was obvious to Jeanene) that Dilip Dhesi, to whom he had taken a fancy, was distinctly smitten. Having recently fallen in love himself, Sebastian felt sentimentally disposed to play Cupid.

He got home at seven-thirty, in yet another taxi, with his briefcase, a case of wine, and a box full of beer, mineral water and etceteras. He let himself through the iron gate which protected the entrance to the block, put down the box, staggered upstairs with the wine and his briefcase, and kicked the door. Giles opened it almost at once, kissed him on the cheek, and sped downstairs for the rest of the supplies. Sebastian took the wine straight through to the kitchen, and then, returning to survey the living-room, began to laugh.

His salon was an elegant affair with olive-green walls, a fair amount of gilt, and accents in Pompeiian red, decorated with engravings and mounted panels of Coptic and Byzantine textiles. There was a good Turkish carpet, and most of the furniture was decent 1920s Vogue Regency. It was a décor with a Walter-Pater-ish, fin-de-siècle feel to it, suitable to an aesthetic and scholarly bachelor. Giles, however, apparently in the interests of cheerful-ness, had gone out and bought dozens and dozens of mixed dahlias, which he had distributed all over the room in every vase, jug, and receptacle that Sebastian possessed.

'Do you like them?' enquired Giles from the door, a little anxiously. 'I thought they'd look awfully jolly.'

Sebastian took the box of beer and crisps from him, put it down on the sofa, and embraced him reassuringly. 'Darling. I think they're lovely.'

'Oh, good.' Over Giles's shoulder, Sebastian suddenly observed that one of the vessels now replete with jolly dahlias was a vase of Samian ware, two thousand years old, in perfect condition, and worth a small fortune. As soon as Giles's attention was elsewhere, he would have to effect a swift substitution in case there was a disaster. He disengaged himself gently. 'I'd better go and wash. It's been a long, hard day, I must be absolutely fetid. If you can unpack the wine and put a lot of glasses out, I'll have a two-minute bath, and then I'll come and help.'

'Should I change?' asked Giles. Sebastian stepped back, and considered him thoughtfully. Giles was wearing a pair of russet moleskin jeans, and a grey Viyella shirt with the sleeves rolled up and the neck open, exposing a muscular throat. He was rangy, but powerfully built, and sunburnt in a way that spoke unmistakably of hard work in the open air rather than gyms and sun-beds. He had a mop of chestnut curls, an angular, brown-cheeked face, and at that moment, an anxious expression.

'No,' said Sebastian, tenderly. 'You look absolutely perfect.'

Swiftly, he showered, doused himself with Acqua di Gigli, and put on a pair of white trousers, a beautiful, full-sleeved, heavy linen shirt which he had bought in rural Greece, and a striped silk waistcoat. Slipping on a couple of rings, he emerged resplendent to help Giles in the kitchen. Together they made crudités, and dolloped hummus and tortilla chips into bowls, while Sebastian filled Giles in properly on the day's events.

By nine, the little party was in full swing. Tim had brought Anthony, Hattie had brought Alice the lurcher, and the air was thick with mutual congratulation like the aftermath of a successful Cup Final.

'Darling,' said Giles, as Sebastian passed by with a bottle in either hand.

'Mmm?'

'Jeanene's just told me she's never been out of London. Isn't that awful? I was just saying, she really must come and visit us at Rodmarton.'

'That'd be great,' said Jeanene politely. 'Gloucestershire's supposed to be really beaut, isn't it?'

'Far too pretty for its own good,' said Hattie, overhearing this exchange as she approached Sebastian for a refill. 'It's got very touristy. You can't move for tour-buses in the Cotswolds all summer, but they've probably tailed off by now. No one's got round to marketing a "Season of Mists and Mellow Fruitfulness Experience", though it's probably only a matter of time. Actually, Giles, I'd love to see what you're doing. Perhaps I could bring Jeanene out to you one weekend?'

'I'll tell you what,' said Giles, 'why not come tomorrow? Sebastian's got to lunch with his Greek monks, and go to Highgrove. If you came to the cottage mid-morningish, I could show you the workshop, and explain what I'm doing. Then we could all go into Tetbury together – Seb can meet up with his monks, and I've been meaning to pop in and see Bremner & Orr, – I don't know if you've heard of them? They're a rather good design consultancy in Long Street who sell some stuff for me. You might be interested. We can get some lunch ourselves at the Snooty Fox or somewhere, and afterwards I'll show you a bit of Gloucestershire.'

Jeanene looked imploringly at Hattie for guidance. One aspect of English English which still had her confused was sorting out polite insincerities from genuine offers.

'That sounds absolutely lovely,' said Hattie, smiling reassuringly at the young Australian, 'I'd really enjoy that. I haven't been out of London for months.'

'That's settled, then,' said Sebastian. 'Dilip, d'you want to come along?' Dil, who was talking to Anthony, jumped when he heard his name, and turned round. Sebastian explained the whole plan to him.

'Sure,' he said, rather constrainedly, 'I'd like that.' Realising that they were all looking at him, he smiled in embarrassment, and fell silent.

'Empty glasses, anyone?' said Sebastian, breaking up the awkward moment. The doorbell rang. 'Dilip, could you get that please? Buzz whoever it is in, and see what they want.'

Dil, glad of a moment's respite, went through to the little hall, pressed the button which released the street gate, and, when he heard footsteps approaching, opened the flat door. To his complete astonishment, he found himself face to face with Edward Lupset dressed as an Arsenal supporter, with utter dismay written all over his face.

'Hi, Edward,' he said, recovering himself and gesturing eloquently at the shirt, 'I didn't know you were a Gunner.'

Edward, looking stricken, opened and shut his mouth like a goldfish, but nothing came out. 'Sebastian's having a party,' Dil continued. 'Are you coming in?'

'No,' said Edward hoarsely. 'I'll come back.' He turned and fled: Dil, standing with the doorknob in his hand, heard his feet clattering down the stairs.

'Weird,' he said to the empty lobby, and frowned in puzzlement. Like many Asian boys, he had never felt that the national obsession had much to say to him, but he was perfectly aware that, post Nick Hornby, the most unlikely people appeared to have acquired an interest in football, and particularly in the Arsenal. Ed, however, seemed an unlikely recruit – if he got into anything like that, it would surely be rugby? More to the point, what was he doing there? Dil felt as though there was something he was not quite getting: he was so preoccupied with his own crucial dilemma that this minor puzzle was not getting his full attention, but he could not rid himself of a feeling that he was being somehow obtuse. Was Edward gay? Insofar as he had thought about it at all, he had always assumed not, but on the other hand, the man had never actually mentioned a girl in his life, even as a friend. Perhaps he was deeply closety, in that public-school way? That might account for the clothes, and also for the way he looked so aghast, poor sod. With Sebastian so obviously newly-wed, it was maybe better not to mention the incident? Dil, whose experience of gay social circles was limited, felt strongly that he was out of his depth.

'Anything?' called Sebastian, as he came back in.

'No,' said Dil curtly. He was tense and nervous, disinclined to talk to anyone, but made an effort, fearing that he was being rude. 'Sebastian, you aren't interested in football, are you?'

'Football, *qu'est-ce-que-c'est?* Why?'

Dil shrugged. 'It doesn't matter. Just a thought.' He turned away to pour himself his first glass of wine of the evening, and slipped quietly into Sebastian's bedroom for a moment or two by himself. It was with a curious jolt in the stomach that he realised immediately that Jeanene had got there first. She was standing by the window, looking out across the rooftops of Coptic Street towards the colossal dark bulk of the British Museum, apparently lost in thought. She had not heard him come in.

He stood in the doorway looking at her. She had put her hair up again, and her nape, rising out of a round-necked grey jumper, shone white and slender against the darkness outside. One or two little wisps of hair had escaped the comb, and were beginning to spiral down her neck again. She had not moved, but as he stood there, hardly breathing, he knew she was now aware of him. He put his glass down gently on a bookcase, and moved silently towards her, until he stood just behind her. Still she did not turn, but her breath came a little faster, and he could see a pulse beating under the tender skin on the side of her neck.

With a feeling of jumping into deep water, he took the final irrevocable step forward, and put his arms round her. She gave a little sigh as his lips touched her skin, and moved at last, turning round to face him.

'I always promised my mum,' said Dil some time later, 'that if I ever brought her a white daughter-in-law, I'd give her six months' notice in writing. I reckon I owe her a letter.'

'Leave it out, Dil!' protested Jeanene. 'You hardly know me.'

'Are you coming home with me?' he demanded.

'Yes.'

'Then I'm going to know you a damned sight better, aren't I?
Look, d'you want to go on this Cotswold taste tour tomorrow?'

'Er—'

'That means yes, doesn't it?' He grinned at her, suddenly
immensely cheerful. 'It's fine by me, honestly. Come on. Is this
your coat?'

He charged out of the bedroom, and found Hattie, talking to
Sebastian. 'Hattie, love. Could you pick us both up from Ealing
tomorrow? Sebastian. It's been a great party. See you tomorrow.'
As they looked at one another, bereft of speech, Jeanene emerged
from the bedroom, head held high, but blushing like a peony.

'Er, goodnight,' said Sebastian feebly.

'G'night all,' she replied, failing to meet his eyes, crossed the
room, and vanished into the night with Dil.

'Lumme,' said Sebastian, once the door was safely shut, 'how
did that happen? He looks like Young Lochinvar or something.'

'Search me,' said Hattie. 'But being swept off your feet by Dil
Dhesi must be a bit like being swept up by a tornado. Oh, well.
Good luck to them.'

'Okay,' said Lamprini wearily. 'What happened?'

'He was having a sodding party. It wasn't even him that
answered the door.'

Lamprini looked at him thoughtfully. She longed to tell him
exactly what she thought of him, but it was obvious he was near
the end of his tether. He would have to be handled carefully if
they were going to get out of this mess in one piece.

'Forget tonight,' she said soothingly, crossing the room to her
mini-bar, and peering into the fridge. 'What would you like to
drink?'

'Scotch, please.'

She took some Perrier water for herself, poured him a drink,
and carried it across to where he sat sprawled in her hotel room's
only armchair. 'Let's think about tomorrow. It *must* be tomorrow.

For one thing, we don't know what this man Raphael's doing after this. For two, I've got to get back to Greece Sunday. Raphael's in Rodmarton, maybe tonight, maybe early tomorrow. Come and look at the map.' She had a Michelin touring map of the British Isles with her, which she spread out on the hotel's inadequate desk, under the light. 'Rodmarton's here, just about fifteen kilometres from Tetbury, on the A433. When is Raphael in Tetbury?'

Edward thought hard. 'For lunch,' he said eventually. 'Say twelve at the earliest, probably twelve-thirty.'

'And he's got this friend, driving him. We've got to separate them. Ed, this is a scenario. We wait at Rodmarton and watch till they leave. They're driving along. I'll have got a hired car. I drive along after them, and somehow, I make an accident. My problem; I'll work it out. They stop, I stop. Then I have hysterics, and I don't speak no English, you see? We know Raphael speaks Greek. So I get him to come with me, maybe to a garage, or the police, whatever he thinks. Once I've got him on his own, you can make a hit.'

'But where am I supposed to be?' objected Edward. 'If he sees me in the car, he'll know something funny's going on. And he'll recognise me. Look, this is crazy, Lamprini. We aren't the kind of people who do this sort of thing. We're out of our depth.'

'No, there's got to be an answer,' insisted Lamprini. 'We're intelligent, right? So we can solve problems...another car?' They sat in gloomy silence, thinking.

'I know,' said Edward suddenly. 'One of my flatmates is a motorbike nut. And he's spending the weekend with his girlfriend's parents. I could take the bike. He's got a suit of leathers, too.'

'Ed, that's perfect. No one looks twice at a young guy on a bike. And the helmet hides your face. Also, bikes are more – slippy? Is that the word?'

'Manoeuvrable?'

'Yes, that's what I mean. You can get behind me or in front of me, and if you stop, you just fiddle with something, and people think you've got engine trouble. Bikes are always stopping. We've got an answer.'

XXIII

Hattie duly collected Dil and Jeanene from Ealing at nine-thirty the following morning, which was grey and dull, though not quite committing itself to rain. As she observed indulgently, though Jeanene looked a little shy and conscious of her last night's clothes, they were both transparently happy and obviously underslept. Even if Gloucestershire turned out to be pretty dreary, they almost certainly weren't in a mood to be critical.

'Jeanene, you'd better go in the front,' she said cheerfully. 'You're the one who hasn't seen any of this before. Dil, you'll have to go in the back with Alice.'

'That's okay. I get on with Alice.' He bent to release the catch on the front seat, and slipped into the back. Alice sniffed at him briefly, raising mild eyebrows, put her head on his thigh, and went back to sleep before he had even finished strapping himself in.

'Heigh-ho for the scenic M4,' said Hattie, as they moved off. 'I warn you, it's all pretty dull as far as Swindon. You can drop off if you like. It gets better after that.'

As they drove westwards, through what Hattie described as the dull bit, it was the sheer size of London that impressed itself on Jeanene; the mile after mile of little rows of houses, shopping parades, big garages, blocks of flats, repeating endlessly. There was a sort of oppression in the idea of the millions and millions of lives being lived in a confined space, as if she were passing through an ant-hill. Dull? Could you learn just to ignore all this? Trying to digest this new consciousness of the sheer quantity of human life which happens within the belt of the M25, she also began to realise that the sameness and repetitiveness of bypass architecture was disorienting her, gradually unsettling her basic sense of where she was. The London she had been learning her way around since July had sometimes seemed grotesquely familiar, mapped out by Eng Lit 101 from Shakespeare to Dickens, but the featureless city which Hattie was navigating was no part of that world of literary reference and cultural heritage. It was more like Sydney, in fact, because it simply existed; mile after mile of it, without any cues or reference points whatsoever. And what went on there? – nothing she knew gave her the slightest clue. But it was Dil's world, she knew. A sort of panic gripped her: what did she know about any of the stuff she'd got herself into, London, Hindus, ancient Greek, anything? She felt as if she were bungee-jumping into the future. She and Dil had ended up spending the night locked in one another's arms talking for hour after hour. Both self-sufficient, private, essentially loners, the sheer relief and sweetness of trusting another human being had been overwhelming for them both. Looking back on the last twelve hours or so, she almost found herself doubting that any of it had actually happened, the whole experience seemed so far outside anything she had expected. His weird certainty was infectious, but she had always been a planner, a one-step-at-a-time girl. Sometimes you just had to jump, though...

Jeanene lapsed into abstraction, brooding about Dil, and staring unseeingly out of the window. Hattie, glancing at her preoccupied face, left her to it, and stuck one of her long-car-journey soothing classics in the cassette-player. A random Mozart symphony washed over them; Dil, in the back, seemed to be dozing. Hattie alone observed their eventual escape from the tentacles of the outer suburbs, and the way the terrain opened out into farmland interspersed with dormitory towns.

'Hey,' said Jeanene, the best part of an hour later, startling her, 'We've just passed a sign for Avebury. Why have I heard of it?'

'There's a huge stone circle,' said Hattie. 'God knows how many thousands of years old.'

'I thought that was Stonehenge?'

'That's a different one,' said Dil from the back seat, waking up at the sound of her voice. 'It's not very far either. All this bit's sort of Weirdo Land. Avebury's south off the next junction, Stonehenge is a bit further south than that, and a bit west there's Glastonbury, which is pretty well Nutter Capital of Britain. It's where the New Age Celts get together.'

'I thought Wales and Scotland were the Celtic bits?' said Jeanene, puzzled.

'Oh, yes. This is something different. According to my mate Digger, Celticness is a state of mind. I bet no one'd say that in Glasgow. I mean, he said *I* could be Celtic if I liked, and I'm not even white.'

'What Dil means is that the New Agers are making it up as they go along,' supplied Hattie, 'so don't expect it to make too much sense. What's going on here is basically a lot of Anglo-Saxon English people trying to get themselves some kind of spiritual identity, only they don't want any of the nasty stuff which goes with it. Half the time I think they're trying to reinvent folk Catholicism without the Church, and anyway, they don't seem to realise there's downsides to being a Celt. Like being screwed by the English, for starters.'

'You're probably right about all that,' objected Dil. 'I wouldn't know. But some of them are serious people. Digger, for instance. He's a total lunatic in some ways, and I don't suppose he knows much history, but I've got a lot of respect for him.'

'Oh, I'm sure a lot of them are worth knowing,' said Hattie. 'At least they're questioning things, and I'm all for questions, and they're stirring things up a bit. It's just that they're settling for such a bloody pathetic collection of answers.' They lapsed into silence, and a few minutes later, a blue sign hove in view. 'Our exit. That's us off motorways for the morning, thank God. It starts getting nice after this. We'll go up through Malmesbury, which is sweet, and pick up the 433 a bit higher up. You'll like Malmesbury, Jeanene. It's got a stonking great medieval church, and a lovely old-fashioned marketplace.'

The rest of the drive was a journey through an implausibly beautiful vista of dreaming shires. The sun was beginning to struggle through the clouds, and was gilding the yellows, browns and russets of the shaggy hedgerows. Languid and a little lightheaded from lack of sleep, Jeanene let the pretty little towns and villages flow past her, the watermeadows, where white mist lay in the hollows, cattle grazed, and pollard willows stood in gaunt rows, the rich, luxurious mantle of trees and bushes lining the road, and standing even between the fields. Again, it meant literature to her, mostly poetry; Keats, Browning, Housman: a landscape described so often it was impossible simply to see it. She was back in Heritage again; but this time, she'd seen where the people in between lived. It didn't look quite the same, once you'd thought about that.

It was twenty to twelve when they reached Rodmarton, which was at the other end of a narrow road so bosky that at many points, even the autumn-lightened trees met overhead, making a brown-gold tunnel. Hattie drove cautiously through the main village, peering at the grey Cotswold stone houses, looking for the school, which Giles had given her as a range-marker. Since it was of no concern to her, she did not consciously observe that several cars were parked on the side of the tiny, triangular village green, nor that one of them still contained the driver, apparently busy in contemplation of a map. The school duly became visible on the right, and as she approached more closely, she spotted an unmade track going left, with a small sign saying 'The Grooms' House'.

She swung up it, and as she had expected, saw a little building-group, marooned by the side of an enormous field: a small, utilitarian brick barn or storage shed, and beside it, two minute cottages now knocked into one. They had arrived. Giles's ancient Morris Traveller was parked on a patch of gravel by the side of the house, up against a grey stone wall, and she slid her own Renault in behind it. As she did so, Giles bounced out to greet them.

'Super to see you. Did you have a good journey?'

'It was fine. Sorry we're a bit late, it took longer than I thought. Is this the studio?' Hattie asked in her turn.

'Yes. It's ideal, really. They used to keep haycarts here or something. The whole lot became redundant when they stopped having horses – they stopped having grooms living in, of course, and the tractors and things they've got these days live in enormous great sheds like aircraft hangars. Anyway, this is so far from the main farm buildings it's inconvenient for them, and not secure enough. I was looking for somewhere affordable round here with a bit of space, and they let me lease it.' He was already walking towards it, as he spoke, and they followed him. 'The door's round this side.'

'I'd better leave Alice outside. She's a street dog, so she's pretty sensible. She'll just potter around, and have a sniff at things.'

The building was immaculately clean, with bare brick walls. A variety of mysterious pulleys and hoists were suspended from the rafters, there were huge plastic tubs containing materials, filing-cabinets, shelves and shelves of interesting objects, a couple of worktables, and a model's throne on a podium. Photographs and working sketches were pinned everywhere, and the air was permeated with the flat, limy smell of fresh plaster. Jeanene and Dil wandered about, looking curiously at samples and models, while Giles and Hattie plunged into an intricate conversation about pargeting.

'It's fantastic, isn't it?' said Sebastian as he came in, immaculate in the sober glory of his best suit. 'Giles is the only person left in the country who can do work of this quality.'

'What's this?' asked Dil, indicating a high-relief modello of a stag embroiled with a rearing serpent. 'It's practically three-dimensional. What's it for?'

'Oh, that's a repair,' said Giles. 'You get that sort of very high-relief plasterwork in some Jacobean rooms. Bits started falling off one in Cambridge, and Rattee & Kett retained me to make it good.'

'What Giles means,' interjected Sebastian, 'is that it was so bloody impossible to do that the best firm of restoring builders in the country had to call him in.'

'Mmm,' said Giles modestly. 'What I'd really like, of course, would be for someone to commission a new one. I love doing repairs, but just for once, it would be nice to design one from scratch.'

'We need to find the right patron,' said Hattie at once. 'I'll have a think about it.'

Jeanene, meanwhile, was looking at a decorative plaster frieze, laid out carefully in sections along a shelf: oakleaves, acorns, an occasional jay half-lost among the foliage.

'Is this William Morris?' she asked. Giles came up beside her.

'Arthur Crofts. You're bang-on for style and period, though. In fact, I think he may actually have done some work for Morris & Co. The original moulds turned up in a barn somewhere, and I've made up a run of it for a client in the States.'

'It's beautiful,' said Jeanene, touching a crisply carved leaf with a gentle finger. Somewhere in the room, an old-fashioned eight-day clock struck the hour, startling them.

'Oh, God,' said Sebastian, 'is that the time? Look, my dears. I'm sorry to break this up, but I'm afraid someone's going to have to drive me to the Talbot.'

'Of course,' said Hattie at once. 'I could stay here all day, but we've got plenty of things to do. It's been very nice to see it at all.'

'I'll just go and get my coat and the keys,' said Giles, disappearing in Sebastian's wake. They followed him out of the studio, and a few moments later, he reappeared, wearing a battered, ancient Barbour. He locked up, and they strolled back to the car, leaves crunching crisply underfoot. The sky had cleared completely, and settled to a clear, pale blue.

'What I think we'd better do, Hattie,' said Giles, 'is I'll take Seb to the Talbot, park the car in Tetbury somewhere, and get in with you three. I'm afraid she isn't exactly the fastest thing on wheels, but I'm fond of the old girl. You won't mind going back to Tetbury after we've had our jolly?'

'Of course not. I'll keep behind you till we get there, so we'll be sure not to lose each other.'

Giles and Sebastian got into the old Morris. Hattie's Renault was obstructing their exit, so she backed a little, and then slipped the car adroitly round them, and further up by the hedge. As the Morris turned in the space in front of the barn, and headed out into Rodmarton, the unwisdom of this became apparent, since the nearside wheels of the car had gone off the gravel into a patch of treacherously yielding Gloucestershire clay. Jeanene and Dil had to get out again to lighten it while she manoeuvred back to safety.

Down by the bus-stop, Lamprini observed the nose of the Morris emerging from the farm-track, let in the clutch of her hired Nissan, and followed it. She was round the curve of the road, and out of sight of Manor Farm before Hattie's Renault escaped from the mud and emerged from the same gap. Edward did not observe Hattie's exit either. Unrecognisable in Alan's leathers and helmet, he was waiting down the village's other street, which ran down to the green at an angle, where he could see Lamprini's car, but neither see nor be seen from the Old Stables. When he saw the blue car emerge, he looked at his watch, and gave her four minutes' start before settling his helmet and starting his machine.

Hattie, meanwhile, pottered slowly towards Tetbury. She was keen not to catch up with the Morris, which she doubted could do more than forty-five or so, and it was a lovely country road, lined with stone walls almost concealed by undergrowth, hazel and beech mostly. The gentle, rolling countryside beyond, visible through occasional gaps, gave them beautiful glimpses of long fields: winter wheat, hedges, and mist. Periodically a car, usually a four-wheel drive, came up behind her till it almost touched, then accelerated round her bad-temperedly when she refused to be hurried. Used to bumper-to-bumper London driving, she paid them no attention.

Apart from the mannerless rich people in their new Isuzus and Range Rovers, the road was mainly populated by motorbikes; quite a few of them, which struck her as odd. Neither the inhabitants nor the visitors she expected to find in the Cotswolds seemed the type for bikes. She was just about to say so, when she came round a bend, and braked hard, thanking her stars that there was nothing behind her. Fifty yards further on, Giles's Morris lay at an angle off the road, its front nearside wing mashed against a stone field-wall. A blue Sunny was pulled up beside it, and Sebastian was standing on the verge, gesticulating lavishly, in earnest conversation with an immaculately dressed and obviously foreign young woman, who seemed to be in tears, while Giles mooched round the car, gloomily assessing the damage. 'I'd better take Sebastian on to Tetbury,' she said, adding this all up. 'He mustn't be late.' She parked the car, and got out. 'Sebastian!' she called, but got no further. The woman, startled, swung round to stare at her, and in that moment, Jeanene erupted from the front passenger seat, her voice shrill with warning.

'Sebastian! *That's the Greek woman!* The one from the pharmacy! The one I thought was trying to kill someone!' Sebastian gaped at her for a long moment, then memory caught up with him: it was possible actually to see his brain firing into life. Dil, meanwhile, scrambling out of the back of the car in his turn, added Jeanene's words up with his accumulated, half-unconscious doubts and worries about Edward's strange behaviour, and shouted, 'Be careful! There's something bloody funny going on.'

The Greek woman, as she absorbed this completely unexpected intervention, stood paralysed with astonishment, but she was the first to recover herself: she turned on her high heels, and raced for her car. As she did so, Alice the lurcher, her deep gaze-hound's instinct to chase anything that fled suddenly activated, hurtled from the back of the Renault, and went after her. The Greek beat her to the car by a fraction of a second and scrambled in, slamming the door as Alice's teeth closed impotently on the handle, and accelerated away.

'Heel!' screamed Hattie, as Alice showed every sign of setting off in pursuit.

'Will someone tell me what's supposed to be happening?' wailed Sebastian.

'Listen,' said Jeanene urgently. 'That's the Greek woman who filled a prescription for a really high-dosage diabetic drug, back in the summer. I thought about it for weeks. The night we met, remember?'

'And whatever's going on,' added Dil, putting two and two together at speed, 'I bet Edward Lupset's got something to do with it. He was the guy who came to your door last night. There's not likely to be two sets of weird things going on; there's a connection. And I can think of an obvious Greek link, it's this Eugenides he was seeing, isn't it?'

Sebastian's face darkened, and he swung round to Jeanene. 'What'd happen to someone who took this stuff if it wasn't prescribed for them?' he demanded.

'Oh, they'd get dopey and disoriented. They'd start hallucinating a bit, and they'd probably go into a diabetic coma and die, in the end.'

'He killed Eugenides,' snarled Sebastian, as the different bits of information suddenly meshed together in his mind. 'The treacherous little bastard.'

A motorcyclist came round the bend, and slowed right down, looking at them curiously.

'That's Edward!' shouted Dil, catching something he recognised in the posture of the figure, the familiar way that he was peering mistrustfully forward, shoulders slightly hunched, and chin stuck out. The biker immediately confirmed his impression by reacting: he hastily opened the throttle, causing the front wheel of the bike to rear alarmingly off the ground, and accelerated down the road.

'Catch him!' yelled Sebastian, incandescent with rage. 'I want to wring his bloody neck!'

'You can't catch a motorbike with a Renault five,' said Hattie. 'I'll go after the woman, whoever she is.'

'I've just thought,' said Dil suddenly. 'She must be Ed's Greek lawyer. I'll explain later.'

Hattie was already heading for her car when a squadron of dirty, powerful bikes roared up the road, temporarily blocking it, and rendering further speech impossible. Dil grinned wolfishly. His eyes were very bright, crackling with energy, and he stood very straight, looking suddenly like a Rajput warrior prince about to give Clive of India hell on a plate. 'We need the cavalry,' he said suddenly, and strode purposefully out into the road to flag down the bikers. To Sebastian's astonishment, a group of them stopped, and regarded them with apparent curiosity. A tall, thin man in worn leathers, straddling his machine with one booted toe to the ground, pushed up the visor of his battered helmet, and looked them over.

'Need some help, mate?' he asked, civilly enough.

'We need to catch a bent lawyer on a big bike. There's no time to explain. Can you give us a hand?'

The biker absorbed this statement impassively, and nodded. 'Who's coming, then?'

'Not us, bro. We're chasing someone else,' explained Hattie, and ran for her car, followed by Jeanene.

The biker assessed the situation, and turned to his friends, idling in the road waiting for him. 'We need two rides,' he shouted.

'I'll do it,' said a powerful, hippie-looking diesel-dyke, wheeling forward, while a burly man who looked like a bricklayer moved silently up beside her. The first biker waved a hand, and made introductions.

'Saffron. Keith.'

'I'm Dil. This is Sebastian, and that's Giles over by the car.'

While these amenities were being observed, the other bikes wheeled aside to let Hattie through. Giles, who had been squatting by the nearside front wheel of his Morris mourning over the damage throughout this exchange, straightened up, and strode forward. 'Who are you?' he asked, bewildered.

The biker grinned evilly, exposing blackened, gappy teeth. 'The Albion Warband, matey. Archdruid Merlin speaking.'

Giles, his face blank with bewilderment, turned for help to Dil, the only person present who looked as though he had a clue what was going on. 'Is that woman trying to do Sebastian in?' he demanded, focusing on the essential.

'I think so. God knows why.'

'Then I'm jolly well coming.'

'So am I,' said Sebastian quickly, before he could change his mind.

'Okay, then,' said the druid. 'All aboard that's coming aboard.' Dil got up behind Merlin, while Sebastian hitched a ride from the formidable Saffron, and Giles doubled with Keith. Merlin waved at the rest of his group. 'Tell the troops I'll see 'em at Glastonbury,' he yelled, then the three bikes roared off in pursuit of Edward, followed at her best pace by Alice, who had been forgotten in the excitement.

Hattie, meanwhile, was already slaloming down the winding country road, as fast as she dared.

'How much time've we lost?' asked Jeanene breathlessly.

'That can't have taken two minutes,' said Hattie, 'she's not far ahead. She'll have to slow down in Tetbury, it'll be busy. And she's got a road full of bikes to contend with, remember.'

They careered down the road, looking anxiously ahead as it dipped and swung through the rolling Cotswolds. When it opened out a little, Jeanene spotted a fleeing blue dot, embroiled in a bluebottle-like swarm of motorbikes, possibly belonging to druids.

'There she is!'

'Right,' said Hattie, praying for a clear road. They were gaining on the Greek, who in turn was gradually being outpaced by the bikes. All too soon, a sign that Tetbury welcomed careful drivers flashed past at speed, followed by a random straggle of peripheral development. 'I daren't slow down,' gasped Hattie, 'I might lose her.' In fact, they caught up with her almost immediately. With a German tour-bus trying to turn in front of her, and occupying the whole of the crossroads, even Lamprini was unable actually to keep going. But she saw the Renault coming up in her rear mirror, and the moment it was physically possible to do so, she swerved to the left, and shot straight down the middle of Long Street in a blare of indignant hooting from all sides. Hattie put the heel of her hand on her horn and kept it there, to warn everyone she was coming. Wailing like a banshee, the Renault stuck to the tail of the Nissan as if it was on tow, the rows of expensive antique-dealers on either side a blur of grey stone and hanging baskets. At the bottom of the road, coming up far too fast, was the Butter Market, with exits on either side of it, a crossroads and a mini-roundabout; cars were approaching from five different directions, all sounding their horns.

'Holy God,' said Hattie, for Lamprini, in the panic of the moment, had allowed Continental reflexes to take over and was hurtling the wrong way round the roundabout, emerging on the right-hand side of the road, and heading straight towards an enormous Land Rover at sixty miles an hour. As the aghast driver stood on his brakes, with a squeal of tortured rubber, Lamprini, desperate to lose speed, wrenched her wheel viciously, and careered up the pavement straight into a plate-glass shop-front, which exploded.

A sunburst of glass shards lifted slowly, glittering, from the point of impact, and crashed musically to the ground, followed by a soft, plumping rain of overdressed teddy bears and hedgehogs in mob-caps. Hattie parked her car on a double yellow line, got out and leaned against it, rubber-kneed, while a crowd of indignant motorists, shoppers, monks, and tourists converged on the blue Nissan. Lamprini emerged from it slowly, obviously shaken. It was self-evidently pointless to try and run, so she stood amid the glass and the teddy bears in her Gucci shoes with tears streaming down her face, and screamed Greek invective at Hattie, God, Jeanene, Edward and fate with infant lack of inhibition. Around her, motorists shouted, and the owner of the teddy bear emporium wailed in the background unheeded.

Abbot Akakios came out of the Talbot and approached with ponderous tread, having observed Hattie standing white and trembling by her car. He frowned magisterially at his country-woman's language – unlike Tetbury at large, he naturally understood what she was saying – and bent, with some difficulty, to pick up a teddy. It was wearing a little cap, and a dinky knitted sweater embroidered with the words 'I'm a Cotswold Bear', and the soles of its feet were made of Paisley-print Liberty cotton. He turned it over and over in his square, hairy hands, as if he expected it to offer him some kind of a clue to the mystery which is modern England.

While everyone was trying to make themselves heard, flashing blue lights and a wailing siren announced the arrival of the police. The officer drew up by the Talbot Hotel and got out of the car, producing a sudden diminuendo in the general noise-level and, as he crunched towards the Nissan, eventually silence, broken only by a small blond child, who, oblivious to the high-octane drama surrounding him, emerged suddenly from the ring of bystanders, picked his way carefully across the sea of broken glass, and chose a bright pink bear out of the soft, furry carnage.

'Lovely Teddy,' he said gravely.

Sebastian, Giles and Dil, meanwhile, were racing down the A433 with the Celtic eco-warriors, in triangle formation with Merlin and Dil at the apex.

'There he is,' yelled Dil, with Merlin's grubby blond mane whipping his face as he leaned forward to shout in his ear. Merlin nodded, and waved a clenched fist to alert his troops.

Edward, at first, though he was conscious of bikers behind him, did not realise for some time that they were after him: he was keeping a wary eye in the mirror for the Renault, though he didn't expect to see it. It was only an unexpected glimpse as he rounded a bend, of a bike ridden by a big fat woman in black and red leather doubled up with a helmetless, dark-haired man in an immaculate suit who could only be Sebastian, that told him that the enemy had unexpectedly managed to summon assistance.

It was many years since Edward had ridden a bike, and he was reluctant to race against pros, but panic spurred him on. Taking advantage of an oncoming bend, which he hoped would conceal the manoeuvre from his pursuers, he took the bike off the Tetbury road, and careered down a country lane going God alone knew where. Merlin, fortunately, took the bend wide, spotted him as he apparently vanished down a rabbit hole, and flung up a warning hand.

Edward hurtled on, the bike shuddering beneath him as he pressed it for maximum performance, the hedgerows blurring to either side. The road opened up a little, and he put on more speed, only to realise he was facing disaster; a tractor with a trailer-load of hay was puttering away from him at twenty miles an hour hugely burdened with great, golden Swiss Rolls, while a horsebox coming the other way was trying to squeeze past it. There was no hope for it: Edward shot through the open gate of the stubble-field from whence the hay had come, and roared up the slope, hoping to pick up another road on the other side of the rise.

The eco-warriors, slowing down for the hazards ahead, took only a moment to spot his silhouetted figure on the crest of the golden field, and streamed through the gate after him.

'Forward on!' yelled Giles; reverting to type. The ancient spirit of the hunt was abroad and the riders were in its grip; a primitive madness, older by far than the bikers' dream of druidry. Though only two out of the six had any more idea of who they were chasing or why than the dog Alice, the simple urge to run down a quarry had overtaken any rational considerations whatever. It was a fairly even contest: the double weight on the pursuing bikes was a handicap on off-road, but the paladins of Albion were equal to the challenge. They roared up and over the gentle curve of the hill, and saw from its crest the rest of the great field spread below them, with Edward crossing it diagonally, going like the clappers, blue smoke spilling from his exhaust. The field they were in was completely hedged, with stone wall visible through the thinning foliage; impassable, except for the bottom corner, where it seemed to melt into a little coppice, the meeting-point of three fields. Beyond, there was red ploughland to the north, with bare, ugly clods gaping at the sky, and winter wheat to the south; and beyond that again, on the far side of the wheat, another hedge, and through the gaps in it, an occasional glimpse of traffic which implied the presence of a road. It was obvious what Edward would try to do: as one, the bikers arrowed down the hillside, making for the wood. Being reaped but not yet ploughed, the ground was hard and relatively easy to negotiate, though Sebastian, urban, urbane and unheroic, clutched the beefy waist of his dreadlocked Boadicea in a deathlike grip as the machine bounced and jolted beneath them, and imprecated his overworked patron saint all the way down.

When Edward shot into the wood, the three bikes were only yards behind him. They caught, as he did, a glimpse of an opening between the trees, a little path, a flash of emerald, the colour of a well-kept bowling-green – then, hastily reining back their growling, farting steeds as the message sank in – they were also able to see that the green was a duckweed-covered dew-pond, presumably made for watering cattle, and that Edward was careering unstoppably into it. His bike went straight into the water, coughed horribly, and died, stuck fast in the clay, while Edward somersaulted over the handlebars and disappeared with a splash.

The knights of Albion leaped off their bikes, and ran down to the edge of the water, which stirred and heaved: heavy bubbles rose to the surface and broke under the thick layer of duckweed, releasing an appalling stink of methane and ancient cowshit. Edward rose from the turbid water like Grendel's mother, water pouring from his helmet, plastered with mud and clumps of weed, his face streaked with dirt and tears. Wild-eyed, beyond all sense, he staggered to his feet, and hauled a gun from his pocket. Holding it in both hands, he aimed it at Sebastian, and pressed the trigger. Nothing happened.

'You little swine!' roared Giles. Before Edward had absorbed the realisation that a revolver bought for cash in a pub carpark is about as likely to work first time as a video similarly acquired, Giles charged obliviously into the pond, strode through the waist-high, stinking water, and punched him in the solar plexus. Edward fell backwards, with another mighty splash.

'Giles, darling,' said Sebastian wearily, 'that was very sweet of you, but could you haul him out, please? And if possible, find the gun? Someone's going to want it for evidence.'

Giles dragged the semi-conscious Edward to the bank, where he was tied up with a variety of belts and leather thongs donated by various members of the warband. While they were thus engaged, Alice galloped up, her thin flanks heaving and her tongue hanging out, exhausted, but evidently cheerful, and under the impression that she had made a contribution.

'We'd better go and tell the feds,' said Merlin, practically. 'Dil, I reckon you'd better come with me; they're more likely to believe you. Saffron love, can you let him have your helmet a minute? If we're going to a copper-shop, we'd better be road-legal.'

Saffron unbuckled her helmet, which was decorated with red and white dragons locked in combat, and handed it to Dil. 'It was an epic ride,' she said, beaming euphorically.

'Yeah,' said Merlin, straddling his bike, 'and when we get back, maybe someone'll tell me what the fuck it was all about.'

XXIV

'What d'you think's going to happen to Edward?' asked Hattie, as Giles came back with the tray of drinks, and dealt them round the table. 'Thanks, Giles. Cheers, everybody,' she went on, raising her glass of Perrier to them all. They were sitting by a wood fire in a pub called the Thames Head Inn, halfway between Rodmarton and Tetbury. Once the police had finished with everybody's statements, Giles, Sebastian, Dilip, Jeanene and the dog Alice had squeezed themselves somehow into Hattie's little Renault, and returned to the cottage to recover themselves. Since, as it transpired, Giles and Sebastian had left the weekend's shopping at Stedham Chambers, and Giles's kitchen cupboards had turned out to contain very little except dried pasta, half a pound of sausages and a piece of neolithic Stilton, Hattie had promptly packed them back into the car, turned round, and taken them back down the road to the nearest pub to get something to eat. She was exhausted. Although no one had actually been killed or even injured, the memory of her hair-raising drive through Tetbury clung round her mind. There was nothing she wanted to do less than to drive, but no attractive alternatives presented themselves, and she was too proud to admit how she was feeling. At least, she reflected, the Thames Head was not unappealing, in its own way. It had far too many exposed beams, and was divided into so many snug little nooks that it felt a bit like drinking in a stable, but it was dark and cosy, and the menu promised well.

Dil shrugged cynically. 'He's a posh boy, so probably less than you'd think. His lawyer'll probably try and say he had PMT or something. But he did try to shoot Sebastian – we all saw him. He wasn't to know he had a dud gun. I mean, it'll take a bit of explaining away, even for a barrister.'

'I still can't believe it,' said Sebastian, taking a reviving swallow of his gin. 'I mean, I know I'm quite annoying sometimes, but why should anyone want to kill me?'

'It's obviously not you in yourself, Sebastian,' said Hattie. 'You must know something.'

'But I don't know *anything*, for pity's sake!' wailed Sebastian.

'You know he killed Eugenides,' observed Jeanene.

'But that's thanks to you.' Sebastian put his drink down on the crowded table, and ran his hands through his sleek hair, visibly thinking. 'We've only got the story together between us. If it wasn't for you, we wouldn't know that they'd got hold of something poisonous, and we wouldn't've been able to identify the Greek lady who ran Giles and me off the road. If it wasn't for Dilip, we wouldn't know there was a connection between Edward and this Greek woman and Eugenides. Come to that, if it wasn't for Hattie, I wouldn't've met Dilip, and none of this could have happened.'

'But you're the missing link, aren't you?' said Dil excitedly. 'As far as I can make it out, Ed and this Lamprini woman must've started some kind of a scam to get money out of Eugenides. They must've thought that he didn't know anyone, see? Then when you turned up, they lost their heads, went into total panic mode. They must think you know lots more than you do.'

'I can see that,' said Sebastian thoughtfully. 'They couldn't know what I knew, I suppose. Eugenides said sod-all about his business, but they might've thought he had. I wonder what they were after? There were a couple of good pictures in the house, and Eugenides' manuscripts are worth a fortune...Dilip, do you think Edward can have been interested in the books?'

'Doubt it. I don't think he'd've looked at books. I know I wouldn't, if I was looking for something to nick. You'd look a bit conspicuous turning up with a furniture van to take them away, wouldn't you? And you'd need a lot of specialist knowledge to get rid of 'em. The old geezer was some kind of retired banker, wasn't he? I'd start looking into the stuff he controlled. The answer's in there, somewhere.'

'It really makes you worry about lawyers,' observed Hattie. 'If I've understood what you're saying, Edward got in touch with this old man for business reasons, realised he was all on his own, and thought, whoopee, I'll do him in and steal his dosh. No one expects lawyers to be altruists, but you don't expect them to murder you! What d'you think, Dil? Was he a freak bad apple, or are there a lot of them out there?'

'We're not all crooks in the trade,' protested Dil. 'The thing is, solicitors get a lot of temptation. You can find yourself handling millions of pounds' worth of property sometimes, and if the client is really dozy or the whole thing's incredibly complicated and no one's quite sure who owns what, you can easily start wondering about letting some of it stick to your fingers. Specially if it's a one-off. If you've got a long-term relationship with a client, it's probably worth more to you than you could make off a bit of fiddling, because if you ever get into that sort of trouble, you can't get out. Like, when one account comes due, you end up robbing something else that's just come in to pay off the first guy. Not every crooked solicitor's lucky enough to have a peaceful, three-generation, Dickens-style property suit he can milk till Kingdom Come. I'd say that only a very small percentage of solicitors are bent from the start, but maybe another twenty per cent will go bent if the perfect opportunity comes up. The rest of us are probably honest enough. What keeps the whole show on the road is that perfect opportunities aren't that common. We've all got to have an audit certificate every year, and if you've ever gone bent, then it's like a little time-bomb in the firm's records, isn't it? Years and years later, someone may just have a bit of information and put two and two together, and then there's you struck off. Eddie must have found something seriously out of the ordinary to go in for this Bonnie and Clyde stuff. People destroy each other's lives every day in the City, but we don't go in for actual murder.'

'I don't think that's a lot of comfort,' said Hattie. The food arrived, and Hattie, who was sitting the furthest out into the room, turned to take the plates one by one from the barmaid. 'This looks like your vegetarian goulash, Dil,' said Hattie, handing it over. 'Who wanted the beef and Guinness pie?'

'That's mine,' said Giles. 'Seb's is the scampi and chips.' Swapping plates across the table, they gradually got themselves sorted out, and conversation resumed, while Hattie went off to the bar for a second round of drinks.

'What I can't get over is how accidental it all was,' said Giles. 'I keep thinking, if Jeanene hadn't happened to be with you, and hadn't recognised that Greek woman, Seb would've gone off with her, and he'd probably be dead in a ditch. We didn't suspect a thing. I just thought she was a jolly bad driver, and it was providential Seb could speak Greek. We didn't have a clue.'

'It's even worse than that,' added Sebastian sombrely. 'I was the only person who was able to get a Before and After look at Eugenides, and it didn't occur to me for a single second that anyone might've poisoned him. I've got a terrible conscience about it. I just assumed there was something organic...well, you do, don't you?'

'Try not to blame yourself, Sebastian love,' said Hattie, returning with fresh drinks. 'Maybe a doctor would've thought it didn't quite add up, but I'm sure nobody else would.'

'We can't afford to be suspicious any more,' said Dil. 'I remember thinking a bit about Eddie weeks ago. I wondered what he was up to, then I thought to myself, be sensible, there'll be a simple explanation somewhere. I'm kicking myself now, of course. The thing is, if you're a Londoner and you started worrying about everyone who acted a bit weird, you'd end up suspecting everybody, all the time.'

'People sometimes do if they get raped or mugged,' said Hattie. 'I've known people get into that sort of state, and they just end up cowering behind a locked door, scared to go out. It's another kind of madness. The trouble is, it's not that easy to read people. We're all too different. Look at us, for instance. There's whole areas of life where we don't overlap at all. If someone behaves differently from what you're used to, you can't afford to worry about it.'

'Too right,' said Jeanene feelingly. 'I really don't know *any* of the codes for here. For instance, if I'm talking to someone with old-fashioned English manners, I don't know what they mean. Like, when someone says, "That would be lovely," and half an hour later, it dawns on you you've actually been told to fuck off and die?' It dawned on her suddenly that both Giles and Sebastian might feel, not without reason, that she was getting at them personally, and she hastily buried her nose in her pint to cover her confusion.

'The point is,' Hattie persisted, ignoring this potential change of direction, 'you can't tell what's normal now, because there isn't really a norm.'

'We've ended up having a proper, old-fashioned adventure,' observed Sebastian. 'That bloody bike-ride's going to haunt my nightmares for the rest of my life. But it wasn't attached to anything. I mean, if you look back at what's been going on, you can't really say there's a proper story with a hero. Well, there's Giles I suppose – he's my hero, anyway. I'll never forget him charging into that grismal little pond like Bulldog Drummond, shouting "Take that, you swine!"'

'Oh, gosh. I'm not a hero,' said Giles, flustered. 'I didn't have a clue what was going on!'

'I'd've thought that was just about a qualification,' said Hattie dryly. 'Seriously, though. Sebastian—'

'Not me, dear,' said Sebastian promptly, 'I've got the wrong kind of shoes. Dil's the hero, then. He's the other one who did proper hero stuff. It'd never've occurred to me to round up those bikers, though they turned out to be perfectly sweet.'

'You're not going to get anywhere thinking like this,' said Dil. 'We haven't been very bright. What's actually happened is we've sort of accidentally solved a crime which no one knew had even happened just by getting to know each other. It's a checks and balances thing, isn't it. One bit of random causality put Eddie into the way of a serious scam, which ends up killing your old Greek mate. I'm sure Edward would've gone on being middling honest if he hadn't fallen over something he thought was just begging to be taken. Good luck for him, bad luck for Eugenides. Then another bit of random causality brought us together, in just the right combination to notice it. Bad luck for Eddie. The great thing is, randomness cuts both ways. It's like the way audits keep lawyers honest. If you can never be sure what other people are going to do, then you can't be sure there won't be a pair of beady eyes in the wrong place.'

'So what you're saying is, there's no point in looking for meaning in contingency,' said Hattie.

'I suppose so.'

'Anyway, it's been a lesson to me, about being nice to graduate students,' commented Sebastian, who was beginning to feel better. 'I think I might write that in art pokerwork, and put it up in my office. Should we have another round?'

'I don't want to move just yet,' said Jeanene apologetically. She was beginning to feel a little drowsy now she was fed and warm, and she was holding hands secretly with Dil under the table. 'It's nice just sitting here watching the fire. What are those things up along the beams? The things that look a bit like bunches of paper grapes?'

'Hops,' explained Hattie. 'They're used for making beer. They grow a lot of them west of here.'

'Let's go back in a minute,' said Giles. 'I've got some whisky, and I think there are a couple of bottles of wine somewhere. I'm sure Hattie could do with a real drink.'

'I could, rather,' said Hattie. 'Actually, I wouldn't mind getting moving.' A sudden thought crossed her mind. 'Giles, there's something I've been meaning to ask you since we got here. Why is this place called the Thames Head?'

'Because that's what it is. I thought you knew. The source of the Thames is just behind here.'

'You never! I never knew where it went after Oxford. Is there anything to see?'

Giles, recognising a kindred spirit, was immediately galvanised into life.

'Absolutely. There's a wonderful monument. I haven't seen it since I was about eight. My parents took me to see it, and I thought it was lovely, but somehow, I've never been back. It's funny, isn't it, the way you never get around to things that're just next door? Why don't we go and have a look at it? I've got a pretty powerful torch in my Barbour, you never know when you'll need one.'

'I've got one in the back of the car,' said Hattie, getting up. Alice scrambled out of her place of concealment under the table, looking hopeful.

'Darlings,' said Sebastian plaintively, 'are we talking about *another* death-defying expedition over wet, muddy fields?'

'Well, just a little one. It really isn't far,' said Giles. His optimism wilted visibly under Sebastian's cold stare. 'You could stay here, and we'll come back for you? Or I'll just take Hattie, and the rest of you can have another drink?'

'Oh, I might as well come,' conceded Sebastian rather grumpily.

Giles looked at him, a little wryly. 'Seb, darling, it might help if you thought of the country as an unparalleled excuse for buying a lot of new clothes.'

'H'm,' said Sebastian, failing to meet his eye. Pulling themselves together, shrugging into coats, visiting lavatories, they drifted out of the pub, and gradually reassembled in the carpark, where Hattie extracted a large and businesslike torch from the boot of her car.

'Lead on, Macduff,' she said. Giles strode off into the raw, damp, autumnal darkness, snapping on his own torch. Following the bobbing beam of light, Hattie, Sebastian, Dil and Jeanene streamed after him as he strode out of the carpark, through a small coppice, and set off confidently along the verge of a field, with crop to one side and an ivy-covered drystone wall to the other. There was very little natural light. Behind them, the lights of the pub gleamed yellow and friendly, and an occasional flash of headlights was visible through the hedges, but overhead the moon was partly obscured, and the sky was midnight-dark, with black, ragged clouds, and before them was darkness. Hattie directed the beam of her own torch at the ground, and they picked their way through the tussocks and nettles as best they could, trying to stay within the circle of visibility. He stopped, some way ahead, and they came up to him hopefully.

'We cross the railway line here,' he said cheerfully. 'There's a stile, and another one on the other side.' Sebastian opened his mouth to complain, then shut it again. 'It's really not much further,' said Giles placatingly. Tightly grouped behind him, they walked together in silence down a straight grass track, wet ploughland dimly visible to either side. 'One more stile.' On the other side of the stile, he gestured with the beam of the torch, which swept up over the gentle rise of a water-meadow, illuminating a stand of trees perhaps fifty yards ahead. 'It's just in there.'

'There've been *cows* in here,' complained Sebastian, picking his way fastidiously like a cat on the damp grass. 'It's *soggy*.'

'It's a water-meadow, Sebastian, love,' Hattie said patiently.

Giles was forging ahead, long-legged, confident, properly shod. They saw him stop, and direct the beam low over the turf. The torchlight picked up a phosphorescent gleam of water, welling up between the blades of grass. 'We must be coming up to the actual spring now.' He flashed the light over the water, and up towards the lowering clump of trees as the rest of them stumbled up behind him.

'Er...' said Dil. 'Where is it then?' There was a moment of stricken silence.

'Oh, God. I've just remembered,' Giles said guiltily. 'Someone told me a couple of years ago there'd been a problem with vandalism, and they'd decided to move it. I'd completely forgotten. I'm terribly sorry.'

As the seconds prolonged themselves, Hattie realised that they were all staring mutely at Sebastian, whose face was unreadable in the dusk, waiting for the explosion.

He seemed to realise it, for suddenly he shrugged, shaking his head, and laughed. 'Oh, don't worry, Giles, darling. I'm not going to scream. It's still the source of the Thames, statue or no statue. I'm glad I've seen it.' Giles watched him in trepidation, as he started walking slowly towards the dark verge of the spring. 'The Romans took springs awfully seriously, you know. I think we ought to be nice to it. Let me think a minute.' Raising both hands in a gesture of invocation, he took a deep breath, and began to address the darkness, his plummy, rather beautiful voice floating gravely over the water.

Salve, magne parens frugumque virumque, Tamesis!
Diversum sortita capis finemque caputque,
Salve, amnis laudate agris, laudate colonis,
Dignata imperio debent cui moenia Anglae!
Tu valeas vigeas semper, carissime flumen:
Te stagnis ego caeruleis magnumque sonoris
Amnibus, doctiloquis te commendabo Britannis.

He bowed his head, and with some ceremony, fished in his pocket for a handful of change, and threw it into the water. He retreated a couple of squelchy steps. 'There. I think that'll do nicely. Give us a kiss, Giles. I bloody well deserve one.'

'Oh, Seb,' said Giles, coming forward to hug him, 'I think you've made me cry. That was lovely. What did it mean?'

'It's an *ode*, sweetie. It doesn't mean anything. They aren't supposed to.'

Dil put an arm round Jeanene, while Hattie kissed her fingertips, and bent down to touch the cold water. 'Give my love to London Bridge,' she said softly.

'It's sort of magic anyway,' ventured Jeanene. She found a couple of coins in her coat pocket, and tossed them into the spring. The tiny splash shocked the velvety silence of the night.

'Let's get back,' said Giles, after a minute or so of silent contemplation. 'Seb's been marvellous, but I don't want to push my luck.' One by one, they bent to touch the water, then turned their backs on it, and began trudging back towards the carpark, Sebastian arm in arm with Giles, while Hattie walked with Dil and Jeanene in a friendly trio.

'I wonder what Edward's thinking about now?' said Sebastian suddenly, as he was climbing over the last of the stiles.

'Dunno,' said Dil, 'but I bet you he's not wishing he hadn't done it. If I know Eddie, he'll be trying to work out who else he can blame.'

In fact, Edward was doing neither of these things. Lying sleepless on the hard bed in a police cell, more uncomfortable than he had been at any time since leaving school, he was thinking furiously. What was on his mind was, as Sebastian could have told him at once, a classic conundrum known as the Prisoner's Dilemma, a problem with no solution.

He had remained almost entirely silent since the disaster of his capture, and intended to maintain this policy until he had the advice of a competent criminal lawyer. Lamprini, he was prepared to bet, had done the same. His overall situation was so bad that it was, perversely, beyond causing him any anxiety. Once the worst has happened, there is a sort of calm to be found in the eye of the storm. The question which was tormenting him was this: was there any short-term advantage to be gained by revealing the contents of the safe-deposit box? That is, could he, by revealing this treasure, get a better deal for himself? If he and Lamprini both kept quiet, on the other hand, it was by no means impossible that, with the papers which he already had, he would be able to forge a convincing document which would gain him access to the box when he was once more at liberty. But if she spoke, and he did not, he would lose out... What constituted the path of maximum self-interest?

Slowly, and with extreme reluctance, he was compelled to acknowledge to himself that in these most special of circumstances, self-interest lay in trust.